———— ALSO ————
GEORGIANA

ALSO
GEORGIANA

✦

Alison Harding

St. Martin's Press
New York

c.1

Library of Congress Cataloging-in-Publication Data

Harding, Alison.
  Also Georgiana.

  I. Title.
PR6058.A624A79   1987   823'.914   87-4353
ISBN 0-312-00559-8

First published in Great Britain by Michael Joseph Ltd.

First U.S. Edition

10 9 8 7 6 5 4 3 2 1

BL   BL SEP 10 '87

To the memory of my father

Author's Note

This is a work of fiction. The 'autobiography' of an obscure nineteenth-century woman – whose name alone provided the initial imaginative impulse for the book – it explores the hopes and difficulties which might have presented themselves to a 'sister' of Charles Dickens' hero Pip in *Great Expectations*.

However, I wished Georgiana's story to reflect a kind of contemporary reality quite different from that of Dickens' novel. To this end, certain literary and artistic figures have been allowed to enter her life, or to influence her progress as a painter. Where I have taken liberties with established fact, I have endeavoured, through the use of records and accounts from the period, to portray these characters faithfully, and without distortion of biographical detail.

While I have sometimes found that reality has corresponded far more nearly than I had anticipated to my fictional projection, Georgiana Curwen herself, and those persons and events most closely connected with her, are imagined, and bear no resemblance to actual persons or events, past or present.

I should like to thank all who have answered enquiries or provided material for research, in particular the librarians of the Devon and Exeter Institution and the Highgate Literary and Scientific Institution; Mr Charles Page of Exeter University; Mr Michael Moon of Whitehaven; and many others – museum and library staff, booksellers, and friends in West Cumbria, London and Devon. I am especially grateful to my editor, for her unfailing patience and support; to my agent, for her consistent interest; and to members of my family, for their tolerance.

Alison Harding, 1986

This is a green and gentle country where I write . . . Sometimes my father drives me to a little beach beside a lake; the narrow strip of sand is white and pure, the water of a blue more deep than any I have known. The sand is coarse – so that when I pour it from my hand I see the fragments of the shells, each shining particle the remnant of a shape which once was perfect: fan or whorl, or butterfly, or razor-shell perhaps. Like these, our lives are tossed and torn apart by circumstance, and whittled by degrees to a minuteness, and non-entity.

The only sound is the quiet fall of curling waves; each pauses, holds its breath, resolves its course, and scatters bubbles on the waiting sand. At home, as I sit and watch the breathing of a sleeping child, I feel once more the rhythm of the lake, the steady pulse beneath the skin, the beating of a heart. For him I fear the ungovernable tide that can destroy a dream, dispel illusion, carry him beyond the shore of childhood harmony; but for myself, I am content to wait whatever Chance may choose to bring. And perhaps, as I tell my mother's story and my own, I will find that the shadow of a pattern falls across the page, that the fragments of remembered days will form some semblance of a shape – though they have long been scattered by the wind.

Dublin, 185–

PART I

Cumberland

' *Also Georgiana Wife of the Above* ... "There, Sir!" I timidly explained. "Also Georgiana. That's my mother." '

Charles Dickens, *Great Expectations*

After a disastrous love affair, the 17–year–old illegitimate sister of Pip (Dickens' Great Expectations), gains recognition as an artist in Victorian England.

I had always known, since the time when I became aware of such complexities, that my mother was of gentle birth. What else, indeed, could account for the delicacy of feature that I beheld upon looking into the cracked glass above my white-painted dressing-chest; what other explanation for my own hands and feet – so small that even when red and chapped with cold they seemed incongruously thrust into my coarse garments and boots, so hated yet so familiar. There could be no doubt – and her own portrait in its shabby frame told me the same story – that my mother, Georgiana Curwen, had been a lady.

Why this should have been a matter of such importance to one so young, I had yet to discover: it was comfort enough, throughout the long cold evenings of my childhood, that I had such a certainty to sustain me.

Her name, I had long since realised, was my own – Georgiana. But it was not until my coming-of-age in the spring of 1830 that I learned that my second name, Frances, had been that of my maternal grandmother. Until that time, so little did I know of my origins that even the existence of my mother seemed to be a fancy spun from my nightly contemplation of her picture, rather than a reality with which I was ever likely to be confronted. The solace I derived from my belief in her gentility had, I fear, far more to do with the upholding of my self-esteem in the face of my fellow servants' hostility than with any notion of her as an individual. As a child I had wept, without knowing why, over her picture; as a woman, I was to weep for her as someone whom I might have known and loved.

I could not even recollect how the portrait came into my possession. It had always stood upon the chest in the room I regarded as mine – an uneasy privilege, since the other servants shared their quarters, and their voluble speculation as to my isolation was a burden I learned to carry with quiet indifference. At first I found their curiosity and its cause exceedingly hard to bear. For it was but a short time since I had, almost overnight it seemed, been banished from the schoolroom where I had shared the lessons, and in some measure the privileges, of Joseph and Horatia, the elder children of Horace Chatterton, lawyer, in whose establishment I had grown up. It was he, so I believed, who had been responsible for my presence in his household, and also, I was sure, for my present unhappy, ambiguous situation – half servant, half dependant, without means or identity and, so it appeared then, without prospect of change.

My only claim to personality lay in my mother's picture. Her features were my own. When, painstakingly, I copied the portrait, using pencil and paper stolen from the schoolroom, I sought to recreate the image I saw daily in the mirror. Her hair was fair and fashionably curled, where mine was dark and straight, but I knew the line of her nose, the gently curving brows above grey-green eyes, and the roundness of her chin, with its hint of strength. What I could not convey, despite frequent redrawing of that face, was the laughter indicated by her slightly parted lips – my own were usually tightened in a far less becoming expression of determined seriousness. When, in years to come, I saw Romney's painting of my grandmother, Frances Curwen, whose colouring and bearing I had inherited, I recognised, and no longer rejected, the implications of that solemn look about the mouth and the questioning directness of her gaze, so like my own.

It was perhaps that same seriousness, coupled with an instinct for independence, which brought about the eventual conflict, for so long dormant, between myself and Horace Chatterton. His wife, a mousy and frivolous-minded, though not unkind woman, feared him to the extent that even the servants connived to protect 'poor Matty' (as they disrespectfully called her among themselves) from the master's contempt when some household task appeared neglected or ill done. Apart from his wrath on such occasions, and her panic at the minor ailments of the children (whose indispositions were regarded as crises, in which the much-tried patience of the family medical man must have been strained to limits made tolerable only by the size of his fees), the establishment ran smoothly – as establishments will where the intelligence of servants is allowed to take over the reins. The servants it was, rather than his wife, who anticipated Horace's return from days of legal proceedings in the City; they saw to the comfort of his occasional guests, to the good ordering of the dinner table, and to the timely absence (apart from their routine appearances to 'bid goodnight to Papa') of the younger children from the main rooms of the house. And it was they, in the persons of Maria, poor Matty's maid and confidante, and of Mrs Parsons, the cook-housekeeper, who warned me, during the weeks that followed my seventeenth birthday, that I had 'better watch the master' and that 'something was afoot'.

I had already sensed that some kind of change was imminent. I knew that Horace and his wife had had, some time previously, a difference regarding myself: she had protested a little (hardly daring to do more) at my removal from the schoolroom and his instruction that I be found something more useful to do than play with the little ones or help Horatia with her drawing. For, though older than I, Horatia had, on account of her delicate constitution, been thought unable to stand up to the rigours of formal education. I privately felt that self-indulgence rather than physical frailty lay at the root of her inability to attend to her books or even, on occasion, to walk as far as the garden. Whilst I eagerly took advantage of her frequent absence from lessons to absorb whatever instruction the governess, Miss Hamilton, cared to impart, I knew that Horatia's ill-temper could when necessary outweigh even her idleness. Her dislike, harmless in early childhood, later became insupportable, and I was outraged when she took my drawings – accumulated under the instruction of an occasional visiting master who conveniently developed a passion for the fortunate Miss Hamilton – to her mamma, who believed them to be Horatia's own. The portfolio was even sent to the principal of a school for young ladies as proof of her advanced skills: though I came to regard their loss as a small price to pay for the larger benefit of her departure, I mourned them for a time as I might have mourned the loss of a child.

For two years past, since Horatia was sent away to be 'finished' at that same ostensibly smart establishment, in the country between London and Maidenhead, I had been given duties of an increasingly menial nature. This had resulted, to my sorrow, in the loss of the companionship of Joseph, whom I had, through many collaborations, protected somewhat against his elder sister's capriciousness and the governess's petty tyrannies. The attitude of my fellow servants, as they now became, added further to my loneliness; I had previously been regarded with indifference or, at worst, suspicion, which now turned to contempt. Had it not been for the watchfulness of Mrs Parsons I should have suffered more. Her kind words helped me through the empty days following Joe's departure for school, from where he returned transformed into a supercilious youth, who had already begun to adopt that air of moral superiority commonly shown toward those whose origins are doubtful, and income insufficient to ensure their status. When, in tears, I enquired of the housekeeper how Joe could be so much altered, she responded merely that his father had much to answer for, adding, frustratingly, that 'such things do happen, though the Lord knows they didn't ought to!'

His father I had long disliked, for on his part a similar air of superiority had always been manifested toward me. This was usually accompanied by a thin smile, which as I grew older I came to distrust, for it seemed to threaten me in some way that I could not in my inexperience define. A small man, whose scented cleanliness and smooth skin increasingly repelled me, Horace did not try to hide the hardness of his nature even from his wife and children. The household could not ever have been in any sense a happy one: an atmosphere of unease dominated, becoming for me intensified each time the master returned home – it seemed more frequently since Joseph and Horatia had been sent away. Even before events occurred which changed my life precipitately, I had determined that I would try to change it for myself.

The theft – for as such I regarded the loss – of my drawings, I laid along with other deprivations firmly at the door of Horace Chatterton. His wife's anxiety to impress and his daughter's lack of scruple derived, I felt, directly from their fear of his censure. Though I blamed their weakness, I blamed his inhumanity more. I knew myself to be more angry than afraid of him. And, I reasoned, he could hardly care if I chose to remove myself from an establishment where my presence must at best be super-fluous, at worst a source of domestic discord. My reasoning could not have been more misguided.

I approached him one Sunday morning before luncheon, when it might have been supposed that his customary coldness would have yielded to some more charitable state of mind. Acknowledging my request, he indicated his study door, beside which I waited while he gave instructions to Mrs Parsons. At his desk, he appeared to examine some papers as I stood patiently, my gaze fixed upon his white hands, which instinctively I found repugnant. He listened to my words, which seemed less confident than I believed myself to be.

'I think it might, now that I am seventeen and beyond the age when I can be regarded as a child, be more suitable for me to obtain employment. I am so little needed, now that I do not assist in the schoolroom ... I know I am of little use in the kitchen, and I wish ...' My voice faltered as I felt his movement toward me. The papers were thrust away and fell from the desk with the violence of his reaction; and taking fright at the look of anger that had swept away his cold composure, I fled across the room towards the door. His hands were upon my shoulders before I reached it. He turned me bodily to face him, and to my amazement it seemed that something akin to panic had replaced his wrath.

'Have you told anyone, anyone at all, of this ... this plan? It is impossible that you should leave my house without permission from – ' and his tone changed to a whisper as he glanced at the door, in evident anxiety that no one should hear our exchange

[5]

' – from your legal guardian; there can be no possibility of it, none at all,' he repeated. My surprise at his words momentarily overcame my fear. I gathered courage, too, from his discomposure, and spoke more firmly.

'From whom then, sir, should I seek permission? If indeed you and your wife are not, as I have always supposed, my guardians, how can you forbid me? How can you be sure that such a one might not wish to remove me from your care, when you treat me neither as your own child, nor even – ' and bitterness succeeded indignation ' – as a useful servant in your household? I am nothing – '

At this, having recovered his customary self-control, he cut short my protest by the simple device of holding my gaze in his, with a stare at once so contemptuous and so calculating that my voice lost its boldness. I was indeed reduced almost to incapacity by that look, which I had seen before during a particularly ugly exchange between Horace and his wife, who had become quite hysterical at its severity.

'If,' he said, smoothly anticipating my thoughts – as though I were an unfortunate witness hampering the progress of a case – 'if you have any notions of precipitate action, I suggest you dismiss them. It is my duty as the representative of your guardian to protect you from your own youthful folly, and you may be sure I shall do so by whatever means may be necessary. Should you try to seek any kind of situation, my description of your character would ensure that you did not remain in employment.'

I knew that he was right. Already, from tentative conversation with Mrs Parsons, I had learned that without a 'character' one was quite lost. Even Maria, wrongfully dismissed from her last situation, had obtained that of Matty's maid only by the intervention of the lawyer himself, who must, I later surmised, have held some advantage over her. For she was, of all the servants, the most in fear of him, and would only say of him – 'he knows everything, the master.' For the present, I could only accept his pronouncement. I knew, however, that I would try again; and subsequent events proved that Horace Chatterton, also, realised that my acquiescence could only be short-lived.

*

In winter or wet weather, my chief means of escape from the oppressive atmosphere of that house, and from the demands made upon me by its occupants, lay within my own power. By diligent application of pencil to paper, and, when I could obtain the materials, of brush and colour, I created page upon page of drawings. Some were attempts at landscapes, following the instruction of the drawing master, who must have proved more successful as teacher than as lover, for Miss Hamilton tired of his advances and attended to the steadier prospect of an alliance with the curate from the nearby church; not, however, before I had learned sufficient to reproduce with accuracy the views from the upstairs windows, which overlooked in one direction a series of gardens belonging to well-appointed houses similar to that in which I lived. Beyond them lay the church, the London road, and some cottages, which I found of greater interest. But my chief attention came to rest upon the objects within doors – here the shape of a chair, there an elaborate mantel clock, perhaps a piece of glassware or the design upon a shawl or other fabric. I never lacked for subjects and rarely tired of my occupation save when some intricacy of shape or pattern eluded my skill, or the demands of Horatia – to dress her hair in yet another style or fetch soothing medication for some imagined injury – disturbed my power to concentrate.

Out of doors, in fine weather, or sometimes in the gentle rain so characteristic of the climate in this part of England, I wandered through the garden, not large but provided with some fine trees and rosebeds. And from there, through a wicket gate, I could reach unobserved the water meadows that lay between the houses and the river Thames. Here my escape was complete.

Tall straggling buttercups reached above my waist. If I sat down they were on a level with my eyes and I could see into the yellow depths holding dusty pollen, sometimes a tiny fly or diligent bee. A narrow bridge led from garden to field, over a dark ditch hemmed with clumps of cow parsley or 'Queen Anne's lace', whose shade was warm and heavy with dust; below it I sometimes saw a flicker of water, deeper, I knew from childhood warnings, than it at first appeared. The creamy white of elderflowers, the colder white of the cow parsley, and the pink-and-white wild roses above, made this a virginal, closed and unsuspecting world, through which I wandered, isolated, yet not entirely insecure.

Sometimes I would sit in the shade of a willow and try to draw a flower, a spray of grass, some ash or aspen leaves. But I lacked the skill to render more than the shape of a petal, perhaps the gradations of seeds along a stem or the patterns of veins upon a leaf. Though I observed, I could not reproduce the changes of colour brought about by light and shade, I could not convey the translucence within a flower: I had, for the most part, to be content to experience them, just as I would sometimes sit and watch until my eyes ached the movement of a piece of foam along the river, or would lie with closed eyes and listen, almost until I slept, to the sound of the water.

Beside the Thames I also caught glimpses of a wider world. Sometimes small groups of people took the riverside path, perhaps to or from church on a Sunday morning; occasionally a boat passed, its occupants fashionably dressed and shaded with parasols, that hid their faces but could not mute their laughter or exclamations of pleasure. Then I longed to leave behind me the repressive formality of the Chatterton household, the complaining voices of Horatia and her mother, the gibes of Maria or Walter, even the less unkind admonishments of Mrs Parsons. My consciousness of a world from which I was shut out increased with each year of my age. My humiliation at being further barred from the company of those with whom I had played as a child was therefore the more intense, and my dislike of Horace Chatterton turned to a furious hatred that I had no way of expressing. I no longer sought with childish curiosity to trace in my mother's face reflections of my own. To think of her as a lady, as part of that world from which I found myself excluded, afforded me pain rather than consolation. And the conviction that she had abandoned me to an existence lacking all kinds of natural affection destroyed within me any feeling for her that I might, in my immaturity, have harboured.

For I knew now that such affections existed. The hasty embraces of the servants, in the darker corners of the house or in the garden at evening, had always been familiar – and meaningless – to me. But the glimpses I caught of shared intimacy between those who walked beside the river or were borne past me in their carefree boats – these were of a different and more disturbing kind, hinting at pleasures and their fulfilment of which I was allowed, by virtue of my situation, to know nothing.

Mingled with my increasing yearnings was the remembrance of a day when I had by chance been wandering through the water meadow at some distance further than I usually ventured. It was perhaps the year before Horatia's departure for school; I remember that she had taunted me with the prospect of her future experiences – the aristocratic acquaintance she would make, the opportunities she would find for unparalleled display of her dress or hair, and the certainty that she would become equipped beyond my imagination with accomplishments fit to ensure her a splendid match with the unsuspecting son of a great house. I succeeded in escaping her further descriptive raptures by inventing some errand to her mother, and thankfully gained my retreat beyond the garden.

Perhaps I was listening too hard to the sound of birds or river, perhaps simply lost in thoughts of my own. Suddenly, beyond the grasses that swayed as I parted them, beneath a willow and shaded by its branches, lay Mrs Parsons in her usual grey afternoon gown, and, embraced within her arms, Thomas, the master's valet, fully fifteen years her junior. Their faces, so close together, were invisible to me; but the passionate tranquillity of their bodies, enclosed by warm grasses and oblivious even to the disturbance of my approach, informed me of yet another world waiting to be discovered. Even in so brief a moment, I glimpsed upon Mrs Parsons' finger the broad wedding-band (had there ever been a Mr Parsons, I was later to conjecture) that I had observed only that morning plunged into a bowl of flour; I saw, too, the coloured scarf habitually worn by Thomas on his free afternoon, cast aside among the buttercups. One day, I was to realise how significant familiar things become at moments of passion; now, all I knew was that a measure of peace was attainable, even to the servants of Horace Chatterton.

*

[9]

During the weeks that followed my encounter with her husband, Matilda Chatterton appeared more than usually agitated whenever she had occasion to address me. She had always, I was aware, regarded my presence as a burden even less welcome than that of her own offspring, whose care seemed quite beyond her capabilities. Though ready enough to lament the cost of keeping me (even in her daughter's cast-off garments) she eagerly made use of my abilities as nursemaid to the younger children. At first I welcomed this – any role seemed preferable to that of pander to Horatia's caprices – but my tasks became increasingly onerous. As well as consciousness that I could not protest at such humiliation, I felt frustration at the loss of my chief refuge from those around me: for had I even found time enough for drawing, my hands were too swollen with kitchen and laundry work to control my pencil. So, despite Matilda's agitation, I resolved to attempt further action on my own behalf, choosing a time when I knew Horace to be engaged in a City case.

Matty's response to my request was as extreme, if less unexpected, as had been that of her husband.

'It is impossible that you should leave – impossible!' She echoed his words. 'I know nothing of your guardian; I can tell you nothing.' Her voice took on a familiar, hysterical note. 'My husband forbids that we should discuss your – your ingratitude.'

'I *should* be grateful, ma'am,' I replied, trying hard to contain my anger, 'but less for what you have done for me than for some certainty as to my future. Have I not a right to know? How may I find any employment if you refuse to tell me what I should know about myself, even to let me go from here?'

To my surprise, Matilda half nodded, even as she glanced behind her in evident fear that her husband might somehow materialise and shrivel her attempt at kindness. 'It is true – you will only continue to be a burden to us, beyond all that can be expected of us. But I cannot tell you what you should do. I know so little – he tells me nothing . . .'

'If I could but know the name of my guardian,' I urged, 'I might make some communication. I have no wish to continue to be an embarrassment to you. If you could but help me – ' I appealed to her, forgetting, in my eagerness to achieve support for my venture, that 'poor Matty' had but one resource when faced with a situation beyond her strength or comprehension.

'Fetch Doctor Wright,' she murmured, her pale eyes filling with convenient tears; 'I feel so weak – you have quite exhausted me. Tell Walter to fetch Doctor Wright, quickly!' I had no alternative but to do as she requested. If her 'attack' were to last until Horace returned from London, he might guess at its cause and further obstruct my purpose.

As I lay in my room that night, however, the small window open so that I might breathe the warm early-summer air and hear, beyond the garden and field, the sound of the river, I felt calmer. I knew that I would find a way into that wider world of which I had so far glimpsed only flitting shadows – shapes that I could draw only in my mind, complex textures and subtle colours I could not as yet interpret, experiences that I longed to understand.

As summer turned to autumn my hopes seemed to have been but foolish illusions. I had little time to indulge my fancies, for Matilda Chatterton was indeed ill, from some 'distemper of the blood' according to Doctor Wright, whose visits took on even greater frequency. Horatia and Joseph were dispatched to their respective educational establishments, and I found myself needed both as nursemaid to the children and attendant in the invalid's room. In some measure I was happier than previously, for Matty preferred my care to that of the regular nurse, and I could see that when unharassed by the presence of her husband there was in her some humanity he lacked. He appeared indifferent even to her sickness, and though hardly at all in London spent little time with her, leaving the house early in the morning and spending the hours after dinner in company of his papers and, so Walter said, his bottle.

It was on one such evening that, without warning, he made it clear that our earlier conversation had not been forgotten. I had left Matilda's room, Mrs Parsons having indicated that she was willing to sit with her that night. Returning from an errand to the kitchen and intending to retire early (for I was weary with incessant demands), I passed Horace's study, from which he suddenly emerged. To my alarm he grasped my arm, and pulled rather than led me into the room; he leaned heavily against the door, as though to prevent my escape. The light from the table, littered with papers and books, showed me that his usually pale complexion was now flushed as though from some exertion; the hand that still enclosed my arm shook despite its strength. A glass and empty bottle confirmed what I had already guessed, and it was evident that he enjoyed my consternation for he laughed as he spoke, his face unbearably close to mine.

'I have a message for you, miss. A personal message from –' he paused, savouring my bewilderment, 'from your guardian. Should you prefer to read it for yourself – or shall I *whisper* it to you?'

'I should prefer to read the letter, if I may, sir.' I tried to move towards the desk where I guessed the letter lay, hoping he would release me, my mind suddenly alert despite the weariness of my body.

'I thought so; then I shall whisper it in your ear, as some small recompense for my efforts upon your behalf. I had begun to think I should never be rid of you; God knows I had the responsibility thrust upon me. But at last, it seems, others – who should have done so sooner – are willing to relieve me of the task.' He laughed again, and turned me with a sudden movement of his wrist, so that now I was against the door, and he almost pressing me against it.

'The message, sir!' I managed to make my request, though I did not know which I feared the more – the message or the manner in which it might be delivered.

To my relief he moved away, reaching a letter from an inner pocket and holding it with his free hand toward the light.

' "My compliments to Miss Georgiana Curwen, whom I shall be pleased to receive in my home at a time to be mutually agreed, but no later than 3rd April next. E. Nicolson." '

The date was that of my birth; next April I would be eighteen, and I was to make many conjectures during the coming months as to the significance of my guardian's stipulation. Meanwhile, a glance at the handwriting, visible as

Horace Chatterton held the letter beneath the lamp, told me nothing more than that it was flowing and well formed.

'When, and to where, am I to go then?' I asked, attempting as I did so to move away from the door. But I achieved neither satisfactory answer nor escape, for he only murmured, 'You will be told', and the letter was sent spinning onto the table, where it lay white against the green of the bottle. I was pulled towards him again, this time feeling against my face those cold fingers, the pallor and scent of which I had long detested. Then I was almost deafened by the knocking that came at the door behind me, and by the voices of Mrs Parsons and Walter, both calling with urgency for their master.

Matilda Chatterton died that night. In the confusion of my encounter with her husband, his news and his manner of imparting it had superseded in my mind all thought of the invalid – on whose behalf I now felt horror and anger that he should have so cruelly neglected his duty to her, even as she lay dying. Her frivolity and self-pity, once so irksome, seemed forgivable to me now, in the light of his incomparable callousness. I could not but pity Horatia, to be removed at once from her friends, from her absorption in ribbons and suitors, to take her mother's place at the head of her father's household.

It was winter when I left Berkshire. I was to travel by public coach to London, escorted by Horace Chatterton, whose legal business, I was informed, allowed him to accompany me. I hated such a prospect, but had no choice in the matter. Since Matty's death he had, it was true, scarcely addressed me; but I had been told that I was to arrive in my guardian's home, in the town of Workington on the coast of Cumberland, in the early part of December. I was daunted at the promise of so long a journey; I knew nothing of the country, or of what awaited me at the end of what would undoubtedly prove to be arduous travelling. As the coach crossed Maidenhead Bridge, I looked out as best I could around the stout bodies of two elderly women who were loudly protesting at the discomforts of their route from Bath. Beyond them and below us lay the river Thames, now bereft of the summer boats; a solitary labourer, heavily burdened, walking the path beside the water, beneath the leafless trees.

At Slough, Horace descended, and I caught sight of him in conversation with a lively-looking schoolboy with whom he travelled outside for the remainder of the route into London. Mist, mingled with snowflakes, added to the grime of the coach windows, prevented my observing much as we approached the centre of the capital. I thought wrily of Horatia, and her jealous raptures on first learning that I would see London. She had prophesied brilliance, gaiety, all the interior delights of the winter Season: here was darkness, the noise of wheels and shouting; a lighted square, then darkness again; a great house, its curtains drawn against the late afternoon chill. And at last, relief from the overheated atmosphere of the crowded coach, from the incessant twitterings of my genteel companions; the descent to the pool of light shed by a lamp, beneath which the outside travellers were already assembling baggage, huddling further into their capes, exchanging words with scuttling attendants, whose brisk patter seemed a world away from the slow drawl of the Berkshire servants.

But I had no time to think of what lay behind me. A small and very dirty boy, half naked in the icy wind, struggled with my portmanteau (conjured up by some magic of the good-natured Mrs Parsons, and filled with my few clothes and possessions), while I walked swiftly to keep pace with Horace. A clean enough lodging and a respectable-looking woman, who dried my boots and brought food (though I could eat but little), removed my earlier apprehensions as to where the night should be spent. When, however, I retired I could not rest. More than once I rose to make sure that the door was firmly locked; several times, cries and clatter from the street below caused me to move aside the window curtain, but I could see only yellow swirling mist and the wetness of falling snow against the glass. The room was very cold; and though I believed myself to be secure, I seemed to feel again upon my face the chill moist fingers of Horace Chatterton . . .

Despite the ceaseless tasks that had occupied my days since his wife's death, at night his form and touch had filled my dreams, until I feared to sleep; the quiet comfort of darkness, once my refuge from petty daytime trials, held no protection against his image. And, all too soon, I came to know that he was in truth not merely lecherous, but evil. Though he had hardly approached me openly, my duties being directed by Horatia or the housekeeper, I recognised his tread upon the stair or along the passage in which my room was situated. Sometimes he paused beside the door, the key to which I now kept safe upon a ribbon; sometimes his step went beyond, to where the servants slept, and I remembered the warnings I had been given by Mrs Parsons and Maria. But no one, it seemed, had warned Horatia.

She came to me in the early hours of a bitter November morning. Her father had stayed in his study until almost midnight. I had thought to hear him pass by, but had not done so – only his step near the stairway, the sudden sharp closing of a door, and now, her frantic knock and weeping. Pity for her overcame my fear that she might be followed; I laid her upon the bed, fetched water from the wash-stand, then with shaking hands removed her nightgown, its fresh whiteness stained and its ruffles, sewn with such care by her mother, now sadly torn. From among my clothes, washed and folded ready for the coming journey, I found her a clean gown; and – for she was a little calmer – I tried to persuade her to come with me to Mrs Parsons, for I knew no one else to whom she could turn.

'I cannot – he will come to know; I dare not for she will lose her place and then I shall be quite alone, for you will be gone . . .' Her weeping began anew, and I could only sit beside the bed, her hands in mine, until the daylight came. Then, while she slept at last, I went about my duties, though they were ill performed. From that night until my departure, Horatia slept with me in my room: I could do no more then but entrust her secret to the housekeeper, and resolve for my own part never to return . . .

I rose yet again and looked from the window. I could distinguish some shapes of roofs and chimneys, the faint light of morning behind them. I was glad of the warm shawl that Mrs Parsons had selected for me from among her dead mistress's garments. As I took it from the portmanteau, I saw by the candlelight the features of my mother within the once-gilt frame, which I had placed, together with my accumulation of drawings, among the folds of a blue dress. Matty herself had handed it to me some years earlier, yet it seemed not one that she herself would have worn, and had been unsuitable in style and length for the young girl I then was. I had ascertained only the day before my departure that it now fitted me perfectly. As I bent to rearrange its folds around the picture I wondered suddenly whether it might have belonged to my mother, to that unknown Georgiana of whom I had lately thought only with bitterness. Her age, in the portrait, could have been little more than my own: had she intended, I wondered, that I should remain for so long in ignorance of my origins? Perhaps, in Cumberland, I should find the answer not only to this but to other questions that I had sought, since childhood, to suppress.

Chapter 2

That winter morning, in December 1829, I left behind my childhood to become Miss Georgiana Curwen. My few illusions, painfully dispelled, belonged to the girl I had been, who, it later seemed to me, bore as little resemblance to the young woman I became as does the chrysalis to its emergent butterfly.

The severe weather had come early. Already, for some weeks before my departure from Berkshire, frost had lain between garden and river, and snow had excited the younger Chatterton children. I took little delight, however, in the wet snowflakes that clung to my garments as I waited, my limbs chilled as much with anxious anticipation as with the icy wind, in the doorway of Osborn's Hotel, to which Horace and I had been driven through the narrow streets of the capital. We were joined, to my surprise, by the youth who had mounted the coach at Slough on the previous morning. This time he was accompanied by a tall sharp-featured gentleman, evidently his father, whom Horace greeted with respect, almost deference – an attitude I had not hitherto observed in him.

'Captain Nicolson, sir – this is a great kindness. The young lady, Miss Georgiana Curwen, this is she.'

He drew me forward. 'The captain has agreed to escort you down to Cumberland, Miss; you will be secure enough in his charge.'

Before I could enquire of him whether this was, as I instantly concluded, my guardian, he had indicated my baggage to the captain's attendant, muttered some words of farewell, and hurried into the street. Glad as I was to see him thus vanish from my life, I could not but wish that he had told me more about the person with whom I was to travel, for several days and through I knew not what hazards. My nervousness was only increased by my remembrance of the name upon the letter I had so briefly seen, and had so often thought of during the weeks that followed: how would its writer now receive me, and for what purpose was I to accompany him so far?

The voice of Captain Nicolson interrupted my speculations.

'You had better wait within, Miss Curwen; you will be more comfortable. There is yet half an hour before we depart and I have still some business to attend to. George here — ' he turned to his son, 'will keep you amused whilst I am gone. You must forgive my haste.'

And he left quickly to execute his commission, while I tried to curb both my bewilderment at his courteous manner (for I had become used to less civil approaches), and my curiosity as to his exact relationship to myself. George escorted me into a small parlour-like room at the far side of a spacious hallway where other persons, all dressed for travelling, were gathering and conversing, with great animation despite the early hour. Even to my inexperienced eyes it was evident that Osborn's was an establishment patronised by gentlefolk; and I should have been still more conscious of my unfashionable clothes and lack of grace had it not been for the goodwill of my young companion, who saw me seated in comfort and ordered refreshment, clearly enjoying his responsibility for my welfare. I had observed a similarity of height and colouring between this new acquaintance and my former playmate, Horatia's brother; yet the likenesses were superficial, for there was a friendly charm and ease in this boy that contrasted only too painfully with the recent superiority of attitude shown to me by Joe.

Upon my enquiring as to our route north into Cumberland, I learned that we were to travel not, as I had thought, by the regular public coach, but, said George, 'by Sir Henry's own carriage, for he is already in town, and Parliament being now in recess he sends his coach north to bring the ladies for the Christmas season.'

At which I concluded, correctly, that the gentleman referred to was a Member for one of the northern counties. But I was quite unprepared for the further news supplied by my young informant.

'That is, Sir Henry Curwen – no doubt a relation of yourself, miss, for we are all connected in Cumberland.'

At my look of astonishment, he repeated, 'Yes, there are so many connections, Mamma says it is a wonder there are any other families in the county. Even we Nicolsons, though only cousins, are reckoned as family, you see.'

He laughed; then upon my changing the subject (which I feared might become too personal, though I longed to know more) and asking where he was at school, he answered readily, 'At Eton, of course; did you not observe my speaking with Mr Chatterton at Slough?' He continued by setting out for me the relative merits of Eton and of Saint Bee's School, on the Cumberland coast, to which he had expected to be sent. His animation was such that I could not help but become absorbed in all he described, to the extent that we were both surprised by the return of Captain Nicolson. In some haste, we followed him outside, to where the coach was already waiting.

It had stopped snowing. Faint sunlight filtered through the haze, and as we rolled through the streets I looked out eagerly. This then was the London Horatia had so romantically evoked – high buildings, dark narrow passages crowded with people such as I had never, in that sheltered Berkshire countryside, envisaged. True, I had observed poor travellers, country folk and their families, trudging along the London road in search of I knew not what possibilities. But here in the city itself, seen from the bright and comfortable carriage in which I sat, the poor were not those who existed solely (as in the novels and Ladies' Magazines pored over by Horatia and her mother) in order to be visited by noble-hearted gentlewomen. Condescension and charity could surely be of little use to those I saw now, clinging to posts or carriage wheels, leaning beside tavern doorways or market stalls. Though I noted with wonder the newer, whiter buildings springing up beside gracious parks and gardens, through which the morning's first gaily-coloured figures already strolled in the winter sun, the images I carried with me towards Cumberland were of those darker streets and more desperate humanity. As I leaned back in the coach of Sir Henry Curwen, I felt I had no greater right to think myself a lady than had any one of those creatures we had so confidently passed by.

As city gave way to open country and we proceeded north-wards, my thoughts inevitably returned to my older companion. He had again addressed me with civility, indeed had carefully ascertained that I was settled in my corner of the carriage before turning his attention to young George, who chattered on unchecked. Occasionally his father gave me a glance, perhaps a half-smile at some particularly lively description, but at no time did he make any remark that indicated his possible guardian-ship. Yet – had not the boy mentioned some mutual connection with the political gentleman in whose coach we were now travelling?

I puzzled over the fragments of knowledge that had been tossed at me, longing above all for some certainty, however slight. It had so long seemed impossible that I should ever know more than my own name: after so much conjecture, the identity of my guardian appeared just as elusive. I had allowed myself few illusions as to that person's interest in my earlier well-being: had he not left me for years in the care of one whose motives and behaviour had proved equally untrustworthy? But I could not link such an attitude of neglect with the man who now sat opposite me, his arm across his son's shoulder in a gesture of fond concern. His was a kind face, I decided; and his expression, as he caught my gaze, was like that of the boy, frank and lively.

'Come, George, we are neglecting our duty toward Miss Curwen.' He cut short my denial and continued, 'I must confess I have been so much distracted by my son's affairs that I have neglected to convey your aunt's greetings to you. Our mutual aunt, Mrs Nicolson, sends her good wishes for your safe journey; she will be unable to meet you herself at Carlisle, but I shall make sure that you are in safe company from there to Workington. She looks forward greatly to your visit, for she has been much alone since the death of my uncle.'

I thanked him politely but my thoughts were now even more confused. Despite our evident relationship, it seemed that the captain knew little or nothing of my circumstances; and my guardian – for such my aunt must surely be – had indicated only that I was her visitor, rather than a responsibility she had hitherto ignored. I could not believe I had any right to be regarded as a member of that extensive family whose connections were (if George were to be believed) scattered throughout Cumberland; even so, I determined to find out more about my Aunt Nicolson.

'I fear I am a little in ignorance,' I began, 'as to the circumstances of your uncle's death, but I hope you may accept my condolence.'

'It was indeed a tragedy.' He proceeded to tell me how Humphrey Nicolson had drowned, only a year earlier, with the entire crew of a Workington vessel returning from the Caribbean, where he had been sent by Sir Henry Curwen to establish some new indigo plantations.

'Fortunately,' he continued, 'Aunt Nicolson became reconciled with Sir Henry, at the persuasion of her husband, before he died. For Humphrey Nicolson was once Lord Lonsdale's agent and consequently in dispute for many years with the Curwens over harbour developments, both at Workington and at Whitehaven. But at last he believed Sir Henry to be in the right, and took on the indigo venture, though that of course ended as I have told you. At least,' he concluded, 'the families communicate once more – else I should not have been able to escort you.'

Captain Nicolson laughed, while I reflected upon this unknown aunt of mine – clearly a lady of strong character, thus to have married an opponent of her family's interests. Her nephew seemed to speak of her with affection, yet I could not feel myself kindly disposed toward her, or view our meeting with anything other than misgiving.

My speculations were abruptly ended by the sudden slowing down of the carriage. We peered through the windows into a gathering twilight that, in my absorption, I had not previously noticed. There was no expected reason for delay. We had just passed through Stanborough, having traversed part of Hertfordshire, and were now level with a pair of elaborate iron gates, at the edge of a park. A few deer were visible close by, sheltering beneath gracious trees; beyond, a lake stretched away towards rising ground, from which the lights of a mansion shone through the mist. The carriage stopped to a noise of shouting and, as Captain Nicolson descended, a look of alarm on his face indicated some possible danger. Through the now open door I observed a further set of gates, round which were gathered some ill-clad men bearing staves and bars, or sharp sickles clearly not intended, at this wintry season, for use in the empty fields.

The captain began a conversation with the apparent leader of the men, who pressed close to hear what passed between them. In spite of my concern, and George's barely suppressed belligerence, I was more shocked than frightened by the pallor and fatigue in the upturned face of the stocky labourer, whose exchange with our escort seemed less ferocious than the heavy implement he carried as a weapon. Behind him I saw a woman's figure – the only one among the group of men – and as she too pressed eagerly forward, I realised that in her arms, beneath her coarse shawl, she carried a child. The light of our carriage lamps, already lit though it was but early afternoon, fell briefly upon her dark hair and pale face. As she looked up, her gaze met mine with a look in which hopelessness and hatred were equally expressed; and I knew, as the folds of her shawl fell away from the closed eyes and pinched features of her infant, that it could not be alive.

The moment passed. Captain Nicolson rejoined us, pulling up the carriage steps and closing the door. We moved slowly away, past the crowd and past the open gates, upon which the shiny armorial crests were draped with filthy rags, as were the eagles that topped the stone pillars of the entrance.

'It is Lord Melbourne's seat, Brocket Hall,' explained the captain, as he leaned back and our speed increased. 'Those fellows are eager for Reform, and seeing the arms upon our coach thought we must be bound for the great house. I told them that we are but travellers heading north, and that since Sir Henry Curwen has sympathy for their cause they would be wiser not to harm his friends or family. They were civil enough then, poor things; but I fear they will gain little support in other quarters, however scandalous their neglect – not even Melbourne himself can right such wrongs without, it seems, insuperable obstacles.'

I sank back, relieved at our escape, marvelling at the power of a mere name to avert such difficulties, yet only half hearing the captain's words. My mind still dwelt upon the dark-haired woman, hardly more than a girl and so helpless against the harshness of her circumstances. I thought too of Horatia – helpless from a different cause, and within her father's house; and I recalled her anguished look at my words of farewell, when it was too late for pity to turn to friendship.

Some hours later, it promising to be a frosty night, we halted in the town of Huntingdon; tomorrow, I was assured, would see us almost into Yorkshire. How far away, already, lay the wide green valley of the Thames, and my childhood.

Few experiences, I have since discovered, are more conducive to weariness of the company of others than is the proximity endured during a long journey by closed carriage. Yet the first days passed with my new-found relations upon the road to Cumberland were as pleasant as I could have wished, given the disparities between our age and sex, and apart from the discomforts of winter travel. I forgot the drabness of my garments and the gaucheness of my manner, so courteous and cheerful were my cousin – for so I must address him – and his son. They pointed out the great houses and antiquities to be seen along our route, and described to me the many beauties of the Lakeland district through which we were to pass. I had hitherto heard only of its splendid scenery, so much admired by travellers and artists: now I learned not only of lakes and mountains, but of the ports and foreign trade of Cumberland, of coal-mining, weaving and farming, in all of which my cousin Hugh took more than a passing interest.

'It is a rich county,' he remarked with feeling, 'but its people are poor, and their pride suffers greatly from their poverty. If London were only less remote, and if Parliament were to do more and dispute less, there might be some end to their wrongs, for they are not afraid of work, only of suffering through lack of it.'

Yet it seemed that Sir Henry Curwen, Member of Parliament, was a gentleman whose preoccupations lay quite as much within the county he represented as in the distractions of London society.

'For,' continued my cousin, 'though ageing now and frequently in poor health, he still insists that he spend more time among his own people than in wasting his good effort waiting in Whitehall – hence the toing and froing of his carriage, as often as every week when Parliament is sitting. But I do believe that even if the railway comes to Carlisle – as surely it must do before long – he will still prefer the comfort of his own coach!'

I could only respond politely, for by now my chief anxiety lay in the prospect of the addition to our company of a further passenger, to join us at Wetherby. As we climbed the hills toward the town, the weather became more severe; it was already dark, and the hour later than expected, for ice upon the road had earlier forced a slower pace. The captain noticed with some concern that I was shivering; I could not tell him that it was less from cold and fatigue than from anticipation of my coming meeting with his wife. For I feared, far more than the hazards of the road, the curiosity and criticism of which I knew women to be capable. My male cousins had made few demands upon me: I had quickly realised that I could both like and trust them, and I was reluctant to give up that ease of communication which I knew resulted from their good nature rather than from my own social adequacy, so soon to be tested in female company.

George, of course, was delighted at the coming reunion with his mother, on whose behalf, it appeared, the carriage had been secured. Though her health was evidently precarious, following the birth of the latest child, she had felt it necessary to visit her ageing parents in Yorkshire, before winter made the roads between the northern counties impassable.

'She must be a very devoted daughter,' I remarked, to which my cousin replied, 'Indeed, for her parents have shown great kindness to us both, and I owe them much for entrusting her to me when I was a young man without prospects.' I was surprised, for I had assumed him to have always been a gentleman of some means, though I knew by now that he carried out work in connection with Sir Henry's mines. I could enquire no further; but I was to learn, during the coming years, much more about such changes of fortune among my Cumberland relations.

As I look back upon that first meeting with Mary Nicolson, I wonder that I could have so misjudged a person. Her resourceful-ness of character, later of such support to me, was, I must suppose, earlier obscured to me by my own fears and by my suspicion of any feminine frailty that resembled, however remotely, the artifices of Horatia Chatterton and her friends. Mary was fair and delicate of feature, her movements quick and eager despite the sober gray of her Quaker gown. Within moments of our entry into the hotel parlour, the tall, almost stooping figure of her husband had enfolded her within the depths of his travelling coats, little regarding the public nature of their reunion. George joined them, embracing both his mother and the lively small girl who as we entered had called excitedly to her father and brother.

I withdrew to a corner of the room, where a young man watched the scene with evident amusement. He turned to me, raised an eyebrow, and murmured, 'Touching, is it not?' I felt first surprise, then anger, at being so addressed. My reactions went unnoticed, however, for he continued, 'My sister never varies – her demonstrations of affection are always extreme, whether toward husband or child – or indeed toward puppy-dogs, for that matter,' he added pointedly. For a heavy-pawed, yellow-haired dog, not yet fully grown, had joined the group, to the delight of the children and the laughing consternation of their father.

At the mention of his sister I felt less suspicious of the young man, though still unsure of the propriety of discussing the family in this manner. In spite of his good humour, I could detect a kind of unexpressed criticism in his tone; I therefore commented, with

[25]

some energy, 'Would that all families were so contented together!' He gave me a sharp look, and murmuring 'Yes, but at what cost!' he moved away, leaving so much unspoken that I seemed almost to have intruded upon his private thoughts.

While he went to shake Hugh Nicolson's hand, with every appearance of brotherly affection, I turned to face Mary, whom George now tugged towards my corner, the yellow dog leaping beside him. The directness of Mary's gaze, so like that of her brother, disconcerted me even more than his penetrating glance; but there was no ambiguity in her words.

'My husband tells me that you are a relation of his Aunt Nicolson at Workington. I hope you will understand her – people are very different in our northern country from those you will be accustomed to in the south of England. No doubt you will find out all about us,' she added, drily, 'though you are very young, and Aunt Nicolson may not care for that.'

'I shall hope to be a useful companion to her,' I ventured; then, feeling I must remember the courtesies, though I disliked her manner of speaking to me, I went on, 'I have found your son charming company during our journey – he told me so much I did not know about the countryside we came through.'

Mary proceeded to exclaim with enthusiasm over the changes Eton had apparently wrought in her eldest child, who now produced with impatient eagerness his gift for her – a pretty box at which she went into raptures that reminded me of Horatia and her ribbons. I do not know which disconcerted me the more – Mary's bluntness toward myself, so different indeed from southern politenesses; or her lack of inhibition when dealing with her family. Accustomed as I had been to coldness or, at best indifference, on the part of others, I was now alarmed by such direct display of attitude or feeling – as though some door within myself would not be opened. Later, as we went to our respective rooms, I still wondered as to the cause of her brother Philip's comments. For despite his cynicism, and my own unease in Mary's company, I found myself beginning, already, to envy her. How I wished, that night, that our journey was at an end; and how I longed, for the first time, for the enveloping security of unsolicited affection, for the warmth of family and home.

The next morning brought me, as I had anticipated, into further conversation with Mary Nicolson, for we travelled inside together with the children, while her husband and brother went outside. It was a fine clear day, though cold, and I felt less oppressed in spirit. Though it was strange to return to talk of domestic matters, I was relieved that Mary avoided (I am sure, now, from kindness rather than from lack of interest) any discussion of my own situation, save for a single remark that increased my own curiosity as to my aunt's character.

'Aunt Nicolson, being childless, should be glad to have some companionship at last,' she observed, as she dressed yet again her daughter's wooden doll, whose Quaker costume was in every detail similar to her own. 'But she has certain – eccentricities, to which you will have to become accustomed; and yet she can be kindness itself save when crossed, as I have learned from experience.'

She smiled charmingly, and I was grateful for her warning, yet it served only to increase my fears as to my welcome in Workington. How would such a formidable lady treat one who had, as far as I could tell, been wished upon her? Would she soon tire of me, and if so, should I be able to find employment in a strange county? For I had no money, and could not believe a guardian so long neglectful and of such uncertain temper would wish to provide for one whom the Chattertons had found so burdensome.

I was diverted from these painful thoughts by George, who called my attention to the surrounding hills, and a tumbling river that wound between them. We were soon, I learned, at Catterick Bridge, where we crossed the fast-flowing River Swale, beside which great rocks lay; beyond lay further hills and deep vales, fertile no doubt in summer but now white with lying snow. We climbed, then, a road so steep and narrow, and so slippery with snow, that it seemed the horses could scarcely manage the ascent. At some distance from the summit, the men dismounted the coach to ease the horses; even so, we moved at such slow pace that we could see without difficulty the spreading panorama of the plains from which we had come. As we turned the last corner, I looked again at the valley below, down which the river, smaller and more precipitous now, fell between boulders and stubby trees, dark against the snow. It was a bleak landscape, yet I felt more hope, and more certainty that I would face whatever was to come, than at any moment since leaving Berkshire.

The road stretched away before us, across a desolate moor, and for some miles we made but slow progress. Then we halted; the little girl woke from her dozing comfort beside her mother, and Hugh Nicolson told us that we were to stop in order to rest the horses before continuing into Westmorland. George at once descended, and having been assured that my presence was not needed, I too stepped down from the coach.

I found myself in a new, almost alien world. All was still save for the light yet piercing breeze that penetrated even my heavy cloak; to the left stood a moorland farm, where the barking of dogs and a drift of smoke from a single chimney indicated some activity within its granite walls. In the distance were yet more hills, topped with snow and sharp-edged against the blue clarity of the sky. I walked away from the treacherous ruts worn by the passage of carts and coaches; beneath my feet the icy ground cracked a little, the snow seeming to shimmer with the colours and deceptive delicacy of mother-of-pearl, like that of the card-case I now carry. A few yards, and I stood beside a frozen stream, its edges fringed with brittle glistening reeds and stiffened fronds of fern. The narrow branches of an overhanging bush appeared as though enbalmed in glass, beneath which the knots and roughness of bark were visible; above, a waterfall was now a curtain of ice suspended between rocks – though silent, it seemed still to be a living thing which might at a touch resume its noisy flow. Years later, I saw in Paris a vase, with crystal traceries laid upon milk-white glass, which recalled the frozen veins and suspended bubbles of the moorland fall: I do not know which was the more beautiful, the natural form or the man-made artefact. But I longed, for the first time in many months, to transmute what I saw into a painting.

I heard a voice behind me, and turned, astonished. It was Philip Earnshaw, Mary's brother, his coat swinging and head bare.

'My sister thought that you might need assistance – the ground is not safe. But I assured her that so independent a young woman would be sure to scorn my help.' His laugh was not unkind, but I was unsure whether to thank him for his trouble or to apologise, since he had followed me unwillingly.

'You are certainly a remarkable female, to be exploring the wild countryside whilst your fellows sit shivering and complaining.'

I detected some note of admiration, and determined that we should not embark upon the kind of conversation I instinctively detested – when gentlemen deliver compliments which ladies deny in hope of receiving more. I had overheard such exchanges in the drawing-room at Maidenhead, and did not know then that even such obvious artifice may lead to true communication, if such is the speaker's objective. I had not yet acquired the more civilised, if less honest approach, and therefore spoke without reserve.

'I cannot think it so remarkable, sir, to seek exercise after such close confinement, and solitude after so long a period of proximity as that of our journey today. I am grateful for your sister's concern, but I am more . . . comfortable, alone. Besides,' I added, more to myself than to my companion, 'it is all so beautiful . . .'

His momentary look of discomfiture did not escape me, yet any hope of keeping Philip Earnshaw at a distance was short-lived. He laughed, and accepted my reply as a challenge.

'Can it be that you are a lover of nature – not merely unsociable but a true solitary? Come, so thoughtful a young lady has surely heard of our Lakeland poets?'

And he proceeded to quote to me, without hesitation, some verses relating to solitude. His voice lost its customary mocking tones, becoming low and musical, and as he continued, expressive not only of the poet's meaning, but also, surely, of some feeling of his own.

I was charmed, yet wary. It was clear he took me for a far more educated person than I was, and it was impossible to enlighten him without forfeiting our communication – which I confess was a novelty I enjoyed beyond expectation. Silence

[29]

could only intensify the moment, and I ceased then even to seek for words, hoping to prolong that instant of unfamiliar pleasure in another's company. He was speaking again, of poetry and poets, of Wordsworth and Coleridge, names which were indeed to become meaningful to me but now served rather only to remind me of my ignorance. Yet, kindly, he sensed my confusion, and continued more prosaically: 'The wind blows more coldly out here across the snow – you would be wise, perhaps to abandon your lonely excursion.'

He looked with some anxiety at the darkening sky. Towards the north-west great clouds were beginning to move across the sun's lengthening rays, which, despite their brightness, held no warmth. A shout from the direction of the road, and George was on his way towards us from where the coach was standing; I should have hastened at once to rejoin it, but for my companion's restraining hand upon my arm.

'Miss Curwen,' said Philip Earnshaw, 'I confess I am curious about you – my brother-in-law makes quite a creature of mystery out of you, and you seem to me to be . . . not quite of the order of most young ladies. I shall seek you out, you may be sure, in Cumberland.' Though once again he spoke lightly, his eyes were serious, seeming almost to reflect the snow's glitter as he looked down at me.

The necessity of replying was spared me; thankfully, I turned to greet George. The coach, it appeared, was ready to depart, and there was some concern lest more snow should fall before we reached Brough, where it was hoped we should spend the night before taking the road for Carlisle. Tomorrow would, if there were no unforeseen delay or difficulty, be the last day on which I would travel with my cousin and his family.

Now, as we gradually left behind the icy uplands, moving with increasing speed as the way grew easier and the threat of snow more imminent, I became conscious of regret at the prospect of this journey's end. My lonely fears of the previous night seemed unreal, almost unfounded, as I sat with little Edith's head resting against my arm in that gesture which a child will make when deciding that an adult may be trusted after all. Though some years would pass before I felt at ease in her mother's presence, the child already drew from me a warmth of feeling that had lain too long unkindled. Beyond tomorrow lay fresh apprehensions – an unknown guardian, a future without shape or certainty. But, for the present, I found myself strangely content to accept the pleasures, however fleeting, of my new acquaintance – and even to hope that something might endure beyond the next day's parting. And mingled with that hope, I knew, was my belief in the assurance I had received from Philip Earnshaw.

Chapter 3

'There can, my child, be no redress – of that, I am certain. My brother cannot – will not – be persuaded. For my own neglect, I shall make what amends I can.'

I knew by now enough of my great-aunt to have no doubt that she spoke truly; Elizabeth Nicolson was not a woman given to wasting words, and would not have lied to me. She had told me how my mother had been sent away from home, had been parted from me when I was a few months old, and had died two years ago, far from her family in Cumberland. As we sat in the upstairs parlour on the eve of my eighteenth birthday, I listened to my guardian – and tried to comprehend.

'Henry is a good man, and would not wish to think ill of any person, least of all his own child. But he believes that your mother acted foolishly, cruelly, with no thought for how sad an example she might prove to her sisters – then young and easily swayed by so strong an influence as hers.'

'But did he not love her as a father should? To disown her, his daughter – I cannot understand it.'

Indeed I could not; I felt only that such a man must be hard beyond imagination: I knew then nothing of the subtle shades of doubtful motivation which may lead us along paths that cannot be retraced.

'I am sure – ' my aunt paused as if finding the words difficult to utter, 'yes, I am sure, that had he loved her less he might have understood her better. For Henry was always hasty in his judgement of women, as I know to my cost – his own wife was such a paragon that he judged us all by her virtues. And yet even Frances had her faults, faults he was blind to till the day she died; she was too clever for him, that's certain – and he's no fool; the people love and respect him, and in times like these such a reputation as his is not won easily.'

But I had already, in my heart, condemned Sir Henry Curwen. No words even from one so upright as my aunt could have spared my grandfather at that moment – as I consigned him, with all the bitterness of which only the young are capable, to that outer darkness of mistrust where he seemed rightly to belong.

My guardian's honesty, at least, I trusted – but her capriciousness was something I still feared, and could not understand. Though she might with profit, or even from mere kindness, have attempted to curb her outspokenness, to have done so would have been to concede – a word with which she was not acquainted. Since my arrival in Workington, I had found no way by which to penetrate the armour of conviction that she wore daily, to battle as it were with those who at their peril crossed her path. 'Formidable' describes her – no weaker adjective could do justice to the strength of purpose and firmness of manner displayed in all her enterprises. Even her clothes lacked compromise: stiff black silks, old-fashioned and so rigidly corseted that any suppleness of limb was totally disguised. She was not only large, and threatening of demeanour: her voice had no soft cadence, no gentle or persuasive tone, but a penetrating clarity that assured the hearer that this was no guileless feminine creature. Her questions demanded answers, without delay; her judgement would accept no contradiction; and, above all, she did not stoop to lie.

At times I was to be grateful for her honesty, but now it only added to my pain; it gave me no hope, and that I needed, beyond anything. For I knew now as truth what my childish instinct had already told me, that my mother, Georgiana Curwen, had been born a lady. I was indeed, as young George Nicolson had so lightheartedly suggested, a relation of Sir Henry

– his eldest daughter's child. Yet I had no claim to recognition, and no hope, as Aunt Nicolson made plain, of any redress for the wrong he had done my mother; there was no way in which I should come to know either his interest or his affection. And, most cruelly of all, there was no way in which my mother might be restored to me, or ever come to know me as her daughter.

We sat for some moments, my aunt and I, in the sunlit parlour overlooking the cobbled square that I had come to think of, almost without awareness, as my home. For as I crossed it, almost daily, on some errand or excursion, it seemed always tranquil, despite the carts that came and went, or the tradespeople shouting at the doorways. An old man, sitting each day beside his window, watched me pass, as he watched every passer-by; he would nod between the geraniums on his window-sill, and nod again when I returned. My aunt's house, with its low roof, somewhat irregular windows and modest doorway, formed part of the upper corner of the square – small indeed compared with any gracious London square, but here a quiet haven from the narrow bustling streets and passageways of the town.

My aunt rose, rather stiffly, and moved towards the door. Her eyes, of a blue I could only compare with the blue of my woollen gown, seemed unusually kind. 'Come,' she said, 'it is warm enough for us to walk further today. We will go as far as the harbour, for I must see about my boats – Humphrey would have wished it; the *Elizabeth* needs repairs and refurbishing, I am told, and it must all be done before the summer.'

We found our bonnets and wraps, for the wind was still blowing cold from the sea, and, with rapid instructions to Emily, who hovered anxiously to know when she should have the teapot ready, we descended the narrow stairway and went out across the square.

The town of Workington as I came to know it had but lately begun its progress towards the industrial port it has since become. Our pleasant square, situated on the edge of the more gracious, modern and respectable quarter, was provided in its farthest corner with an almost hidden passage to the winding, often precipitous ways of the lower town. At first my aunt walked with a speed that I found difficult to match, especially since the streets, for the most part still unfamiliar to me, became increasingly crowded as we neared the harbour.

Away to our right lay the widening Derwent, its nearer bank lined with the empty hulls and half-built vessels of the boatyards. Below us men laboured at the new pier, the project of Sir Henry Curwen and now almost completed. It was clearly a necessity, for even though many of the smaller fishing-boats were away from port, the moorings were busy with all manner of craft. Some, squat in shape and bearing Irish names, were being loaded with coal or slate; others, with taller masts and complex riggings, brought cotton for the mills, tea and coffee, fruit for the markets; on certain days, I had learned, boats left with passengers for the Isle of Man or for destinations on the Scottish coast across the Solway. From the time I had first reached Workington, weary with a day's journey through mist and sleet from the city of Carlisle, and filled with an inner dread that with each mile increased in proportion to my weariness, I had loved the sudden sight of those many masts, glimpsed between the chimneys and gables of the dockside buildings.

That December afternoon, now more than three months behind me, I had, in obedience to my great-aunt's bidding, retired upstairs to rest before facing her again at dinner. We had communicated little upon my arrival. For a few moments only – yet how long they seemed! – I stood in her small parlour, my cold hands knotting and re-knotting the ribbons of my bonnet. Then, with an abruptness that I thought must signify displeasure, my guardian addressed me: 'You are like her, as I thought – and yet – you are not like!'

I knew not what to say; I almost wept – while Emily, who had already scrutinised me on the doorstep, regarded my portmanteau with suspicion before carrying it, with a pause at each step, up to my room. This, though not large, was comfortably furnished, warm with a fire and fragrant with the scent of jessamine from a vase near the bedside. Such unexpected kindness from my austere relation gave me encouragement; I crossed to the window and drew back the heavy curtains. It was not yet dark: below me lay the town, the harbour, and the sea. Where the clearing western sky met the line of the horizon, rays from the late sun were turning the grey of the water to a silvery green; above stretched delicate bands of crimson, green and gold. Even the higher storm-clouds were touched with a rosier light, which brightened the calmer waters within the bay. Here a long low black mass of rock jutted seaward on the one hand; on the other lay the curve of the wooden pier. And between, seeming to rise from among the rooftops, were the masts of numerous vessels, their dark thin spires hung about with fine traceries of ropes, like so many autumn cobwebs.

Although since then I had looked many times, and with undiminished pleasure, upon the prospect from my window, we had rarely ventured down through the old town to the harbour. The early months of the year had been severely cold, with frequent wild westerly gales that caused me to imagine, as I heard the wind beating at the safety of the walls, the plight of those aboard the tossing boats at sea. All I had known before were the drifting pleasure-seekers on the river Thames; here I came to learn of other, harsher destinies – like that which had claimed my guardian's husband, Humphrey Nicolson. Though Aunt Elizabeth seemed, on occasions, to become removed in thought to regions of experience where I could not follow, she rarely spoke of my uncle save in some practical connection. The refurbishment of his boats, at last returned to harbour, was clearly a matter of importance. So I dutifully followed her, though I longed to pause, to linger beside some shadowy passage or curious crooked doorway – above all, to stand for a moment on the stone stair leading to the quay and look out beyond the boats to the glistening open sea.

At length, she did stop. And I stood beside her, gazing up at the *Elizabeth*, while my aunt simultaneously straightened her bonnet, inspected my own, and called out, 'Captain Sharpe! I wish to speak with Captain Sharpe!'

As we waited, in that spring sunlight which so falsely makes us feel the breath of summer's warmth, the vessel might have been the phantom ship of which the poet Coleridge writes –

becalmed upon the still and silent ocean – so little movement did she make, so little sound responded to the calling of my aunt. 'Captain Sharpe!' Again no answer: only the almost imperceptible flapping of a lower sail, left loose though all the rest were neatly furled. From behind us came the cries of gulls, fighting for their quayside spoils, remnants of the morning's catch; and from further along the wooden pier on which we stood, all the bustle of departing passengers, their farewells echoing across the water as their boat receded.

With more patience than I should have dared to attribute to her, Aunt Elizabeth waited; and I should have thought her unexpected tolerance ill-rewarded had not, at the instant we turned to go, a figure appeared on deck. Within a moment he had run along the nearest spar, from which he leapt the narrow gap between boat and pier, to arrive with a gallant, if inelegant, bow beside us.

'Your service, Mistress Nicolson, ma'am,' he said, smoothing his hair and fastening the brass buttons on his faded waistcoat. 'And yours too, miss,' he added, bowing again, as though charm could erase the unfortunate impression he gave of having just awoken from his winter sleep. For this captain was no handsome dashing buccaneer, such as may haunt a young maid's dreams – but a nimble, wiry man of middle age and height, reddish hair turning to grey, his quick glance and movement like those of a wayside squirrel.

'My niece, Miss Curwen – now residing with me,' stated my aunt.

Captain Sharpe's manner became warm as well as courteous. 'In that case, miss,' said he, 'I hope I may have the pleasure of conducting you aboard the *Elizabeth* – once her repairs are completed, that is, and she is fit to be seen again. A fine fast ship she is – well protected, too,' he added, indicating the gun mountings along her side. 'Now then, ma'am – ' and he turned once more to my aunt, with whom he entered into lengthy discussion of various items of work soon to be undertaken.

As they conversed, his deeper voice (its rough though not unmusical tone like those I had heard among other of my aunt's Workington acquaintance) seemed to arouse in her a lively, yet gentler than usual, response. Then I became aware that this more kindly animation, which gave warmth to her cheek and brightness to her eyes, stemmed from the mention of her husband. 'Ah, yes,' she was saying, as the captain pointed out some damage inflicted by a storm during the latest Caribbean voyage, 'you are right, it was indeed near there that we once almost lost the ship and ourselves with her. How well I remember that fearful tempest, and our certainty that Humphrey would bring us through safely — as, of course, he did! You had been with us but a short time, then — and have learned a good deal more about the sea since those days, I'll be bound!' She laughed, almost merrily; then looked up at the *Elizabeth*, and once more tightened her lips and frowned.

Hitherto, I had seen Elizabeth Nicolson but as a sharp-tongued vigorous lady, sombre in her widow's garments — and with preoccupations I had thought entirely sober and domestic. Now, briefly, she became again the eager, spirited young woman who had gladly followed her seafaring husband to far-off places; a traveller, whose voyages, begun and ended at this obscure Cumbrian harbour, had required fortitude as well as devotion — which had clearly earned her the censure of her brother, Sir Henry. My aunt's independence of the Curwen family, must, I realised as I wandered further along the pier, have prompted my mother's choice of her as guardian to myself. She had spoken of making some amends for her neglect: yet how could I remain where I had no place, no purpose? My existence, cause of my mother's disgrace, must surely become an embarrassment even to one so seemingly immune to opinion as that straight-backed, black-bonneted figure who now beckoned me, with an authority I could not dispute, to return to her at once.

We looked for a few minutes at my aunt's second vessel, the *Hope*, newly painted and almost ready to set sail. But there was not time, I gathered, to linger talking with her captain, one Brathwaite, who smartly acknowledged our presence in a manner less eccentric — and less interesting — than that of Captain Sharpe. The latter waved at us cheerfully as we retraced our steps, and Aunt Elizabeth nodded briskly at him.

'I have promised Sharpe that you will visit his wife one day soon — she keeps indoors, poor thing, and would be pleased to have company. It's my belief some air would cure her quickly enough; but some women are like plants in a hot-house — the very thought of a cold wind makes them shrivel, however pretty they look!' With this judgement, which seemed to me a little harsh (though I did remember poor Horatia and her wilful assumption of delicacy), she set off at a smart pace.

Our return through the lower town, though necessarily slowed down somewhat by the steepness of the ascent, took an erratic course of a kind to which I had become accustomed when walking with my aunt. Having covered a distance at great speed, she would stop suddenly, in mid-flight as it were, to accost with characteristic vigour some unsuspecting citizen for whom she held a vital communication that must not be delayed. The person — male or female, respectable-looking or of dubious appearance — would seek in vain to escape her instructions or admonishments; until at last, with equally dramatic abruptness, she would discard him and continue her progress with renewed energy. While she remained stationary, I would perhaps become absorbed in noting the sounds and colours of the street-market; or, as today, would pause to look along a little court, scarce wider than a cart's breadth, where cats and children played and a sleeping man lay in the shadow of the wall. As usual, my aunt's departure took me unawares, so that I found myself hurrying after her — whereupon, as if determined to elude pursuit, she took an unexpected turn in through the doorway of a linen-draper's shop.

Here, when I caught up with her, she was engaged in critical inspection of a display of coloured silk threads. As the draper, with whom I was already acquainted, reached up for yet another box to open for her scrutiny, his young assistant, blushing deeply, ran forward with a second chair; this he offered me, with a sympathetic raising of an eyebrow and a glance in the direction of my companion. Ashamed of such tacit conspiracy, I hastily attended to the silks, as my aunt turned to me, saying, 'Now, since these are for Isabella's chairs, they must be right. You are of an age with her — tell me, will she prefer these — '

indicating some peacock blues and greens '– or these darker, violet ones?'

I was at a loss, for I knew that she would already have decided and my opinion was therefore quite superfluous. The embroidery in question, intricately worked designs unlike my aunt's usual practical needlework, had been in evidence since my arrival; it was destined as a summer wedding-gift – for another Curwen grand-niece. Predisposed as I was to hate the very name of Curwen, I was seized at that instant by a quite irrational vindictiveness toward my unknown, doubtless charming, cousin Isabella. With a conviction I did not feel, I stated my preference.

'I am sure, aunt, that Isabella would much rather have the violet – it is so *very* pretty!' And I was rewarded by seeing the chosen silks most carefully wrapped up, while the blue and sea-green that I loved were packed away again by the eager assistant. When, in time, I recognised the violet silk embroidery *in situ* in my cousin's drawing-room, I felt a tremor of guilt – that, but for my wilfulness, its effect might have been a trifle less funereal among the pastel shades of its surroundings.

Following our return my aunt was more than usually disposed to silence. By now I was well used to her dismissal of my conversational attempts, or to her brisk concluding remarks following which there was no option but to pursue one's own thoughts. But on this occasion even Emily refrained from that ingenious provocation with which she instinctively responded to her mistress's mood. The teacups were removed without the faintest clatter of spoons against delicate china; the door was tactfully closed behind her, with but the merest hint of hesitation. Then I rose and drew across the velvet curtains, shutting out the mist that had succeeded the mild spring afternoon.

There were so many questions that I wished to ask – yet I was held back by a sense of defeat. Had I travelled so far but for this? – Oh, I knew not why I had come, or for what I had hoped! When I looked out from the coach window at the wind-bent trees and huddled cottages on the roadside between Carlisle and

Workington, all earlier conjecture had been swept away by fear – fear of what I might discover, fear of what I might not find. The very town had seemed to me, on that winter day, a fearful place! Behind me lay the winding, windswept road, my childhood gone; before, lay the dark monotony of roofs and walls, beyond which a widening river slid from blackened stones toward the shore; only a narrow frill of foam – like a petticoat's white beneath a widow's gown – relieved the uncompromising greyness of the sea. And in the weeks that followed came a further dread: that my aunt, each day observing me, might find me wanting in some way, might cast me out as suddenly, upon a whim, as she had sent for me.

Yet it seemed that those fears had been but shadows of the despair that now took hold of my young heart. My aunt could not have known, as she sat in silence, her hands unwontedly idle, how my anger was succeeded by a craving, long suppressed, for what could not be mine – some warmth of feeling to enfold me, as I had seen my cousin Hugh enfold his daughter in his welcoming arms.

Later, after dinner, we took our places once again in the parlour, she with her embroidery, I with my sketchbook and pencil. I had thought to try to draw some details of the harbour as I had seen them that afternoon; perhaps I might make an excursion later in the summer, to capture something of that strange blend of action and tranquillity – the noise and movement of folk and goods, the gentle sway of masts, the easy glide of waves upon the shore . . . And yet – I might not be here in summer. Should I not leave Workington, my hopes and longings unfulfilled, behind me; embark perhaps on some small boat for an unknown land? I saw again the *Elizabeth*, on which my aunt had sailed – but she had had reason thus to depart, and a husband with whom to share the danger and uncertainty. And I saw the *Hope*, her painted figurehead sharp against the sky, bright gilded hair that glittered in the sun, red, parted lips, and a blue eye that stared mockingly down upon me . . .

I looked across at my aunt. Her head, bent over her work, was turned away a little. Perhaps I had imagined that hint of gentleness beneath the harsh surface, the laughter upon her mouth, now drawn in a tight line against adversity. Her hands, pale upon the coloured fabric, their fingers long and tapering, were such as my mother's might have been. My own hands, restored now to a smoothness that might almost be termed elegant, toyed still with my pencil, but refused to obey my inclination. For I remembered suddenly, as from some dim recess a half-forgotten treasure comes unsought-for to the light, the touch of Philip Earnshaw's hand upon my arm, the sound of his voice as we stood beside the frozen stream.

He was still in my thoughts when, at the customary hour, I said goodnight to my aunt and left her to turn down the lamps, a ritual she refused to delegate to Emily. In my room, I recalled my hopes that Philip might fulfil his promise when my cousin Hugh paid Aunt Nicolson his New Year visit – an event that caused as much domestic preparation as if he had brought with him his entire family. But only George, whom I was glad to see again, accompanied him; and I soon dismissed as mere masculine self-indulgence that assurance Philip made with such conviction. Some lingering hope had stayed with me, despite myself. But the chance that he might find me, should he choose to seek me out, must be remote, for I could see no future now for me in Cumberland.

'Georgiana!' My aunt's voice aroused me from my thoughts. She stood in the passage, her bedtime candle flickering; I could see by its light a look of sadness upon her face.

'Georgiana – there is something else. I had thought to give this to you tomorrow, for then you will be of age and whatever it contains should be legally your own. But there can be no reason to delay any longer – so much harm has been done already, not least by myself, by delaying and indecision. Goodnight – we will talk of all this again tomorrow, if you wish.'

She gave into my hand a small packet neatly tied with a brown ribbon. Had I known then what a Pandora's box of emotions this was to let loose upon my as yet unformed personality, I should perhaps have rejected the package – containing as it did my mother's letters, written during the last years of her life, to myself, her unseen daughter.

*

For some time I sat in the low chair beside the fireplace; unheeded, the last flames flickered and died. When at last I rose, I raked neatly the few embers for use next morning – a duty I had always performed whilst I had the care of Matilda Chatterton's room. I found it difficult still to leave such tasks to Emily, who usually knocked before she went to her bed in case there should be something I needed. She appeared to take a grim kind of pleasure in such attentions, and would have been affronted had I rejected them. Tonight, however, her knock must have been gentler than her usual peremptory rapping, for I had heard it not, as I sat by the dying fire, holding in my hand that little package of letters . . .

I lay awake in the darkness, the unopened packet beside me. At length, towards dawn, I summoned courage enough to light my candles, and slipped the topmost letter from the ribbon that held it with its fellows. It bore a date and an inscription upon its outer fold:

> *March 1827* These letters, written by me to my daughter Georgiana Frances Curwen, are all I can give to her as proof that I did not willingly abandon her & in the beleif that those who parted us have not destroy'd the bond of love between us – for I have kept it alive in my heart. GMC

To my present shame and sorrow, I felt no warmth for the woman who wrote those words. For I knew that no such bond existed. I did not believe in it, so cold was my heart, so unresponsive my affections: my childhood feelings had long since withered from lack of nourishment and any remnant had been locked away in bitterness. I yearned only for the living – for that which I could touch and hold.

The letter, which I then unfolded and read, was the last that my mother had written.

> Rochester february 1827
> Today I have been walking in my garden – it is a consolation to me to see the new shoots coming among the dead leaves of Autumn. Yet I cannot find it in my heart to care about the Spring: a winter darkness seems to cling about me, to penetrate

[43]

all my being, to chill my limbs & make me move so slowly, as though my strength will never be renew'd. Even my baby (Pip they call him) has no claim to make me long for life – he is a curious little thing, such large eyes & frail limbs that I fear he too may not live long. And yet such infants are oft tenacious, like those green shoots springing even where feet have trod the ground till it is hard. When I nurse him, it seems my life is ebbing away into the hard ground while his body struggles to grow. But I am glad I can nourish him, even as I nourish'd you my daughter long ago – for it gave me a bond with you, as with this little one. One cannot care so much for the children one has not nurs'd. Tho' I griev'd when each in turn they sicken'd and died, I mourn'd so much the more for you – my living child cruelly taken to grow & blossom in some stranger's garden where I may never enter.

I hope that when you read these lines you may beleive in my love for you & will soften your heart to one who did not lightly abandon you. Always I felt that one day I should see you again, hold you in my arms & see in your face the likeness of him I lov'd so dearly. Now I know that Patience is but a lure to draw us away from that happiness to which we should hold fast while 'tis in our reach: waiting, trusting in God as we were taught to do, has given me nothing to call mine, no life to which my children may look with pride as I beheld all my own mother achiev'd. But I could not be like her, I knew, in strength of mind and diversity of talents, for which my father worship'd her. So willful a child as I could not but disappoint such parents – the one so gifted, the other so fill'd with truly moral purpose. How could they know that brilliance & virtue seem'd only to stifle my spirit, that I needed to walk the hills, to ride the horses, dance the nights away & shock the neighbourhood, to make for myself the freedom of which the poets write. Had I been a man I should have done these things, father'd a hundred bastards had I wish'd – & they would have laugh'd & call'd me wild but would not have refus'd me entry into their drawing-rooms!

It is fruitless I know to have regrets, just as it is useless to try to fight those who are stronger than oneself. My strength seem'd all to leave me when I found that your father was powerless to help me. Our happiness was like that of children – founded on illusion, part of a daydream from which one would not wish to waken. And yet – my dreams have kept me alive. At first they fill'd me with false hope, that Alexander would somehow descend god-like & transport me from the dreariness to which I was condemn'd, away to some green valley (O, Wastdale in the Spring!) where we wander'd together when young. Later I dream'd that when my children were grown & my duty to their father – whose kindness has not wavered tho' I never lov'd him – at last fulfil'd, I should return to Cumberland, to lay my head in my Mother's lap, to walk again beneath the beeches in the garden & run to greet my Father's carriage at the gate.

Now all my dreams are faded save for one – that you my daughter, a second Georgiana, may go there for me. Tell my Father, if he lives, that I love him still tho' he has wrong'd me: I know now that I shall not see him again nor walk on the hills where my heart is. Forgive, if you can, the frailty that caus'd me to be parted from you – for that, I cannot forgive myself. I thought then only that your future would be assur'd, not counting in my foolishness the cost of losing your affection. This is the last letter I shall write to you. Like all the rest, it is written in greif, and with love.

Georgiana Curwen

Her name, and the last few lines preceding it, were faded and blurred a little, as though she had penned them even as her tears flowed. Yet my own eyes were dry, though strained from reading in the dimness of the almost burnt-out candles. I felt only a weariness beyond belief.

I do not know what strange impulse caused me then, with sudden resolution, to dress myself, almost mechanically, in my daytime garments. Shift and petticoats, gown and woollen stockings, cloak, bonnet and gloves, all came to be placed upon my limbs as though some invisible nursemaid were at hand to fasten the buttons and strings in the now-fading darkness of my little room. Then she guided me down the stairs, helped me pull back the bolts of the street-door, and pushed me out into the square, where I stood shivering in the half-light of that early

[45]

April morning. I had no thought that this was my birthday. I knew only that I could not return to my bed, beside which it seemed my mother stood, holding in her hand the letter I had read, from which her presence had somehow been conjured up, as though her words had brought alive her portrait from within its frame.

Unwittingly, I retraced the route my aunt and I had taken but half a day ago. Past the old man's window, its curtains drawn behind the red geranium; along the cobbles of the passage, slippery with falling mist; past the linen-draper's stores and the clog-maker's shop; down a narrow stone stairway, my gloves becoming soiled with grime that clung to the twisted iron hand-rails. Mist lingered still around the mast-tops as I reached the quay, where fisher-girls were beginning to gather with their baskets. The first herring-boats were in; the sound of laughter and cursings, as the men made fast and brought in their catch, reached me as I leaned against a warehouse wall, waiting the moment when I might slip past unnoticed. Beyond the fishing-boats stretched the old wooden pier, and the deeper water where the *Hope* and the *Elizabeth* were moored; and further still, dark beneath the drifting cloud, lay the open sea.

The place was deserted, save for the ever-hungry seagulls – and one boy, seated at the very end of the pier. He moved, briefly, to look at me, then turned his face seaward again. Wrapping my cloak more closely round me, I sank down upon a capstan and listened, for I know not how long, to the faint tinkling sound of ropes against masts, and the deeper sound of the water as it flowed round the wooden pillars toward the shore. It was near to full tide, and the sea's roar, as it tugged and worried the pebbles between the jaws of great grey waves, seemed to threaten the town itself. Away from the shore and the quay with its scurrying figures, behind the warehouses and chimneys of the dockside, the streets and houses rose more steeply. Some of the rooftops shone in the new sunlight which penetrated the dispersing mist. Even as I watched, the cloud was lifting from the tall trees beyond the north-eastern limits of the town. And though my knowledge of the area was scanty still, I had no doubt as to the name of the white building upon which the sun's rays now rested: it was Workington Hall, seat of Sir Henry Curwen, and my dead mother's home. Behind and to the east rose the Lakeland mountains, their tops still hidden by folds of mist, their lower slopes already bright with the new green of springtime – the season of my birth and of my mother's death, so far from the hills she loved.

Chapter 4

For a few bitter moments longer, I gazed landward. But though I resolutely pulled my wraps around me and turned to face the ocean, still I saw before me the shining whiteness of Workington Hall, set among its graceful trees, remote as any fabled castle in a childhood story. Thus is the unattainable printed upon one's too-receptive mind, as clearly as the most familiar detail of a much-loved landscape.

How long I should have stayed there I cannot tell, had I not felt a tugging at the fold of my cloak. It was the same child I had noticed earlier, seated at the pier's end, staring out to sea. He was, I judged, about eight or nine years of age, though the care written upon his brow gave him the aspect of one far older in experience.

'Miss, if you please,' said he, 'will you look and tell me if that dark thing upon the watter is a boat, now? I believe it must be, but my eyes are sore wi' looking so long and hard.'

His anxiety was clearly great, and I at once turned again toward the open sea, peering in the direction indicated by his outstretched arm and pointing finger. Something dark was indeed to be seen upon the greyness. I waited several minutes before pronouncing my opinion that it was the looked-for boat, but that it was moving very slowly and could surely not make harbour for some time yet.

'Oh, miss, I'm right glad if it is, though I wish Father could hurry – all the other boats are in by now, and he will get a poor price for his fish with being so late.'

He turned as if to leave me, but I hurriedly addressed him again.

'I am sorry to hear it – but tell me, is there something more, or do you weep only at the price of the fish?' For I had seen his eyes fill with tears as he moved away, and felt, besides, strangely disturbed at his urgency and evident distress.

The boy looked up at me, his hand pulling at the great lock of black hair that fell across his brow.

'It is just that I need my father to come home quickly, for one of the babbies is so sick, and I cannat tell what I should do. If he's too long coming I fear she may die, and Father will be angered that I left her to come and look for him.'

His tears started again, and I walked quickly beside him as he began to run along the pier. With his bare feet he could move more swiftly than I along the slippery boards.

'Wait! Wait – I will come with you and look at the baby if you wish. Perhaps there will be something I can do until your father comes,' I added, as he stopped, then took my hand without a word.

He led me back the way I had come, past the sailing-boats now busy with men and merchandise, through the crowd of women and girls at the fish quay. Some looked at us curiously. One called out 'Peter!' and made as if to speak with the boy but he ducked out of her reach, pulling me away past the open doors of a warehouse and along towards a stair similar to that down which I had earlier descended. Then, oblivious to all but my own painful thoughts, I had not noticed the rotting doors and sunken roofs of the close-packed cottages. Now, in the brightness of the sunshine, it was evident that the buildings were much neglected; and though some of the little children already playing upon the precipitous steps, even at this early hour, wore garments neatly patched, others were in rags long past cleaning or mending. I trod carefully to avoid the mud and heaps of refuse on the stairway, which in wet weather must have resembled some kind of filthy waterfall – shaded not by leafy branches but by lines of tattered laundry hung between the gables of the cottages.

Peter had let go of my hand as we climbed the steps. I followed him to a doorway where two small girls, dark-haired and ragged like himself, seemed to be disputing the ownership of some pebbles and fragments of coloured glass that lay on the doorstep between them. From within came the sound of a wailing child; as we entered, and my eyes became accustomed to the dimness of the room, I heard the boy exclaim, 'Are you crying still then? What can be the matter with her, miss? She was just the same all the night – if only father would come, he would know what to do.'

I bent down to look at the baby, huddled as she was in a great shawl that had seen better days but had at least kept her warm in that chilly room, where the hearth was empty save for one half-burnt piece of driftwood.

'I think your baby is very hungry, and that is why she cries so much,' I said, for though she was clearly weak she seemed not to be feverish, and her cry was not the feeble sound of a sick infant. 'She should have some warm milk, perhaps some porridge or broth,' I continued, remembering the nursery at Maidenhead where I had had care of the youngest child, then about a year old, as I guessed this one to be. I looked about me but could see no evidence of provisions: some bags and boxes on a shelf near the hearth were, as far as I could ascertain, quite empty.

'Do you have no food at all?' I enquired of Peter, who had by this time picked up the baby – but she only cried more frantically as he tried to rearrange the shawl around her. The two girls had left off their play at the doorway, and were standing beside their brother, amazed at the intrusion of a stranger.

Peter hesitated, then, 'There is some food, yes,' he said. 'But I promised Father I would keep it hid, for they – ' he pointed accusingly at the two younger children ' – they would take it all, they are always so hungry, and after it is gone there can be no more till he sells his fish. But I fear he is too late today, with the boat coming in so slow – '

He broke off and ran to the door, evidently hoping he might see the fisherman already mounting the steps. But he came inside again, his dark eyes looking anxiously at me to see what I would do.

'Find me what you have,' I said, no longer hesitating. 'I will take you with me when we have fed the baby, and I shall give you food to bring home with you, so you will not need to go hungry whilst your father waits to sell his catch.'

Any thoughts I might earlier have entertained of never more returning to my aunt, I now dismissed. She would, I was certain, let me have food for these little ones, for she could not even, despite occasional sermons against wastefulness, let the birds go hungry in the garden when the weather was severe. Only a few days before, when a sudden hard frost had reminded us that winter was not yet gone, she had reprimanded Emily, who on opening the back door had exclaimed crossly when half a dozen sparrows sought refuge in her kitchen. 'They are all God's creatures,' my aunt had pronounced as she scattered crumbs from the breakfast table. Since she rarely invoked God at all – and then only when rational argument was insufficient for her cause – I knew she must indeed have the sparrows' interests at heart.

From the depths of a chest beneath the table Peter produced a bag that still contained a little meal, sufficient I surmised to make a pan of gruel. One small sister was dispatched for water, the other to fetch sticks with which on her return the boy managed to conjure up a fire. The transformation wrought by food and warmth was such that, when at length the absent fisherman returned, he stood upon the threshold of his home and stared at what was happening within. Peter, worn out with the efforts of the previous hours, was curled up in the only chair, and fast asleep. His sisters had crept close to the blaze, warming their bare feet and brown fingers and listening as I told them a tale such as I sometimes told the Chatterton children; while I sat on a footstool, the baby on my knee – a situation that afforded me as much satisfaction as it seemed to give the child.

The sudden appearance in the doorway of a tall heavily-bearded figure filled me with alarm. I had for the present quite forgot the long-awaited father: but now reality returned, to break – as with the breaking of a spell – the temporary calm I had achieved. The boy awoke and rushed with a cry across the room; the girls followed him, and I stood, still holding the infant, feeling (as indeed I was) an intruder and usurper of another's place beside the hearth. For what seemed too long a moment, the fisherman continued to stare at me. When at last he spoke, it was not with the quicker, sharper voice of Workington folk but with a slow and gentle intonation that I later realised was an Irish way of speaking. Despite the softness of his speech, however, his words held no welcome.

'Happen, miss, you'll tell me who you are and just what you might be doing in my house. Then maybe you'll get out so I can come to my own fire and get a bit dry – God knows I've been long enough getting here.'

But without waiting for an answer he strode into the room, shaking off the clinging children, throwing into one corner a large heavy-looking bag and into another his salt-encrusted coat, such as I had seen worn by other fishermen down on the quay. His fatigue, his soaking garments, and his eagerness to reach the fire gave him an air of helplessness quite strange in so substantial a man – a figure in whom pathos was most pitifully at odds with his rough words. I had seen such weariness, mingled then as now with a certain menace, only once before – in the faces of the would-be rioters on the road from London. But, more wisely than I knew, some instinct warned me that I should not (as my cousin Hugh had done) rely upon the name of Curwen to protect me. As carefully as I could I answered him, not wishing above all to give the children any knowledge of my nervousness.

'You must excuse my intrusion, sir,' I said, 'for I found your son in much distress as to your safety, and concerned as to the little ones – I came but to see what I could do. In case your return might be delayed much further, I have given them food – of which a little yet remains should you require it. I shall stay no longer – if you permit, I should be glad if Peter might show me my way. I am not yet quite familiar with the town.'

I gathered up my cloak. The father would not, I was certain, himself take kindly to the offer of provisions; but I hoped I might yet keep the promise I had made the boy, who came to my side and took my hand, as the fisherman turned again from the fire and spoke.

[52]

'He's a good lad, sure enough. But he'll learn not to ask for anything from folk like you. I've seen them often enough, the ladies with their white hands and their charity – which you find is just another way of asking you to work for next to nought in their husbands' mills or mines. That's why I keep to the fishing – if I drown I'll at least die free, not the slave of some Lowther or Curwen, curse them.'

His bulk seemed to fill the room, blocking out what remained of the blaze behind him. The bitterness of his words – the fruit I guessed of harsh experience – did not dispel my anger at his injustice to myself.

'You do me a wrong,' I answered, 'to suppose that I care, any more than you yourself, for those who mask self-interest with kindness. I thought but to help the child, when I found him weeping and watching for your boat – *that* could bring me no profit . . . Nor,' I added, half to myself (but with more truth than prudence) 'do I have cause to love the name of Curwen . . .'

His eyes, dark like those of his children, seemed less contemptuous as he looked at me again.

'Aye,' he said slowly, 'you've more spirit and less airs than most, I'll admit – and you put me in mind of someone, though I cannat think why . . . But you'd best be gone, for I'm worn out – I've a sister will look to the baby, when the fool has finished wasting her time with the men at the pier, that is!'

I remembered the girl – black-haired and laughing – who had called after Peter as we hurried past the boats. But I had no wish to stay. The fisherman sank into his chair, too much concerned, I hoped, with his own affairs to enquire further into mine. The dark and dankness of the room, moreover, with the fire now almost out, began to oppress and chill me, so that I was thankful to regain the brightness of the outside world.

Yet even this, as I climbed the hill with Peter, did nothing to dispel the dark uncertainty that lay ahead. I did not fear the censure of my aunt, nor Emily's silent curiosity; nor did the keen remembrance of my mother's words upon the page, her image in my room, cause my reluctance to return. It was the colder, unknown land I feared – that arid, loveless, childhood

[53]

land I had thought to leave behind at Maidenhead. And when I came, with faltering step, out from the shadow of the hidden lane into the sunlit safety of the square, I knew that this – the refuge I already loved – would undermine my resolution to depart.

For some weeks following my birthday, and my encounter with Peter, I saw the harbour only from my window. To my aunt and Emily, the dampness of the tenement cottage and my overlong exposure to the early morning air were cause enough for the fever that now confined me to my room. As the outside world receded, becoming in the early days of my illness part of a misty realm that lay beyond the curtains of spring rain, I ceased to long for the distant lands that beckoned as I stood upon the pier beside the boats. My thoughts (the aimless wanderings of a fevered mind) drifted like leaves on a wayward breeze, which pays no heed to conscious wish or will until, at last worn out, it sighs and lets the weary travellers fall to earth. So I returned, an exile from reluctant banishment, to find an unchanged shore – the constant presence of my aunt. Her hands, astonishingly light for so large and dominant a woman, seemed as they touched my brow or rearranged my covers (thrown for the hundredth time awry by my restless limbs) to convey assurance and a comforting concern. Though few, her words convinced me that I was no burden to her, as of course I feared – but rather a welcome charge, whose care had begun to fill a place left vacant by her husband's death, and her own childlessness.

Meantime Emily, grimly attentive, maintained an impressive fugue of commentary on the successive stages of my sickness. As recovery followed days of ceaseless care, her scolding increased in proportion to the improvement in my condition, till on the morning she pronounced the doctor a scoundrel, his potions worthless and his attentions quite unnecessary, I knew that both her temper and my health must be restored. At last I could venture downstairs and, before long, out into the garden, where summer had now succeeded spring and the walls were bright with roses. The sweetness of their scent, borne on the slight sea-wind that even on the warmest day rustled the branches and blossom of the pear tree, was indeed a more certain cure than the most potent physic.

Though I had leisure enough, as I sat in a shady corner or at the open window of the drawing-room, to contemplate my future or review the past, I lacked the desire to do so. Contentment – a state I had rarely known save in far-off moments of childhood peace among the water meadows – for the present kept at bay the bitter knowledge of rejection that had overwhelmed me but a short time before. If I thought at all of the Curwens, it was only to dismiss their actions as beyond my power to comprehend. And when I relived those moments of alarming insight, those glimpses of my mother's inmost thoughts, it was with a detachment which I then mistook for mere indifference. Such cold clarity of vision, I now know, is but the shield with which instinct hides our least protected tenderness of feeling: that instant hardening of the heart one feels when young may often cushion one against disaster. It is only with constant onslaughts of grief or pain that our youthful armour is penetrated by experience, never again to prove sufficient for such severe encounters.

One episode alone disturbed my hard-won peace of mind. A question which I put to Emily as she gave my room its daily upheaval (a process I considered not at all needful but to which I submitted rather than provoke an outburst of reproaches) gave rise to a disturbing revelation.

'Where is my mother's picture? It used always to stand on the dressing-chest there – has it suffered some damage, Emily?' I had noticed its absence some days before, but had felt too weary to enquire; now its whereabouts assumed a fresh importance to me.

'There, I knew you would be wanting it sooner or later – and I told the mistress she were wrong to put it away but she never listens to me as you well know – '

'Come, Emily,' I said with increasing impatience, 'you should not criticise your mistress in that way – she must have had good reason. But I should like to know where it is.' Emily continued as though she had not heard me, a technique she had long ago developed.

'It weren't right, I told her so myself, but she would listen to that Doctor Richards, drat him for a useless interfering busybody. For you had been rantin' and cryin' – we was that upset to hear you. Shoutin' in your sleep you were, and callin' out at your poor mother not to kill the babby – you kept sayin' she were tryin' to kill it, and it were all your aunt and me could do to stop you cryin' so . . .'

She paused for breath and waved her duster expressively.

'So your aunt took the picture away, for the doctor said it might be that upsettin' you so. And it's put away safe so never you worry about it, child, for I dusted it only the day before yesterday lest you should be wantin' it back – which I told 'em you was bound to before very long as is only natural – '

I managed to stem the flow of words only by rising from my chair and moving towards the door.

'I shall ask your mistress about it when I am ready to do so, Emily,' I said firmly. 'I have no need of it now; as long as I know it is safe I shall be quite satisfied. Please let us say no more about it.'

Then I made my escape downstairs, where I said nothing to my aunt about the portrait. For I had indeed no wish to look upon it nightly. My mother's letters were locked safely in the drawer of the table beside my bed. One day, I knew, I would read them – one day, when I could be sure that her words would not destroy the calm I now enjoyed. Meanwhile the strength of purpose that so often grows from physical weakness stayed with me: I would not put the portrait back into its place until I felt its power diminished, and my own restored.

Though distanced now by time and lack of contact with the world beyond my room, I had not forgotten Peter and his family. No fever could erase the glimpses I had had of children's lives more cruel than any I had seen – bounded by crumbling cottage walls and sustained only by a diet of meal and scraps. Though warmed by an affection I might envy, how cold was an existence shadowed by such lack of means, how frail were Peter's hopes – daily beset by fear or by his father's bitterness! I remembered still the troubled look, mingled with eagerness, when I gave him the provisions that my aunt, without delay or query, had supplied at my request. 'I hope my father will let me take it,' said he, with so much doubt that I too wondered how the boy and his precious bag of food might be received.

When I questioned Emily, she merely muttered words so Cumbrian and obscure that I could not, as she well knew, understand their meaning. Aunt Nicolson was unusually evasive. But I did at length discover that a basket of fish had been found upon the doorstep; and I could only surmise that the boy, or perhaps the fisherman himself, had by this means repaid their debt. When, as my strength increased, I looked out into the darkness beyond my window, and saw between bright drops of rain the lights of some ship at anchor in the bay, I wondered where, at that moment, Peter's father was; at sea still with his fellows in the fishing-boat, while his family slept uneasily at home; or back beside their meagre fire, his children (motherless as I had been) curled up like dozing puppies at his feet?

My recovery, aided by the warmth of lengthening days, was almost accomplished when at last the boy returned. I had been seated for some time beneath the pear tree on a sunny afternoon, and had almost fallen asleep; my sewing lay unfinished in my lap. A faint tapping roused me; as it grew more insistent I realised that it came from the wooden door set into the wall. I crossed the grass, stood for a moment, then opened the door so suddenly that Peter fell into the garden at my feet.

'Oh, miss, I thought you would never come!' said he, getting up and wiping his dusty face with an even dirtier hand. 'That old cross woman – the fat one as always opens the front-door – she said you was restin' i' the garden and couldn't on any 'count be disturbed!' He gave a perfect imitation of Emily's most portentous voice, making me laugh despite my glance at the kitchen window in case she should be watching.

'Anyways she be shakin' her broom at me from the upstairs so I reckoned I could try to make you hear at the other door there. I've been so many times and always they says the same thing – that you can't be seen today – so I'd almost giv'd up. But I've got something for you, miss, and if I wait any longer it will get lost, sure enough.'

And he brought out from under his jacket not, as I half expected, a fish or crab or any other likely gift, but a small, quite terrified, white cat. I could only exclaim, 'Oh, Peter!', as the little thing clung to his chest, its claws digging deep into the cloth – as fierce indeed as any captive crab brought struggling from the shore!

'Oh, Peter!' I cried again, 'I cannot keep it – is there no one else who would take it?'

Even as I spoke the kitten leapt from his arms, ran across the grass and took refuge beneath my chair; as we tried without success to reach it, it spat protestingly, its sea-green eyes glowing in the shadow. The boy kept watch while I went to the kitchen for milk, wondering as I did so how I could possibly reject the gift. The problem unresolved, I returned to Peter, who lay contentedly upon the grass, half his attention on the cat and half on his task of pulling daisy heads apart. He sat up smiling and scattering petals, as I placed the milk beneath the chair.

'This is a proper garden,' he said, looking about him, 'not just a bit of earth and sticks, but flowers – trees – ' I thought at once of the steps where his sisters played, and wished I could, by some sleight of hand, transform their bleak surroundings . . .

I sat and listened while Peter told me more about his father, and about the fisherman's pretty sister who now cared for the children while he was at sea. We did not hear my aunt's approach: only when her shadow darkened the sunlit grass did I realise that she had been standing for some moments, watching us.

At once Peter, most alarmed, made for the garden door. But I caught up with him and led him back to where my aunt waited, silent still, for my expected explanation.

'I think you remember Peter, aunt,' I began, ' – his father kindly sent us some fish whilst I was ill . . .'

'Yes,' added the boy, with surprising boldness, 'and he said he wished he had not been so rough when you only meant to help us – but he did feel sorry when he knew you was ill, miss, and he says you are to let him know if ever you need assistance, for he would gladly give it to you. Though he is very proud, ma'am,' he continued, turning to my aunt, 'he would not forget such a kindness. We might have starved had you not sent us food that day. But my father is doing well at the fishing now . . .'

He looked up at my aunt, and I saw that, quite unwittingly, he had (like those fortunate sparrows) hit on the very way most likely to soften her heart towards him.

'I am glad to hear that,' she replied, 'and you must thank him for the fish and take back his basket with you. Come now, your young lady is very tired, I think, and you should go home; but you may come again to see her this day week.'

Peter followed her to the kitchen door. I turned to seat myself once again beneath the tree. There, curled up among the sewing on my chair, lay the small white cat, forgotten and asleep.

June had succeeded May before I was considered strong enough to leave the confines of house and garden. To my delight, the old man often sat in his open doorway across the square, the geraniums flourishing tall in his neat white porch, where I eagerly listened to tales of his seafaring days or of the hillside farm where his youth was spent. I visited Mrs Sharpe, at first formally and accompanied by my aunt, later to take flowers or other small gifts of which the invalid (lonely now that the *Elizabeth* had left port) made excuse to detain me longer than mere courtesy required. Though my aunt relaxed her vigilance somewhat, the harbour, with its steep descent and crowded streets, was still forbidden me.

To my relief, the coming wedding of my cousin Isabella provided my two attendant dragons with an irresistible diversion. Together with Susan, a red-cheeked girl who helped in the kitchen, Emily and her mistress accomplished a quite superfluous second spring-cleaning. It was likely that members of the Curwen family – including the bride herself – might in the coming weeks pay calls upon their relative, who (whatever her reputation for independence) would not be found wanting when there were rites of hospitality to be observed. I was allowed to occupy myself in the garden, sadly neglected since Humphrey Nicolson's death. Here, with Peter's assistance, I tied back roses or clipped the straggling herbs, feeling at last both useful to my aunt and at ease with my surroundings. Only the thought that soon I must meet with those who bore my name arose from time to time to disturb the surface of my peace.

For it was clear that Elizabeth Nicolson, her guardianship renewed, wished the world to recognise me as her ward and niece. Presented thus to callers, introduced to her acquaintance in the town, I had, moreover, been nursed with more than dutiful care. For my part, to remain in Workington was unwillingly to become a Curwen – yet to feel rejected still, whilst Sir Henry would not accept me. But whatever her quarrel with her brother, my great-aunt, I already knew, had none with his only son and heir, my uncle Richard Curwen. For he and his family often came to Workington, Emily said, from their estate near Cockermouth, inland along the Derwent. She told me too of Isabella's holiday visits to my aunt, and her brothers' schoolboy exploits on the shore. And I was, despite myself, most curiously drawn to those unseen cousins who might, had circumstance allowed, have been part of my own childhood.

Almost imperceptibly, I began to know them. There was James, the eldest, a lawyer, already married and looking to obtain a seat in Parliament: he sounded kind, respectable, and dull; another brother, Henry, had taken orders and might, I was impressively informed, one day become the bishop of Carlisle! The third son, Charles, was clearly Emily's favourite – it was he who had been soundly thrashed for cockfighting with collier lads from the town, and had often stolen Emily's baking when it was scarcely out of the oven. As for Isabella (the youngest, predictably spoiled and adored by all), she sounded so alarmingly accomplished and complete a young lady that I resolved that, given forewarning of her arrival, I should at once take refuge in visiting Mrs Sharpe. While I could scarce admit such cowardice to myself, I hated the thought that my own inadequacies, though fewer than six months ago, might be exposed to the critical eyes of my far superior cousin.

So as the days passed, and the imminence of visitors became increasingly alarming, I lengthened the walks that I took after luncheon, or would linger over whatever reading Mrs Sharpe had chosen we should share. It was, accordingly, long past the accustomed time for callers when, on an afternoon in late June, I let myself through the side door into the garden. I paused to inspect the progress of some additions to the flowerbed, and to gather fresh roses for the dinner table. The air was warm and unusually still. So, having ascertained that no one was in sight, I pulled off my bonnet, abandoned my wrap, and sat down on the grass beyond the pear tree. Knowing that my aunt always rested at this hour between tea and dinner, I yielded further to temptation and took off my thin slippers, delighting in the feel of the sun and the touch of the grass beneath my feet. For some blissful moments I sat there; then reluctantly I gathered up the flowers, my wrap and shoes, and walked up the garden to the kitchen door, thinking to attain the back stairs and the safety of my room without detection.

But I had been observed – by neither Emily nor my aunt, but by a stranger, who sat at ease, his legs outstretched from his perch on the kitchen table. His coat, thrown carelessly down, occupied one chair; a stick, as used for walking tours, lay across another, beside his broad-brimmed hat.

'You had better not let Emily see you,' he remarked, as to the most familiar acquaintance. 'She always told me I should come to no good if I left off my shoes – and I must confess she was correct. But perhaps you have by some miracle charmed her into approving all you do: that seems very likely, since I see you have even introduced a cat into the household.'

He indicated Minou (whom Peter had first named Minnow for her quickness) lying outstretched in the sun, next to Emily's pot-plants on the window-sill. Whereupon I realised that he must, from the open window, have observed my indecorous progress through the garden. As I stood there, silent and staring at him, I became conscious of the slippers in my hand, my bonnet full of roses and my bare feet beneath a crumpled gown. My confusion only increased when he smiled, held out his hand and continued, 'You are, I am sure, my newly discovered cousin Georgiana. Though I admit that you look more like a sun-browned dairy-maid than a Curwen – a very pretty dairy-maid of course!'

[61]

He bowed with a politeness at odds with his disconcerting words. And though in height he was little taller than myself, his bearing and graceful movement gave the lie to his own careless appearance. I recognised at once the fair curling hair and laughing eyes, the determined chin and expressive smile – all so familiar to me from the portrait of my mother. Such likeness left me in no doubt as to his relationship. And, from the description Emily had given, I knew that this could only be my cousin, Charles.

But I found wit and voice enough to answer his effrontery – though I knew that my complexion was indeed darkened by the sun (the effect of gardening without a bonnet, for which my aunt had several times rebuked me). 'Then you, sir, must be that thief and reprobate of whom I have heard Emily speak so fondly: surely no gentleman could stoop to such deceptions – nor, moreover, address a lady whilst still in his shirt-sleeves. I should, if you will allow me, prefer to be introduced in the drawing-room, in my aunt's presence.'

As I passed him to reach the stairs, he spoke again: 'Well then, since we already understand each other, let us make a bargain. If you will consent not to betray my shirt-sleeves, I shall not say a word about your shoes or your bonnet. And I will even forgive you for leaving me now, if you will promise to appear in the drawing-room, and not vanish back into the underworld from where Aunt Nicolson has rescued you!'

I could not help but smile, as he looked at me with an expression of conspiracy and earnestness combined. Then I ran upstairs, for I had heard the closing of a door, and Emily muttering as she returned to the kitchen. As I quickly restored my hair and garments to correctness, I suddenly recalled that other, long-expected, guest – Isabella. The knowledge that even now she might be in the house, awaiting my appearance, caused such apprehension that I thoroughly repented my agreement to descend. But I did so, resolving that I should meet her with all the reserve of which I was capable: toward her brother, too, I would behave coldly, for in retrospect his easy assumption of familiarity annoyed me greatly. He was, I must not forget, a Curwen, and to be recognised as a duty, not a friend.

But my resolutions were in vain. For Isabella was not in the drawing-room. Charles, with one of my roses displayed upon his coat, was standing beside the small table from which my aunt was, despite the lateness of the hour, dispensing tea. Beyond her, and seated in an armchair near the window, was a second gentleman: as he rose, I saw that he was Philip Earnshaw.

Chapter 5

I have always disliked drawing-rooms. Even the most charming has an air of dust-covers whisked aside, of objects tastefully displayed for admiration, drapes correctly hung, their folds calculated to a nicety to suggest the acceptable degree of luxury. The very prospect from the window seems on occasion ordered to please the eye rather than to engage the heart. As for the occupants – they sit or stand to a pattern as regular as that of the carpet beneath their feet, their groups predestined to form and re-form, moving, as in a dance, from introduction to conversation, withdrawal and polite farewell. The room itself appears to impose restraint – allowing only the most artificial kind of communication to glide over its polished surfaces.

And yet (though preferring as I did the lamplit intimacy of my aunt's parlour, or the kitchen sights and sounds so comforting to all the senses) I welcomed at that moment of recognition the formality which of necessity distanced me from Philip Earnshaw. As he rose from his chair to look across the drawing-room towards me, I tried to compose my thoughts – and, I hoped, my countenance – just as I had earlier smoothed over the disorder of my dress. The room's familiar dimensions, the furniture and flowers arranged to withstand the critical glance of the most superior Curwen relation, momentarily became unreal, taking on the shimmering whiteness of the moorland where Philip had, with almost equal unexpectedness, appeared beside me. Then, our isolation, and consequent communication, had seemed complete. Now, however, little response was required of me other than to extend my hand, incline my head, and murmur appropriate phrases as first Charles, then his companion, was briefly introduced. My aunt – perhaps sensing my apprehensions on such an occasion to be entirely understandable – indicated a place beside her on the couch, from which she continued to organise her teacups and pronounce her opinion on the education of young George Nicolson.

'I am quite sure, Mr Earnshaw, that the boy would have benefited far more from attending his father's school. Whatever its advantages, Eton is too grand for a country boy –and it lacks the sea air, too, which he would have had in abundance at Saint Bee's. The Nicolsons are of northern stock and should be proud of it: there's no sense in turning a healthy lad into yet another of your pretty gentlemen – all looking alike and fit for nought but decoration and amusement as far as I can see. It is like trying to transplant good old-fashioned herbs to a hot-house – they grow sickly in a week and lose all the good that's in them!'

There are those to whom the unwritten laws of the drawing-room seem not to apply. I had already learned that my guardian was one such, for she regarded it as her duty to express her convictions – usually with a disregard for convention that was as absolute as it was well-intentioned. As she paused for breath I could not help but venture to look at Philip, half expecting him to counter her onslaught upon his relations' judgement with some equally outspoken argument of his own. But his reply, though to the point, kept within the bounds of courtesy – and his expression remained quite inscrutable.

'My sister's chief care being always the health of her children, I do believe, ma'am, that she would have sampled the air at Eton had such a course been practicable: as it was not so, doubtless she found it necessary to base her decision upon hearsay, which is often unwise. When last I saw him, however, George seemed in remarkably sound health despite his exposure to such hazards – did he not, Charles?'

[65]

'Indeed, yes – but I'll grant you the Cumberland air is far superior to any south of Morecambe Bay, aunt. And it has a wondrous effect upon your roses, too. Their scent is quite delicious, is it not, Miss Georgiana?' Charles turned to me with a hint of amusement in his tone. 'Surely the roses in even your sheltered southern gardens cannot compare with them?'

'I believe not, sir,' I replied, attempting not to notice his indication of the blossom in his buttonhole. 'But I think that they bloom somewhat later here, and are, in consequence perhaps, the sweeter for being awaited longer.'

'Just as we, cousin, have waited over-long to make your acquaintance!'

The skilful compliment took me quite unawares. And before I had time to reply in a suitably cold manner, Charles continued: 'I trust you will find us not so barbaric as our London relations tend to consider us – living as we do so far from the centre of civilisation. Our Workington theatre has much to commend it, if you are fond of such pastimes. Philip, I know, does not believe it can compare with the kind of entertainment to which he is accustomed at Cambridge – but I shall not allow him to judge without first sampling it. Perhaps we may tempt you, aunt, to accompany us, so that Miss Georgiana too may become convinced that there are advantages to Cumberland?'

My pleasure at the notion of a theatrical excursion quite dispelled the annoyance occasioned by my cousin's compliment; I hastened to assure him that his native county appeared to offer a bewildering variety of distractions. Aunt Nicolson, however, was not to be so readily committed. Somewhat to my disappointment, she merely remarked that she would first wish to ascertain the nature of the play, and should it prove to be one of Mr Sheridan's composition she should certainly avoid it!

'For,' said she, 'I cannot believe that such a production would contribute greatly to my niece's education. She ought first to hear Shakespeare, and thus gain some understanding of what is truly great in poetry – do not you agree, Mr Earnshaw?'

Appealed to in this way, Philip could hardly avoid giving his judgement in the matter. I expected at once that he would expound the merits of the Lake poets – just as he had before. Yet he did nothing of the kind.

'You may indeed be right, ma'am,' he said, looking for the first time fully into my own countenance, as I momentarily forgot reserve and eagerly awaited his words. 'But I believe that if Miss Curwen wishes to learn more of poetry, and thence of life, she should study the work of Lord Byron.'

Here was cause for consternation indeed! I knew nothing of Byron save his reputation – which was such that his poetry, however sublime, was not usually recommended to young ladies in polite drawing-rooms. But, though instantly anxious on my aunt's behalf, it was not this particular challenge that caused me almost to weep with shame and anger, so that I had to turn my face toward the window in an effort to calm my sense of outrage: it was Philip's bold assumption of my ignorance – not merely of literature but of life itself – that cut so sharply through my frail composure. There was no mitigating sympathy in his glance; his tone was calmly dismissive. How could he thus presume to judge the extent of my experience! How, moreover, could I have hoped that one so assured of opinion, so scornful of domesticity (as I had observed him to be in relation to his sister), and so cruelly unfeeling as he now appeared to me, might have sought me out in order to fulfil a thoughtless promise? No, if he had looked for me at all, it was but to amuse himself with the spectacle of my deficiencies of education, my ignorance of the world. Had he been in full possession of the facts regarding my birth and lack of prospects he could not have been more accurately unkind.

To my astonishment, Aunt Nicolson appeared (when I succeeded in attending once more to the conversation) to have remained quite unperturbed by Philip's suggestion.

'As to the character of Lord Byron,' she was saying, 'I have often felt him to be misjudged somewhat. He was after all a patriot as well as a great poet – and a traveller, too: he knew much of foreign people and lands – which my husband always believed to be a necessary thing in a man, if he were not to remain narrow and prejudiced. There is nothing like travelling abroad to increase one's knowledge, after all . . .' and she proceeded to enquire after Charles' own plans for a tour of Europe in the coming spring.

Thankfully (though for her own rather than for Philip Earnshaw's sake) I concluded that my aunt's literary preferences, like her choices in other matters, were quite arbitrary and unpredictable. But my agitation did not readily subside, and I therefore rose when Emily appeared, prolonging as best I might my unnecessary assistance with the removal of the tea-things. And when Charles proposed an inspection of the improvements I had effected in the garden, I at once accepted – with a gratitude that was as heartfelt now as it would but an hour before have been unthinkable. I could respond, with instinctive certainty, to his easy communication, more readily than I could bear Philip's incomprehensible disdain.

The gentler outdoor air served to soothe my spirits, oppressed beyond bearing by the confining atmosphere within the house. But it would have been hard indeed to resist the combined charms of the garden, where I had spent so many peaceful hours, and of my cousin Charles! While Philip discussed with Aunt Nicolson the latest architectural developments beyond the square, Charles embarked upon a precise examination of the flowerbeds. With persuasive eagerness he exclaimed at the profusion of flowers – and if he noticed that I called them by their old-fashioned cottage names (learned long ago from the old fellow who had tended the Maidenhead garden) rather than describing them with botanical correctness, he gave no sign that it mattered at all. He ascertained to his satisfaction that the pear tree of his boyhood was still in good heart and promising a splendid crop; and he listened, quite without condescension, to my account of Peter's assistance in my horticultural endeavours.

Finally, as he and his companion prepared to continue their walk along the banks of the Derwent to Workington Hall, he undertook to obtain from the gardeners there some plants he had noticed to be lacking from Aunt Nicolson's border. My protests that it might prove unwise to move them when summer was already upon us met with good-natured disagreement. 'And,' added Charles (voicing a fear I had not dared express), 'you may be sure that Sir Henry takes not the least interest in the comings and goings of the plants in *his* gardens – he will talk of politics and Reform and nothing else at dinner tonight, and I for one will be exceedingly bored by it all. How fortunate you are to be spared such an ordeal – I shall leave the conversation all to Philip, since he and Grandfather appear to agree so well.'

It was proposed, as the gentlemen departed, that my cousin should return very soon with the promised specimens. Moreover my aunt, I learned, required him also to assist her in going through some books and charts of her late husband's, with a view to Charles selecting some of them for himself.

'I know,' she said, as we seated ourselves once again amongst the comparative disarray of the parlour, 'that Humphrey would have wished Charles to have them. For though he intends to farm, he is a keen sailor and may have reason to make voyages on his own behalf some day – he's the only one of that family who is likely to do so, that's for sure.'

I could no longer wonder (as I had done during Emily's descriptions) that my aunt preferred Charles Curwen to others of his family – not excepting the apparently incomparable Isabella. Even had he not so closely resembled my mother in feature and in colouring, I should have felt as fierce a pang of envy at the possession of such a brother. Indeed, so short-lived was my first resistance to his personality that I could not help but compare him with Philip – though it pained me to do so. For though the younger by a year or two, Charles exhibited a natural assurance of manner, a spontaneous warmth of interest, that made his companion appear hard, almost withdrawn, beside him. There was nought of femininity in Philip's features; and whereas Charles was quick of movement and thought, ever seeking to display his skills, mindful always of the onlooker, Philip cared little for those who watched, nothing for either their good opinion or censure. Charles from that first meeting seemed to me to inhabit the summer air, through which he moved with a grace and confidence that quite outshone the

[69]

other's wintry stillness – much as a swallow might appear, momentarily, to outfly a hawk. And yet, though I did not at that time understand it to be so (being dazzled by the surface brightness of the one, alarmed by the chill, unfathomable depths of the other), each had assumed an arrogance that was entirely masculine – Charles by believing one would find him altogether delightful (as one did) and Philip, in his cynicism, by courting rejection from all quarters.

In appearance, I was forced to recognise that Philip was the more impressive. His height and broad forehead, his mass of hair almost as dark as my own, could not fail to strike the least susceptible observer as distinctly handsome. But when I tried to recall the colour of his eyes I found myself remembering only the nature of their expression – at our first meeting eloquent of a message I knew not how to decipher, but today remote, beyond such communication. We had hardly spoken; I had found his presence disturbing, yet had felt bereft at his going, almost as though some irreversible catastrophe had left us, each quite alone, at the far poles of the earth. When, during the week that elapsed before Charles was engaged to visit us again at Portland Square, I thought of Philip Earnshaw, it was rather to wonder at his strangeness than to remember with any gladness our earliest encounters. So it came about that I sought to erase such memories from my mind, resolving to indulge myself with no further hope of friendship with him.

As for Charles, I could not help but smile at his parting concern for the rose he declared his favourite, which he retained, even as he walked away, in the buttonhole of his coat. So complete was my innocent acceptance of his goodwill, that it did not occur to me to question the direction in which this charming will-o'-the-wisp, my cousin, might lead me.

Emily, next morning, left me in no doubt as to *her* opinion.

'Master Charles,' she pronounced with evident satisfaction, 'is just as wicked as ever he were! But that Mr Earnshaw – he's a right black Yorkshireman if ever I saw one. I cannat bide a man that frowns so much, and hardly a word out of 'm – not that I was wantin' to listen, mind,' she added self-righteously. 'But

[70]

nothin' good ever came out of Yorkshire, that I do know. Mr Charles, now – he always did have a sweet nature, even after a beatin' (and that were often enough, too). But he'll not settle down till he's ready, whatever they might say; and Sir Henry were just as wild, till he set his eyes on Miss Frances – you'll mind how *that* ended, Miss Georgiana.' . . .

How could I not remember! Though I had, it was true, heard it first of all in my aunt's more sober words and not in Emily's much-embellished version, my imagination had been caught at once by the tale of my grandfather's unlooked-for courtship, as a young man of radical convictions, of the Curwen heiress. Her arrival in Workington from Ireland had caused a stir among the more eligible families of the county: orphaned by her father's death (within but a year of his attaining the estate), she became at once an even more alluring object of competition and speculation. But as occasionally happens (though far more frequently in fiction than in fact), Fortune favoured the deserving: her cousin, Henry Christian, the ambitious, high-principled and impecunious younger son of a Maryport merchant. Rumour had it that the imperious Miss Curwen had herself dictated that their marriage be in Scotland, in order to avoid the more public ceremonial; whatever her reason, she had insisted upon her husband taking her name for his own, had promptly placed her fortune at his disposal, and thereafter proved a devoted consort to the man who became chief employer and benefactor in the town. Whilst Henry Christian had compromised his principles so far as to accept Miss Frances' person, name and capital, he remained adamant on one point: he steadfastly refused the peerage offered in reward for his duties, conscientiously performed, as Member of Parliament for Carlisle.

'Why,' he had said, in the presence of my aunt herself, 'should I want to join the likes of Lowther and Muncaster in the Lords, when I can meet them every month at the dinner table, should they see fit to invite me? I had rather remain in the Commons, where at least a man may make a useful speech or two – I'd sooner keep my feet on the ground, on good Cumberland clay, than wear a coronet and have my head in the clouds!'

[71]

Henry Curwen had won Aunt Nicolson's support in this at least – despite their quarrels over other matters, of which I as yet knew little. But she had, on her own admission, disliked her brother's bride from the outset. Herself an equally strong-minded (if less flamboyant) figure, she had clearly found Frances capricious and given to sudden enthusiasms which, even had she had the means to indulge herself thus, my aunt must have found uncongenial to her own puritanical nature. She cared little for the literary and artistic circles in which my grandmother, it seemed, had delighted – the patronage of which had led (so Aunt Nicolson averred), to a certain neglect of her young family – including, of course, my mother.

At this point my aunt had abruptly ceased her narrative. She had evidently forbidden Emily, on pain of dismissal, to reveal to me whatever she might know of my mother's history: for, on the sole occasion that this dangerous ground had been approached, Emily had declared that she would 'say no more about *that*' for it was as much as her place was worth! But I had of late become determined to discover the truth. As the lethargy induced by physical frailty receded, I found my thoughts returning, almost against my will, to the letters in my drawer. Though my mother's portrait had remained unsought in another room, her image in my mind was clear as a reflection in the stillness of a pool on a summer day. And though my resolution had preceded his appearance in my life, the recognition of her in my cousin Charles had strengthened my desire to know her history . . .

Meantime Emily, who rarely lost an opportunity to assert her long-standing right to concern herself in affairs of the family, had returned to her favourite theme – in which I too had no small interest.

"Twill be just the same, you'll see. There was many a heart got broke when *she* got wed – and there'll be more than enough tears for Master Charles when he goes that way. There's even a lady over in Westmorland who refuses to marry till your cousin's wed, they say, in hopes of giving him her fortune. It would be temptation enough for some young men, I reckon . . .'

'Fortune or no,' said my aunt, appearing at that moment at the door of her parlour, 'it's high time your young hero did as his grandfather wishes and gave some thought to his land – and time some work was done this morning, too,' she added, as Emily grudgingly withdrew along the passage to the kitchen. 'And let us hope that your cousin confines his breaking of hearts to the young ladies of the next county, if only for the sake of his Workington friends and relations.'

I wondered for an instant at the note of censure in her remark, but she did not pursue the matter.

'Come, Georgiana,' she continued, 'I wish to know if you have given thought to my proposal of securing a drawing master for you. There is a Mr Jameson, who has moved from Ambleside, where he used to teach Miss Wordsworth, to Cockermouth – so Charles was telling me. Isabella has had some instruction from him, too, and they evidently think most highly of him. It's little enough I know about such things, but he is said to have known Mr Constable, for what that is worth. And,' she added as an afterthought, 'he is an Edinburgh man.'

That the good opinion of Mr Constable was of no little consequence, I was later to discover. However, not even this – nor yet his Scottish credentials (from the studios of painters as eminent as Mr Nasmyth and Mr Raeburn) – had saved my drawing master from that fate peculiar to his profession: the daily battle against circumstance which compels artists of talent to impart their skills to others, in whom affluence generally exceeds ability. A respectable decline toward obscurity is all that men of this kind may hope for – if indeed they survive such struggles at all. As for the woman who would become a painter – she must not aspire even to respectability. If she will confine herself to the drawing-room school, to the painting of pretty views and the decoration of teacups or cushions, or even to the filling of pages in the albums of other young ladies, then her acceptance in society is guaranteed. But let her venture beyond such bounds, to the observation of her fellow human beings; let her try to depict them in their poverty or nakedness, their degradation or passion – then must she remain (in reputation at least) in that limbo to which other such immoral creatures are cast. Even a girl who so far risks her soul as to become an actress on the stage, perhaps the model or the mistress of an artist, has a greater chance of salvation (in society's terms) than one who would paint or write the truth as she may see or feel it.

How could I at that time have foreseen the social snares and moral mazes into which my desire to draw might take me? For, when I considered my aunt's proposal, all reservation fled. Until today, I would have rejected any suggestion that I might choose to stay in Workington. Yet now, almost as though some knot or bond had been, without my knowing it, untied, I found myself able to contemplate those hopes and possibilities before unthought-of. And I could not but feel gratitude – from which affection often springs – toward Aunt Nicolson, for her concern as to my future course.

'I think I should like it very much, aunt,' I began, 'but I do fear that since I have done so little drawing of late, someone of such authority may find me sadly lacking.' (Especially, I thought, if my work should be compared, as it must surely be, with that of Isabella!)

'Why, child,' came the swift reply, 'I saw you but the other day with some sketches of Minou, and one of Peter in the garden, and I thought that they were very like – but then, I'm no judge of these things. It would be best, perhaps, if you were to gather some of your work together; when Charles comes he shall take it home to Cockermouth for this Mr Jameson to see, and he shall say whether you are like to make some improvement by his teaching.'

'But suppose that others should see my drawings – I could not bear that, aunt . . . And besides, they may become lost or – or – mislaid in some way . . .' I was indeed distressed at such a thought, for I could not help but remember that theft, so long ago, of my childish work, so important to me then.

'In that case, I shall instruct Charles that he is to deliver them into the hands of Mr Jameson himself – and to no one else. There, that is settled; and you must, for your part, have all prepared for when your cousin comes again.'

Already, indeed, I had begun to think what I should choose to send – and to regret the wasted hours of weakness and despondency. Only lately had I felt once more the lure of the empty page, the power to express upon it the movement or the colour of something seen, that must be caught, pinned down and wondered at. I could achieve already a degree of likeness with my pencil; but how should I, without aid, make my hand obey my will? Mr Jameson, perhaps, might teach me how . . .

There arose, as I sat musing, a sudden commotion from the direction of the kitchen. The sound of voices raised in indignation; a door banged shut; then a clatter of clogs on the cobbles of the street, a renewed assault on the door, and a further shout from Susan, the maid. Emily reappeared at the parlour threshold, a look of agitation on her face, which generally bore an expression of grim placidity.

'You had better come, miss – it's that boy again. Lord knows what he's wantin' for 'tisn't his regular day and I told him as much. But he'll not go, though I sent Susan to chase him off, like. She bid him wait till the afternoon, but I don't doubt he's in trouble again – which is no surprise to them as knows *his* kind of folk.'

Between Emily and Peter there had developed an unremitting feud. It stemmed, on her part, from that hostility so often shown by those who have attained a measure of respectability toward those who have not. She had an intolerance of anything masculine (with the one exception of my cousin Charles) and consequently turned every encounter with the boy into a battle. Aunt Nicolson, well aware of the situation, chose on this occasion to overrule her.

'You may go and see what he wants, Georgiana. Tell him to wait in the garden, Emily; and let him have something cool to drink, for it is excessively hot this morning. And Georgiana – you must take the strawberries for Mrs Sharpe. I meant you to do so yesterday.'

I accepted the rebuke, for I had, in my haste to escape the house after luncheon, quite forgotten the promised fruit.

'Yes, aunt, I will take them now – and perhaps Peter may go with me to carry the basket.'

My preparations made, I went out to where the boy waited. He was leaning against the garden door in an attitude of such dejection that it was clear to me at once that something was sadly amiss: usually he would have been found playing on the grass with Minou, or making faces at Susan, who did not share Emily's dislike.

Our way lay through the churchyard on the far side of the square. A bleak enough place in winter, when mist gave to the shapes of its uncompromising stones an eerie quality of distortion, and persistent dampness glistened on the bare branches of the surrounding trees, it felt gloomy even in summer daylight. The morning was, as my aunt had observed, already very hot. The unusual stillness of the air made the blue hardness of the sky oppressive; the heat, and anxiety about my companion, quite dispelled the lightheartedness with which my day had begun.

The boy was strangely silent. He carried my wicker basket as if it were an intolerably weighty burden, setting it down with a sigh when at last I stopped beside a flat gravestone at the farther end of the church. Many of the stones were worn, of a grey granite that had acquired the deceptive softness bestowed, through time, by their coats of lichen or moss; others were of Cumberland slate, cold and green as a winter sea, and bearing inscriptions whose incised messages remained clear and final. Across the churchyard came the sound of a stonemason at his work; a blackbird flew in protest from beside the monument where we sat. The faint but unmistakable cries of sea-birds rose from the marshes that stretched away beyond the churchyard wall, down to the edge of the lower town and the black rocks of the shore. And the sea-wind, which in autumn would rattle around the corners of the church tower, now barely rustled the grass and wild flowers that grew in profusion at its foot; small butterflies hovered there, where warm sweet scents mingled with less welcome odours – of smoke drifting up from the pits, the acrid perfume of the yews, and a pervasive smell of rotting vegetation that rose perhaps from the reedbeds, or from the churchyard itself.

At length, though I had begun to dread what he might have to say, I bade Peter tell me what was the matter.

'Father said not to speak to anyone at all,' he faltered, 'but I must – for his leg is hurt very bad, his head too, and he'll not be able to work, surely. There was a fight, miss, yesterday, in the afternoon – a terrible fight down on the shore there ...' He indicated vaguely in the direction of the harbour. 'And 'twas something to do with Mary, that I know, for she came back cryin', very late – she says she'll not stay and I think she means to take the baby with her.'

For a few moments I could say nothing. I could not bear to think of such violence, so close – yet far removed from the tea-table politenesses to which I was now accustomed. Though once or twice I had heard brawling away beyond the quiet streets of the upper town, we led a sheltered existence, safe in our gardens and drawing-rooms.

'Where is your father now?' I asked then.

'We have taken him out of the town, miss – across the marsh there, to a safer place. For Jem thinks the man that hurt him is like to die, and then – then they'll come and look for him at home. And if they do, then the law will mebbe put my father in prison ... or ...'

Across the churchyard, the tapping of the mason's hammer continued.

'Is there no one to care for him – a doctor who would go to him, or his friends, perhaps?' I persisted.

Peter looked at me with the steadiness born of despair.

'No,' he said. 'Doctors will not come to the likes of us – how should we pay them?'

How indeed! I had forgotten, almost (and to my shame, so easily), that there existed a world where one could not command such advantages.

Suddenly the boy reached out and crushed, with his brown fingers, a spider which at that moment chanced to emerge from a crack and run across the stone between us.

'No, miss,' he continued, his voice so low that I had to bend my head to hear his words more clearly, 'there's only Jem – that's the one who works the boat with him; and the old man, Jem's father he is, who goes with them sometimes. 'Twas they took him to the hut – but now they have gone, for they must get the boat out to sea again.'

He stood up.

'My father may hang if he is found.'

Chapter 6

All motion, at that moment, seemed suspended. Islanded above the town, the marshes and the sea, we might have been the sole inhabitants of that stony landscape, bounded by graveyard wall and yews. The mason had ceased work, his hammer silenced by the midday clock, which called him to refreshment in some distant shade. Peter and I were, for a time, as if carved in alabaster, unmoving as the monuments around us.

The sun's heat, burning down from an unpitying sky, could not prevent me, suddenly, from shivering. The chill came from within. It was clear that Peter did not expect my aid: he had no illusion as to his own defencelessness, nor to his father's likely fate. But I felt anew, in him, the bitter loneliness of childish grief – far greater surely for a loved and living father cruelly cut down, than for an unknown mother lost, like mine, so long ago.

And – what must be *his* thoughts, out there alone beneath that same fierce sun, which only yesterday had seemed to me to shine upon a carefree world? Now it drew from the marsh a veil of mist, which rose from the spongy bogs as from some nether land where – guarded only by golden iris spears and glistening ranks of reeds – the fisherman lay. I pictured the struggle they must have had, to carry a man of such weight and size along the shore and narrow paths to shelter.

'Father's worrit for the little 'uns', said Peter, as if reading my mind. 'I – I must try to get work, miss, for he would not have me beg, that I know'.

I rose and gathered up the long-forgotten basket.

'Come,' I said, 'let us take these quickly. My aunt, I am sure, will give you more work in the garden, at least for the present, until we see what – what happens to your father . . .' At the boy's look of alarm, I added, 'and don't fear, I shall say that he is not well or – or gone from home. And who knows – perhaps they will not need to search for him . . .'

I spoke with a reassurance that I could not feel. For even were the fisherman not pursued, he might die where he lay, his injuries uncared-for. As we walked in silence to the farther gate, I looked once more across the marshes to the sea. Between the ocean and the sky, a band of fog had formed; already white wisps and tendrils reached across the water to the shore, where within hours they would mingle with the rising vapour from the reeds . . . I stopped, and with sudden resolution flung down the basket and turned to face Peter.

'Listen – listen carefully! Do you see the mist – out there, look?' I seized him by the shoulder. 'Now, tell me, is there a way to where your father is hidden – from this side of town, I mean, without going along the shore?'

The boy nodded.

'And tell me, could you find your way there – even if, as I believe it will, the fog should become quite thick by evening?'

He nodded again, his eyes wide with puzzlement.

'Then I shall try to find a doctor, as quickly as I can. You must see – ' I spoke urgently, sensing my companion's instant fear ' – if his hurts are not attended to, he must stay there, perhaps to be found and taken. But if he can get stronger, he may escape the law – by boat perhaps, with Jem, or by some other means. It is a chance, surely?'

'I am afraid to go – for he will be angry. Yet I think you must be right, miss – only do not come yourself, he would not wish that. But – but who else can I trust. . . ?'

'I have a little money, I will use that if need be – for I do believe your father is in need of more skill than I possess. And . . . I think I know of someone who might go.'

For already I had remembered the young doctor whose attendance during the later stages of my illness had afforded me relief from the overbearing manner of his superior, Doctor Middleton. The latter would, I knew, be of little use to the likes of Michael Stephens, being elderly, stout, and given to lengthy condemnation of the faults of the labouring class – among whom he rarely went, preferring to collect his fees in comfort and to the accompaniment of a glass of good port to sustain his efforts. Emily had scorned the younger man, but his gentleness had seemed to me to compensate his inexperience; and though I could scarce expect him to go without payment, I hoped that his ready sympathy might outweigh any other scruples.

'Come,' I said to Peter, 'let us see if Mr Richards is at home – he lives close by Mrs Sharpe and sometimes attends her in the mornings.'

We hurried, as fast as the heat allowed, to Mrs Sharpe's. That lady, who rarely rose before afternoon, was still upstairs in her room – and, said her maid, had sent that morning for Doctor Middleton. By way of excuse, I made enquiry as to what book I might prepare to read to Mrs Sharpe. The ensuing dialogue between invalid and attendant, the search for the required volume, and other necessary politenesses occupied fully half an hour – during which I paced the airless over-furnished parlour, pausing only to look through the window (closed and half-curtained even on so hot a day) into the street, where Peter waited. The sight of the boy standing there in anxious anticipation renewed my resolution, which else had dwindled to nothing, as the minutes lengthened and still the doctor did not come. I was summoned at last to the door of Mrs Sharpe's room: she thanked me, in her plaintive voice, for my kindness in coming, and bade me convey a grateful message to my aunt. I was on the point of descending the stair, my hopes quite gone, when the doorbell rang, and the maid hurried down ahead of me to admit a somewhat breathless Doctor Richards.

'I beg your pardon, but I – I wish to speak with you – on another's behalf, about an urgent matter.'

He hesitated. 'Very well,' he answered. 'Mrs Sharpe will be a few moments preparing for me. Mr Middleton has been detained at the Hall – a slight accident to your kinsman, Sir Henry, I believe. If you can tell me at once – '

I told him Peter's story, leaving aside the likely consequence for Michael Stephens should his assailant die, and making clear the need for utmost secrecy. 'The man has enemies who may look for him or – or harm the children, perhaps. If only you will go, I wish to give you whatever fee is suitable . . .' I looked up at him, dreading his refusal.

'Tell the boy to come to me,' he replied, with a decisiveness that surprised me, 'this evening, at about nine o'clock, and I shall be ready for him. As for the question of a fee – we will speak of that later if need be.'

There was scarcely time for me to thank him. I found myself on the doorstep, where Peter waited patiently. To his questioning look I answered simply: 'He will go, tonight.' Slowly we retraced our steps along the dusty cobbles, back through the churchyard, to Portland Square.

Three days elapsed; long days, during which I saw neither Peter nor Doctor Richards. So great was my anxiety that, though I tried to busy myself with the preparation of my work for the inspection of the drawing master, I had little heart for the task. When my aunt enquired if I were not feeling tired, or ill perhaps, since I had been so little out of doors, I evaded her questioning as best I might. But when she announced her intention of calling Doctor Middleton, I at once agreed, hoping that (as indeed it proved) his assistant might take the opportunity of visiting the house. I disliked the thought that I must thus deceive my aunt – yet the belief that Peter and his sisters might suffer if I did nothing gave me the necessary spur.

When he came, I asked Doctor Richards how his other patient did.

'Not badly,' came the reply, 'if one considers where he must recover and how little help he has received. I have seen him a second time, and he is now in no serious danger, for his fever is less and his injuries will heal, given time. But I fear the leg will be far too frail for him to go to sea again – or not, at the very least, for some months.'

'Is there something I can do?' I asked eagerly. 'And Peter – is he with his father still?'

'No, I have not seen him since the first evening – though I believe he took the man some food yesterday: he is in the town somewhere, perhaps.' The doctor looked at me keenly. 'You should not, I think, allow yourself to become too concerned on their behalf. If I may advise you, Miss Curwen – it is not safe for a young lady such as yourself!'

Had he guessed, I instantly wondered, at the fisherman's reason for remaining hidden? As calmly as I could (for I must not let my own fears betray him) I expressed my gratitude, offered once more a fee, which was refused, and inwardly blessed Aunt Nicolson's timely interruption with sherry, which Doctor Richards hastily drank before departing.

That evening, once again, the town of Workington was closed in mist. Within doors, it became needful to light the lamps, and such was the chill dampness of the air that we sat wrapped in heavy shawls until bedtime. So weary was I with yet another day of waiting for Peter, that I could summon little concern at my aunt's chief news – which was that Isabella's wedding to Mr Wordsworth might now need to be postponed. For my grandfather had evidently met with a mishap while out upon his favourite bay horse – 'Far too spirited for a man of his years, of course, but he'll listen to no one's advice on that score,' commented my aunt, with much energetic waving of her sewing-needle.

'Charles sends word that he may not now visit us on Sunday – he must wait to see how my brother does, and will be needed to ride round the farms for him. He will let us know when he can come. And Mr Earnshaw is gone back to Yorkshire: I must say I had thought he would stay a longer time.'

Philip's departure gave to me, at least, no surprise. There had been something so conclusive in his formal parting handshake, in his sombre glance as he left the drawing-room, that I sensed, even then, the closing of a door – for what reason I knew not, save that he had realised, perhaps, his error in seeking me out.

Inexplicably, I experienced now a sensation almost of release, as from some unseen threat that his proximity had imposed. Yet Charles – Charles was already in some strange way familiar, a part of myself: in the moment when he had gravely suggested that we might inspect the garden, I had turned to him, as in refuge from one who had briefly pursued, idly caught and scrutinised his prey, then rejected it as unworthy of his attention. And it had been my cousin of whom I had thought, for a fearful instant despite my more pressing errand, when Doctor Richards had spoken of an accident at the Hall.

Now I was impatient – almost to anger – that my grandfather should prevent Charles from coming again. All, it seemed, revolved round Henry Curwen's whims and wishes: why, his falling from a horse (a common enough occurrence among men of his class) had the effect of a major event – of altering weddings, even! I determined that he should never make *me* so change my mind! His power in almost every sphere seemed undisputed. He ruled – not merely his own family but the whole of Workington itself, just as his rival, Sir James Lowther, Earl of Lonsdale, dominated Whitehaven, the sister town. Yet in public life, I knew by now that Henry Curwen far outstripped his neighbour: mills and mines, harbour and shipping, agricultural matters of all kinds, were of importance to him – Reform, but a word to other men, was to him a practical affair. The people, in response, were loyal to his cause; and at election time the blue ribbons and rosettes of the Radicals were worn with a degree of fervour that dashed the hopes of any Lowtherite supporter.

Nevertheless – this man had cast out my mother, causing untold grief; my aunt, unpredictable in many things, remained firm that he had erred in doing so. Why then should I be bound, as others were, by duty to him? And must I, now that circumstance had made a lady of me, do as Doctor Richards had implied and (from the safety of the drawing-room) ignore the needs of such as Peter and his father? A well-bred young girl was allowed to care for little beyond outward show: the cut of a coat, the set of a hat, the dainty frills upon a shirt should indicate (to one correctly informed) the status and acceptability of a man. Society, like a well-kept garden, serves to foster such delicate blooms, to nurture those who keep within its bounds: those without (from the worthiest fisherman to the most renegade agitator) one must dismiss as weeds, which grow or perish unregarded.

Such, I believe, was the mental air breathed by my grandmother, Frances, as she tended hot-house intellectuals in her drawing-room. Such was the climate that caused my mother to grow faint from surfeit, impelling her to seek escape amid the freshness of the hills. For a man, it seems, may safely move (as the doctor himself had done) where he chooses – from the fugitive's rough shelter to the civilised comfort of his own fireside: but a woman, if she be a lady, must remain untouched by harsher truths, protected by the nets cast close around her, that she be not robbed of those most precious fruits – her virtue and her reputation.

It was with a heavy heart that I retired that night. I had never, in my short life, felt concern so great as now I felt for Peter and his family; what little I had done would aid them not at all if, as I feared, the fisherman were found.

Towards dawn I woke from an uneasy sleep to hear the steady beat of rain upon the clematis that grew around my window – left wide open in defiance of Emily's wrath (for she believed fresh air a sinful thing, rather than a gift from the Almighty!). There was distant thunder, and even as I looked the harbour was illumined by lightning which flickered across the dark waves towards the rocks. My dread of storms (cause of much mockery in the Chatterton household) was no less on this occasion – yet the strange play of light upon water, around the swaying masts and across the shore, held an unwonted fascination that almost outweighed fear. But when the thunder became louder, rattling the window as I banged it shut, I withdrew behind the sheltering thickness of the curtains, and lit my candle as if to keep the elements at bay. Even so, a flash would sometimes penetrate the shadowy corners of the room; I found it quite impossible to sleep; and I thought, safe as I was with Minou curled beside me, of those who lay out there amid the storm. If Peter did not come to Portland Square next day, then I would try to find him.

*

Susan, the little maid, went with me. A cheerful girl, from Ennerdale, she was fond of the boy. Moreover, she often accompanied me when my aunt had errands in the town; it was therefore no unusual occurrence when I asked to take her with me on pretext of sketching to be done before the morning should grow hot. After the storm, the air was less oppressive, and the streets, though slippery underfoot, had a rain-washed look about them. As we trod the shining cobblestones, and passed the labourers in their blue-dyed shirts, the women with bright kerchiefs bound about their hair, I felt released, eager to find the boy, almost believing that all might yet be well.

At the door of the cobbler and clog-maker's shop, near the corner of the close from which the steps led down to Peter's home, I told Susan to come no further. She looked troubled (as well she might at this departure from custom) but I said firmly: 'I wish you to wait for me here. You may try some clogs for me – we are much the same size, I believe, and I should be glad of them when winter comes.'

After giving her the necessary money (for I had in mind that I might need the clogs should I have to traverse the rough ground of the marshes) and assuring her that I should not be long gone, I made my way into the close. I ignored as best I could the curious stares of two old women who sat in adjacent doorways, their black skirts stiff with grime, the shawls knotted across their shoulders seeming heavy and incongruous in the summer sun. A younger woman, bearing coals upon her back, in a basket so large that it half filled the narrow stair, stood aside to let me pass, and I bade her a shy 'good morning' when, unexpectedly, she smiled at me. The children clinging to her skirt shouted merrily despite their rags, while a grey whippet, scrawny as themselves, leapt about them, its eyes as dark and sad as those of the boy I had come to find.

The door of his cottage swung wide open in the breeze. I hesitated to go in, for though there appeared no sign of occupation – not even a sparrow pecking in the dirt where the little girls had played – some premonition warned me that I was not alone. As I waited, my hand raised to knock, there came from within the sound of a woman's voice. She sang – a mournful song such as I have heard but once since that day, among the cottage girls in the fields of Ireland, near my home. For some minutes more, so sweet was her voice and so still the world about us, even in the midst of a busy town, that I almost forgot my purpose in coming: until, of a sudden, she broke off singing and began such bitter weeping that I dared not disturb her with my knocking. Then she came to the door in a flurry of red skirt, carrying the same child I had held in my own arms on that April morning. She was the girl I had seen on the quay – laughing and tossing her black curls as though no care could touch her. Now her lovely hair was matted, and the laughter gone from her eyes; her brow was marked with the deep bruising of a heavy blow, and the brown of her complexion scored as if by a cat's determined claws. Her expression, as she faced me on the threshold, made me shrink back, for it was one of unmitigated malice.

'I know you, my *dear*!' She spoke softly, with deliberate emphasis. '*And* I knows who you're lookin' for, too. And 'tis a pity, for you're come too late, to be sure.'

At my look of consternation she smiled mockingly.

'Aye, he's gone! And if you think to fool me, as you fooled that brother o' mine, with your dainty graces and your charitable ways, you'll not be doin' so. For you're nought but a bastard yourself; and there's a deal I know that you mebbe don't yourself, fine miss – for there's others o' your kind, at the Hall, no less, that's as bad as any man when you gets to lookin' at 'em!'

In my shock, I could find no words to answer. As I made to move away, she pulled at the muslin of my sleeve, then gestured toward the baby on her hip.

'And for what he's done to me and mine, I wish that Michael may hang – aye, and Peter with him for all I care . . .' The girl's voice, though harsh, was unsteady; despite the cruelty of her speech, it seemed to me her grief was greater than her anger.

'I pity you . . . And I – I wish you well, the child too . . .' I faltered. Then, as she stared at me in surprise, I turned away and slowly, my own eyes filled with tears, began to climb the steps.

*

[86]

I read my mother's earliest letters at this time – when my days were filled with apprehensions for those friends (for such I chose to call them) whom on a youthful impulse I had thought to help. So deeply grieved was I, so shamed and startled by the words the girl had spoken, that for hours I could think of little else: till at length I reasoned that, whatever evil she might know, she could do me no further harm. For she was gone, I guessed, to Maryport, as Peter had said she intended; but those words stayed with me – drawing me, at last, to look once more at the packet I had locked away.

My mother's hand seems, when I see it now, almost childlike – little better indeed than that of my own young son. Yet when I saw it first I was conscious less of its lack of form than of its density: page upon page of closely written lines, some wavering and uncertain, others clear and bold, as if her purpose were quite firm despite her troubled mind.

> Rochester 3 april 1826
>
> This day, my daughter, is your birth day – almost the same as that of my own mother Frances Curwen. How we children us'd to love that day, when she would gather us to her knee & give to each a gift – which she said was an ancient custom that brought good fortune to the giver! My brother (older and always more severe) us'd to scold and make the little ones await their turn –
>
> What can I give to you, save these lines? As on so many days I can only think of you and wish that all may be well for you – but my love too might have been yours, & that I can never forget. Once – long ago it was – I sent you a gift, a little ring with hair lock'd in it & pearls set round, that my mother gave me as a child. But I know not if it came to you – I was foolish perhaps to entrust such a thing to others. And for so long, as I lay unable to do more than look from my chamber window, I hop'd for word from you, hop'd too and despair'd that news might come to tell me how they fared at home. Now – it is too late

The ending to this letter had been roughly torn away, as if the words were far too bitter to be read by any save herself. The next, however, was more resolute:

Tho' I shall not ever know you more than by your name – as Georgiana Frances, which I gave to you – I shall write if I can sufficient that you may know & understand your mother a little. Had I been able I shd have wish'd to give you not affection only but that understanding of another's needs which I & those around me often lack'd. Tho there was love enough in my parents home there was little time for us children save on special days – allways I felt confin'd, driven to run & hide from the bustle of folk who fill'd the drawingrooms or saunter'd up & down the stairs as if they own'd the house. Did Mary, the Scottish queen behave so (I us'd to wonder) when she sought refuge long ago – were the Curwen children of those days as weary as I of the noble names, the artists who wd paint us with our dogs & horses?

What a burden it seem'd – that heritage of ours, how wearisome the small-talk of the scented women in the evnings after dinner. My mother much preferr'd the company of men & said that even drunk they could converse, whilst women drunk or sober scarce could think at all! I lov'd best the library where my father work'd, amid books that smell'd of leather like the harness-room in summer. How I long'd to do as he did, make laws in Parliament & fight for the better days to come as he said he shd allways do. And how I read – Gibbon & Rousseau & Burke – to his alarm for he beleiv'd the drawingroom & boudoir to be my destiny. He fear'd clever women I think – yet ador'd my mother. She had her own life & freinds: she told me how when the Revolution came to France their talking went on far into each night; & how she later held me in her arms when news of further massacres was brought. But soon she could not bear such things – a poet & scholar whom she lov'd was kill'd in Paris; then came the wars that made all England fear the emperor & hate the French –

My willful nature anger'd her I fear, so oft my mother call'd me an ungratefull child! She told me that a woman rules men best by guile & once she quoted Rousseau's words on female education, laughing & saying he dug himself a pit by such philosophy! And Mary Wolstencroft I read but later lost the

[88]

book (my brother said 'twas burn'd & rightly so) yet I remember it still — how bitter I feel at her fate, for she was destroy'd by love as I have been.

Your father, Alexander Grieve, I truly lov'd, because he shar'd my thoughts not mock'd them as some did. He car'd not for hounds or guns, nor profit & trade as other men: I knew his gentleness from childhood for our families play'd together til prevented by that bitterness which made the Curwens & the Lowthers enemies. Sir James, his uncle, & my father were at odds in ev'rything, united only in their anger when (beleiving as we did that all oppos'd our love) we left our homes to take the boat for Ireland. Had we succeeded in escaping thence, America was our goal — where we intended (as the poet Southey & his freinds had tried) to live in peace with others of like mind; to till the land in harmony with freinds, all equal — men & women both, in witness that liberty & brotherhood were not destroy'd! Although we fail'd, our dreams were good — tho our parents (like the Capulets & Montagus of old) parted us so cruelly, our union was as true as any made in church: & tho' our youth & hope were taken from us, starcross'd as we were, there remains in you our daughter proof that once we lov'd. But if as I do fear such circumstance of birth shd cause you grief, I ask you to forgive, tho you may not understand —

That day I could not forgive, nor could I truly comprehend. For — like a child with many fragments of a toy, which when rightly put together make a whole — I saw little then save the pieces on the page. My mother's image had begun to take on flesh, yet to me was only partially alive — as though I started painting her anew, the outline known, the detail indistinct. And as I read her thoughts and feelings, joys and woes, I felt as a stranger might who happens on some tale in a dusty book — which he takes up, reads, is moved by for the moment, and sets down again.

For present pain and laughter are more real. I felt more pity for an Irish girl, whose child I held for barely half an hour, for Peter and his father — living yet, not laid in some country churchyard far away. There is perhaps some shutter that the young can draw against the sufferings their elders feel, making them judge too harshly – as I judged my mother then. So may a watcher from a window close his mind against some drama in the street below: a carriage passes and a woman falls beneath the horses' feet; some stranger pauses, gently lifts her head; the carriage moves away. Indifferent, you turn your face toward your fire, and draw the curtain close. And only when the doorbell rings, the message comes, does the truth begin to quicken in your heart: in dread you then descend the stair, go out and hold in yours a lifeless hand, and look at last into the face of one you should have loved . . .

So then I could not share my mother's pain – and puzzled too how one who knew so much of books, whose childhood had been blessed beyond the dreams of many, could in one moment cast it all aside. As for my father, Alexander Grieve (no more than a name to me as yet) – why had he abandoned her? And did he know I lived? Though I read further I could find no clue, save in some lines my mother wrote again that month, when the birth of her last child was soon expected:

24 april Rochester

It is wrong, I do beleive, to lose ev'ry hope. Tho weary enough in truth of bearing children by one I have never lov'd, I am not so weary of life that I do not hope to see, before long, the swallows return to their nests above my window. How empty the land appears in this corner of England – the long line of the marshes stretching away beyond the church tower – then farther still I am told lies the sea. Tis strange how the sea is allways blue to a child: I remember it so from Cumberland & I wept at my brother saying the Sollway was not the Ocean, for that lay beyond the isle of Man. Will you love the sea & the ships as I did then?

At the least I know now that you do live – why that certainty was so long deny'd me I cannot tell. But I do not willingly think my father kept me ignorant – some grave mistake must have led him so to keep silence. My letters perhaps did not reach him, thro' malice surely contriv'd by one who gain'd thereby; from Alexander but one short letter found me – & that too late. Was it Chance alone that caus'd such mischeif? Had I strength enough I should discover the truth, that you, if not I myself, might gain a father's love once more. Wrongly I trusted those who should have help'd me when I was alone – but the law which should protect the weak is a weapon in the hands of those who profit by others woe.

If the child I carry now should live, some joy may yet be mine. That a marriage made on my husbands part out of pity, & on my own in despair, should have borne fruit at all is a wonder to me – yet they lie – all my little ones – in the churchyard yonder. I will not beleive that such things are punishment for sin; my love for Alexander was no sin. If I err'd twas in yeilding you to others, for which your loss is punishment enough. I thought to keep you – but they lied to me. O never put faith in lawyers – for they lie. And do not Georgiana marry save in love & trust, for 'tis a bond that tightens ev'ry day til life itself is gone.

Chapter 7

When at length Charles visited Portland Square, he did not come alone. I was seated in the garden, a sketchbook upon my knee, when I saw him approach, my aunt leaning on his right arm and on the other a young woman whom I knew at once to be his sister, Isabella. She moved so close beside him, lightly in her floating summer gown, that I felt once more, as she looked up at him with unconcealed affection, that pang of envy I had known at Emily's tales of my cousins' childhood. For there seems to be, about those who grow up in such old-established families, a kind of natural confidence and ease, a happy grace which makes their youthfulness look charmed – however dark the days that lie ahead.

Even my aunt, as she walked with them across the grass, appeared less forbidding and remote, despite her customary black; there was a warmth in her voice as she conversed – as if they might be her own and not her nephew's children. Charles was taller than I remembered, his hair now bright in the sunlight as he inclined his head, laughing at some remark of his sister's. She herself was small of stature, with that delicacy of feature which turns to sharpness in later years, softened by light brown curls which were prettily rather than fashionably arranged. I might, had I been less nervous of our meeting, have been more readily aware that, more than any other attribute, it was her eyes – large and of an almost violet hue – that justified those claims to beauty I had heard so oft repeated. Now, as I rose from my chair, rehearsing in my mind the phrases long-prepared, I hoped only to conceal my agitation – all too easily aroused by my aunt's announcement, earlier that day, that my cousins were expected.

But Isabella forestalled me. Leaving her companions, she moved impulsively towards me, holding out her hands and saying as she did so: 'I am glad – so very glad – that you are come home, at last, to Cumberland!'

I had no doubt of her sincerity. My cousin's voice, though low and gentle, held conviction; her glance, direct and without guile, confirmed her welcoming words.

'Forgive me,' she continued with quick concern, 'I am too hasty, I fear – but I have so long wished to meet you. And Charles – Charles has told me – ' She broke off, stood back a little from me, and gazed at me again, as though she sensed the depth of my uncertainty.

'You are very kind . . .' I began, hesitantly. Then, to my own surprise, I took her hands in mine, and – as if her goodness touched some spring within – spoke with a truthfulness that equalled hers. 'And I am glad indeed to know you – cousin!'

For face to face at last with Isabella, I found (as I had done with Charles) my hatred of the Curwens dissipated, my cold armour of reserve superfluous and the warmth of my affections, so long unexpressed, now called upon to give response.

I was disarmed – and yet perplexed to find the imagined object of my fears so readily displaced. Where I had anticipated haughtiness, or daunting beauty – here was a modest graceful-ness: of the superiority which her accomplishments, so often praised, had led me to expect, I saw no trace. There was, above all, in her an innocence which (as I came to know) her brother lacked. Though charm came just as easily to Charles, in him it was not without a certain calculation – which, if I saw it now, I might mistrust. And where in him a subtlety lay hid below the surface – Isabella was all openness, simplicity and genuine goodwill.

While my cousin took the low chair next to mine, I turned to where Aunt Nicolson and Charles stood watching our encounter. A look – almost of complicity – appeared to me to pass between them; then my aunt shook her head briskly, as if denying some emotion that she felt, and busied herself in arranging her skirts as she sat beside Isabella. Charles greeted me eagerly, with a disconcerting note of satisfaction in his voice, and a glow, as of some inner purpose, in his eyes. His hand, as he helped me to my chair, held mine for the minute only that such courtesy required – yet his fingers seemed to burn with an intensity that set my own afire.

If, as I do believe, seduction may be accomplished (whether by touch, or word, or look) in such a moment – it was so then. All that followed – pursuit, fulfilment, parting – lay in that instant as do the curled petals within the flower, which is gathered, cherished until it opens to the sun, and worn on some gallant's coat in triumph, for an evening, or a day.

It was so then: though I did not foresee pain or anger or despair (or any of those griefs concomitant with love) as I sat in the summer garden with my aunt and cousins. I listened as they talked of pleasures they had shared, of future plans, of the coming wedding – to be held more quietly in consideration of Sir Henry's health. No longer did I feel excluded or alone but, thanks to Isabella, part of that larger whole – the family to which by right I now belonged, despite the past, my doubtful birth, my mother's loss and death. And, as I felt Charles' gaze upon me, or responded, laughing, when he reminded me (with such delightful gravity of tone) that I should require his assistance to place the plants he had most carefully remembered – how could I not, for the duration of an afternoon, feel most happily alive, most peacefully content?

At length my aunt, who could rarely be persuaded to remain inactive for so long as on this occasion, stood up and spoke with her usual brusqueness of manner: 'Come Charles, we have a great deal to do: the day is but twenty-four hours long and three-quarters of that will be gone before you have all done gossiping. Let us go and look at those books of your uncle's – then you may take some of them with you when you go.'

As soon as we were left together, I turned to Isabella.

'Cousin – if I may call you so without impertinence – I must thank you, truly, for your kindness to me. I – I had expected that you might scorn me,' I continued, in a low voice (for I felt some emotion at expressing such thoughts to her), 'since you must know something of my situation – and of my mother . . .'

She sighed as she looked gravely at me. 'I wish only that I might do more – for I do believe, as does my brother, that it is wrong for Grandfather to remain so obdurate; even Papa, I think, is glad that Aunt Nicolson has received you at last – but I know he can say little to Sir Henry for fear of making him even more unwell. He flies into such a rage if your mother is spoken of – and it appears he is quite immovable with regard to yourself. And yet' – she sighed again – 'he was so full of affection to us as children, and I cannot bear to think of his causing you distress.'

'You are very good,' I responded. 'But I must confess I feel much bitterness toward him. Though my guardian is kind – even if I fear her still, and do not dare to question her too much.'

Isabella laughed, her blue eyes for a moment as lively as her brother's (though her animation was in general less – and I heard her once described, by Mary Nicolson, as 'but a mouse – though a very charming one!').

'We are all afraid of her – even more than of Grandfather, whom I for one could always persuade if need be. But Charles, I know' – her expression became serious once more – 'has displeased him greatly by his reluctance to manage the farms – for he maintains he will not do so till he has a wife in view.'

What kind of woman, I wondered, might one day satisfy the capricious-seeming Charles? With such a sister, he must seek one, surely, to match her in gentleness and virtue . . .

'Indeed, my brother is so difficult to please! He collects young ladies' hearts like pearls on a string – and he finds, I believe, the pursuit more to his taste than the prospect of possession. Mamma tells him he will one day lose his prize, as punishment for so much trifling – but he only laughs and says that most girls have no heart to give, and his own is the more secure!'

I was glad then that I, being a cousin merely, must remain immune: for whatever kindness he might show, he could never think me worthy any greater interest. Already my lack of worldliness had earned me Philip Earnshaw's scorn; I was grateful only to receive from Charles such attention as I might have known had he been, perhaps, my brother. Yet – had I been one such as Isabella had described, he would not have found me heartless; nor could I think any girl would wish to spurn him, whom so many had admired.

'But you are fortunate,' I ventured (almost despite myself), 'that you have possessed, throughout your life, a brother who – '

'Who is so close – with whom I share so much, you mean? Ah yes, that is true, and always, since we were children, has been so. For Charles tells me all his secrets – or he used to do,' she modified, 'until he went to Cambridge. I know little of his life there, for I went there only once, when Mr Earnshaw – '

Isabella coloured suddenly, and looked away, as though some painful thought disturbed her. I was, for my part, startled by her mention of her brother's friend: for though my reason had rejected him, I had not succeeded in erasing memories of his presence, which had moved me so. But if Philip had by some harshness caused my gentle cousin grief – that were a cruelty which one never could forgive . . .

But she, to my relief, had recovered her composure. And I saw, as she proceeded to describe to me her future home and husband, that whatever might have caused her past distress, it had no power to cloud her pleasure now.

'I do trust,' my cousin was saying, 'that when I myself am married you may come to visit me. For John – that is, Mr Wordsworth – will have the living at Brigham, which is not so very far from my home at Cockermouth. And though I shall be much occupied, I know – for the parish is a large one – I shall not wish to lose my family or my friends.'

I found her eagerness engaging – yet a little sad. She would, I did not doubt, become a fitting helpmeet to her husband in his work, for her warmth and thoughtfulness must soon endear her to those within his charge. But – would her life be no more than this – a short flight from her parents' to her husband's home, with no experience of the larger world? I thought her not unlike some captive butterfly which, when released from the safe room where it first saw light, flutters beyond it to the summer

[96]

flowers, among whose sweetness it hovers briefly – not apprehending that its wings, though frail, might take it further than the garden where it lives and dies. Yet if, like my mother, a young girl should try to reach the freedom of the fields – borne by imagination or ambition's wings to attempt the more dangerous flight of independent thought – she may be caught by some arbitrary hand, then flung out and left to fade in some obscure place. And if by persistence or good fortune she achieves escape, she must struggle on against the blast of others' censure till, her wings grown ragged and her colours gone, she is cut down by the bitter frost of autumn. So I wondered even then how I should choose, were I offered, by some future circumstance, such a security as Isabella faced.

'Forgive me,' said my cousin, placing her hand upon my arm. 'You look sad – and I have perhaps grieved you by chattering so.'

Then I resolved to put to her a question which had troubled me.

'I must ask you, cousin – if I may without offending you: how is it that you – and your brother also – can accept me as you do? For I know that you must go against Sir Henry's wish – and fear you may incur his anger, lose his affection – which I am sure is of no little consequence to you!'

Isabella looked at me, and for the first time I saw true beauty in her solemn gaze.

'It is because we think it right,' she answered steadily. 'And – though harsh – Sir Henry will not, I believe, be so unjust as to punish us for doing so. Aunt Nicolson has told us how he loved your mother – and it may be, when he knows that all save he accept and care for you, that he will undergo a change of heart. If Grandfather could see you, he would know that Charles is right, though he is usually most incorrect in his descriptions of young ladies! For you are, indeed, much more a Curwen in appearance than I am myself – or any of us, saving Charles, perhaps . . .'

'I feel only gratitude toward you – but I cannot think that anything will make Sir Henry change his mind.'

And in my heart I knew that I could never – even should he alter – find that forgiveness which, were I as good as Isabella, I might show toward him. For I had lost, through him, that which could never be regained: my childhood here in Cumberland; a mother whom I might have loved.

'There is one thing more,' said my cousin then. 'There is something I must give you, Georgiana – for by right it should belong to you.'

She took from the beaded purse she carried with her a small leather case, which she unclasped and handed to me. From it I drew out a locket made of gold, oval in shape and engraved with an intricate design: a girl's head with flowing hair, above which another head – a unicorn's – was poised; on the reverse a second unicorn stood rampant, and in the space beneath it were engraved initials: *GMC*.

'Open it,' said Isabella. 'There is a little spring – look!' I pressed it, and saw within two portraits done in miniature.

'It was your mother's – or it should have been, for Grandfather had it made, with his own and our grandmother's likeness, to be given to her on her wedding-day. My father kept it, when his mother died: it is she whom you resemble most, as you can see. Papa, knowing that I should meet you, sent the locket by me. He cannot come himself, Sir Henry would be greatly angered; but I know that he does wish you well – for your mother's sake.'

'I will write to him,' I answered. 'I will write to thank my uncle for his kindness.'

'And I shall tell him so.' Then, seeing that I wept, Isabella sat in silence whilst I restored the locket to its case.

It was agreed before my cousins left us that Aunt Nicolson and I should join them shortly in an excursion to the lakes and mountains beyond Cockermouth. Whether by chance or by contrivance on my cousin's part, my recent lack of spirits served to give excuse for such an expedition – which, when offered as a cure for my fatigue, could not without unkindness be rejected by my aunt!

'I trust,' said Charles, as he prepared to take in charge the drawings I had carefully assembled, 'that you are now recovered, cousin, from your indisposition.' Then as I looked at him in surprise he continued: 'Your guardian has kept me well posted, you see, with regard to your health of late – and I grieve that in tending the garden you have, it seems, neglected to care for yourself. I have suggested she should be stricter with regard to your footwear – or lack of it – lest you fall victim to some dreadful chill.'

I laughed at his gravity of tone, then blushed at the recollection of that earlier meeting, when I had thought to escape the garden undetected.

'It seems to me, sir,' I answered, with pretence at equal concern, 'that you should yourself have a care lest your own health be harmed by an excess of application to certain duties – for I am told that you are far more zealous than need be in riding after foxes on the fells.'

He shook his head and frowned.

'Now that occupation, though it affords me much amusement, can only be regarded as essential for the welfare of the farms – whereas your own preference, which I seriously deplore, seems to be for exploration of the lower town, which holds far greater hazard to young ladies than the field or covert to a sportsman like myself.'

At this remark I became at once alarmed. Could he know, somehow, of my efforts to find Peter and to help his father – or was it but idle speculation that led him to speak so?

'On the contrary, cousin,' I replied, as lightly as I could, and hoping to divert him from that dangerous subject, 'I much prefer the safety of Portland Square – though my guardian speaks of taking me one day to Keswick, where I may try some further drawings. She hopes to call on Captain Nicolson and his family, whom I myself should gladly meet again.'

'Indeed – I had intended to ride across there very soon, for Isabella wishes to visit them and requires an escort. We might accompany you.'

He spoke immediately to my aunt, whose acquiescence to his plan amazed me: soon all was settled between them.

Triumphantly, Charles turned to me and said: 'Your good health, Miss Georgiana, is assured – and your flowers need fear no longer the loss of their attendant spirit, for the air of the hills will work wonders, as you shall find!'

[99]

I could not fail to be delighted at the prospect. But when I expressed my gratitude, he gracefully rejected it.

'Do not thank me, cousin: it is only right that we should show you something of the splendours of the Lakes – if only to persuade you to remain among us, instead of seeking, like the swallows, a warmer climate when the winter comes. Now tell me, truly, is there nowhere you might choose to go – if that were possible?'

I protested that I should enjoy whatever might be chosen for me – then, beguiled by his air of disappointment, added (suddenly remembering my mother's parting letter) that I should like, one day, to visit Wastdale.

Charles looked at me keenly. 'Ah, that is indeed a lovely valley – and at its best in springtime. Yet the lake itself is a most gloomy and impressive place, even in the summer – it is more to my friend Earnshaw's taste, for he prefers the wild romanticism of the poets, at any time of year. Whilst I – ' and his voice became more serious ' – I care more for the domestic, whatever tales you may hear to the contrary. The fields and cottages, the lanes and wild-flowers of the sheltered vales, are far more to my liking than the rugged mountain-tops. And I shall one day make my home in some green valley – but that will be when I, not others, choose to do so!'

His eyes, for a moment, seemed to darken, and his lips – more often curved in laughter – took on a bitter, almost angry set. Then, as I glanced at him in some anxiety, he smiled again, and asked if I had ever learned to ride a horse. On my confessing that I had rarely approached one, and was as ignorant of riding as of flying, he laughed and said easily: 'I think we must teach you, cousin, how to sit on horseback, else you will miss one of the delights of living near the hills and lakes. Now, through the winter days, you must diligently sew your riding-clothes in readiness, and I shall find you a safe mount, which that boy of yours might look after in Aunt Nicolson's old stables there: how is that for a plan?'

'Perhaps, sir,' I answered, not a little sadly, 'I should not presume too much upon my guardian's goodwill – or indeed, upon your own.'

Though I longed to do so, I could not yet believe in such a

certainty as Charles envisaged for me. For I feared not only my aunt's disfavour and my own shortcomings, but those hidden pits which Fate prepares for the unwary who, where the grass is greenest, find themselves unwittingly entrapped. Yet my cousin – despite my doubts – was not readily deterred.

'I cannot answer for Aunt Nicolson,' he said, 'though I am as sure of her goodwill toward you as I am of mine – which I shall prove to you, cousin, never fear. For the present, we must be content to go to Keswick – which you will like well enough, I believe. But in the spring, you shall ride to Wastdale – it is a promise – and I myself shall take you there!'

His enthusiasm – like all else about him – charmed me. And when he left us I felt touched beyond expectation by the kindness of his words.

'I shall hope, cousin Georgiana, that my sister may continue to find in you – not a relation merely, but a friend!'

'I should like it, of all things,' I answered simply.

For I knew that not only Isabella but her brother had become, already, part of the happiness I might, from that moment, hope to find in Cumberland.

How is it absence has the power – I wonder now – to transmute liking into longing, longing into love? I watch, as I sit beside the window, the sunlight play upon the polish of a table which, though it has no life, shimmers as though its surface were indeed alive. The fluttering shadows of the roses, too, cast by the sunlight on the wall beside me, seem to shift and dance, their leaves and stems – even their pointed thorns – enlarged, swollen to a softness beyond reality. So, after he had gone, thoughts of my cousin Charles began to form themselves, creating from his earlier presence something – someone – new: a brighter, larger image which (as happens when one loves) became, for me, himself – till time and circumstance diminished him again.

For often, after parting, memory can blur the outline of things seen, may – by its softer light – ease harsh reality, make bearable the prickle of the rose. And yet, it is the touch remembered or a look relived, a word that is printed clear upon the pages of the mind, which will (by a strange reversal) sharpen the edges of perception once again, renew past pain or bring back, through some alchemy, the sweetness of a long-forgotten moment. So I remember now Charles' touch, like a burning coal upon my skin; or hear, among the echoes of my mind, the cadence of his voice across the garden.

Yet I thought of him, at first, not as a lover but as one who had shown me kindness which, in my limited experience, was unparalleled. He, and my cousin Isabella, embodied at this time a way of life – which my mother (with a wilfulness I could not understand) rejected. And, though I had not forgotten all that Peter and his father meant to me (another world, where artifice and wealth were not), I was in spite of them seduced – not only by my cousin as a man but by all that he, with his sister, represented: affection and security, the safety of a name and home. For there can be, when one falls in love, a penetration of the mind which may precede – and be as potent as – that entry of the body which confirms the mental act: in this way then I was prepared (though ignorant of either cause or consequence) both to become a Curwen and to love my cousin Charles. My acceptance by the family (save for Sir Henry) being accomplished first, my other captivation was complete.

Chapter 8

Quite by chance, on the morning following my cousins' visit, I discovered Peter's hiding-place. From the back window of the parlour (which being set across the house looked out over the garden as well as toward the square) I happened to see Minou, her fur shining from the fine rain that was falling, leap from a branch of the pear tree to the top of the garden wall. Impatient of my own confinement by the weather's unexpected change, I flung on my cloak and brass-buckled clogs (those duly purchased by Susan) and went out quickly across the grass, now slippery with wet moss and scattered petals from the roses. To my annoyance – for I was anxious lest she should fall victim to some idle stone-throwing lad, or even worse, to the wheels of a passing cart or carriage – Minou avoided my outstretched hands and ran further along the wall, to vanish above the arched doorway leading to the disused stable-yard. Already my curiosity had been aroused by Charles' intention, which he had indeed confirmed before leaving Portland Square, of finding me a pony very soon: accordingly I did not hesitate to follow Minou, passing through the heavy wooden door which, to my surprise, I found unbarred.

Beyond it, in the cobbled yard, amid heaps of mouldering straw, lay some rusting harness and a long-abandoned chaise, its cushions torn and soaked; the white cat stared at me, hissed, and disappeared up an unsafe-looking ladder. Determined still to catch her, I gathered up my skirts and in a moment reached the loft – where upon a pile of dirty sacks I found Peter, fast asleep. Minou's eyes glowed from the darkness of a corner; and even as I blessed the chance which had caused me to pursue her, the boy awoke. His initial look of fear was succeeded by a cry of happy recognition; but he was clearly apprehensive still, and I hastened to assure him that – save for the cat – we were alone.

'Aye, she'm nowt but a nuisance, that'n,' said Peter, trying to pull the straw from his hair. 'I know'd as she were bound to give me away sometime – for she'll not keep away whativer I do . . . But, you'm not angry, miss?'

'No, Peter,' I answered at once. 'But anxious for you, yes – and for your father, too.' I scarcely dared to ask the question which was foremost in my mind – and yet, I had to know . . . 'Oh, tell me, is he – ?'

'Nay,' he said, 'they didn't get him yet, but they tried at the house – twice they came for him, and to Jem's place, too, but Jem's wife, Rosa, she didn't say owt, and they went away. But they know as the little ones are there, and mebbe they reckon as he'll go back for 'em. But he'll not, for 'tisn't safe, miss, that's for sure.'

'And his leg – is it mending, as Doctor Richards said?'

'Aye, except he will try to use it, which he didn't ought to – and he curses something terrible at it, too!'

The boy grinned, looking for a moment like the happier child who had helped me in the garden, before such trouble had come upon him. But now, he was filthier even than when I saw him first – and I realised, as my eyes became accustomed to the dimness of the loft, just where, in the three weeks past, he must have been.

'Peter!' I exclaimed, 'you have been down the pit, surely – oh, why could you not say? If it was money you were needing, we would have helped you – anything rather than that!'

''Twas Father said I must, to give Rosa what I could get for taking the others in, and Jem being short of a man in the boat without him, too. And – and I could not tell you, miss' – his voice sounded as if he were close to tears – 'or come to you, for he were that angered about the doctor even, and said there was danger as you knowed nowt about. But I reckoned I could sleep here safe enough wi'out botherin' you or Mistress Nicolson – for I comes when 'tis dark, over the wall and through the door there; and they'll not follow me to my father so easy as from Jem's, see.'

'Then you must stay,' I said quickly, 'and I'll not tell anyone, you may be sure. But may I not try to find other work for you – something easier than the pit?' For it grieved me, remembering his delight in playing with Minou among the grass and flowers, to think of him, so young in such a place. I had seen, besides, the miners trudging homeward through the town, such weariness betrayed in every step, their hair and garments stiff with sweat and dust; and their eyes – their eyes seemed so vacant in those blackened faces, as though their souls had fled the brightness of the day, back into the darkness whence they came.

But Peter laughed.

'Why, miss, 'tis not so bad as all that! Sometimes I helps with the ponies that pulls the wagons with the coal – and sometimes I has to go right in where the men can't get, me bein' so small like, you see, when the tunnels ain't big enough for 'em.'

He felt some pride, I could tell, at doing a man's work, difficult or hazardous as it might be.

'And I'm safe enough down there, any road,' he continued, 'it bein' so dark mostly, and I can get away quick if anyone asks about my father. 'Tis better than the sea, miss, I knows that,' he added defiantly. 'I hates the sea – and I'll never be a fisherman, for certain.'

He shivered, and I saw him again as he had been that morning in the churchyard – the world's cares written on his brow, his childish mouth set with a bitterness beyond his years. I wondered what would become of him. His hatred of the sea I understood: so many times he must have watched and waited on the pier, since infancy familiar with the perils of the wind and waves. For to those who must earn their bread by such dangerous means, the sea is no guileless maiden, blue-gowned, with shining tresses and a sparkling laugh – but a hard mistress, with a voice which threatens and has the power, at her merest whim, to destroy men who consort with her.

And yet I shuddered at the thought that any, whether child or full-grown man, should toil his life away below the ground, in order to provide, at best, such meagre food and shelter as this boy had always known. Since then I have, in truth, seen others in worse case – in cities where the poor must breed and die like rats among the excrement of richer folk, places where hope and dignity are trodden underfoot, crushed by the dainty silken slippers of society. But now I only longed (without the spur of pious aim or Christian charity) to lighten, if I could, the load which fate had bidden Peter carry: for I knew that they must work, without respite, who have not the more kindly hand of Fortune to guide their lives.

I said no more, at that moment, of my fears for him, nor of the plan already forming in my mind. He was, I saw, tired out; and so I left him to sleep longer, reassuring him that I would come again when I could do so undetected. Leaving the heavy door unbarred as I had found it, I regained the house – to the sound of Emily's scolding as I shook the raindrops from my hair.

'Why, Miss Georgiana, your aunt's fair put out at you goin' off like that i' th' middle o' the mornin' – wanted you most particular she did and couldn't find you nowheres. Soakin' wet you be, too!' added Emily, shaking her head as she took my cloak and hung it by the stove. Without replying, I removed my clogs, put on the slippers I had left beside the kitchen door, and went at once upstairs to the parlour.

Aunt Nicolson was seated at her writing-table. As I entered she put down her pen and carefully sealed the letter upon which she had been engaged; then she looked at me – her expression of reproach more effective than any spoken rebuke. At length her silence, so far removed from her habitual eloquence, became too much for me to bear.

'I beg your pardon, aunt: you wished to speak to me, Emily says. I – I was looking for Minou and – ' I faltered, only too aware that such excuse must appear insufficient for an absence of more than an hour, and for the quantity of dust and hay which had clung, unnoticed, to my skirt. Yet, as I waited for my guardian's response, I felt a sudden sense of injustice at being so severely regarded – as if I were a child to be reprimanded for some trivial misdemeanour.

'I have no wish to enquire into your actions, Georgiana; but you must know that such thoughtlessness causes concern, especially in the light of your – disappearance – on an earlier occasion.' She could only be referring, I was sure, to the events of my birthday, and I had indeed grieved at causing her such anxiety then. Her next words, however, roused in me a quick anger which overwhelmed my more conscientious feelings.

'I fear that I must ask you, therefore, to inform me of your purpose should you wish to go further than the square – and that you should on no account do so unaccompanied.'

'But aunt,' I cried, 'you cannot, surely, mistrust me so? I own I have been lacking in consideration perhaps, but I have never wished to distress you: how could I, indeed, when you have been so much more than kind to me? But I am not a child – I am of age – and should not be confined in such a way!'

I was not only angry but alarmed at the prospect of such restriction; moreover, the knowledge that I had already, of necessity, deceived her, only served to increase my determination to resist her request. But at this my guardian stood up; her blue eyes revealed no conceding softness as her gaze met, and held, my own.

'Yes,' she replied quietly, 'you are of age, Georgiana, and remain here by your own choice. But whilst you do so, I may not allow you to act in ways which, for a young lady, might prove unwise, possibly unsafe. For at times like this – an election spoken of, the people agitating for Reform, even for revolution in some quarters, I am told – any kind of violence may occur. Why, even here in Workington, where the family name is respected and so many are loyal to Sir Henry, there is now, Charles tells me, some feeling against the Curwens!'

The gravity with which Aunt Nicolson spoke, together with her unexpected mention of my cousin, for the present checked my indignation. In the momentary pause as she resumed her chair, I remembered that, should I defy her further, I would not only forfeit her goodwill but might, by a few incautious words, endanger Peter and his father. Though inwardly rebellious, I tried to restrain the tears which threatened – and which my aunt seemed to interpret as contrition, for her voice was gentler as she continued:

'Come now, you must know that Charles asked me most particularly to ensure that you do not go alone into the town. He is much concerned, for only last month, he said, one of their best men from the pit was set upon by some ruffian down by the shore – and he may yet die of his injuries, it seems. One of those wicked Irish it must have been: they come across in search of work, and finding none (for there's little enough for the men who belong to the town, heaven knows!) they cause nought but mischief till they go home again – or are deported to the Indies, as they deserve!'

Silently I listened as she expanded upon a favourite theme – the need for severity in dealing with such lawlessness among the poor. As my conviction grew that, from her description of the incident, it must have been the fight involving Michael Stephens, I could only be thankful that I had succeeded in keeping my temper and my counsel. And I prayed now that she might not detect, as I sat with folded hands, eyes fixed upon the curled legs of her writing-table, the increasing turmoil of my thoughts.

'Let us hope, at all events, that they will find him when they search the marshes as they intend to do tomorrow – for we're none of us secure with such a villain at large . . . Why, don't look so alarmed, Georgiana – they are certain to catch up with him soon!'

She turned briskly, to pick up the letter from the table.

'There, I have written already to Keswick – it was about that I wished to speak with you; for I have to send word today to give Hugh and Mary sufficient notice of our coming. Now Isabella, when I talked with her about it yesterday, proposed we should drive up through Cockermouth and Lorton Vale, which I remember as a *very* charming route . . .'

But for me, the joy and certainty of yesterday were gone. The charm of the intended route and my cousins' promised company belonged, from that morning, to a future dream which, if I disobeyed my aunt and were discovered, might not become reality. I could allow myself to feel no warmth of gratitude at Charles' concern for my safety, since he had (though with good intention, surely) lost me my freedom at the very moment when I needed it most.

For Peter's father must be warned, and quickly, of the impending search. I would wait only until Aunt Nicolson retired, as she always did, for her rest in the late afternoon. Emily I would placate with some excuse – the loss of a glove or handkerchief in the garden would suffice – in hopes that I should find the boy still sleeping in the stable-loft. If by an unlucky chance he was already gone, I must myself seek out Jem or Rosa before nightfall, so that the fisherman might, by some means, evade pursuit. Beyond such reasoning I had no plan, for my acquaintance with the country was so slight that I could think of no safe refuge for him. I knew only that I would try to help him and, if need be, face whatever consequence might follow – even, perhaps, the loss of all that I had found in Cumberland.

It was a warm, calm evening. The rain had ceased but an hour or two since; its moisture clung still to the churchyard grasses, which bent and shook with their burden of shining droplets, each a fragile silvered world, poised until the wind should blow it off. I could smell the salt in the damp air, the breeze too light as yet to ruffle the surface of the sea. For the Solway stretched out before me, still and golden in the sunlight, which lay upon the water and the Scottish hills beyond with a brightness that, even as I watched, intensified, merging its gleams and sparks to form an endless-seeming flow of liquid fire. Due west rose the mountains of the Isle of Man, black against the white-gold of the sky, across which massed ranks of cloud strode landward, grey armies whose sun-tipped shields and swords dazzled my eyes as I waited there, alone, on the high ground above the marshes.

From here the promontory curved inland, following the river's wooded banks and rising, on the nearer side, with almost precipitous steepness to the Hall, the ancient fortress of the Curwens. Uncompromising yet serene it stood above the

Derwent, small tumbled cottages about its feet on the seaward slope, up which the townsfolk must have fled in times of siege, to reach the gatehouse and crowd within the walls. At the far corner rose the square battlemented tower, from where, four centuries ago, Sir Christopher Curwen rode to meet, with five more knights of illustrious name, the six knights of Scotland who had challenged them to battle on Carlisle Plain. Yet now, new stonework shining in the evening sun, it seemed that little could ever have disturbed the peace or safety of that house. How gently green and luxuriant were its tall trees – chestnut, oak, and beech – beneath which my mother had waited for my grandfather's carriage; and how, suddenly, I pitied her the loss of her childhood home! In my stubborn pride, I had avoided taking walks which I knew would lead me to the high wall which edged the parkland; but I pictured my mother playing with her sisters upon the grass, or riding, carefree, from the gate to meet her lover – my father – Alexander, whom she had lost and I would never know . . . For she had been bereft, as I had been – as had, indeed, the boy for whom I waited still, beside the church.

Looking out across the firth from her high window, that other Georgiana must have seen (by another summer's light) the sea and sky and hills as I saw them, in all their tranquil splendour. So might they have looked, perhaps, to the defenders of the town, seeking Saint Michael's sanctuary against the sea-borne foe; so, too, to Sir Christopher, Lord of Workington – now lying there, stone-encased, beside Elizabeth his lady, stone hounds asleep at head and foot, in the twilight of the chancel. And even so, who knows, to those earlier guardians of the shores, soldiers who built their forts (outposts of Rome) from the great wall at Carlisle down along the Cumbrian coast, at Bowness and Beckfoot, Maryport and Moresby and Ravenglass . . . At Ravenglass – where, unless disaster overtook him first, Peter's father would find safe harbour by tomorrow morning.

''Tis the only landing-place, you see, miss, where it don't dry out too much when the tide drops – that's why Father wants to try for it – but 'tis a long way to go, sure enough. And

Ravenglass was once a great port, so Jem says, but now only the fishers know it well enough to use it; for 'tis hard to get in there – wi' the bad currents, and quicksands, and a great sand-bar, he says, that's so wick wi' sea-birds you cannat even hear the sound o' the sea sometimes, they make such a great noise wi' their cryin', like.

'But my father should be safe enough when he gets there, for there's other Irish folk, and people as he knows from up i' the hills – a wild lot, he said they be, as comes and goes wi' all kinds o' things . . .'

Here Peter had paused and looked at me warily, as if fearing he had told me too much. But I knew already, from Emily's tales, of those who, lacking better livelihood, used their knowledge of that coast for their own illegal ends, for trafficking in rum or wines, tea and tobacco, even graphite from the Keswick mines. And I had heard that few who traded from these ports – even respected merchants, owners or captains of ships – would turn away from easy profit; some, it was rumoured, had built their gracious lakeside houses with money from the sale of slaves in far-off places, despite the reformers' zeal or Acts of Parliament. Such evil men, grown rich on others' suffering, were a greater danger, surely, than an outlawed fisherman, forced by poverty to steal in order to survive! So I felt no shock at Peter's words – only a fear (of which I dared not speak) that Michael Stephens, once at Ravenglass, might never see his son again.

I had found the boy, as I had hoped to do, on my return to the stable-yard. He was standing at the pump, trying to remove the sleep from his eyes and the coal-dust from his face, when, late in the afternoon, I slipped through the doorway from the garden. Upon hearing that the marshes were to be searched next morning, he had stared at me, first in alarm, then with increasing determination.

'I must find Jem, and the old man, too,' he declared, pulling at his dark hair, 'for they'll be bound to try and catch the tide tonight – right up the shore 'twill be, nearly to the edge of marsh, and my father will get to the boat a bit easier, like.'

He told me then how they had already planned to take the

fisherman, as soon as his leg was strong enough, down the coast – beyond Whitehaven and the great headland at Saint Bee's – to Ravenglass, where he had friends, some (so I guessed from the boy's description) being fugitives, like himself.

'He'll not be followed so far, surely,' concluded Peter; 'but I'll need to go quick as I can, else I shall miss Jem, maybe – and I must get back along the shore from the town to tell Father, for the boat cannat wait for too long . . .'

He looked at me again, anxiously – and at once I knew what I should do.

'Let me go and warn him that the boat will be coming – you can show me where the path goes, down from the churchyard. It will not be dusk for a good while yet – I shall find him, I am sure. And then,' I added, seeing his uncertainty, 'it will matter less if you meet with some delay. Stay here, whilst I go to the house for my cloak; I will leave by the side door – you can follow me, when you are sure no one is watching you, up to the church. I will wait there until you come.'

Aunt Nicolson, I knew, was by now resting in her room, and Emily busy in the kitchen. Quickly I found what I wanted – my own cloak, and another, old but warm and serviceable still, and a heavy ashen stick from the stand beside the door. Before leaving, I took the letter I had penned that afternoon, and placed it upon the table beside my bed, so that my aunt would find it if she came to look for me. Sadly, yet with resolution, I left the house which I had thought of as my home, and crossed the square – to wait, in the brightness of that summer evening, beside Saint Michael's church, high above the Solway.

At first the path was clear, as the boy had pointed it out to me: almost a cart's breadth, the turf and stones treacherously roughened by the passage of sheep or cattle driven from the beach, up the hill to the common land beyond the churchyard. But when I came down to where the track divided, the wider way continuing toward the shore, I took another, narrow path to my left, turning south, so that the town now lay behind me. There was sand beneath my feet; I stumbled a little on loose pebbles or tufts of coarse grass; and though I could no longer see the waves, I could hear them driving the shingle up the shore, loud above the sound of the wind in the reeds, which grew tall on each side to a height beyond my own, their tops the colour of hair bleached almost to whiteness by the sun.

Hemmed in, I began to lose direction: the sound of the sea grew fainter as, almost imperceptibly, the ground rose a little, growing firmer with each step. Then came a sudden clearing, where I saw a rough, low hut, roofed with reed and coarse cloth, like pieces of sail; beyond, a small fire, still faintly smoking, where a long-haired dog fed upon a carcass of some kind. Of human inhabitants there was no sign: but they could not be far away – herding cattle perhaps, or combing the beach for whatever the tide might yield, hoping, like many another, to find amber or the sparkling stones which might lie among the pebbles. The dog barked; I quickened my pace, clutching my stick and then almost running to where the track, so Peter had said, should start again. Though I found it, it was now even harder to follow, at times almost vanishing beneath the grass and iris, which here grew in profusion; until at last I came to a great bank of sand, like a barrier before me – once, when the sea reached so far inland, the line of the shore.

There was now no choice. Slowly I climbed the bank, and from its height looked for the landmark by which I must find my way. I could see only the cruel glitter of the waves, the far-off ceaseless ripple of turning water; an endless sea of rushes, with here and there a patch of iris, green shafts among brown, their tips barbed with yellow flowers. There were cattle, black shaggy beasts, browsing patiently; and close by, on a lichen-covered rock, a small brown bird repeated its song. Then, not far away along the ridge I saw it – the blackened frame of a wreck, lying at a crazy angle among the reeds.

Quickly I removed my clogs lest I should turn an ankle when crossing the rough ground, pitted with holes which in autumn would fill with rain or spray driven in by the westerly gale. From the far side of the curving spars a faint track ran through thorn bushes, stunted and bare of leaf even in summer. As I trod the mean turf, flies buzzed about my head, with an incessant movement which – weary and impatient as I was – only added to my haste: for I was conscious of the distance I had come, and of how time was slipping past.

At last I reached a tall smooth stone, embedded deep in the ground; a pace or two beyond stood another, and a third; then more again. Almost without realising, I touched each one as I passed it, impelled by some sense of ritual, buried deep as the stones themselves. Ten I had counted when I came to one wider and flatter than all the rest: behind it, outside the rocky circle and sheltered by thorns, was a small stone hut, arched over with a thatch of turf and rushes. Meadow-sweet grew there, and pale lady's-smock; shells, white and smooth with age, lay scattered among the daisies in the green grass of the hollow. I heard the cry of a sea-bird far above my head, the whirring of some insect in the warm air, and, far away, the sound of the rising tide upon the shingle. Perhaps long ago some hermit had lived here, or the Romans, maybe: I do not know, but will remember, always, the stillness and lonely quiet of that place.

If I had pitied him before – when I first saw him standing in the doorway of his home, his strength exhausted by his struggle with the elements – now I felt both anger and compassion at the fisherman's plight. His large frame sprawled upon a makeshift bed of rags and reed, the pallor of his face quite alarming in the dimness of the hut. He lay as though he had fallen there, like some massive tree brought low by the force of the wind. So still was he, indeed, as I bent low through the narrow opening, that he might have been one of the great stones near which he had taken refuge.

He stared at me first as though unseeing. Then with a curious smile, almost childlike, he ran his fingers through his wild hair and beard – which I remembered as black but which shone with the silver that age or suffering bestow upon a man, even in his prime, as he was, despite his weakness. Looking down at his leg, bound with cloth to a crude splint, he said: 'Yon doctor friend o' yours put me in this now – so you'll pardon a man for bein' incapable o' greetin' you politely as you're accustomed to, surely.'

He inclined his head ironically, and I felt suddenly disturbed by his words: for I realised that, however helpless, the man was little changed in spirit, had become indeed more bitter and independent even than before. Yet – he did not seem angry at my coming.

'There is no time for such mockery, sir, however you may wish it! I am come to warn you that you cannot stay here longer – Peter has gone for Jem and the boat will come for you soon, to catch the tide.' I spoke with increasing urgency, as I saw the doubt and weariness which showed upon his face. 'Believe me, it is not safe for you now – there is to be another search tomorrow!'

'Why,' he said, 'it matters little enough if they take me now – I'll not get to sea again with this!' He struck at his leg violently with the flat of his hand – and it hurt, I could see, from the look which he gave me then. 'Now get you back to your home and leave me be!'

I feared such despair far more than I had his anger. And I felt no little bitterness at being so readily dismissed.

'Think of Peter!' I cried, 'and of your friends and your little ones – how can you grieve them so? For their sakes, you must get to the boat, and to Ravenglass. And do you think I have come so far to have you send me back again?'

With tears in my eyes, I brushed the hair away from my face, and shook the sand from my skirts – then suddenly reached out and touched his shoulder:

'Come, Michael,' I said, more gently, ' – as far as the tinkers' hut, where we must wait for Peter.'

For a few moments he was silent.

'Aye, we'll try, then!' There was a hint of acknowledgement in his grim tone, and of grudging admiration in his next words: ''Tis a lonely path through the marshes for a young lass: but there's some Irish in you, for sure. And I'll maybe see Ireland again myself, who knows, one day!'

He pulled himself up stiffly and tried to stand, cursing as the weight came onto his injured leg. Without speaking he took the stick from me, then the cloak, which he wrapped awkwardly about him. I went before him through the low doorway, where he almost fell, but again refused to take my helping arm. Slowly he came out into the light – like some wild creature emerging into the sunshine.

At first, he would not lean on me: but as we went the roughness of the terrain took, with each step, its toll of weariness and pain. When we left the stones to strike out across the treacherous ground toward the wreck, he stumbled several times and fell against me, so that before many yards were gone his weight rested hard upon my shoulders, his free hand clutching, each time he fell, the heavy fabric of my cloak. When at length we reached the blackened spars, the fisherman sank down against them, his face sweating and pallid, eyes grim with effort.

'Let us rest here – there is time,' I said; and he murmured 'Aye,' with an expression of such anguish that, despite his attempt to hide it, I feared we might go no further. But before long my companion picked up the stick once more, and (my support this time accepted without question) we continued along the ridge, until – most difficult of all – we descended the steep bank of sand, down to the narrow hidden path which led to the tinkers' hut. By now, the man's weight was almost more than I could bear; each breath seemed to cause him pain, every pace to be an act of will, which – had I been able at that time to make such reflection – I would have wondered at.

A strange slow-moving pair we must have looked, as we came out into the clearing. Several dogs were now at large there, a ragged child running among them, while a man and woman heaped wood on the fire, its leaping flames the colour of the sun sinking low beyond the reed beds. I stopped in alarm. The fierce grip on my shoulder eased a little as Michael looked across towards the hut.

'Those are friends – they'll not be botherin' us.'

He spoke almost in a whisper, his whole body shaking, yet seemed suddenly to regain strength as he gestured towards the reeds.

'Over there now – 'tis a quicker path to the shore. We will wait for him there.'

The tinkers watched us cross the sand to where the track started, and here, in the shelter of the tall reeds, Peter's father rested at last. I could not sit – I was too anxious for the boy to come; but I loosened my cloak and flung it down, being hot with exertion and glad to feel the cooler evening air. So long and wearisome had been our traverse of the marsh, I had lost all sense of time; now the chill of the breeze against my cheeks, the fast-setting sun, and the deep violet hue of the clouds banked in the northern sky, told me that it would not be long before twilight. Since leaving the square, I had not thought of Aunt Nicolson: at this moment, perhaps, she might be looking for me, or reading the note I had left . . .

My companion lay silent, his head upon his outstretched arm. There was no sound about us – only the steady beat of the breaking waves, unseen yet ever-present. A flock of oystercatchers flew overhead, their barred and angled wings sharp against the sky, their cry a faint low bubbling murmur, becoming almost bell-like in clarity and sweetness as they passed, then fading, echoing, and fading again. Still Peter did not come; I looked over toward the tinkers' hut, but saw no sign of him, only the movement of smoke from the fire round which the family was gathered.

'Aye, vagrants and vagabonds all – but better to be trusted than finer folk, I'm tellin' ye!'

Michael's voice, and his dark eyes watching me, took me quite unawares. I sat down on my cloak beside him, sighing as I did so, for I was apprehensive about Peter, beginning to fear that somehow his plan had gone amiss.

'An' it's like enough to a tinker lass you are yourself, so I'm thinkin' – so you'd mebbe best come wi' me to Ravenglass, away from such folk as yon Curwens!'

He gazed at me intently as he spoke; but my astonishment was such that for some moments I could not answer him – nor do anything save look at my hands, stained brown with mud; at my feet in a peasant's clogs; and my gown, torn and dirty with stumbling so often while crossing the marsh. Then the full meaning of his words came to me:

'So, you know who I am – and yet you do not hate me for it?'

'Aye,' he said, 'you put me in mind of – of someone, so soon as I set eyes on you that day. And then – why, I knew sure enough you were one of them; I was thinkin' to hate you for't, that's for sure – but you're not the same as others as I knows of, else you'd not be here – and helpin' a man as you knows nothin' of, and has no cause to be carin' for at all!'

'It is true,' I said, 'that I have no reason to help you, or Peter either – yet I do care . . . But I – have no wish to go to Ravenglass, all the same.'

He laughed then – but I could not tell if his eyes were bright with something more than laughter.

'Nay, lass, 'twas jestin' with you I was!'

But he reached out a hand, and grasped me by the arm, with a strength quite at odds with the weakness I had witnessed earlier; and this time I could not doubt that he meant his words:

'Let me tell you, now – before you go back to your aunt, as go you must. Have a mind who you trust, for there's some as will talk sweetly wi' you, but will care not what harm they bring to folk. And 'tis strange . . . the law is different for such as them, so it seems . . .'

He almost muttered to himself, and shook his head, becoming for some minutes lost in thought. I stayed beside him then, not fearing that his hand still rested upon my arm, nor that he was, in truth, a fugitive – a vagrant, as he had said, and a violent man, as indeed I knew. And though I dearly wished for his safety, it meant we should not meet again, that I might never learn how he fared in Ravenglass, nor if he would get to Ireland as he hoped . . .

But where was Peter – and why did he not come? I could bear such waiting no longer and sprang up, flinging my cloak around me, ready to run down the path to the shore – so that I might at the very least see whether he was somewhere near. But his father called after me, to have patience a little longer, lest I be seen and so endanger all of us.

'Don't fear, now,' said Michael, as unwillingly I returned, marvelling at his calm certainty when so much – his life, indeed! – was in jeopardy. 'Don't fear, the boat will come, lass, you'll see!'

Chapter 9

It was true, as I had said: I had no wish that day to go with Michael Stephens. Yet, one night, soon after his escape, I dreamed I was indeed in Ravenglass.

It was full tide. I saw, as I left the boat by which I had come there, grey waves lapping high up the granite walls of a row of cottages, which stood like a bastion against the sea; their foundations were built upon the shore, their windows deep inset, like narrow eyes which watched all night and day the incessant flight of sea-birds above the sandbank that lay beyond the anchorage. Slowly I walked along the landward side of the cottages, pausing at each in expectation of seeing someone who I felt was waiting for me. There, in the doorway of the very farthest house he stood, his tall figure stooping a little, his hand shading his features as he looked along the street toward the sea. But, as he stepped forward, I saw that he was not anyone I knew: not Peter's father, as I had expected, nor was it (as I hoped quite suddenly) the countenance of Philip Earnshaw turned to greet me. The outstretched arms were those of a stranger, whose face was as blank as the paper in my drawing-book, save for eyes which held no warmth, for which I longed – eyes which looked at me indifferently as he raised a hand in a motion of rejection. And though (still searching in my dream) I returned, despairing, to that place, he was gone – to where, I never knew . . .

For I awoke then, and lit my candle thankfully, to keep such images at bay for the remainder of the night. And yet, though relieved, as a frightened child might be, to find myself in the safety of my room, I felt an inner certainty that one day – for a reason still unknown – I must go, in truth, to Ravenglass. So may it sometimes happen that, most strangely, the very name of a place or person yet unseen may haunt the imagination, conjuring dreams which – long before their time – take on reality. For thoughts will follow where the body may not go: down the untrodden path, or across uncharted seas. So, though I remained behind, and after his departure returned to Portland Square, as Michael himself had bidden me, I wondered sometimes (as I wonder still!) how it might have been had I chosen differently, and gone with him.

That evening, as I stayed beside him, he seemed to me a man whose strength would not, had I ever needed it, have failed me. Then, at last, Jem and Peter came. And, feeling the boy's loss as with him I watched the boat, so long awaited, sail into the coming darkness, I knew that it was the enfolding warmth of a father's love I sought – and must seek in vain. It was not my mother's arms I longed for, as I had at Maidenhead, but the unchanging affection which I saw in Michael Stephens' care for his children. His parting words, before he left us together on that lonely shore, were for those whom he had (by such cruel chance) to leave behind.

'You'll not forget my little ones? I will come for them so soon as I can, and fetch them to Ravenglass – you must tell them so, Peter. Aye, you are a good lad, that's for sure!'

He kissed his son, awkwardly enough, then took my hand in his, looking for a moment as if he would say more; yet he did not. And so he left us; and that distant harbour, in the days which followed, became for me a haven of the mind, a refuge from the anxious conscience which, from the hour of my return, so troubled me.

I had anticipated my guardian's anger, Emily's reproaches, the disgrace inevitably consequent upon my having wilfully (and at once) disregarded the restriction my aunt had laid upon me. Though I had tried, in the letter I had left for her, to explain my absence as needful only to aid a friend whose trust I could not betray, I did not believe that Aunt Nicolson would wish me to remain with her. I did not regret what I had done – yet I was not so strong in spirit that I could bear the thought of homelessness, or poverty, or lack of love. For my affections had become more strongly rooted than I dared to contemplate. The kindness of my aunt and cousins had erased much bitterness: had I not longed, since my journey northwards with the Nicolsons, for the security of family and friends, for some barrier against the Horace Chattertons of the world, whose cold-eyed lust I feared (when I dared to think of it again) as I feared nothing else? My home, so I wished to think, was here in Workington; whilst my heart already, though I knew it not, was centred on my cousin Charles.

It was of Charles I thought, as I stood for a moment in the half-darkness of the garden. The boy had gone, exhausted, to his bed in the stable, leaving me at the side door, where roses (fewer now that July was almost past) still faintly scented the air. Would my cousin care, I wondered, when he heard of my disgrace, and learned that I was gone? Would he take another, perhaps, to Wastdale, in the spring?

I looked up to where the parlour curtains were drawn, only a narrow gleam of lamplight to tell me my aunt was there, having dined, an hour ago, alone. For I had heard the church clock striking nine as we hurried across the square, and I knew that, at so late an hour, my absence could not go undetected.

Yet – in my room, the letter lay on the table still, folded as I had left it. It appeared not to have been touched: but I had clearly inscribed her name upon it – as my aunt must have seen if she had, as I expected, come in search of me. By now I was almost overcome with anxiety and fatigue, desiring nothing more than to remain in the reassuring quiet of my room. But I summoned resolution enough, even so, to change my gown, and to arrange my hair as neatly as I could by the flickering candlelight – as if I might, by such familiar action, restore the courage I had lost.

At the end of the passageway, the parlour door stood slightly ajar; I hesitated there, then saw, as I pushed the door further open, my aunt's figure beside the window which looked out across the square. She turned towards me, and for an instant I wondered if she had been watching for me.

If so, she said nothing of it. She crossed the room to where I stood, took the small silver bell from its place on the stand beside the door, and rang it vigorously.

'Susan may bring our coffee now,' she remarked – as she might have done on any other evening after dinner, before taking her place as usual beside the fire.

'You look pale, Georgiana; I think a little of Humphrey's brandy might not come amiss . . . It is two years now, almost to the day, since he should have returned – ' She paused for a moment, they continued briskly, '– and I cannot think he would have wished good brandy to sit idly in the cupboard there when it might be of use to someone. It was something my brother and he never could agree on. For Henry always said he'd as soon have a glass of water as all the fine wines in the cellar – and his is full enough, Lord knows! But Humphrey knew a good bottle when he saw one – even at sea he would have none but the best, as this is, you may be sure!'

So we passed the remainder of the evening. Susan brought the coffee, and removed the cups, doubtless hastening, round-eyed, to report to Emily on her mistress's unlooked-for self-indulgence. Aunt Nicolson talked to me, as never before, of her girlhood in Maryport, of her husband's travels; and even of his quarrel – hardly mended before his death – with my grandfather. At first I knew hardly whether I should smile or weep, so profound was my relief, which was equalled only by my puzzlement. For it was almost as though she understood my fears and wished (without saying as much) to reassure me in some way: not once did it occur to me, at that time, that my guardian herself might fear a future empty of affection, might regret the loss of one whom she had chosen – after so long an interval – to bring into her home. All I could comprehend was that, if my aunt had been grieved or angered by my absence, she did not show it; and if she had found and read my letter, I never knew.

Only once, that evening, did she give any sign that she might have guessed something – yet even her sudden question might have come about by chance.

'Tell me, Georgiana – what has happened to that boy – Peter, is it not? He seems to have been very remiss of late – and you will need his help to get the garden to rights in the autumn, which will be on us soon enough, once August is out, and that wedding of Isabella's over with at last.'

I was on my guard at once – despite the drowsiness induced by a warm fire and my aunt's generous filling of my glass. Though the fisherman was, I hoped, by this time some way upon his journey, I could not risk any mention of his name. But I could perhaps, now that he was gone, make it easier for Peter to avoid returning to the pit – or to Jem's house, where he might be seen and questioned about his father. He would be safer, surely, in the upper town, where he and his family were too poor to be of interest to anyone.

'He is here, aunt,' I said – glad that in this at least I could tell her the truth. 'He has no home now, and has been sleeping in the stable. That is where I went this morning: I followed Minou and found him there. I – hoped that you might allow him to stay . . .'

I looked at her in trepidation, not daring to expect that she would agree without further question.

'Ah, then it *was* he, just as I thought!' Aunt Nicolson nodded at me significantly. 'Emily told me only yesterday that she had seen someone in the garden, down beyond the pear tree. I said that it was just the boy come again but she would have it there was someone dangerous about – such as that fellow Charles warned us of, you remember?'

'I am sure Peter will be useful, aunt,' I urged, not wishing her to dwell further upon the subject of intruders. 'He will work hard, and he might perhaps be of help to us if – if you should obtain a pony one day, for Charles suggested it, did he not?'

Although his proposal seemed to me unlikely to find favour (for my own place in the household could not but remain uncertain) I had hopes, even so, that it might prove an added reason for Peter to remain longer: for I feared that he might – if I did not do something quickly – have no choice but to return to working in the pit.

'We shall see – I don't doubt that your cousin means well enough, but he does not always think of consequences . . . But Peter may put the yard to rights – I had intended doing so in any case: and if he were not here we should need to get Emily's nephew over from the Dragon to do the work. She says he's busy enough as it is, for there's so much coming and going, with mail-horses every day and folk looking for carriages, when they come from the boats – '

As she paused for breath, and to give the fire an emphatic shake with the poker, I sighed, and wondered how much longer I could keep awake . . .

'Why yes – let the boy stay if he will. Then perhaps you'll not be fretting your days away with not knowing where he is, and we shall have some peace again!'

With this pronouncement she rose and replaced Humphrey Nicolson's brandy in the cupboard beside the fireplace, where, as far as I knew it remained, untouched, until some years afterward – when I myself removed it.

Each day I waited for the blow to fall – for my aunt to give voice to some indignation or reproach; for she did not, I well knew, easily keep patience with those who crossed her, nor could she tolerate deceit. I could only surmise that on this occasion she must have had strong reason for such restraint; yet I feared that her anger, when it came, must be the greater for it. But still she said nothing to me. The burden of my conscience grew daily harder to bear: so that even as I tried to be more than usually helpful to her (less from apprehension than from sadness that I must myself keep silence) I sometimes felt it would have been easier, almost, had I been forced by Aunt Nicolson's wrath to defend my actions.

As it was, I gained some recompense in Peter's pleasure at being given the task of clearing the yard and stable – already, as he and I both knew, his own domain. On making her inspection (surely the first for many months) my aunt raised her hands in horror at the sad state of the chaise, which though old-fashioned might have been serviceable yet. At first she was for making a bonfire of it, then abruptly changed her mind and sent for Emily's nephew, Josh, to come from the Green Dragon to give his expert opinion.

'Why ma'am, 'tis a week or two's work for a joiner, right

[124]

enough. Old Ben down at the yard, he would do't, mebbe – but then there's all them fancy cushions needs makin' good and a coat or two o' varnish – 'twill take a month an' no mistake. Though you'll not be wantin' it yet, I'm thinkin', any road . . .' Then he shook his head. 'Now a new one might be a better notion, mistress, if you've a mind to't – very quick an' smart they be, some o' them – '

But his suggestion was brushed aside, my aunt declaring that the old was always better than the new – and what had been smart enough for the Captain was smart enough for herself.

'I had thought,' she continued, 'that it might be ready to take us up to Keswick but I see that'll not do. We must make the best of it and hire from the Dragon after all – and you shall drive us, Joshua!'

Josh Pratt looked doubtful at this honour but was too wise to express any reservation. He slipped away, as soon as he was able, in the direction of the kitchen, where I later found him drinking a mug of ale and teasing Susan, to Emily's manifest annoyance.

Despite Aunt Nicolson's declared intention, the matter of our visit to Keswick remained (to my own doubting mind, at least) in question. Although I had begun, in some measure, to believe that she must intend me to remain with her, it was impossible – while she continued to avoid all reference to my absence and my letter – for me to feel any peace, or any certainty as to the future.

At last, one morning, my aunt called me to her.

'Georgiana – there is some news from Mary, and not before time, I'm thinking. She and Hugh will expect us on the twelfth, and we shall remain with them for three nights. So *that* is settled at least.' Then she frowned. 'But I cannot think why Isabella has not sent word; it is most strange – unless . . .'

She glanced at me sharply, and her look and manner were such that I could only guess the delay to be connected, some-how, with myself. Perhaps, I wondered sadly, my cousin had repented her hasty kindness, had even (her welcome notwith-standing) decided to withdraw her friendship. I did not wish to believe it of her: but I still remembered Michael's mistrust of the Curwens, and Sir Henry's continued domination of the family.

But to dwell upon such matters could only add to my despondency. So I applied myself the more eagerly to assisting Aunt Nicolson, who on that same morning had determined to attack the accumulated possessions left, since his death, to gather dust in her husband's study. For some hours we worked, our efforts punctuated by my guardian's exclamations or reflective reminiscence. It was almost as if she hoped, by making such a vigorous assault upon the past, to exorcise the perpetual presence of Humphrey Nicolson from her mind.

While she sorted papers, books and maps, I found much to interest me. There were books of political thought which, when winter came, would help me to understand the world in which my grandfather had moved; trade and agricultural publications, many relating to the Isle of Man and Cumberland; collections of nautical papers connected with Turkey, Greece, the Caribbean – which at once fired my imagination. I longed to travel to such places; yet I turned with equal fascination the pages of a book of Hogarth's work, finding here those images of London I had carried in my mind for many months. Glimpses of cruelty and despair, of men and women ruined or degenerate – I had caught them but fleetingly from the window of a carriage: but they had not left me, for sometimes I had seen such faces in the streets of Workington. Later, when I saw in gracious galleries the noble features of the aristocracy, painted by Gainsborough or Reynolds, I admired what artists made of them – but I remembered the reality my mother's letters hinted at, of gentlemen who drank themselves to death, women who trifled with men's fates and charmed their money from them, the vicious world which Rowlandson and Hogarth knew.

The study walls were hung with pictures, of ships and seascapes by painters from Whitehaven or Carlisle. Among the heavy gilt-framed oils and above the bureau, an engraving – the more conspicuous for its smaller size and the plainness of its frame – caught my attention. Aunt Nicolson observed me looking at it.

'Hmm! If *that* ship had gone to the bottom of the China Ocean we'd all have been spared a deal of trouble. There were more folk's lives ruined than I care to think – and Humphrey could have told a tale or two of some of them, if he'd not had sense enough to keep his counsel. So don't ask me anything about it, niece, for I've no more mind to speak of it than he did!'

Indeed, I was about to question her, just as she thought. For the ship was none other than the *Bounty*. I knew already that the famous mutineer had been my guardian's cousin: so I had been curious to hear more of Fletcher Christian, and was now the more so since I saw that the subject was unwelcome. But she was always reticent when speaking of her own relations. I could not press her futher; yet I noted the name – *P. Heywood* – pencilled at the foot of the engraving, and remembered it when Aunt Nicolson, long afterward, came to speak of it to me.

I had just returned from delivering yet another bundle of papers to Peter's bonfire in the garden when there came the sudden noise of horses' hooves on the cobbles in the square; and a masculine shout, followed by a rapping at the front door. Aunt Nicolson went quickly to the window, then spoke to me with an imperative tone against which I could not have protested even had I wished:

'Go upstairs, Georgiana – at once! And wait in the parlour until I come to you.'

Even as Emily – muttering at the impatiently repeated knocking – crossed the hall to admit the visitor, I almost ran from the study, along the passage to the back staircase. But, having gained the parlour, my curiosity was such that I was drawn (without thought of decorum) to look out of the window.

Below, in the square, beside the chestnut tree, two horses were standing – my cousin Charles seated upon the larger, a fine golden-coloured creature with dark mane and tail. The second horse was riderless and, though a sturdier, less elegant animal, clearly spirited, for my cousin had much ado to hold it in check while waiting, evidently, for his companion. He was, I thought, too much occupied with his task to glance up at the window; so for some minutes I watched him, his hair sunlit and awry as he pushed it back with a careless hand – with which he then caressed the neck of his own mount, becoming a trifle restive beside the other. Despite his strength (evident now in his mastery of the horses) Charles looked to me, as he sat there, the most perfectly graceful of men. He seemed, in his coat of a darker green, to be at one with the swaying green and gold of the chestnut leaves, part of an ancient dappled landscape – of hounds and horses and forest trees – upon a mediaeval page.

I did not wish to be noticed, watching him. For a few moments I sat at the table in the parlour; but the thought that he was there – so near, yet not intending to come into the house – roused in me an impatience that almost angered me, so intense and unbidden was it. At length I determined to go to my room, where I would not be tempted to look out at him again. But as I passed the top of the stair the door of the study opened, and I heard the second visitor exclaim as he crossed the hall:

'Why, Lizzie, I've no thought to seek election in the spring – and as for the leg, 'tis well enough now and there's an end of it!'

The voice, though commanding enough, was not unpleasant, with more than a little of the Cumbrian intonation I had come to like. But as the speaker continued, I was taken less with the sound than with the content of his speech.

'The day I cannat ride about my land, and look about the farm – *that* is the day I dread. They can keep Westminster, and all their blue ribands, all that electioneering rubbish. I'm getting too old to care – why, not even Burke would argue with me any more if I met him in the corridor of the House tomorrow, things are come to such a pass! A Radical's a radical no longer, and even if they get Reform – as they will in a year or two – 'twill be a milk-and-water thing compared to what Fox and I and t'others fought for!'

Quite motionless, I stood there. The trembling, restless pleasure caused by my cousin's presence was entirely gone. And then I heard – with that kind of chilled detachment that one feels only at moments when another's words seem to dictate the course one's life must take – I heard my grandfather continue:

'As to that other matter – I shall never change my mind! You'll do as you like, as you always did, and I cannat stop you.

But I'll have no part in it, remember that . . . I'll let myself out, thank you kindly. Good-day to you, Lizzie!'

He closed the front door behind him emphatically – at which I remembered my aunt's injunction and returned to the parlour. As Sir Henry mounted I glimpsed grey hair (still curling and unruly, like that of my cousin) and, when he bent to gather up his reins, a fine almost patrician profile. Then, rejecting Charles' assistance, he pulled himself stiffly into the saddle, where he sat straight-backed, broad of shoulder like a farmer or fell-man rather than the gentleman I knew him to be . . .

Aunt Nicolson stood beside me – aware at once that she had no need to tell me who her caller had been.

'Yes,' she said, as I looked at her, 'that was my brother, Henry Curwen . . .' She sighed, wearily as it seemed to me. 'He came in answer to my letter, in which I told him of our plan: it would not have done to go with Isabella and not tell him of it.'

Together, we watched my grandfather, Charles beside him, ride to the eastern corner of the square. Then: 'Did he consent?' I asked quietly – as if given unexpected courage through having seen, at last, the man whom I had thought to hate: against whom, indeed, I did not at that moment feel such consuming fury as I once had known, but rather a dreadful, cold indifference – almost a lack of feeling rather than a positive emotion.

'He was less angry than I had expected,' came the reply. 'He does not forbid us to go; he cannot, in truth, do so. But he will not accept you, and refuses to see you, even once.'

'But I have no wish to see him, aunt,' I cried. 'Indeed, I believe I should rather die than do so!'

During the silence which followed, I resolved, suddenly, to ask my guardian that which I needed now, above all else, to know.

'Aunt, do you wish me – truly – to remain at Portland Square?'

At this Aunt Nicolson regarded me steadily, almost as Isabella had done. And she must have seen in my eyes another, unspoken, question; for in answering the first, she answered this as well:

'Yes, child, I do wish it. I had doubts, it is true, until but a few days ago: but whatever 'twas that happened then, I believe you meant well, and we need not speak of it again. Yes,' she repeated, 'your home shall be here with me: if you choose, it shall be so, Georgiana!'

And so, on that day week, I went with her to Keswick.

Yet tho, like so many did, I fear'd his anger, there were other, happier times – when we sail'd in my father's boats on Windermere, when people came from Yorkshire or even London to see his Regattas on the lake. Or the agricultural shows he held in Workington, when the people feasted & the day became a holiday for all, when he would carry my youngest sister, Harriet, upon his shoulders thro' the throng, my mother at his side, laughing & beautiful & proud, as we children were, to be with him.

But tho I was born to it all, there seem'd, as I grew older, no part that I should ever play, save to decorate the drawing-room & wait for suitors – whom I often sought to frighten if they came to ride with me, for I could lose them fast enough on the hillsides if I chose! Only Alexander seem'd to understand, when we talk'd together, how I would have chosen, if I could, to work, not to inherit; and that a woman, like a man, might long to change the world. And tho I was glad to go with my father to see my brother Richard's hounds & horses meet at Cockermouth – I vow'd that I should never marry such a man, to settle on a dull estate & make its boundaries the limits of my knowledge . . .

It was clear to me, from such letters, that my mother had dearly loved her father – as I might perhaps have loved my own had I ever come to know him. Little by little, piecing together the fragments which I had read, with the descriptions my aunt from time to time had given me, and matching them now to the man whom I had seen and heard that morning, I came to understand that Henry Curwen was, despite his faults, a person of distinction (of greatness, some might have said) within his sphere. Yet it had not been he, but his son, my uncle Richard Curwen, who had sent my mother's locket to me: Richard, who had known from childhood of her rebellious thoughts. Was it from him, perhaps, that my cousins had learned the kindness they had shown toward me?

'A man of principle, and of impulse': thus had my aunt described Sir Henry. She had told me how, in the Commons, he had denounced corruption, threatening (with a passion no less convincing for its frequency) to retire to his farm if justice were not done to those who laboured on the land. He had even once appeared (so the story went) in the garb of a Cumbrian peasant, bearing a meagre piece of bread-and-cheese to show his well-fed fellows in Parliament how the poor must fare, tilling the earth while their landlords make empty promises. And though not born a Curwen, he had become, by his own endeavours, one of the greatest to bear that name – which his daughter Georgiana had betrayed, even when his rivalry with Lowther was at its most intense. Yet my aunt could not explain why his anger had been prolonged, to be visited after so many years upon myself – unless he blamed my mother still for his wife's decline and death; or unless his mind had been (as I had begun to think) strongly persuaded by some other, unknown person . . .

I was certain only that Henry Curwen's principle remained unyielding; that his impulse had led him to a point from which he could not, without dishonouring the name he had adopted, contemplate return; and that the compassion for which he was renowned had, through some blinding of his vision, not focused upon so near an object as his daughter. Yet she had loved him until her death. From such delicate threads, it seems, is the fabric of affection woven, that it takes but one wrongly placed for the whole to go awry; for a life to become misshapen and (like a child deformed) to be rejected by those who seek perfection elsewhere, when they might, if they looked more closely, find beauty – however flawed – in what they already know and love.

And whom, I wondered then, might Charles resemble more? The set of his head and shoulders, as he rode away, had been like our grandfather's, stubborn and uncompromising. Yet he possessed, as I had seen already, the wilful, laughing charm of my mother; and he was, I felt instinctively, as capable as she of bitterness and passion. Did he find, as she had done, that inheritance of birth and land an intolerable burden; or was he, like Sir Henry, above all a son of Cumberland?

Charles came again to Portland Square on the day following, this time alone, and bringing the awaited letter from Isabella. The plans for our expedition were duly conferred upon with Aunt Nicolson, who proved, after her brother's visit, to be more than ever determined to act independently of him. My cousin brought, too, the news that my portfolio of drawings was approved, and that the lessons might, if my guardian consented, commence at some time in September. I had, during the turbulence of the preceding weeks, almost forgotten that such a proposal had been made. But now my joy was quite as great at this as at our going to Keswick!

'Why, Jameson was greatly taken with your work,' declared Charles, 'and Isabella tells me he's not a man easily pleased. But, little cousin,' he added, solemnly, 'you shall have to apply yourself even more diligently now. You must take your book away with you, and sketch all that you can – I shall sit for you beside the lake, and you may draw me in a suitably pensive, poetical pose! Do you promise?'

'Indeed, I do not!' Then, fearing my quick refusal might seem too discourteous, I relented: 'But I should like to try a drawing of your horse – for he looked so splendid – '

Too late, I realised my mistake.

'Ah, then I was right – you did see me yesterday.' Charles laughed softly. 'So now, Miss Georgiana, you are revenged upon me for watching you in the garden! I feel inclined – almost – to refuse your request ... But come, he is in the yard, which I must say is quite transformed, and fit at last to leave a horse in – mine is something of an aristocrat, and likes good quarters. Come now, you shall make his acquaintance!'

Peter was already in the yard, talking to the horse and feeding it wisps of hay with a fearlessness that astonished me, for it was so much greater a creature than the pit-ponies to which he was accustomed. As we came through the doorway from the garden, my cousin called to the boy to have a care;

then, as he turned, and came towards us, I saw Charles frown suddenly, his mouth tightening as if in anger.

'Come here, boy!' His voice was harsh. 'Have I not seen you before, in the town perhaps or – yes, on the shore, some weeks ago it was. There was fighting – you were with a tall black-bearded fellow, I am sure of it!'

Peter tried vainly to wriggle from my cousin's grasp – then he looked at me imploringly: 'Oh, miss, tell him it wasn't so – you are wrong, sir, I swear it!'

'Indeed, Georgiana, I am certain it was he: it was the day I came with Earnshaw – you remember, that afternoon – '

His eyes met mine. And I remembered only too well – but I was not thinking now of roses and laughter, but of Peter's father, whom at all costs I must not betray.

'You are mistaken, Charles. It cannot have been Peter, for he – he was with me in the garden, and then came with me to Mrs Sharpe. Indeed I returned from there just after you arrived, and so I am sure you must have seen some other boy.

'And now – you must look to your bonfire, Peter – I see it is smouldering yet, and my aunt will wish to know it is quite safely put out.'

Charles released the boy then, and allowed him to run off into the garden, saying as he did so: 'You must have a care with these people, cousin. It does not do to be tender-hearted with them – they will lie and cheat you all the same.'

'But surely,' I cried (in spite of my wish to be cautious), 'there may be exceptions: poor folk who are good, and honest, too – just as some of better birth may lie and cheat!'

I was indeed angry at his unjust remark. But as I gazed at him, my cousin looked away and (I remember well) shrugged his shoulders as if in denial of what I had said.

''Tis not impossible – but come, here is the Emperor waiting for you to be seated upon his back.' With which Charles suddenly lifted me up, so swiftly that I could make no protest. 'You see, he accepts you as worthy of him – and he is called the Emperor because I saw his likeness in Paris, in a famous picture of Napoleon, who seemed to me at the time far less imperial than his horse!'

He looked up at me, his expression curiously triumphant.

I had no choice but to smile back at him, forgetting our difference in the pleasure of the moment, and in my certainty that he had now quite forgotten about the boy. Indeed I could not help but feel delight at being seated, for the first time, on horseback; my cousin assured me that, when he came to find me a mount, it would be – though perhaps less splendid – as carefully selected as his own.

And then, as he helped me down, there came an instant of such sweet proximity that afterwards I wondered at myself for allowing it. Yet I did not choose it so: for it was Charles who, taking my hands, bent his head toward me, and with the lightest of touches, kissed me upon the lips. It was not the passionate conjunction of a lover's kiss – and yet it seemed to me, remembering it, to be the key to all I had longed to find in Cumberland.

'Shall you like it, little cousin – now that you are one of us?' He regarded me gravely; and when I made no reply: 'Or will you, after all, go south again – as at first I feared you might?'

My hands, I realised, were still in his. Then, as he let them go, and stood back, not smiling, but with a look of such urgent questioning in his eyes, I knew my answer:

'I shall stay. Aunt Nicolson wishes it – and now, I cannot want it otherwise!'

For there could be no longer any question of my going back, neither to where I had come from, nor to what I had been. When, after Charles had gone, I restored my mother's portrait to its place in my own room, it was because her image could no longer frighten me away. What she had rejected I had now – as far as lay within my power – embraced, so that I would go (my future at Workington assured) with more certain step to Keswick with my aunt and cousins. Though my thoughts were often with Peter's family still, and though I was drawn, in mind, to Ravenglass, I knew now who I was, and where my heart belonged. It was as if the past, which had so alarmed me, had at last receded: for in seeing my mother's features, I saw my cousin, too.

Yet – though his likeness was familiar, what, beyond this, did I know of Charles? That he could be obdurate as Sir Henry, passionate as my mother, I felt certain – but there was more, much more, of which I was not sure. His harshness with Peter had made me momentarily uneasy; and though I happily accepted his delightful domination of myself, I sensed even then that behind it lay a quality I could not analyse – someone whom I did not know, and would perhaps discover.

Chapter 10

The road inland to Cockermouth winds steeply uphill, past the gates of Workington Hall. In the brightness of that August morning I caught glimpses, as our carriage passed, of my grandfather's house, white against the green grass, which glistened still with dew beneath the shadowy darker green of the surrounding trees. The square gatehouse looked deserted, the driveway empty at this early hour, while the Hall itself had yet the air of a fortress, undisturbed by changes beyond, or dramas within, its massive walls. But the iron gates at the entrance were wide open, guarded only by the high pillars to each side – which were surmounted, I saw, by unicorn heads of stone, like the unicorns engraved upon the locket which should have been my mother's.

I was wearing the locket now. Although it was the only jewellery in my possession, I had hesitated before putting it on. But my muslin gown, though new, had looked so plain to me – and I longed, on looking in the mirror, for something more impressive to wear on the occasion of my first excursion from Portland Square. Finally, I had consulted Aunt Nicolson. She had, with her usual decisiveness, given me an unequivocal verdict.

'It is yours, child. There can be no question of your right to wear it. Richard would never have sent it to you otherwise. He is the last person in the world to offend against propriety – too correct for comfort sometimes, that he is!'

Her air of disapproving conviction had led me to suspect (rightly, I was later to discover) that my uncle Richard must, despite his evident good nature, have crossed swords with her more than once. But my aunt's next remark quite disconcerted me.

'Why, Georgiana,' she pronounced with satisfaction, 'you appear remarkably well this morning! Indeed – except that your complexion is so brown, your looks are very much improved of late. You put me in mind of Frances Curwen as a girl, when she came from Ireland first. My brother, of course, was quite bewitched by her – and so it was till the day she died. Poor Henry, I have often thought ... but there, he got what he wanted and welcomes no sympathy from anyone, least of all myself!'

My guardian had thus dismissed the subject, to become absorbed in a multiplicity of instructions to be left, on our departure, with Emily and Susan. Now I glanced at her as she sat beside me, bolt upright in defiance of the inviting comfort of the carriage cushions. She was peering out, tight-lipped, at some half-built cottages at the roadside, a mile or so beyond the Hall gates.

'At it again, I see! That brother o' mine won't rest till he's pulled down every cottage in or out of Workington – swears they ain't fit to live in; but 'tis useless, to my mind, building new for folk to turn them into hovels again within a fortnight. You'll not change the habits o' the peasantry overnight – leastways, not by giving them more than they know what to do with. That's *my* opinion, whatever Henry argues to the contrary!'

The image of the fisherman's home came at once into my mind – the filthy steps where his children had played, the rotting roofs and walls I had seen in such tenements and courts in the lower town. There was cause indeed for any landlord to search his conscience! And I was, as so often, amazed at the curious contradictions of kindness and intolerance of which Aunt Nicolson was capable. She had been generous enough to Peter – yet had condemned all Irish as villains; she clearly opposed her brother's radical principles, and would not, I felt, have found herself out of place in some far more despotic society than that of her own time. Yet she had accepted me, where Sir Henry had not – a puzzle I had so far failed to unravel.

As we left Workington behind, following the course of the River Derwent towards the hills, I remembered the young woman I had seen among the band of labourers, desperate for Reform, on the road north from London. My own fortunes had changed so greatly since then, as hers could not have done – if, indeed, she had even survived the bitterness of that winter, when, it was said, men had frozen to death in the fields. Now, for the first time, I felt something of gratitude toward my grandfather, that he at least, while so many remained indifferent, still used what power he had in the cause of those less fortunate.

But would my cousin Charles, I wondered, be as kindly disposed as Sir Henry to those who laboured on his land, when he should come (as was soon expected) to the management of the Curwen farms? He had been harsh enough, after all, to Peter, who had surely done nothing to merit such treatment; yet, Charles' anger on that occasion had perhaps, in part at least, stemmed from his concern for my safety. And then, remembering yet again (for I had relived the moment – more often than was wise) the look he gave me when I assured him that I should stay, I tried to anticipate how I must behave toward him – for we were to meet my cousins, within the hour, at Cockermouth.

The Globe Inn, where Charles and Isabella were to join us, seemed – even at ten of the morning – to be at the centre of the universe! The wide yard was already crowded with all manner of vehicles, from farm carts and old-fashioned curricles to the lighter 'cars' of which my aunt had spoken so slightingly to Josh Pratt. He now brought our carriage to a halt with a flourish of his whip; but Aunt Nicolson declared herself unwilling to descend into such a press of people and Josh was dispatched to look out for my cousins. My companion then contented herself with passing audible comment upon the family whose vehicle had drawn up beyond our own. The gentleman of the party appeared quite at a loss to reconcile the varying claims of his several female companions, who were remarkably encumbered by a miscellany of articles, including numerous hat-boxes and a sad-looking canary in a wicker cage. I, for my part, found the spectacle of such comings and goings altogether interesting; but Aunt Nicolson became visibly impatient at our delay.

'Look, there at last is Isabella – she, at least, seems calm enough, in spite of this dreadful crowd!'

My cousin indeed appeared unperturbed, merely remarking as she joined us, 'I declare I had quite forgot 'tis Monday morning and market-day besides – why, there is Mr Gibson, a tenant of Father's, to be sure.' She leaned out and saluted a large fellow of distinctly agricultural appearance, who returned her 'good morning', blushing furiously as he removed his broad-brimmed hat.

'Ah, here comes my brother. He is quite out of temper, I fear,' Isabella lowered her voice as he approached, 'but he will recover as soon as we are out of town, I dare say.'

From Isabella herself I had anticipated some reserve, but saw straightaway that her goodwill remained undiminished. Not so Charles! He bowed stiffly, glancing round impatiently and murmuring to himself that "twas no better than a bear-pit, and where the devil had that fellow got to!' At that moment Josh appeared, looking very red and cheerful, and quickly leapt up in front, my cousin calling that he would soon follow, as we clattered from the yard.

I had never before seen Charles so ill-humoured. Even my aunt, as Isabella and I settled back into our places, declared with concern: 'Why, Charles has barely a civil word for any of us – surely the prospect of escorting us cannot have displeased him so! Whatever ails your brother, Isabella?'

'Indeed, aunt, it is something quite other than ourselves, I do assure you. It is that Papa has at last issued an ultimatum – under persuasion, I am sure, from Sir Henry himself – and poor Charles is sadly put out. But they are quite right – it is time that he made up his mind to some sensible course; and since I am so soon to be married they are naturally of the opinion that a good match would be the making of my brother!'

'And who, pray, is the young lady lucky enough to be chosen to be my nephew's salvation?'

I guessed that my aunt did not altogether approve such pressure being put upon her favourite, in spite of her own declaration that he ought soon to settle down.

'There are several eligible ones,' continued Isabella, 'but it is Miss Morgan-Price from Kendal whom my parents prefer; and she has a fortune, which is most necessary, Charles being the youngest of my brothers. Unless of course Grandfather should do something more for him – which he has always said he will not do until Charles has shown himself seriously capable of managing the farms.'

'Well, there is something in that,' my aunt conceded. 'But I have told Richard often enough that there's more than one way of getting a horse to water, and forcing a young man to marry never did any good! Charles is as stubborn as all the Curwens – though your father was never as forceful as *his* father, that's for sure. Ah well, 'twill all come right in the end, I don't doubt; and most like Charles will get his way as usual – whatever that may prove to be!'

With which seemingly irreconcilable statements she settled herself back among the cushions at last and, considerably to my relief, confined herself thereafter to remarks about the scenery.

To our left, as the road grew narrower and more winding, rose a range – almost a wall – of hills: among them one which I came to know as Skiddaw, a majestic mountain crouched like a sleeping creature in the sunlight, above the expanse of a lake whose edges were fringed with trees. A summer haze lay about the hilltops, which seemed to shimmer, almost receding as I gazed, quite entranced by their strange shapes and varying colours – from burnished gold and amber on the bracken-covered higher ground, to delicate shades of green where the grassy slopes merged with leafy oaks and birches above the deep rich blue of the water. Closer to the roadside, clumps of thorn and willow grew; and between them I could glimpse flashes of light where a river flowed fast among dark boulders. Then, at a sudden turn, before us lay the vale of Lorton, a wide upland plain sheltered by hills and edged with luxuriant woods; here white farmhouses and cottages lay among the fields, and a church tower rose tall between graceful trees.

Charles, mounted upon the same horse that I had seen at Workington, had ridden ahead, and now waited for us at a narrow bridge where he motioned us to stop. A mill and a row of cottages stood near by; beyond these, a larger building, the Swan Inn, where, in a shaded low-walled garden, we were to take our luncheon. Our general approval of the arrangements, and the tranquillity of our surroundings, seemed before long to have restored my cousin's spirits; and he showed himself, indeed, quite disinclined to move from his rocky seat beside the river when my aunt, restive as usual, proposed that we should walk to see the church, which was evidently newly restored.

'I think, aunt,' he declared, 'that you should go with Isabella, whilst I remain to watch the horses, since Josh needs to take some refreshment before we continue. And Georgiana, perhaps, may like to sketch the mill or the bridge from the garden here: it is very charming, after all, and we shall not return this way when we go home from Keswick.'

I could not but feel some apprehension at being thus left alone with my cousin; yet it was impossible, without arousing the curiosity of our companions, to voice objection to his plan. Besides, I reflected, Charles would not, surely, approach me other than with formality now that his future marriage seemed (whatever his reluctance) to be a certainty. My reservations were further dispelled by the calm courtesy with which he fetched my things from the carriage, obtained a suitably low stool from the inn and placed it according to my instructions, before retiring to the farther side of the garden where the Emperor, in company with the carriage horses, was grazing beneath the trees.

For some time I worked, uninterrupted and quite at ease; so that when at length Charles returned to his rock and sat pensively beside the river, I could not resist including his figure in the composition I had already made. The addition was almost completed when he suddenly rose and came across to me, pausing, and for a few moments saying nothing. Then:

'How strange! I see, cousin, that you have done exactly as I prescribed the other day – for there am I, at the centre of your picture and seated, if not beside a lake, at least beside a tinkling stream: even more desirably picturesque, would you not agree?'

[141]

The innocence of his tone immediately convinced me that he had contrived not only my undertaking the drawing, but his own inclusion in it. But I was firmly resolved not to enter into such skirmishing of wits; and therefore looked the harder at my work, replying, 'Indeed, you have my thanks, for I have little taste for reproducing a landscape empty of inhabitants. But I shall look to Mr Jameson, rather than to yourself, to instruct me how better to achieve figures of correct proportions, so that they appear more natural – rather than posed, as I fear this one to be.'

I took up my pencil again, determined to complete the drawing to my satisfaction, rather than be deflected by my cousin.

'But at least your landscape will be peopled as you wish – not hedged about, as mine is, by restrictions, or crowded with those whom others choose to thrust into my life!'

Charles appeared not to notice my startled look, but continued speaking with a low-voiced bitterness that commanded my entire attention.

'Be thankful, cousin, that you have no need to order your life according to parental expectations; that Aunt Nicolson, whatever her shortcomings, will never try to change you – will not ever wish you to be other than yourself!'

Listening to him then, I seemed to hear an echo of my mother's words, more meaningful than when I had beheld them upon the written page. And as, without thinking why I did so, I reached out a hand to touch the fabric of his sleeve, Charles turned abruptly, ceasing to stare before him at the rippling surface of the water, and looking now directly into my own countenance.

'Why, even Isabella – my own sister! – appears neither to care nor understand what they would have me do; that I might have plans – or hopes, at least – of my own. But you – you are from a different world: though one of us now, you seemed from the first to be not the same as we Curwens. How is it, Georgiana, that you seem to belong to a place where such things as money, pride, possessions, are not, or matter not?'

How could I tell him that I did not, at that moment, wish myself in any other place than this! that any other would seem barren, and myself bereft, were he not there; and even the peaceful meadows of my childhood, or that safe-seeming harbour, Ravenglass, would, without him, be but empty landscapes in my mind.

'And why – why should it be – that I speak so to you, whom I have known but a few short weeks, words which I cannot speak to those whom I have known throughout my life, thoughts which I have scarce been able to confess even to myself?'

He gazed at me still, but more gently, his anger spent as quickly as it had flared; so that I felt compelled to make some kind of answer – yet it was not the answer which my feelings would have had me give.

'I think, cousin, that perhaps you should not say them – but I cannot, for your sake, wish them unsaid! Indeed, I would do anything – '

I did not continue, for I had a sudden sense that, having told so much, Charles would be too proud to welcome words of pity or even kindness. And so it proved: his manner changed at once, as he looked away, saying, 'There is nothing, nothing that you can do – unless . . . Unless it be to forgive me for a tedious, peevish fellow . . ,' He glanced down to where my hand remained on his arm. 'Why, cousin, how very brown your fingers are – '

'Too brown, indeed, to please my guardian!' I answered, hastily removing them again.

'Indeed, she is wrong: too brown perhaps for a young lady who spends her hours sewing trifles in the drawing-room, or tinkling the piano keys to the detriment of any sensitive ear. But no, I prefer hands which are not idle but of use – like yours, in the garden perhaps, or at their present occupation.'

'I cannot think that picking roses or sketching water-mills are *useful* occupations.' I laughed in response, glad that his dark mood seemed to have dissipated. 'And yet I should like to think that I might, some day, have sufficient skill to make drawing or painting the means of supporting myself, rather than mere pastimes.'

The confession made, I immediately regretted it – as one usually regrets the expression of those hopes which, once voiced, only clamour the more insistently to be fulfilled. I knew moreover that such a notion must be considered, in most quarters, not only impracticable for any young woman, but improper – even immoral. Yet my cousin did not, as I half feared, mock, or even disparage, my ambition.

'Have you told Aunt Nicolson of this?' he queried. 'Does she know that you wish to become independent in such a way?'

'Indeed, no!' The very thought of her opinion alarmed me. 'She knows only that to draw has been since childhood my chief, almost my only, pleasure. That is why, I believe, she has secured Mr Jameson to teach me. But I cannot think she would approve my having such a purpose. Nor do I wish her to think me ungrateful, as she might, were she to learn that I should like – above all things – not to depend upon her goodwill alone.'

It was true, in addition, that I had become of late increasingly aware of my guardian's need (unspoken though it was) of my companionship. But I could not tell my cousin so; nor that I had, already, tried to its limit her tolerance of my wilfulness – so that conscience, as much as reticence, must prevent my causing her yet more concern.

'I cannot, therefore, tell her – ' I faltered, troubled that Charles might think me dishonest.

'Nor shall I do so!' he declared, ' – just as you will, I know, keep your counsel as to my own confidences.' He paused bending down to retrieve one of my pencils from where it had fallen, disregarded, among the grasses at my feet. As he handed it to me, his eyes took on that laughing, almost challenging expression which I had, from the first, found myself unable to resist. Then he took my hand (brown as it was!), raised it to his lips, and relinquished it again with an air of great solemnity, as if a compact had been sealed.

'It seems, Miss Georgiana, that we are fated to keep each other's secrets, does it not? And yet . . . how little we know of one another . . .'

And how much, I thought, I at least had already concealed! Would Charles have spoken to me so freely, accepted me with such goodwill, had he known how I helped Peter's father to escape?

'Come – shall we walk together to meet Aunt Nicolson and my sister? The picture is almost done – you will add colour to it later, I believe. You see – I am acquainted as to the procedure!'

Although my cousin was at ease once more, I found it impossible to be so. Silently I gathered up my book and pencils, wondering why I longed now to be alone in some far place (like the green hollow where the fisherman had lain), surrounded by the sea and sky, hearing only the high call of a bird, or the breeze among the rushes. Yet, but a few moments ago, I had wanted only to be here with Charles, to whom I had listened with such eagerness – with a feeling which I could not quite, as yet, acknowledge to myself.

Perhaps, already, I had some inward fear of love's fragility – of an emotion delicately poised, like the balance of a clock, between despair and joy. A single word or look (so little!) sets it on its course; another, misheard or misinterpreted, arrests it, throwing into disarray that harmony which seemed, at first, so near perfection. A whole world, mutually made, ceases at last to turn. As for love – it is but a word printed on misty glass by a childish hand: no sooner written than a breath makes it vanish again, as though it had never been.

We had walked no more than a hundred yards toward the bridge when my cousin stopped, looking across to where the river widened at the mill. Not far from the great slow-turning wheel an old man sat in the sun on the low wall beside the water, where patches of white foam drifted and spun and scattered their way downstream. Two women were spreading linen to dry on the warm stone, while at a little distance children played in the shadows of the river-crossing, their shouts and laughter echoing in the clear air. It was, altogether, a scene of rural peace such as the painter Morland might have chosen to depict; and I could not help thinking as we stood there how crowded and oppressive Cockermouth (and Workington, indeed!) seemed in retrospect to be.

'What do these people know or care, I wonder, about such notions as Reform?' Charles turned to me. 'Can they wish for more than they already have? Hard work, perhaps, but shirts to their backs and no threat of war to take them from their homes; clean air to breathe and a decent landlord? Why should they agitate for more?'

'They look content enough, it is true . . .' I answered slowly, reflecting that they were, at least, more fortunate than some I knew. 'But tell me, who owns the land – someone of your acquaintance?'

'Wragg is his name – Augustus Wragg; he is a curious fellow, reputedly rich and certainly reclusive by nature. I have met him but once . . . Come, I will show you the house, it is easily seen from the bridge there.'

I remember it clearly still – just as I have pictured it so many times since that afternoon. Lorton Grange: a long grey-stone building whose tall chimneys and steep-pitched roof rose almost black against the silvery green of willow and birch growing close to the walls. It appeared to have no gardens, only an expanse of smooth turf, with a few sheep grazing, between house and river; and behind, numerous tumbling barns, orchards, and a sloping meadow which stretched up to the churchyard and its surrounding trees. Even as we looked, two figures, one dark-skirted, the other with a white parasol, were stepping along the church path in our direction.

The sight of my aunt and Isabella caused me to glance at my companion. Charles was gazing at the house, with a wistful intensity which made me conscious, suddenly, that this must be the place – the green valley – of which he had spoken once before.

'It is much neglected – yet beautiful!' I murmured. For this, of all the houses I have known, seemed to belong most naturally – to grow, almost – within its setting. It was perhaps the hazy summer light, the nearby movement of trees and water, which muted the colours of its lichened stone, and softened without concealing the strength of its buttressed walls.

'You would not change it – if – ?'

'If it were mine? How I wish that it were!' Charles smiled, but not without a certain bitterness. 'I should put it to rights, yes – but to what it was, the ancient manor farm of Lorton, rather than make it into some impossible Palladian mansion, such as seems to be the fashion.'

Then he told me how, as a boy, he had once been taken by a cousin (then rector of the parish) to call upon the owner,

Mr Wragg, who had become withdrawn from society following the deaths of his wife and young son.

'He showed me his botanical collection, I remember – some rare specimens he had collected in the woods and from the fells above High Lorton. He seemed to take a liking to me, and would recall it perhaps if I were to approach him – it is rumoured he wishes to sell . . . Aunt Nicolson knows something of him, for he is related to the Lowthers and knew Humphrey Nicolson long ago.'

'I had thought,' I ventured, 'that you would prefer to be nearer to Workington, and Sir Henry . . .'

For a few moments my cousin was silent, staring at the water, where it flowed in patterns of light and darkness among the rocks, and beneath the ceaseless weaving flight of swallows from their nests below the bridge.

'That would please him,' he said at last. 'But I have reason – good reason – to wish otherwise. To live at Workington Hall, to follow in his footsteps as the father of the town – for that is what they call him! – is impossible for me to accomplish. I had rather leave things be than go about, as Grandfather does, with the troubles of the world upon my shoulders.

'There have been changes enough. I should like nothing more than to live here in peace, with fishing and riding enough for my leisure; to travel when I become bored at home –' he laughed, turning his back to the view of Lorton Grange ' – and to have someone like my sister, or like yourself, little cousin, to return to and share it with! Come now, is that not a delightful prospect?'

Charles offered me his arm, and I took it gladly for the dusty roadway was slippery with loose stones. But as we descended the slope from the bridge, I reflected that I, being penniless, could hardly prove as delightful or suitable a prospect as his parents' choice – Miss Morgan-Price of Kendal!

Chapter 11

The Vale of Keswick, seen from the height of an adjacent hillside, has been described as a kind of earthly paradise: 'the peaceful retreat of some favour'd mortals undisturb'd by the Cares and Concerns of the World'. We came there from the high pass of Whinlater, as the deepening shadows of late afternoon lay across the valley, like the shading on a bright silk gown; dark hedgerow patterns trailed upon the spreading skirts of the hills, their hems marked by a silver thread which widened into a curving train – the shining waters of a lake, stretching almost out of sight into the folds of yet more mountains. The faintly smoking chimneys of the town, safe on its slope beneath the benign gaze of Skiddaw, only added to the misty quality of the air, which seemed – as in no other place that I have seen – to be filled with a gentle golden light. And though I have known the vale to look quite otherwise – hemmed in by a mass of storm-bearing clouds, or swept by winds which whipped leaves and branches across the face of Derwentwater – it is thus that I remember it: a place of sunlit calm, remote from the world of strife and effort which we had, for the present, left behind.

Yet, as our carriage laboured up the steep main street, the inhabitants of Keswick looked sober enough mortals. Broad-shouldered, black-clad country folk for the most part – until we came to where a group of smart gentlemen and ladies clustered, like so many coloured summer butterflies, about the pillars of the market-hall. This curious high-towered building (the erection of which Aunt Nicolson remembered as the cause of much amazement to the less progressive-minded townspeople) stood like an island in the middle of the roadway, which became so congested that Josh had much difficulty in getting the horses through. As we passed, I was surprised to note that, in spite of the fine weather, most of the ladies carried large umbrellas, while the men bore assorted burdens of fishing-rods, luncheon-baskets, and heavy walking-sticks.

'Tourists!' exclaimed my aunt, in a tone of scorn such as she usually reserved for the recalcitrant Irish.

'But aunt, we are only visitors ourselves — not natives of the place, after all!'

The look which Aunt Nicolson directed toward Isabella would have sufficed to quell the opinions of an entire army, let alone my mild-mannered cousin, whose eyes, however, met mine with a look of rueful resignation.

But within minutes we halted at a neat-looking square-built house, pleasantly set among ash trees and shrubs, and separated from the road by a low stone wall upon which several children were seated expectantly. I recognised George Nicolson and his sister Edith at once: the former looking a good head taller, despite the hazards of his southern education, and the little girl far rosier than when I had seen her last, pale-faced and muffled against the winter cold. Now they were almost into the carriage before we were out of it; while their young companions, having witnessed the arrival, scattered down the hillside by a path at the side of the wall.

'Great heavens, what a wild kind of welcome is this!' my aunt chided, smiling nonetheless, as Isabella laughed and allowed herself to be escorted with all ceremony through the gate to where Mary Nicolson waited, a small child in her arms and another clinging shyly to her gown.

I hesitated for a few moments, unwilling to intrude upon the mutual greetings and exclamations, and held back too, perhaps, by a keen remembrance of Mary's forthright manner at our last meeting. Then suddenly Charles was with us once more, directing Josh as to the disposition of horses and baggage, declaring his approval of the house and the views from its garden – over the deep valley of the Greta on the one hand, and through the trees toward Bassenthwaite Water on the other.

But it was neither the charm of the winding river nor the distant serenity of the lake which caused me to stand there, forgetful, momentarily, even of my cousin close behind me. I felt, for the first time, the powerful immensity of mountains. From afar they had seemed aloof, untouchable, almost illusory: shining guardians of a land one might never reach. Here – within the kingdom – their strength was palpable, in the turf and rock beneath one's feet, in the contours of their bodies stretching above and beyond the town of Keswick, whose slanting roofs lay on the limb of the hillside like coloured patches on a giant's coat. As for the details of our domesticity –a white flutter of skirts about the door, children calling and running across the grass, the flash and ring of harness as the carriage pulled away from the gate – all seemed as frail and small, in their mountain context, as the humming dusty gnats which danced about our heads in the evening sun.

Now I was aware of Hugh Nicolson's hearty handshake and words of welcome; of Mary's quick appraising glance from myself to Charles, engaged in conversation with her husband; and of little Edith's hand in mine as we went through the low-beamed doorway into a wide, cool, dark-shadowed room. A room which I saw, as my eyes became accustomed to the dimness, to be – in its quiet simplicity – unlike any other drawing-room I knew. Wild flowers and grasses, and bowls of fragrant herbs stood on the high mantel-shelf and wide slate window-sills. The furniture, well-made rather than elegant, was for the most part plain, except for several pretty, comfortable-looking chairs, brightened – as were sofas and window-seats – with many-coloured cushions. One table was piled high with books, another with stones and fragments of rock, all strange shapes and colours; yet more lay among the plans and papers scattered upon a substantial desk standing across one corner of the room. Save for some heavy window-curtains (needful as well as the wooden shutters on winter nights) the walls were devoid of the usual fussy drapes or hangings, being adorned instead – to my immediate delight – with numerous pictures. These were not the formal portraits or heavy oil-painted seascapes with which I had become familiar at Portland Square, but smaller, delicately executed watercolours of lakes, rivers and falls, mountains and lonely cottages; there were some miniatures of children, too – the young Nicolsons, evidently – and a few half-finished sketches pinned beside them, so that I wondered who might be the artist of the family. And I thought, as I looked about me, that such a room might appear to some to be in the worst kind of disorder – from the music-sheets which littered the pianoforte, to the spinning-wheel with its bobbins and half-spun fleece heaped beside it. But for me, it conveyed an atmosphere of gentle industry; a harmony as natural, in its way, as that of the landscape which lay beyond the windows.

We were an easy, cheerful family party that evening. Any constraint I might have felt was soon dispelled, when I found that Mary was now far more kindly disposed than I had feared; she seemed, indeed, to approve of my continuing at Working-ton, for I heard her remark to Isabella that 'Aunt Nicolson is so greatly improved in temper, it is to be hoped your cousin will remain with her the longer!'

To my relief, Charles left us early, promising to return on the morning that we were to go from Keswick, and having, in the meantime, 'urgent business' to attend to. That this was in connection with his future plans I did not doubt; but I had no wish to betray my consciousness of his purpose. For Mary Nicolson, I felt sure already, had little liking for my cousin despite her friendship with his sister; and her sharp perception might, had he stayed, have detected my own increasing intimacy with him.

Late that night, looking out across the darkened vale from the room I was to share with Isabella, I thought of Charles, riding beneath the stars along the lakeside path to Cocker-mouth. How he had longed to make Lorton Grange his home – and how I longed to have the means (as another woman might) to enable it to be so; to give to its neglected rooms the tranquil, living warmth which I could feel around me in this house. But I could be no more to him than a ready listener, to whom he might, without fear of prejudice, confide his bitterness, his secret hopes. Whilst I must now conceal from him – as from others – the truth I could hide no longer from myself: that I, who had not sought to love, yet loved my cousin Charles.

Next day my aunt felt bound to renew her acquaintance with the shopkeepers of Keswick – who I felt certain could scarcely have forgotten her, even after a lapse of ten years or more. Her descent upon the premises of several unwary tradesmen proved indeed no less energetic than her Workington excursions, so that by mid-morning Isabella and I were far more fatigued than Aunt Nicolson herself. To our somewhat wry amusement her purchases included three umbrellas, for none of us had thought to bring one away, and the clouds were gathering even as we walked down the hill. At first she asserted that at thirteen shillings apiece they were excessively dear, their price amounting to open robbery of unsuspecting visitors. But the shopkeeper, remarkably, stood his ground; and she finally conceded that 'we may as well take them, expensive as they are – for when it rains in this mountainous country 'tis as if the heavens were taking the vengeance of the Lord!'

Later, at the bookshop near the market-place, I was persuaded to buy pencils of the superior Keswick graphite; and (less willingly) a copy of Otley's *Description of the Lakes* – published in the town and, my guardian allowed, a bargain at four-and-sixpence! 'I do believe,' she added, 'that it is a wiser purchase than Mr William Wordsworth's guidebook – which is very poetical, I'm sure, but less *useful* than Mr Otley's.'

I glanced anxiously at Isabella, wishing not to offend her by my choice; but she seemed not to mind the critical reference to her future father-in-law. And I was glad indeed to have chosen as I did, when I received from her at Christmas-time a gift of the poet's work, with an inscription in his hand.

We proceeded, cheerfully enough, to the post office; but our visit to Mr Green's Exhibition proved a disappointment, despite the claims of a highly persuasive poster. So I was relieved, on reaching our meeting-place with the Nicolsons, to find that George and I were designated to walk to the lakeside, to arrange boats for our afternoon excursion to the islands. While we undertook the errand, Edith was to try the dress she was to wear as bridesmaid at Isabella's wedding; my aunt was delighted to watch proceedings at the dressmaker's – but I was more than happy to escape them.

George proved as informative a companion on this occasion as during our journey from London. Before long I was able (with the additional aid of Mr Otley) to identify some of the mountains on the farther side of Derwentwater; and, when we reached the landing-place, the large white house which stood four-square upon the nearest of the islands. I thought it ugly-looking, and a sad intrusion in so lovely a place – an opinion which George at once confirmed.

'My father says it is quite monstrous that Mr Pocklington should have built it; but he bought the island, and the woods opposite, too, and would listen to no one's advice as to what to do with them. And because of him, Keswick Lake – this part of it at least – is now spoiled. But at Windermere, Sir Henry's house is quite different, they say. I have never been there; but my parents have seen it and think it very fine; and it is called Belle Isle, which means beautiful, of course.'

What was it my mother had written? – *"Tis a magick isle, the house like some pretty, elvish palace rising from the green trees and blue water of the lake . . .'* Her father had made a garden walk about the island, and the children had a little boat, in which my mother often stole away to drift among the lilies and the sedge, where timid moorhens nested and the heron scarcely moved at her approach. She had been happier there, she wrote, than at any time save the hours spent with her lover, Alexander – even as I had been happy, lying beneath the willows by the Thames . . . where I had seen, among the scented summer grass, two other lovers lost, in their heedless sleep, to the world about them.

Was it there, I wonder, that my seduction first began? For this, that I fell in love with Charles? I know only that as I stood beside the lake, remembering that peace which I had (though a child) discovered, I was able to imagine – without shame or apprehension – such a moment shared with him.

[153]

I believed, even so, that it could not be. And turned, with an inward sigh, to where George stood, eagerly scanning the water for some sign of the boatman. Two empty boats were moored at the landing, and soon we spied another moving slowly away from Pocklington's Island; its return was evidently expected, for several other persons were by now waiting at the water's edge. One of the gentlemen stared curiously at us, and bowed slightly; but I was anxious not to be detained in conversation, wishing to ascertain from where I might sketch the lake, if time allowed, later that afternoon. Leaving my companion, therefore, to negotiate with the boatman, and promising to return shortly, I took the path along the lakeside.

Glad to be at last alone, after the bustle of the morning, I was content to breathe the sweet air, to hear the small birds busy among the branches; and, turning aside from the path, to gaze out across the water from a little pebbled bay, fringed with rushes and overhung with silver birch. Here, seated upon a low grassy bank, I watched the changing sky, and the gentle, swelling breathing of the lake.

The golden light of yesterday was gone. Instead, the edges of the hills were sharply clear, the distance across the water so reduced that I could see, above the tree-tops on the farther bank, the deep-gashed clefts and fissures which marked, as random wounds, the grey metallic armour of the mountain-sides. They seemed to gather round the lake – inexorable close-ranked knights, their jagged knives piercing the grey-white breasts of clouds, reflected swan-like in the water far below. Then suddenly their images were fragmented, blurred by a movement of the wind, which twisted the cloud about the pinnacles and ruffled the surface of the lake, bringing its waves to the waiting pebbles at my feet.

I sat for a few more moments, conscious of the darkening sky; of the cool breeze shaking long trails of birch which lay like hair upon the water; and – more insistent than the rustle of the leaves – the sound of a nearby stream running from among the trees beyond the little bay. Reluctant to go without finding it, I pushed my way between tall ferns and moss-encrusted rocks, coming at last to where it flowed into the lake. Here the stream ran clear and shallow across the stones, whose many colours gleamed and changed as I took a handful from the water, wondering at their smoothness and their curious shapes. But as I laid them aside to dry, intending to take them with me, something else caught my attention – for I was not, as I had thought, alone.

Someone lay outstretched upon the grass, a little way upstream and not far from the water's edge. He appeared absorbed in thought – his head resting on his arm, and a book lying open on the ground beside him. Perhaps I had seen the movement of his hand as he turned a page – or perhaps the whiteness of his sleeve against the green turf: I do not remember now. But as I hesitated, wondering if I should go further or retreat, he turned his head and, on seeing me, laughed aloud.

'Why – Miss Curwen. So you have yet a taste for solitude?'

'Indeed, sir, I have no wish to – to trespass on your own seclusion. And I shall not remain to do so!'

My astonishment at finding Philip Earnshaw in this place was equalled only by my eagerness to go at once. And though I knew myself to be discourteous, his own discourtesy to me at our last meeting had been the greater, I was certain!

As I bent to gather up my little heap of stones, he was there beside me, moving with a swiftness which, as he observed, quite startled me.

'Forgive me – I have alarmed you. But don't go – I should much prefer you to stay.' He looked at me gravely; but I turned away.

'No! George expects me, at the landing – and besides, I do not . . .' I faltered, feeling his gaze upon me, and puzzled by his insistence.

'Miss Curwen – wait!'

This time his tone was so imperative that I glanced back at him. And saw in his eyes – not the harshness I had remembered with such pain, but that serious, compelling, penetrating look which had drawn me to him when we stood together by a winter-frozen moorland stream, so many months before.

'Wait!' he repeated. 'I trust you will allow me to go with you to find my nephew. But first – I know that I offended you when last we met; indeed, I see you are displeased with me still . . . But I did not intend it so – and I had good reason, I believe, to be concerned on your behalf . . .'

Philip seemed reluctant to continue.

'And I would wish to be of assistance to you, should you need – '

'I thank you, sir,' I responded coldly. 'But your concern did not show itself as kindness. As for assistance, I should never request it, save from those whom I now regard – as I could not formerly – as my family, and my friends.' I felt not a little proud that my acceptance by my guardian and cousins gave me the right, at this moment, to speak so.

'Yes. And I am sure that Charles Curwen would prove more than willing in such a circumstance!'

Philip spoke with such deliberate scorn that at once I countered, not troubling to conceal my anger.

'My cousin is – or so I thought – your friend, Mr Earnshaw. And you do him, as well as myself, an injustice by making such an imputation!'

Then to my amazement he seized my arm – even as I turned to go, determined to return to George alone.

'In truth, it is out of friendship both for him and for yourself that I speak as I do. For I know Charles well – too well perhaps; and I respect and admire his sister, who will prove, I am certain, a true friend to you. But he has a reputation for being – thoughtless, toward young ladies; and should you come to care for him, as is too possible, I fear, such a situation might be hurtful – even dangerous – to you. I can say no more without betraying the confidence of another, and that I may not do. I ask only that you believe me, Miss Curwen!'

I had no choice but to believe one who spoke with such conviction: yet had he been any other man than Philip Earnshaw, I should not, I think, have heeded him. But my bewilderment was great: for though he had said no more of Charles than I already knew, I could not understand the urgency with which he warned me of danger; nor could I bear that he should discern (so easily!) those feelings I had but lately acknowledged to myself. So I remained silent; but my distress must have been apparent to him, for he continued, in a gentler tone:

'For your own sake – and for his – I beg you to trust me; and to allow me to help you if needful. And yet I hope, Miss Georgiana, that such need may not arise . . . Call me a realist – or a cynic, just as you choose.'

He smiled; but though I sensed that he wished now to reassure me, I could not respond, save to murmur, 'I shall – remember what you have said . . .' Then I looked up at him, saying more firmly: 'Yet I do assure you, sir, that I do not feel myself endangered by any person – least of all Charles, whose kindness to me has been, like his sister's, that of a cousin only.'

'So be it!' For an instant, Philip's gaze was as gentle, almost compassionate, as his words had been; then eyes and voice assumed once more that strangely cool detachment with which he seemed to observe, on all occasions, those whom he encountered.

'Let us take the path, Miss Curwen; it is easier than the way by which you found me. And George will be delighted, I hope, that you have done so – unless, as usually happens, he is too interested in the conversation of his favourite, the boatman, to notice that I have come at all!'

'Then you are not expected by your sister?'

'No, indeed! For all that Mary knows, I am still across the border in Westmorland, where I have been for a day or two with Mr Wordsworth, about the design of a cottage which he hopes to build at Rydal. But finding that Mr John Wordsworth was to come today to see Miss Isabella, I came some way with him – then struck across the hills and along the lakeside. He has gone first to pay his respects to Mr Southey – an old friend, and of course, our neighbour at Keswick. And I have had a splendid walk at so early an hour – very wild, and very beautiful!'

He had the air of a man to whom such exercise was a familiar pleasure; and as he described to me the lonely route by which he had come, I could not help but envy him that masculine freedom to wander where he chose. My mother, too, had chafed at her confinement – and had lost, in trying to escape, her lover and her liberty for ever. Should I, perhaps, have gone with Michael Stephens after all? Have gone with him to the unseen harbour, Ravenglass; to some cottage or rocky cavern in the mountainside, among those to whom the genteel drawing-room, the gracious garden walks, belonged to a distant, prosperous, alien world? To go, I knew, meant also poverty and homelessness; whilst with my aunt in Portland Square I had the certainty of her affection – and the new, uncertain pain of loving Charles.

I hated Philip Earnshaw then – as one so often hates those who confront one with a cruel truth. He strode beside me, silent again, and remote as the mountains fading into mist above the lake: while I recalled an image which, since leaving Maidenhead. I had resolutely striven to suppress. For his words had quite dispelled that other, momentary, youthful dream of happiness with Charles: of a love enclosed and islanded beyond the world, oblivious to claims of duty, law or piety; of a man and woman bound – not by social fetters but by passion's silken threads.

Instead I saw again Horatia's anguished look, as she fled from her father to the safety of my room: a look which told me of her suffering at his hands, more clearly than her weeping or her faltering speech might do. And I remembered Mrs Parsons' warning words, Maria's fear of her master Horace Chatterton; my own recoiling from the chilly smoothness of his fingers, and my dread on that winter evening when I left for Cumberland. This was the reality from which I sought, in my safer dreams, to hide; which – thanks to Philip Earnshaw – I relived once more.

Chapter 12

'There now – you have made it exactly right, this time! For you must always hold the carders *so*, else the wool does not come away from them correctly and then it will not spin so well, you see.'

Edith Nicolson looked up at me earnestly, then selected another piece of wool from the grey fleece which lay in a heap at our feet. We were seated together beside a window, beyond which the rain, drifting rather than falling against the glass, had quite obscured the bulk of Skiddaw and even the tower of Crosthwaite church below the town. Though it was, I had been assured, 'just a mist' rather than the regular Lakeland downpour, it was sufficient to necessitate a change of plan, the postponement until tomorrow of our boating excursion, and an afternoon at the spinning-wheel for Edith and myself.

As a pupil I had proved, it must be admitted, less than apt. Several times I was admonished by my small instructress for allowing the wheel to stop or the yarn (so impossibly thin and frail) to break entirely; whilst the art of combing the wool into its delicate attenuated rolls, ready for spinning, had eluded me until, quite unexpectedly, the rhythmic movement of the carders became as natural and familiar as if, like Edith, I had known it since early childhood. But mastery of the wheel would take, I guessed, a longer time: yet I was determined to try, for I remembered seeing, in a dusty cupboard at Portland Square, an ancient-looking wheel which might, if my aunt allowed, help to pass my days when winter came.

Now, the gentle occupation and the children's chatter came as welcome distractions from the thoughts which had shadowed my return from the lake with Philip. He had gone, almost at once after greeting his sister, to seek out his friend at Mr Southey's – for Greta Hall, the poet's home, lay but a short distance away on the hillside above the river. The youngest Southey child was of an age with Edith, having been, indeed, among the group who had watched our arrival the previous day.

'But we do not expect him this afternoon,' added my companion, somewhat wistfully, 'for in wet weather Mrs Southey becomes anxious, lest he should take a chill – and maybe, so Mamma says, die as his sister did. I have seen her picture, and she was *very* pretty – but so too is Miss Edith Southey, after whom I am named. And perhaps she may come to see us, instead – may she not, George?'

'I think she will not . . .' he answered, without looking up from the table where, for the past half-hour, he had been polishing some of my stones. For they might, he claimed, prove of use to his father, whose study of minerals and rocks was a part of the work he undertook for Sir Henry.

'Now this one, Miss Curwen, is interesting, I am certain – '

And George held out for my inspection a small smooth pebble – blue-grey like a pigeon's feather and faintly veined with red, which glowed, as he rubbed it with his finger, to an almost living brightness. When I found it again in a box of oddments which (on a last nostalgic impulse) I took with me to Ireland, I thought to have it cut and set one day in silver, as a brooch or other ornament. But I am glad now that I did not: for it is all I have to remind me of those Keswick days, since when so much has changed . . .

I left the window-seat to look more closely at another stone which George declared of interest; and when I returned to his sister saw that a group of people was approaching the house by the field pathway from Greta Hall. Hugh Nicolson was among them, with Philip and another gentleman whom I guessed, from her description, to be Mr John Wordsworth, so eagerly awaited by my cousin Isabella.

The two remaining members of the party were identified at once by Edith who, throwing down her carders, ran to the door, exclaiming as she did so: 'See, George – it *is* Miss Southey after all! And Mr Hartley, too, has come – oh, how glad I am it rained this afternoon!'

As she vanished into the hall I wondered – hearing the confusion of greetings and animated conversation – if I should escape by another door on pretext of fetching Aunt Nicolson, who was resting after the efforts of the morning. But Edith quickly reappeared, tugging by the hand a laughing, slender, dark-haired gentleman – who bowed and blushed on seeing me, then looked about him helplessly, and bowed again. He made as if to retreat, then almost danced across the room towards me; whereupon George frowned reprovingly at his sister and (with a grace that did credit to his Eton education) made the proper introductions.

This was the only time that I encountered Mr Hartley Coleridge: yet his personality was such that I was affected strongly by our meeting – which I should have remembered always even if there had not proved to be an unexpected link between our lives. His frank kindness toward the children (to whom I myself was becoming increasingly attached) immediately endeared him to me. And on hearing of his death but a little while ago, I felt a sense of loss more keen than is usual for a man whom one has scarcely known.

At first he seemed to be all contradictions: small in height, yet with a presence more compelling than that of many a taller person; shy, but exhibiting a liveliness which combined strangely with his poetical appearance – flowing locks, already touched with silver, and ruffled shirt beneath a multiplicity of waistcoats and a bright blue long-tailed jacket. But it was his eyes which chiefly drew my attention, being strikingly large and dark, and expressive of an indefinable melancholy – even when, as now, he stared at me with a gaze at once rapt and alert.

For he was much surprised at the mention of my name,

which he repeated, looking at me so hard that I should have thought it, in another man, discourteous.

'Miss Georgiana Curwen? . . . But no, that cannot be . . .'

'Indeed, sir, there *are* two Miss Curwens – myself and my cousin, Miss Isabella, whom you know already, I believe.'

I had observed that she had followed him into the room, and was now standing beside John Wordsworth and Miss Edith Southey. Then I could not help but smile at my listener's evident bewilderment, which, added to his simplicity of manner, quite disarmed me.

'I must beg your pardon – yet it was not your cousin I spoke of, but another – ' Mr Hartley stammered a little, but seeing that I was all attention, continued, 'I mean that I have met, long ago – why, twenty years it must have been, for I was the age of young Nicolson or thereabouts – another Miss Georgiana Curwen, here at Keswick. It was at the Regatta, which every year was held on Derwentwater: I should not have remembered her, perhaps, had she not spoken to me, very charmingly, for quite some time – while her father was in conversation with my own father and my Uncle Southey. They talked of trees, for the most part – some scheme for replanting beside the lake, and a dispute of some kind between the young lady's father and Mr Wordsworth, the poet, of Rydal . . . I forget it now – but Miss Curwen I did not forget, for I saw her again, though for a few moments only . . . And she was, I am sure, of your own height, though less dark, perhaps – '

He broke off, his earlier confusion returning as I tried (with no great success) to conceal the emotion which his words had roused.

Not since my birthday morning, when I read the letter penned by my mother's hand, had I felt such apprehension – or such grief. But then I had turned my back upon the past, had fled from the presence conjured by her words; and I had not mourned for her, but for myself. Now, so suddenly and keenly did I feel the loss, the certainty of death, that I wept – as I should have done that day.

'Forgive me! I wish that I had said nothing of it, yet I could not – '

My companion's distress was so apparent that I was ashamed of my own weakness, and spoke as calmly as I could: 'Mr Coleridge – I am, I think, grateful that you have told me. For the lady whom you saw was – can only have been – my mother, whose name was indeed the same as mine!'

He did not answer; but I sensed that this stranger's understanding was such that I need not fear to tell him more, and continued, 'Having but lately come to my guardian at Workington, I have had so little chance to meet with those who knew my mother as a girl, that I hope you will describe her to me. She died, some three years since; and it came as a surprise – a shock, rather – that you should speak of her. But I do not regret your doing so, I can assure you, sir.'

'You shall hear all that I am able, after so long a time, to bring to mind, Miss Curwen,' he replied.

Then with a sadness of voice and look that I could not comprehend – for it seemed that he must have suffered sorrow greater than any I had known – he took my hand, saying, 'One always hopes that those who are young and fair will by some grace escape the worst that life can hold: yet I fear that she – like another whom I knew, more intimately, long ago – was not favoured by whatever Destiny it is that must decide such things. And though I do not know her history, I can share your grief a little – for I have met with few young ladies who were so kind as your mother was to me!'

We were prevented from talking further by Isabella's approach with John Wordsworth and Miss Southey. But after tea, when others of the party were occupied at the pianoforte, Mr Hartley sat beside me in the window-seat, and told me of his second meeting with my mother.

It was late in the same summer that he saw her again – the summer of 1810, he recalled, 'For that was the last year – save for one brief visit – that my own dear father came to us at Greta Hall, before he became ill ... and ...' His voice became unsteady, as if the memory caused him pain; I should have understood it better now, knowing as I do much more of the poet's sad addiction and the madness which estranged him from his family and friends.

'And I had been at school for some time here at Keswick under Mr Dawes – with Robert Jameson, the painter, and with Lloyd, another friend who lived across by Windermere. It was to his home at Brathay that we were walking one afternoon, and stopped beside Loughrigg Tarn – where we were throwing stones, and wading, as boys always like to do.

'When the two ponies came by, I thought little of it – until I saw that she, Miss Curwen, was riding one of them. Jameson spoke with the other rider – a young man whom he knew from Edinburgh, I think he said – but they did not stay long. And she said nothing, tho' she smiled, and knew me again, I am sure; I would have thought her a boy, with her hair so short – for she wore a cape and sat astride, too – had I not met her that other time at the Regatta.'

In those few moments, while my companion turned away to stare at the hills, now partly visible beyond the drifting clouds, I knew that my mother had been real: not a distant voice, speaking from beyond some unimaginable void, nor some fiction woven by an ageing servant's fancy, but the living girl whose picture had entranced me as a child. That her image had remained so clearly with this man (now near to middle life) might have seemed strange, had I not known from her portrait how she must have looked at him – so sensitive a youth – with eager laughing eyes that afternoon.

'But tell me,' I asked, as Mr Hartley gave me his attention once again, ' – the person who was with her, did you learn his name?'

I felt I knew the answer, though my companion did not. For even as he shook his head and murmured, 'No, I think that Jameson did not say' – I was certain that only one who shared my mother's thoughts, and her love of lonely places, would have gone with her so far from her summer home, Belle Isle. Yet his was a face and form of which I could envisage nothing, though I believed him to have been my father – Alexander Grieve.

What kind of man was he, who had loved and then abandoned her? Not cold nor heartless, surely, else he would not have planned to go with her to Ireland. Yet he had perhaps regretted such a risky venture; or his gentle nature (of which she wrote with such sad conviction) had maybe proved unequal to the storm of anger which awaited their return. Unless some further cause had added fuel to Sir Henry's wrath, which brought about their parting and her marriage to another . . .

If so, I guessed that Hartley Coleridge knew nothing of it. But his friend, he said, had recognised the other rider – and perhaps –

'The Mr Jameson whom you mentioned – can he be the same, I wonder, who has lately taught Miss Isabella? For my aunt has engaged him to give me drawing lessons, but we are not yet acquainted.'

I tried to speak calmly and to wait with patience, while he thought for a minute or two, looking puzzled, then at length replied: 'Why yes, I believe that he did do so; yet I think it must have been some time ago, when I myself was away from Keswick. Now Sara, my sister – she would have remembered, for she and Miss Dora Wordsworth *did* have lessons with him. But she is gone to London, to Hampstead, having married just a year past – else I should have introduced you to her, for she knows a good deal about painting, far more than I.'

He smiled, tugging abstractedly at his long beard; while I wondered whether I should find the courage, when we met, to question Mr Jameson about my father. But even if I did so, might I not regret the asking: or might it not prove wiser, for my peace of mind, to leave the past untouched, to rest content with what (by chance and not intention) I already knew?

For the present, I could only wait. Mr Hartley, to my surprise, offered to write in my book the address of his sister Sara, in case, he said, I should wish to call on her if ever I returned to London. Then he talked with such admiration of my future teacher that I firmly resolved to work harder at my drawing; for it was clear that I should learn from an artist who had earned respect, and did not merely follow fashion, like so many of his profession.

'He is very gifted, as you will find, Miss Curwen. And I wish that I had had such a way with pupils when I taught in school' – my companion sighed – 'but 'tis too late now, I fear.

[165]

Jameson is older than I, of course, though he remains unmarried, like myself . . .'

Then he glanced wistfully to where John Wordsworth stood, with such evident contentment, beside my cousin as she played and sang a tune for little Edith. It seemed hard to me, even then (when I knew so little of him), that such a man as Hartley Coleridge should, by some caprice of fortune, be deprived of the domestic happiness he craved. Yet as we joined the others at the piano, I could see that they cared for him greatly; and it is thus that I remember him – laughing, rather than melancholy, and surrounded by his friends.

That evening we dined late, the guests from Greta Hall declining to stay, and departing before darkness might make their path too treacherous. Mr Hartley pressed my hand kindly as he left us: had I foreseen that we would never meet again, I should have felt sadness, rather than a gratitude not unmixed with relief that I need face no further painful retrospection. After the revelations of the day, I was fatigued – as one must be when, without warning, one is confronted by the past.

And so I welcomed all the more the gentle ebb and flow of conversation during dinner; the soothing glow of lamps and candlelight, the sense of well-being – unfamiliar to me until then – which seems to emanate, unbidden, from the voices, gestures, glances of those who are gathered in so intimate a fashion. Mary, her smaller children sleeping and her vigilance relaxed, presided with a gracefulness which any fashionable hostess might have envied; and even Aunt Nicolson – usually so discordant a presence, whatever the company – appeared almost benign, her angles softened, her pronouncements less emphatic in response to the lively descriptions proceeding from young George, seated beside her in evident consciousness of his privileged status. From her frequent smiles, her laughter (rarely heard at home), it was clear that she found his assertions an enjoyable challenge.

How long it seemed since she and I had left the quiet routine of Portland Square! Emily, no doubt (her duties reduced by our absence), was dozing even now in her high-backed chair beside the kitchen fire; Minou – privileged creature – curled on another, or maybe stalking moths among damp grasses in the garden. And Peter? Down at the shore, most likely, helping Jem to prepare the boat against the next day's work; or, bare feet slipping on the wet black stones, searching intently among the wrack for wood, or ends of rope, or other useful spoil to be carried up the steps to Rosa's cottage. The pattern of his life, I knew, was far removed from mine, even in Workington: yet there I had crossed the unseen line between the upper and the lower town. There I felt drawn toward the barren shore; and even in the sheltered garden I could hear the sea – was conscious always of a harder world which lay beyond the square.

Here at Keswick a less arduous harmony prevailed: the curtains drawn, the heavy shutters barred, we were enclosed, for a time, within the safety of our charmed retreat. But even as my own content increased, and I shared, without reserve, in the general good humour, I became aware that Philip, seated next to me, was not at ease. He had seemed disposed to silence – for which I was thankful, having no wish to resume our dialogue of the morning. There was an air of distraction about him as he performed the expected courtesies; his fingers – long and finely-shaped, and almost as brown, I noticed, as my own – gripped with unnecessary force the delicate stem of his glass; and so preoccupied did he become, that his sister was obliged to appeal to him a second time concerning the all-important question of boats for the following day.

Thereafter he was more collected; yet still from time to time his gaze was drawn toward my cousin Isabella. She had shown no more than her usual frankness (appropriate to her brother's long-established friend) in their earlier exchanges: now absorbed, with gentle animation, in all that her future husband had to say, she was oblivious to Philip's scrutiny, to the sudden tightening of his lips as he looked away. Perhaps his admiration – openly declared to me that morning – had meant more than friendship for my cousin: if so, having lost his heart to her, and witnessing her present happiness, how bitterly he must regret that loss! ('I pity him,' I reflected, 'yet – I do not think him capable of suffering so *very* much . . .')

'Did I not observe, Miss Curwen, when we met today, that you follow the fashion among young ladies – by taking with you a sketchbook on every excursion, faithfully to record each vista from the stations recommended in the guide? Such admirable enterprise deserves – '

'Deserves to fail, I do assure you, Mr Earnshaw!'

In my surprise at Philip's breaking silence in so arbitrary a way, I did not ask myself the reason for the careful modulation of his tone, the calculated coolness of his look as he addressed me. And I felt no pity for him now – but indignation that my purpose should be misinterpreted as altogether idle.

'Indeed, contrary to your assumption,' I proceeded, with the calmness born of youthful certainty, 'I have always taken up my pencil in order to please myself rather than to entertain others. I do not intend – as your female tourist might – to adorn my journal with "impressions", to be raptured over on returning to an admiring circle of relations. No: my intention is quite other!'

'But it is the duty of a lady to entertain others, is it not? Their approval, surely, is her reward for undertaking the rigours of an education. And if it is masculine admiration that you wish – then I must see your work before I am qualified to compliment you on it!'

Did he suspect me then, of seeking the admiration of my cousin Charles? I could not let him think so – nor would I choose to have Philip see my work!

'I am certain, sir, that my sketchbook would not be worthy any gentleman's attention – however frivolous or otherwise my purpose in carrying it to the lakeside. But did not *I* observe – ' (I was determined to turn the tables if I could) – 'that you carried with you this morning the very book you recommended for my own enlightenment? I am sure that your intention in reading the poems of Lord Byron cannot have been other than to please yourself – unless you foresaw our meeting, and the opportunity to improve my education.'

'Either purpose – my own pleasure or your instruction – would be to my taste: perhaps the two might be combined, Miss Curwen!'

It was clear that Philip had outwitted me. And I was ill-equipped to counter his sophistication, not yet worldly-wise enough to play the coquette's part – by giving arch reply in hope of gaining proof that even such a man as he might be successfully provoked. His words, whose meaning then I did not fully comprehend, were double-edged – far different from the easy pleasantries of Charles. Yet my silence seemed to confirm his low opinion of me; for, having waited for an answer and receiving none, he continued:

'As for your drawing, I think I understand: you hope to achieve a masterpiece, do you not? To distil onto your canvas the very *essence* of our mountains, waterfalls, and lakes? Why, I believe that the south of England is filled with aspiring Turners or would-be Constables, each vying to display his own vision of the Sublime to gratify the gaping London critics at the galleries! They visit here for a month – even as little as a week! – and at the prettiest times of year, then finish off the work in some city studio.

'And yet, in the north are painters who know each rock and stone; whose truth to Nature lies in observation, not in sentiment – men like old Harden at Brathay, who cares at least as much for people as for prospects. There is some of his work here – in Hugh's study; my father knew him well, before my parents removed to Yorkshire . . . I will ask Mary to show you, if you wish . . .'

His scorn, while it lasted, was emphatic enough; but strangely, some other notion had disturbed him, for he frowned and tapped with his fingers upon the linen cloth. Hastily, I thanked him; then added, with a sudden access of courage, 'I regret that I must, so it seems, displease you. For I am either to be dismissed as a female tourist, or accused of too ambitious a purpose. Is there no way I may be allowed a private, serious aim?'

I did not care, as when we met at Workington, that Philip might think me foolish or ill-informed. For I had gained since then (as he could not be aware) acquaintance with a world as harsh as any he might know, with lives led in ugly tenements, where rotting walls and fetid corners sheltered children

[169]

desperate for food and warmth. Already I rejected in my mind the pastel shades and dainty execution of an accomplished lady's work: but I did not – could not, in truth – envisage what might be within my powers, as yet so limited and ill-defined.

'To have any such serious aim can only be praiseworthy, to whatever end. And yet – ' Philip paused, as if considering his words – 'have you not thought that when you marry, as must be expected, you will find that other occupations will have stronger claim; that your obligations – husband, children, home – may be at odds with any private purpose you may entertain?'

'But I think I shall not marry, Mr Earnshaw.'

My swift reply appeared to disconcert him. Then he laughed: 'You cannot mean, I am sure, that you have no wish to do so. That would be to deprive some gentleman who might otherwise be thought most fortunate – like my friend John Wordsworth, blessed indeed.'

He spoke lightly, yet with sufficient irony for me to think my conjecture right in respect of Isabella. But I continued, this time more firmly: 'A wife is only a blessing, sir, if she has a fortune to contribute. I have heard that only lawyers have the means to marry for love, while a clergyman must do so for money – though I do not think such to be the case with my cousin, whom I believe to be truly happy in her choice. As for myself, I shall allow necessity to concur with my own preference for a single life – with my cat and my sketchbook for company!'

'Neither of which would prove, I think, greatly supportive in adversity,' he murmured drily – yet with a smile which, momentarily, reminded me of Charles.

And at the thought of Charles, my resolution, formulated with such clear conviction, could not help but waver. His words, idly spoken as they must have been at Lorton yesterday, might almost have persuaded me that he felt – not love, but something more, perhaps, than the careless trifling of which Philip had, with such urgency, been swift to tell me. Yet even had my poverty not barred me from the possibility of marriage to my cousin, I should have hesitated still.

For neither the memory of Lorton Grange, nor my love for Charles could blind me to the sombre warning in my mother's words, set down so plainly that I had, without question, accepted them as truth. '*Do not marry,*' she had written, '*save in love & trust, for 'tis a bond that tightens ev'ry day til life itself is gone.*' And though I longed to make a home about me or to nurse a child, to care for someone like my cousin Charles (who I thought as near perfection as a man might be) – yet I could not, even so, believe, as is expected of a woman, that to spend a lifetime thus might bring me perfect bliss. Though glad that Isabella had found so gentle a future husband, I should not have wished for myself a marriage which appeared to me, even then, almost oppressive in its certitude. For how might I, so bound, be able to create that other, more elusive world, through my painting – which I hoped, more than ever now, might in some way become my livelihood?

As I looked about me at the pictures, shadowy in lamplight upon the walls, I considered what I might, with patient application, be enabled to achieve. For these were the work of another Earnshaw sister, Charlotte, now in Yorkshire with her ageing parents; Mary had been oddly reluctant to tell me more of her, but I had observed that she drew with skill and boldness far removed from the genteel style of most young women. Were I to achieve such competence, I thought, I should not be content to rest at home. I should wish to travel as Aunt Nicolson had done, to see and paint those far-off places where the traders sailed from Workington: strange, exotic names – Saint Helena, Dominica, Barbados, or Saint Kitts – which were, at Portland Square, more talked about than London or Carlisle!

Philip was regarding me intently. Then, as I returned his gaze more steadily than before, he leaned back in his chair, declaring – with a hint of anger in his voice: 'I do believe, Miss Georgiana, that you are determined – that you may, indeed, even succeed!'

Whether he alluded to my remaining unmarried, or to my painting, I chose not to enquire. For we seemed at every turn to stray too close to that dangerous ground on which debate nears open conflict. Whereas with Charles I acquiesced, content for the most part to be drawn toward some unknown joy, my will, with Philip, stood in opposition to his own – even when, as now, some inner voice might warn me against the wisdom of so

[171]

doing. Though I had accepted his advice that morning, I did not intend to let him influence me further: and I wished, above all, to hide from him the nature of my feeling for my cousin.

'It is strange,' I remarked, 'that a gentleman may continue in his single state – for whatever reason – without attracting to himself the pity or the censure of the world. Yet if a woman – even one as young as five-and-twenty! – does so, she is held to be deficient in some way, even when she has the advantage of a fortune.'

My companion continuing silent, I pursued my theme: 'Is not a woman better suited to survive alone – if only in her domestic capability – than a man, who always requires attendants, such as maids or housekeepers, to supply his daily needs? Might not Miss Southey – to take an example – be better able to live independently than Mr Hartley? It would appear to me to be so, yet the world would deem their situations quite the opposite!'

'Miss Edith Southey,' Philip pronounced, 'is that remarkable and rare creature – a woman whose intellect is equal to a man's; and her strength of mind does not prevent her from fulfilling a domestic role when needful. But she is in truth exceptional.'

Whilst I could not disagree with his judgement of a family friend, I was amazed at his cool assumption of her qualities as altogether masculine in nature – as though such gifts might not be suitable for female minds! But then he continued more gravely: 'And Mr Hartley, it is true, is far less fitted to adapt to life's demands, though his powers of imagination – like his father's – are greater than those of other men. I saw that you did not, as strangers often do, dismiss him as of little consequence – and you were right to estimate him as you did!'

His warmth surprised me, for I had not thought to gain his good opinion in anything; and I answered truthfully, 'I could not have behaved otherwise toward him, sir. I – do not wish to explain my reason, but I am, in no small way, indebted to Mr Hartley.'

'Then I may tell you that which only one of your ready sympathy will understand: Hartley Coleridge, I think, has lived too long within the shadow of the great, so that his genius – for such it is – has had too little scope. For greatness, however worthy, sometimes casts a darkness over those who live in its proximity: even John, and his sister Dora – who is to be a bridesmaid to Isabella – feel on occasion overshadowed by their father's eminence. Yet though Hartley can never be so great a poet as William Wordsworth, or as his own father, even – as a man he is loved by all who know him. There is scarce a cottager within ten miles of Keswick who will not welcome him to his fireside; and some are so loyal to him, indeed, that they believe that Mr Hartley gives ideas for poems to Mr Wordsworth!

'But I need not say more – for you have already, in so short a time, discovered his character.'

I could only feel glad (despite his apparent disregard for female intellect) of Philip's clear defence of one who by society's standard had not found success. And did Hartley Coleridge, I wondered, find in the solitude of hills and lakes that refuge which my mother sought, when she found the greatness of the Curwen name too much to bear?

'Do my observations sadden you so much, Miss Georgiana?'

'I find it sad,' I answered (wary of the glance with which this man seemed able to discern my thoughts), 'that those whose lives are most advantaged may not find happiness, or may end their days obscurely ... Yet' – I was thinking now of Peter, of the weariness of the returning fisherman, and the cold hearth of his cottage on that April morning, months ago – 'there can be little hope where poverty and toil make life itself intolerable.'

'There can be none at all, where the poor are kept in ignorance of their rights: where music, paintings, poetry and all that educated men enjoy, are meaningless – and even the necessities are denied to those who seek no more than honest work and a roof above their heads!

'And that is why I know, as Sir Henry does, that we can wait no longer for Reform; that the next Election must put men in office – after half a century lost in wrangling! – who will bring some justice to the labouring class.'

The passion with which Philip spoke compelled respect: I could not think him, now, a cold observer who cared nothing for his fellow men. He paused reflectively, his dark eyes gazing at the glass he held – as though within it lay some message or some vision which he did not choose to share.

'But do not credit me with overmuch philanthropy! I must, in part at least, make a living wherever gentlemen require cottages – whether for the poor or for their own rural amusement. And from Mr Wordsworth I shall gain quite as much wisdom as I am able to give. He takes a great interest in architectural matters; and his cottage at Rydal, when completed, may prove a model for others who would build and settle here.'

He resumed, for the remainder of the evening, that appraising air – the cynic's stance – with which I was familiar. Yet I had recognised the kinship of his thoughts with mine: a mutual anger at injustice, and a consciousness (felt, for my part, rather than expressed) of others' suffering. And I had glimpsed, I thought, a part of Philip's self which he, for reasons of his own, preferred to hide.

But there were other possibilities I did not comprehend, as I listened to the rain which beat incessantly about the mass of Skiddaw, beyond the curtained windows. I knew that I loved one man – but did not see that another had (in ways more subtle, less defined) already bound me to him; that my cousin Charles and Philip Earnshaw both might claim a portion of my heart. Nor could I know, surrounded as I was by such domestic peace, that there exists another kind of love, which since I came to Ireland has enriched my days – though perhaps like those other loves, it cannot last.

Chapter 13

Charles' arrival next morning surprised us all. I had spent an hour or two at the lakeside, sketching ferns and flowers beside the hidden stream, happily absorbed while Aunt Nicolson and George explored the nearby paths. Returning, we found my cousin established in the garden, giving the smaller children, to their excitement, rides on his horse, the Emperor. Clearly he was in holiday mood – allowing the little ones to discover sweets and ribbons in the depths of his pockets, producing from the same source some useful items of fishing equipment for George, and finally discovering a couple of bottles which Hugh Nicolson at once pronounced an admirable choice. On learning that a boating picnic was proposed for the afternoon, Charles adopted an air of concern, sighed, and spoke most solemnly to Aunt Nicolson:

'I do declare, aunt, that you are in serious danger. If you remain much longer in Keswick, I fear you will become a veritable Laker!'

Only half an hour before I had heard her maintain that the town was sadly changed: 'Quite spoiled with idlers – tourists and the like – and most of them Southerners!' She pointed out one individual in particular (a harmless enough fellow, I thought) as having rashly admitted to being a linen-draper from Tunbridge Wells. My aunt had earlier noticed him purchasing a pair of brown worsted stockings, evidently in anticipation of attaining the summit of Skiddaw; whereupon she had advised him that his choice (of stocking, rather than excursion) was unwise. He had compounded the offence of being a southern visitor with that of refusing to change his mind – to her obvious chagrin; and I wondered now whether Charles might regret his remark.

As it was, she countered shrewdly: 'You, sir, are in more danger from idle gallivanting than I! At least I've nothing to lose by it – a farmer, gentleman or no, should only picnic when the harvest is safely in. Or have you come into a fortune all of a sudden? Made your peace with your father, and spending his money to prove it, is that the way of it now?'

The question hit home, I could see. But though he coloured a little, and frowned, my cousin rallied quickly.

'I have no quarrel with my father, aunt. At least, he understands my situation rather better than he did, I believe . . . and perhaps . . .' He altered course then, enquiring as to where his sister might be, while I wondered if my aunt knew more of Charles than he had guessed, as her severity would seem to indicate.

'Why, Isabella is gone with Mr Wordsworth to meet his father again at Rydal – she is quite a favourite there by all accounts. His parents are quite won over, John has told me, for all that they were so opposed to his marrying. Now, you would do well to follow his example, and make a match which is both prudent *and* to your liking!'

'I think I should willingly forgo the prudence,' he answered, without hesitation, 'if I might but find as good a woman as my sister.'

Aunt Nicolson gave him a sharp look, then spoke with a wry finality of tone: 'In that case, Charles, you will search long and lose a good deal in the doing so: you had better think hard before taking *that* path! . . . Now there,' she concluded, 'is a lady who could well take you in hand, nephew – were it not that you gentlemen don't care for a woman to be clever, and she is something of a blue-stocking, by all accounts.' My guardian nodded vigorously toward the wicket gate.

Miss Southey, accompanied by Philip and a frail-looking boy, had at that moment entered the garden – and I thought as she approached that any man would surely find her charming. Yesterday, her watchful gaze and self-composure had alarmed me, and we had spoken little; now I noticed more the graceful walk and gestures, the expressive smile, which Charles (however clever she might be!) must of necessity admire. Whilst I had nothing save my doubtful name, no skill except a little with my pencil . . . I endeavoured to suppress such foolishness – as if by doing so I could dismiss my cousin from my thoughts. And Miss Southey greeted me kindly, while the boy smiled shyly and made off at once with Edith Nicolson: he, in his sister's special care, was to join our afternoon excursion to Saint Herbert's Island, in the centre of the lake.

So too was Charles. He had, it appeared, secured a room at the Royal Oak in town, and would remain to escort us home with Isabella from Keswick. Now, our party being complete, he prepared to stable his horse, passing close beside me on the path to the garden gate. He paused for a moment, and addressed me directly for the first time that morning: 'Do not forget, little cousin – you are to paint his portrait: it shall be your first commissioned work!'

And with that, he led the Emperor away.

Sunlight on Derwentwater; and the curving bows reflected as they part the stillness of the lake. A scatter of spinning drops, a hesitation of the shining blade before it strikes the undulating smoothness, and the boat moves on through fragments of its imaged self. Below us, pebbles and tangled weed and sudden darting fish appear, distinct and bright – yet transitory in their dimmer, flickering world. Ahead, the slanting shafts illuminate another boat: white sail, white dresses, coloured parasols, the bobbing shapes of half a dozen hats. And all around, the ever-present mountains – fringed with woods in gentle shades of green, their crags and pinnacles deceptively subdued – have in the softer, distant light a gracious air, the clouds too high above to threaten mortal plans!

How I envied, but a year or two ago, the occupants of those remembered boats, which floated idly down the Thames or moored beneath the willows as I watched – not thinking then that I should ever find a way into the peaceful sunlit places of my dreams. Now, childhood is past: Charles, close beside me, and Philip, bending to the rhythm of the oars, are part of a life of privilege and ease in which I share – forgetful, on this summer afternoon, of other darker-shadowed days.

Voices and the ring of laughter across the water: ropes are tossed, ladies assisted at the landing-place; the children and yellow dog, released at last from sedentary confinement, rush to explore the island. Then our smaller craft, more leisurely, drifts through the shallows to the shore. Philip offers me his arm; but Charles, more swift than he to claim the privilege, has seized my hand, and laughing at my hesitation, helps me to firmer ground.

In that instant, I have no choice, no will. Touch and look compel the quick response which love must always give: so sudden and complete the interchange of feeling that resolve is useless, conscience undermined – until the dictates of convention intervene. Reluctant, I turn from Charles, remember Philip's presence, glance toward him – but he has already moved away. Slowly we follow him across the brightness of the grass, to where the others wait beneath the shading silver birch.

My cousin – I could not help but notice – paid a good deal of attention to Miss Southey. At first I was thankful that he did not seek me out. Conscious that my feeling must, at all costs, be concealed, I knew I should remember Philip's warning, and endeavour to forget those moments at the shore with Charles. Yet such mutual recognition could not be denied: so much a part of me, already, was the certainty of loving him, it seemed to heighten the perfection of the wooded island, set within the shining oval of the lake. I deceived myself, perhaps – so swiftly may the senses weave the fabric of illusion, from a single thread.

Meantime Charles, throughout the afternoon, played the model gentleman and guest – devoted to Miss Southey's needs or teaching her brother how to row; readily discarding hat and jacket to assist in the impromptu cricket match; and providing a masculine arm when Aunt Nicolson requested him to escort her to the ruins of Saint Herbert's chapel. I was surprised by her assumption of female helplessness – until I saw Miss Southey at my cousin's side, and guessed that my aunt had her reasons for thus occupying Charles. As I watched them take the pretty woodland path, I resolved again to think no more of him: his character must be as faulty as I had been told, and only grief could come from hoping otherwise!

Accordingly I relieved Mary Nicolson of her duties, and remained at the lakeside, where the smaller children were hunting minnows in the pools among the stones. I showed my charges how to make little boats from pliant reeds, and for some time we sailed them along the edges of the lake; at length, however, the children deserted this pastime to play among the trees, and I found myself alone.

'Why do you avoid me, Georgiana?'

My cousin threw down his hat, scattering the heap of miniature boats abandoned at my feet.

'Why,' he repeated, 'have you spoken not a word to me today?'

I stood up quickly, provoked to anger that he should assign to me the neglect of which he had been guilty.

'Should you not go? I hear the children calling . . .' Suddenly I wished that he were anywhere other than beside me.

'I am being pursued,' he explained, laughing. 'The hounds, including I may say that beast belonging to the Earnshaws, are hot on my trail!'

'Then why do you not hide from them?' I spoke coldly.

'Because they are certain to find me in any case. Indeed they will be vastly disappointed if they do not – I may as well make it easier and get it done with. Besides,' he added deliberately, 'I think it is time I was allowed to forgo duty in pursuit of my own pleasure.'

'Is Miss Southey to be considered a duty, then?' I could not help the question, but at once regretted having asked it.

'Good – then you noticed, as I hoped you might,' he replied promptly, and with satisfaction. 'Yet I wished Aunt Nicolson to notice chiefly – that she should not reprimand me as if I were a schoolboy still! Do you think,' he looked at me wickedly, 'that Uncle Humphrey Nicolson was being prudent in marrying our aunt – or could the match have been to his liking, after all? . . .'

Another time I might have found his query diverting. Now I was indeed convinced that he amused himself at my expense – and worse, admitted to doing so! I answered him firmly: 'You are wrong, cousin, to make such speculation – and even more mistaken to think I have any interest at all in your motive with regard to Miss Southey.' With that I turned aside, determined that if I cared at all, he should not know it.

But he was too quick for me, and stood in my way, his arms folded, and a look of amazement – which seemed genuine enough – replacing the laughter of a moment before.

'Can it be, cousin, that you believe me seriously to be concerned with Miss Southey?'

'I believe you to care for nothing – *seriously*, sir!'

'Then I shall prove to you that the truth is quite otherwise, indeed. And first, with regard to Miss Southey: item, she is older than I – five-and-twenty at least – and I do not care for that. Next: item, she is a scholar, with work published; and, though I prefer an intelligent woman, Aunt Nicolson is right –I do not care for one as clever as all that.

'And third,' Charles paused, and looked at me coolly, ' – which you may disbelieve, or not, as you wish – I have already made my choice, and it is not she.'

My cousin reached out his hand, and gently touched my arm.

'Look,' he continued, 'are they not well matched?' And following his gaze, I could see Philip and Miss Southey, with Hugh and Mary at some little distance beside my aunt, walking back from the wood towards the lake.

'She is far more suited to Earnshaw than to myself. They have known one another since childhood – and he is far more scholarly than I. Though I must say,' he turned to me, his eyes bright with eager speculation, 'I was much intrigued at Cambridge that Philip sometimes disappeared for days, without giving reason, and would return looking quite as though he had spent the time in extreme dissipation – I suspect him of leading a double life, and intend to find him out one day!

'But come, Georgiana – we understand one another now, do we not?'

In truth, I did not know whether I understood him at all – but I acquiesced, even so. For I could not sustain my anger in the face of his good humour; nor did I wish to disbelieve his argument with respect to Miss Southey.

He went on persuasively: 'Now, I shall try to make my peace with those children – can you not hear them, baying for my blood, the wretched creatures? And then we will go together to inspect the ruins: you must not leave the island without doing so. I shall speak to Aunt Nicolson – do not look so alarmed! It will all be quite proper, I assure you. And besides – Earnshaw has deprived me of a lady's company, and I think I deserve some compensation, after all.'

Strange, I reflected, that Charles and Philip should so readily point out each other's failings to me. (I have learned, since then, that men are always quick to commend their own virtues to a woman – if they suspect her sympathy to be engaged with some less worthy fellow.) But it had to be conceded, whatever secrets his friend might suspect him to have: Philip's height – more languid than commanding as he bent toward her – and his dark seriousness, were better fitted to Miss Southey's grace than my cousin's volatility could be. As the latter returned, walking lightly across the sunlit turf to where I waited, Philip's cautionary words of yesterday were fading from my mind: I thought that I should never – no matter whom he chose to marry – love another as I must love Charles.

We went by a winding path, through trees and up gently rising ground, to where the hermit's chapel, centuries before, had stood. But the ruins, though picturesque enough, delighted me less than the expanse of lake which stretched before us – almost white where the sun lay full upon it. Islands, trees and hills, even clouds, appeared suspended – painted almost – against the water and the sky, the air so still that we could hear a faint yet constant echoing sound – the roar of the great waterfall at Lodore on the wooded mountain opposite. As we descended to the shore, Charles gathered grasses, harebells – blue as the butterflies which rose from among the scattered stones – and delicate ferns, which he presented to me with unexpected gravity: 'As you see, cousin, I am determined to make amends!'

Then, while we walked along the narrow beach, I asked him about Belle Isle – of which I knew no more than my mother had described.

'It cannot, surely, be more beautiful than this!' I exclaimed, certain that nothing could exceed the tranquil scene about us.

'It is less wild than here, but I prefer it so,' he answered. 'There is an ordered kind of harmony about Belle Island – different from romantic isolation such as this. But you shall see it for yourself, I believe, before so very long.'

I looked at him in surprise – for nothing had been further from my mind. But he went on to tell me of his parents' plan to live there after Isabella's wedding.

'Until then, they remain at Cockermouth, being closer to the church at Crossthwaite where she has chosen to be married – which pleases the Wordsworths and our Keswick friends. But afterward, Sir Henry wishes them to take Belle Isle, for he has not lived there himself since our grandmother died: he cared so greatly for her, and there are other reasons which he will not speak of.'

My cousin frowned, and I recalled the way in which Sir Henry seemed to dispose of all the Curwen fortunes: only my mother had, I thought, rebelled entirely against his domination.

'And what of yourself?' I asked.

'I?' He smiled suddenly. 'I intend to live at Lorton Grange.'

'But how can that be? I am glad of it, but – ' I remembered his bitter speech at Lorton, and Aunt Nicolson's remarks of this morning.

'I shall tell you. Let us sit for a moment; there is time.'

Charles spread my shawl on a flat boulder, where I sat while he leaned against it, looking before him and speaking with a quiet determination quite unlike his usual careless tone.

'It is not settled yet – it cannot be until I have ordered my other plans. But my father agrees to my wish to live away from Workington – provided that I will farm Grandfather's estate and find a wife to his liking. He is getting old and impatient, but will waive his desire to have me live at the Hall if I satisfy him in other respects; that is my hope at least. I called upon Mr Wragg at Lorton on my way to Keswick this morning; he remembered me – as I thought – and will not sell to another. And whilst he makes up his mind as to when he can sell to me – I shall see Sir Henry and seek his approval.

'What do you think, little cousin?'

For a moment I was silent: glad of his hopes, yet unwilling to encourage them in case – as I feared – he might find the conditions impossible to meet.

'Perhaps you might try to do as Aunt Nicolson suggests: to combine prudence with your own wishes. If not, then . . .'

'Then what – if the two cannot be reconciled? Would you counsel prudence, Georgiana?' He looked at me keenly.

'For myself,' I answered slowly, 'perhaps not – but I have little to lose by following my own wishes. For you – it must be as she said, that you would risk a great deal should you choose unwisely . . .'

Charles was gazing at me still. And as I finished speaking, a strange expression – almost of recklessness – came into his eyes.

'Come,' he said abruptly, 'you shall help me to decide.'

He reached across to where my flowers lay on the rock beside me. From among them he took four grasses.

'There!' He held them out to me. 'One for each way that I might choose. This:' – looking at the first – 'Aunt Nicolson would have me travel the world like her own husband – she worshipped that man, I do believe. If she could give me his boats, to sail as he did, she would die happy: but alas, I cannot help her, and we shall discard that choice at the outset.'

He replaced the grass among the collection at my side.

'The second: Sir Henry would have me be master of Workington Hall – a Reformer like himself, or a farmer; and I must marry money to save the estate from impending ruin – or the possibility of that, I should guess. And third: my parents would have me wed Miss Morgan-Price at once, to gain her fortune and her farms in Westmorland.'

'And the last?' I asked.

Charles smiled – but his eyes were hard as he held up the fourth of my grasses.

'That is the imprudent one, which allows me to do all that I wish – to go to Lorton with a lady of my choice, and live peacefully thereafter. Now, you shall tell me what I must do.'

My cousin's fingers were playing with the fringes of my cotton shawl, twisting them into knots until I felt bound to pull them free. Then he turned away, staring at the lake; and I felt such a longing for his happiness, that it was as much as I could do to keep my thoughts from betraying themselves.

'Tell me, Georgiana,' he repeated.

I shook my head – intending to refuse: how could I, after all, advise him in such things? Accustomed as I was to his usual lack of serious intention, I thought him capricious in making his request. Yet his voice held a note of challenge, which – as when I met him first in Portland Square – I could not easily resist . . .

I took up one of his grasses.

'Tell me – what like is Miss Morgan-Price of Kendal?'

'Why – like other women one meets: young enough, pleasing enough, and sufficiently rich. Perfect, in short – save that Sir Henry's principles may not tolerate the match: her father made his fortune selling slaves. And they say he even married one of them, after a fashion. But when she followed after his ship, in hopes that he might take her back with him – he ordered his men to shoot, and left her to the sharks.' He shrugged his shoulders. 'But his daughter is the mildest of girls, thank heavens!'

'And could you be happy, married to her?' I persisted, knowing that whatever he replied must cause me pain.

'She would look well enough in my drawing-room, if that is what you mean.' Charles laughed carelessly. 'She will do as well as any other.'

Then he glanced down at me – a look of such bitter distaste that I could bear no more. Flinging away the grass I stood to face him.

'How can you say such things? Must others always choose for you? Maybe the last way would be better after all: be master of your own fate, Charles – even if you lose a fortune, you could gain the chance of happiness at least. There!'

I held out the fourth of his grasses.

'That is all I wish for you: to make your home at Lorton and to be content, in whatever way you wish.' (Even, I added silently, with the lady of your choice, whoever she might be!) 'And now, let us go back; we have been away too long already, I am certain.'

'No, Georgiana – wait!' I had gathered up my shawl, anxious to go at once.

'Wait! What of the happiness you say I am to seek? It is unkind to give me only half of what I want: of what use is Lorton Grange if I am to live in it alone?'

'I do not understand you.' His tone – half mocking, half pleading – told me nothing. I became impatient.

'I do not know what more I am to say. You have already promised your parents that you will marry – if not Miss Morgan-Price, then another.'

'True, cousin. But I have yet to tell them that I wish to marry *you*!'

... Sometimes you hear a lover's words and know them to be true; sometimes they sound like truth – and yet you find them to be false. Then, I had no means of telling either way: and even now, remembering, I do not know if Charles had cleverly contrived his speech, or merely spoke on the impulse of the moment ...

At first I turned away; I could not listen, would not look at him. This must be, surely, the kind of thoughtless – cruelly thoughtless – game he liked to play, against which I had been warned. And in part at least, I had only brought it upon myself, had allowed him to take advantage of my sympathy.

Yet I could not believe it to be so. His very coolness carried more conviction than assurances of love – undying passion and the like – which, that afternoon, he left unsaid. When at length I did look up, it was to feel again the powerful certainty of touch and gaze, as when we had stepped ashore. I knew that Charles had meant those words – however they had come about.

'You must not speak of marriage to me, Charles. It is impossible: not imprudent or unwise – impossible!'

'But my parents would care enough for you if they but met you; they speak kindly of you already. And Isabella loves you as a sister might!'

[185]

'No – she cares for me out of pity, because Sir Henry will not. And, you would cut yourself off from him forever if – '

'He would rather I married one of Curwen blood, than a girl whose father killed a woman out of malice!'

'I will not listen, Charles. You cannot wish it if you think more soberly.'

Whatever foolish dreams I might have entertained, I must dismiss them now. If I loved my cousin, I could not give him further cause to speak so recklessly. I had counselled him to follow his own wishes: yet I meant he should resist decisions forced on him by others or by circumstance – not wilfully destroy his life by marriage to myself.

'You cannot tell me not to think of it! I shall speak to you again – when we are away from Keswick. For you care for me, Georgiana: and you cannot tell me otherwise! It is true – is it not?'

But this time I did not answer – I seized my shawl, and left him standing there beside the lake.

He caught up with me at the farther end of the beach. Without speaking, he handed me the flowers which in my haste I had left behind: they were drooping now, in the heat of late afternoon. Quickly I crossed the pebbles, and dipped the stems in the water for a moment, glad of its coolness upon my fingers as I did so.

'Perhaps you should take off your shoes, cousin.'

Charles was beside me, his shadow long upon the stones. I felt weary, and should have liked nothing more than to do as he suggested, regardless of the others waiting our return. I said nothing, but took his hand; together we climbed the slope toward the path.

As we went slowly home across the water, I sat with my arm round Edith, watching the wake unfurl and ripple outward from the boat. Far behind, Hugh Nicolson, the Southey boy and George were fishing still; their rowing-boat, a shadow dark against the lake, seemed not to move – but I heard the splash of oars, and saw the sudden gleam as yet again a hopeful line was cast.

There was little conversation. Even the children were quiet and content, whilst Aunt Nicolson (I was convinced) was dozing upright in her seat. But I noticed Mary lean across to Philip; and my cousin – with whom I had exchanged no further word – nodded and reached into the pocket of his coat. When the sound of flutes began to fill the evening air, my aunt started, and awoke; the boatman, smiling, matched the rhythm of his rowing to the music, while Miss Southey softly sang the words. To our delight, the fishermen had heard: from the direction of the island, as they followed, came a second song, in answer to our own.

Then Charles and Philip played a melancholy tune, so sweetly that it saddened me; but as the echoes faded and the flutes were put away, the presence of the mountains closed about us – keeping at bay, a little longer, the complexities I knew must lie beyond the silent lake.

We had not long returned when I descended to the drawing-room, where for a time I sat alone in the seat beside the window, watching the darkness gather round the hills. I should never tire of seeing them, I thought, if Keswick were my home – yet I should be glad, tomorrow, to return to Workington. The calm of lake and mountains could no longer check my apprehension, or dispel my thoughts of Charles. I knew I must not let him seek me out or speak to me again of future plans; despite his declared intention, I could only think he had behaved impulsively and must regret it soon. In Portland Square, perhaps, my resolution would not weaken easily . . .

I scarcely heard the opening of the door, and Philip's footsteps as he crossed the room. Before I could make excuses or escape, he was beside me.

'Do not go – I hoped I should find you here. You leave tomorrow afternoon, my sister tells me?'

I nodded, surprised at his agitation, which I did not think my own departure warranted.

'And I go early across to Rydal, to complete my business with Mr Wordsworth. Tonight I dine at Greta Hall, and shall soon go there with Edith – so I shall not see you again!'

'But we shall meet again at Workington, perhaps – ' I broke off in some confusion, suddenly recalling that my cousin might not come there.

Philip smiled grimly, clearly mistaking the cause of my uncertainty.

'I cannot think you will regret my absence, Miss Georgiana. You will have sufficient to occupy your attention, unless I misjudge my friend Charles Curwen. No, do not be offended – ' I had risen from the window-seat – 'I have no wish to say more of that – it is out of my hands entirely. Only, should you want to find me, my sister will send any correspondence after me – I shall go to Paris next, Berlin also, I think.'

I held out my hand to him.

'I am sorry you must go so soon, and I am grateful for your kindness. I do not wish,' I added, quite without premeditation, 'to lose your friendship, Mr Earnshaw.'

'In that case – I shall leave this with you: you may regard it as a loan if you prefer, and return it when you choose.'

He handed me a small package, seemed about to say something more, and then to change his mind. But as he turned to go, and even before I had thanked him, the door opened again, and my cousin entered the drawing-room.

Charles regarded us both with frank curiosity, and I was at once struck by his air of defiance as he addressed his friend: 'Why, Philip, I thought you were already gone with Miss Southey: she was waiting for you some little time since – she told me so herself.'

As he crossed the room Philip answered him ironically: 'Then you have lost interest in that lady, after all? I think you should explain your inconsistencies to Miss Curwen, Charles: after all, your behaviour today has been distinctly erratic, even by your own standards.'

My cousin laughed and turned to me.

'But we had a charming walk to the ruins, did we not, cousin?' Then to my consternation he added, 'Though I regret that you would not assist me to decide my future, Georgiana. You see, Philip, she has utterly refused to be my mentor, in spite of everything.'

I did not doubt that his nonchalant tone concealed his serious intention – yet he seemed only to provoke his friend the more.

'Indeed, Charles, I should have thought it sufficient that you make errors on your own behalf, without inviting young ladies to connive at your doing so. I think Miss Curwen is worthy of better than to be drawn into your own dilemma. She can have no notion of the pitfalls awaiting any friend who tries to help you salvage something from the flotsam you choose to call your life!'

I was horrified at Philip's unconcealed contempt; and even more alarmed to see the anger which my cousin scarcely attempted to repress.

'You, sir, should not intervene in matters which concern myself and my family – to which Miss Curwen, in case you have forgotten, now belongs. She is my sister's friend, is shortly to become acquainted with my parents, and will, I trust, have cause to be glad of her return to Cumberland.'

Philip turned to me, and bowed slightly: 'My regrets, Miss Georgiana, for this unexpected diversion from my bidding you goodbye. I think, Charles, we should continue our conversation elsewhere, rather than embarrass and distress your cousin. Come, I must speak urgently with you before I go to Greta Hall.'

As they left me, Charles looked at me with such grave concern that I could not feel him as guilty as Philip appeared to judge. Indeed, I knew only that I bitterly despised myself for having caused – unwittingly enough – the anger which had passed between them.

I sat there still, exhausted and bewildered by events which seemed, increasingly, to indicate that there were other happenings of which I knew too little. Surely such a breach between two friends must have some cause beyond the present one – and had not Philip, warning me of Charles, spoken of another's secret, which he could not at that time confide to me? I had no means to understand it all: Philip, who might have helped me do so, was leaving even now; and Charles I must not be persuaded by, ought not to see again. Perhaps in

Workington (I hoped, more desperately indeed) I might see my way more clearly than I could tonight.

The outline of the mountain, when I looked for it again, was scarcely visible against the deeper darkness of the sky. As I went upstairs to light a candle and prepare my dress for dinner, I carried Philip's package with me; and in the remaining moments opened it, though I cared little what it might contain. Then I could not help but smile – for his meaning was so apt, though bitter enough, I thought. It was the book of Byron's poems which I had found him reading by the lake: a grey-bound volume, inscribed (I noticed with surprise), *'To Philip, in gratitude, IC'*.

But more disturbing in its implications was the note which Philip had himself addressed to me: *'It is time, I think, that Miss Curwen should commence her proper education; and she will, I trust, be the wiser when I shall return!'* He had placed it between the opening pages of a poem whose title then meant nothing to me: 'The Corsair' – which I was to read not once, but many times, in the months before we were to meet again.

Chapter 14

It seemed as though my aunt had re-acquired her taste for travel. Perhaps, indeed, she had never truly lost it during the two years which had elapsed since Humphrey Nicolson's death: now, casting off at last the heaviest of her mourning clothes, she was clearly bent on getting her money's worth from the newly furbished chaise. To the delight of Josh Pratt, and Emily's manifest alarm, whole days during that mild autumn of 1830 were devoted to excursions. Together we explored the coast – Saint Bee's to the south, Allonby and Maryport to the north; inland, Wigton in particular was favoured by my aunt – for reasons which only too soon became apparent to me.

Added to the impetus of her own delight in perpetual motion, was Aunt Nicolson's determination to expand my social opportunities. Possibly the thought of my matrimonial prospects had not entered her mind before our Keswick visit and the imminence of Isabella's wedding. Soon after our return, however, it was clear that I was being prepared, in no small measure, for a future in the county. We called upon all the leading families of the neighbourhood; invitations were forthcoming, as a matter of course; and I found myself, accompanied always by my tireless relative, sampling all the attractions of an autumn season in Cumberland society. That the notion of matrimony had become firmly embedded in her mind was proved to me one afternoon, when she stated emphatically that she did not see why I should not do quite as well as Isabella.

'After all, you shall come into a tidy sum one day, child!'

The implications of this prospect so disturbed me that I could not help saying in reply, 'But, aunt, I have no wish to be beholden to Sir Henry. And I cannot think – '

At which she cut me short in no very civil manner, with: 'It is no business of my brother's where I choose to leave my property – and he may do as he likes with his own! Besides, Humphrey would not have wished me to consult with anyone but himself.'

The notion that my future might be decided by her communing with his spirit might have amused me, had I not become alarmed at the thought of proving an object of interest to the eligible gentlemen (and their no less speculative mothers and sisters) whom I encountered during our forays from Workington. I did not suspect my aunt herself of any such unpleasant calculation: she was merely fulfilling (with her usual thoroughness) her duty as my guardian.

But Aunt Nicolson, during our outward journey, would always catalogue most impressively the niceties of history or pedigree of the family on whom we were to call; and I was always encouraged, as we returned home, to a minute examination of the manners of this or that young man – to whom I had been introduced, unfailingly, as 'my great-niece from the South'. My own status was, moreover, reinforced by Aunt Nicolson's own impeccable credentials: by birth a member of that far-flung family, the Christians of Maryport and the Isle of Man, she knew every respected landowner in the district, and was held in awe by most of them – as much for her ability as a woman of business as for her connection with the Curwens. She could discuss the import price of tea or the crash of a Carlisle bank with any man; and though I knew she had scorned her brother for changing his name to that of a wife whom she disliked, she was not above quoting Sir Henry's authority when it suited her to put down the pretensions of others.

But as we drove on that autumn afternoon to Wigton, I wondered whether, like my mother, I should soon weary of calls and politeness, pedigrees and suitors. I had rather, surely, be at home preparing the week's exercises for Mr Jameson, than trying to attend to the witty conversation of young Mr Dykes of Ovenby Hall, where we were bound for tea. Son of a gentleman farmer (whose acres – a thousand or more, in the vale between Wigton and Carlisle – my aunt pronounced more fertile and far less well-stocked than Sir Henry's), Mr Dykes had paid particular attention to me on the brief occasions of our early acquaintance. It was clear that he was an attractive proposition for any young woman, being (by his own account) an exceptional hand at whist, and an expert at negotiating the hazards of the hunting-field. On learning that I did not care for cards, and had but lately begun my riding lessons, he pursed his well-fleshed lips and stared at me in disbelief, murmuring 'I say, Miss Curwen' at half-minute intervals throughout our exchanges of information. Even so, his increasing enthusiasm for my company had lately extended so far as his appearance, on an admittedly superior mount, at Portland Square – in every expectation of a hearty welcome and further entertainment.

Now, as the chaise passed between the high stone pillars of the gateway to Ovenby Hall, I heard my aunt pronounce, in tones of some satisfaction: 'I believe, Georgiana, that Mr Dykes has serious intentions: have you thought of him at all? He would be a steady enough husband, I dare say, if managed properly; and at least he does not defy his parents when it comes to such important matters as marriage – his mother has told me as much herself, on more than one occasion.'

Somewhat wildly, I answered that I had no thought of marrying – why, I had scarcely become acquainted with the gentleman! At which my aunt, to my immense relief, nodded and leaned back against the cushion.

'Quite right, child, never marry in haste – but at least you are forewarned in this case; young women should always keep their wits about 'em, and have their answers ready! But,' she added ominously, 'there are always men who think a lady's "no" means "yes" – *and* girls who take advantage of the fact. Still, you've a better head on your shoulders than most, or so I should hope!'

Aunt Nicolson's warnings were not lost on me when, in the course of the same afternoon, I found myself assiduously escorted through the rose-walk and avenues, the picture-gallery, and even the well-kept stables of Ovenby Hall; and, despite my protestations of ignorance, was assured that a particular mare was 'well-suited to ladies' and would be at my disposal when next we honoured Mr Dykes with our company. His suggestion was admittedly attractive; and it was, moreover, flattering to be singled out by one who was in all respects so much the English country gentleman. Yet when he called again at Workington – this time to assure us of his attendance at a Grand Concert soon to be held in the Assembly Rooms – I felt more inclined to Emily's opinion.

''Tis that Mr Dykes again, miss,' she announced, 'and too smart, for my taste, 'e is! All fancy weskuts, and boots as never set foot in a field, for all 's a farmer – *supposed* to be, any road. Not like our Mr Charles, as can do a day's wuk wi' the men when 's a mind to, as well as ever Sir Henry afore 'm.'

How could I censure Emily, I thought, as reluctantly I followed to the drawing-room, for a comparison I had already allowed myself to make! For, conscious that the less encouragement I gave to Mr Dykes the more he sought me out, I suspected his motive in so doing. Whereas Charles could hardly want me for my Curwen name; and he had too little fortune of his own to be tempted by whatever small inheritance my guardian might leave me. No, I could not doubt that he, at Keswick, had preferred me for myself. Though still resolved that I must not let him think or speak of marriage to me – yet I could not find it in my heart to wish he did not love me.

Time after time, since returning home, I had recalled his words, his look, my own response to him. And if my aunt had thought (as later I surmised) to divert my affection from my cousin, she did not succeed. Little though we saw of him throughout those autumn months, the glimpses I caught of him – riding through the square on some mission for Sir Henry, or among the crowd at some public gathering – only made me long the more for the sound of his voice or laughter, made me more certain that he was beyond comparison with all the other men I met.

Charles had visited us only once before becoming, as I guessed, caught up in all the social obligations of his sister's wedding. Since our conversation on the island, I had known little peace of mind – yet my apprehensions vanished when I saw him. With him he brought, to my delight, a pair of black fell-ponies – natives, he said, of the Caldbeck hills where they had roamed throughout the summer. Having seen them installed in the stable eagerly prepared by Josh and Peter, he smiled at my thanking him.

'You forget, cousin,' he said, 'that I intend to take advantage of them. For in the spring we shall ride to Wastdale, as agreed.'

Then seeing my hesitation he added quickly, 'Come, Georgiana – you will not deny me that pleasure. I wish only that I, rather than Josh, could teach you now, as I should were I less occupied at home. For my parents intend to remove to Belle Isle before the winter; and I have promised to help my brother prepare for the Election in November – *that* will satisfy Sir Henry. You see, I am a model, dutiful fellow these days. And all for your sake, indeed!'

'I had rather you did it for your own sake, or for theirs,' I replied at once. I could not let his action alter my resolve; for he had no love of politics, I knew, and had spoken once of his plans to go abroad when the Election came. But his answer was as firm as my own.

'I shall only mend my ways for good cause,' he persisted, 'and what better than to please you? You know the future I have chosen for myself – and you shall see that my intention will remain unchanged – ' he paused ' – whatever Earnshaw may have told you to the contrary.'

'But I did not discuss the matter with him!' I was shocked that my cousin might have thought it. 'Philip Earnshaw cannot know what passed between us.'

'Perhaps not; but he has forfeited my friendship nonetheless, and is gone to France, thank God, where he can do me no more mischief. Besides, the fellow's hardly a saint himself – and his notions are become too revolutionary of late: he will find plenty in Paris of a like mind to himself!'

Charles spoke with a cold dismissiveness which saddened me; yet nothing I could say would soften it, of that I was convinced. Hearing him, I knew why the Curwens had acquired a reputation for unyielding stubbornness. Nor would a man as proud as Philip wish to make his peace with one for whom he had expressed such scorn . . . And once again, as we walked in silence through the garden to the house, I could not understand why their friendship had turned so easily to anger and mistrust.

When we reached the steps my cousin suddenly stopped and turned to face me.

'Georgiana – there is one thing more, which I will ask you now, since I shall not see you for some time. That boy – ' He glanced back toward the stable-yard. 'I see he is still with you, and I do not think it wise – he is not to be trusted.'

I began to protest, but he silenced me.

'Do not keep him, I beg of you, cousin. You cannot know these people as I do: they are wild – their ways are not like ours, believe me!'

'But he is a child, Charles – how can he harm me? We have fed him and found him work, that is all, as one would surely do for others if one only could. How can I turn Peter away? How will he face the winter with his father gone? I cannot – '

I faltered, almost in tears and certain that I had revealed to Charles my knowledge of the fisherman. But to my surprise he merely struck at his boot with his riding whip, and frowned, saying abruptly, 'No matter – let it be; I did not think to grieve you so much. Let him stay till winter's out, then maybe – maybe there will be no need . . .'

His manner was strange, equivocal – but I dared not ask what he meant. Then to my relief his good humour prevailed: as we went to join Aunt Nicolson he looked at me with an air of assumed resignation.

'You see, Georgiana, how you can command me! But how I wish,' he added, 'that Sir Henry would relent and see you, for you sound exactly like him when you speak so passionately. I think it is you, not my brother, who should follow in his footsteps and seek to change the world! How should you like a seat in Parliament and the chance to bring about Reform? You might do very well – after all, you have succeeded in reforming me already, have you not, little cousin?'

Changed he might be – yet the ardent pressure of his hand on mine had told me that his feelings had not altered since our leaving Keswick. Even so, I told myself again that Charles must marry money: he must seek a girl who, like his sister Isabella, welcomed those certainties which I might find so irksome. And he could not, surely, want a woman who ignored the social rules as I had done in helping Michael Stephens. For a lady might dispense accepted charity, might visit, with her little covered basket on her arm, the sick and poor; but she must not help them to evade the law, or to escape the penalty of any crime – however justified their cause, however desperate the need to lie or steal, or even kill. Misfortune had made them what they were; and Chance, which had made a lady of me, might as easily abandon me again, and make me one of them.

But did my cousin know, I wondered, that I was by birth a bastard? When, rashly, I asked my guardian how much – or how little – my relations knew of me, she had turned on me with an unaccustomed anger which caused me to regret the question.

'I have chosen,' she replied, her blue eyes colder than I had ever seen them, 'to restore you to your rightful place within the family, against the wishes of my brother. He does not forget the past; but my duty is to your mother, who placed you in my care – though I learned of it too late. If you are wise, Georgiana, you will assist me in that task. You are a·Curwen: let that be sufficient. Though sometimes,' she added, softly yet bitterly, 'I thank God that I do not bear the name myself!'

Was I glad or sorry that the Curwen name was mine? I knew that my mother, like my grandmother before her, had kept it rather than assume her husband's: yet I wished that even that small remnant of my father had been given to me – who had nothing save the hidden knowledge that his blood ran in my veins. Charles had thought me like Sir Henry; and I knew, from the picture in the locket which I now wore every day, that I resembled Frances Curwen still more closely. Yet there must be something of my father in me – something which my mother would have recognised . . .

I will describe him to you, daughter, for you cannot ever know your father, and will wonder one day why I left my home & parents whom I lov'd, the safety of a place where everyone had known my name, the blest familiarities of field & hill. But I would not have you think that he alone had influence over me: For there were others, some whom we knew, who like him at Oxford had rebelled against the shallow thought & self-complacency of academic life – children, as we, of a generation whose ideals were crush'd by fear of Revolution as in France, shock'd by the corruption of the English court, and fearful that Napoleon at last would land on English soil. Young as we were, we thought we could establish new societies, far from the suffering & decadence of European life.

Alexander, when I knew him first, was a dreamer, not a rebel. Poetry & scientific study were his passions – which he read or spoke of constantly, beleiving that together they could hold the key to happiness, that each without the other meant a partial vision of the world. I lov'd him for his dreams, and the gentle way he talk'd of them to me. For all our talk at home was politics or farming, now that my mother had become devoted to her husband's work, had lost the friends – the dilettanti of her younger days – whose painting, writing, causes, she had shar'd or aided with her wealth. But tho a scholar, Alexander lov'd the lonely hills as I did; he car'd for growing things – trees & flowering plants, & sometimes we plann'd the garden we would make together in some far-off place.

Each of us had felt confin'd at home – he because his parents (Scottish & devout, relations of Lord Lonsdale) had always meant him for the Church – I had seen them with him at our gatherings on Windermere. And, in the Summer when we came to know each other well, he was at Kendal, studying at home, & I at Belle Isle with my mother – though I should have been at school in Yorkshire still. But I had been unhappy there & ran away, meaning to go to London to my father, for the Commons were in session & I thought that he, indulgent to me allways, would protect me from my mother's anger. Only, the mistress of the school caught up with me at York, & lock'd me in a room until my mother came.

I know I was a trouble to her allways, yet she let me stay at home & let me wander as I wanted at Belle Isle – until my meetings with your father were discover'd. For we had seen each other almost ev'ry day sharing our thoughts, our hopes & fears; & we kept our love alive with letters all the winter, untill summer came again. Then all was renew'd: we plann'd to go from Cumberland, when I should be of age & Alexander's studies were complete. For we knew by now that our parents would not agree to marriage – so much at odds were the Lowthers & the Curwens that even the common people fought each other in the streets when the elections came & my father tried yet again to keep his seat in Parliament. Nothing was more important then to him – for the gentlest of men is harsh when his belcifs are threaten'd, even by the ones he cares for most.

I tell you all this, Georgiana, so that you may know that Love is sweetest when the heart & mind are one – a marriage strongest when both thought & senses coincide. For often men think women have no intellect, that they are but a pretty toy or ornament, a chattel to be bought then put aside: such would I have been had I married any of the men who courted me at Workington. My parents would not have wish'd me such unhappiness – yet they fear'd the kind of freedom which I sought, which I thought to find by going with your father to a different land.

Yet he was afraid for me – anxious that I would suffer hardship with him, or would grieve for all that I had left behind. Perhaps that is why he did not try to find me when my father parted us; yet he would have come to me, had they told him of your birth: for we had often talk'd of children, knowing the joy that they would bring . . . How his eyes – so black, I remember – seem'd to burn when he told me all that he must write one day; how often he would toss back his hair, very long & dark, when he became impatient at the waiting we endured or at some foolish speech he heard at Oxford, or at some injustice which he longed to right.

As an infant you resembled him, I thought – although a
mother allways seeks to find her lover in the features of their
child . . .

My mother's presence did not alarm or anger me, when once
again I unlocked the drawer in the quiet of my room, from
which I saw the sunlight on the distant sea. It was the morning
of Isabella's wedding – to which Aunt Nicolson had gone alone.
Charles had protested against my exclusion: yet I did not wish
to go, to be the object of collective scrutiny or risk Sir Henry's
wrath. I would rather spend the day with Mrs Sharpe, who
needed me; and I could picture my cousin well enough, in the
grey church at Crosthwaite beneath the shelter of Skiddaw. For
she had wished me, before leaving Keswick, to sketch her in her
wedding-clothes, with Edith, all frills and excitement, in
attendance; the completed drawing, with another of Miss Dora
Wordsworth (whose quiet demeanour had impressed me
strongly at our meeting) was to go with me to Brigham when I
paid the promised visit to my cousin.

So I imagined Isabella, happy with her grave, solicitous lover
– so different, surely, from another bride whom I remembered
at a wedding I had seen at Maidenhead. My memories of the
service (seen from my vantage-point as nursemaid to a fractious
child of the Chattertons) were scanty and unfavourable. But the
bride, I thought, resembled some kind of sacrificial creature:
small, white-clad and terrified beside her enormous husband,
vows exchanged in an uncertain whisper, with a look of
resignation boding ill for future harmony. Marriage, then, had
seemed a fearful thing to me: it had no sanctity, fulfilled no
natural law, was merely the outward confirmation of an inner
hell; and as for protecting children – it had not saved Horatia
from her father's lust.

But now my mother's letter gave me hope – though it could
not restore the happiness which she had lost. I felt, in those
lines, the meaning of her love for Alexander Grieve; and I knew,
as I read of him, that my father would have loved and cared for
me – whether she had ever married him or no.

*

It is strange how often Chance will take us gently by the hand down unexpected ways – only to leave us at the centre of some dim-lit stage without a script as guide, while she resumes the role of watcher at a drama of her own devising. Or sometimes she plucks us from the quiet corner where we sit, tosses us into the mire, delights in leaving us to panic there: sometimes we manage – through efforts more defiant than heroic – to emerge again, and struggle home with mud on our boots and anger in our hearts.

And always, afterwards, we wonder if we should have spoken rather than remaining silent; should perhaps have listened to the warning voice which often precedes impulse. Or maybe those who challenge Chance are not so foolish after all: they have, for a time at least, the illusion of control – may even, on occasion, seem to outwit Fate. For however carefully we tread (hoping perhaps to avoid disaster by acceptance of the stones cast on our path), some subtle trick of misdirection leads us to confusion. Faced with incomprehensible events, we turn – so often – to the shelter of deception, or the consolation of a person whom we should not trust.

It can have been no other than some fateful whim, some fancy on the part of Destiny, which led my aunt to drive to Allonby that day. It was a late October morning; the sky and sea a summer blue, yet with a warning touch of winter in the wind, so that we took a carriage from the Dragon rather than the open chaise. Mrs Sharpe (frail, but in brighter spirit than usual) went with us; and Susan also – for I had grown fond of her cheerful company and knew that she would enjoy the drive and a walk along the shore when we reached our destination. I was glad to leave the town behind, fraught as it was with all the fever which preceeds a great Election – when even those without the power of voting seek to influence the outcome, conscious that sometimes their united voice may be worth a thousand slips of ballot paper.

Even as our carriage left the square, another passed us. Its speed, the pairs of sweating blue-black horses, and the crest – muddied and scarcely recognisable – upon its side, all testified to yet another journey from Westminster to Workington. In that brief moment I caught sight of my grandfather's commanding profile; Charles beside him, and opposite, another gentleman – perhaps the cousin who hoped to take his place in Parliament in Sir Henry's stead.

'That brother of mine will wear himself out, and that's a fact!'

'But there can be no doubt of the Election – surely, Elizabeth, the seat is safe enough.' Mrs Sharpe folded her thin, gloved hands upon the rug which Susan had carefully arranged about her.

'Nothing is certain,' stated my aunt portentously. 'There are riots again in France, so I'm told, and that will make the Whigs unpopular – for all *they* are after is Reform. But Henry will not give up on it, after all his years of fighting: and right or wrong, he'll wear himself out for it, I say – and who will thank him when he's gone, I wonder?'

'The poor of Cumberland,' I thought, 'will thank him – those for whom he found work and provided cottages.' The words came unbidden to my mind, with an unexpected pride in all Sir Henry had achieved. Strangely, my early hatred had (without my knowing it) grown less of late; and when I recalled my mother's wish that I should tell him of her undiminished love, I did not reject the notion altogether. 'Maybe, one day, I shall seek him out,' I reflected as we turned toward the coast. 'And yet – how I wish he would accept me for myself!'

As always, the sight of the open sea and the Scottish mountains (close today, presaging rain before the evening) made me long, ungratefully, to discover what lay beyond them. Yet it was pleasure enough, on reaching Allonby, to escape from the confinement of the carriage, which Josh had brought to a halt as my aunt directed, so that she and Mrs Sharpe might enjoy an unimpeded view of the Solway and the dark-brown sands. The shore was almost deserted, as if swept clean of the summer's visitors – for then it was much favoured by families from Carlisle or lesser inland towns. Neat houses, of a pinkish stone much prettier than the grey or black of Workington, looked prosperous as those of any southern watering-place; and here and there a bathing-machine, awkward among the graceful wide-sailed fishing-boats, waited idly for the winter tide to reach its painted wheels.

With Josh and Susan, I walked almost the length of the cobbled pathway above the beach; then, bidding them continue, sat on a wooden bench to take some notes, as Mr Jameson had advised when there was not time to make a sketch and I wished to record the light or colours of a scene. So it came about that I observed a man and woman seated on another bench not far away, their backs toward me, faces toward the sea. At length they stood, still deep in conversation; and then I knew – almost before I had seen the familiar features, the set of his shoulders, his height as he straightened up – that Philip had returned to Cumberland.

I could not credit it. He should have been in France, or perhaps Berlin by this time. Only a week before I had received a note, brief but amusing, saying that Paris was unpleasant, though safe enough for foreigners; and that soon he must go to see some German buildings which might prove of interest to English architects. What reason then could have brought him here, to Allonby?

Even as I wondered, he leaned toward his companion, taking her hand, still speaking earnestly. She seemed to hesitate, then took up her bonnet from the bench; but as they began to move away she turned her head, and stared across at me.

I remembered the sound of singing, a woman weeping at a cottage door, a child I had once held in my arms . . . Wildly, I looked to where a boy was galloping a pony along the sands, his shouts ringing above the noise of the receding surf.

When I dared to seek her gaze again – she was gone, walking rapidly with Philip toward the centre of the town. But she had recognised me, I was certain: and I recalled, though against my will, the curses and mocking laughter of Michael Stephens' sister – the Irish fisher-girl.

Chapter 15

' "A painter has but one sentence to utter" – remember that, Miss Curwen! Imagination – inspiration, even – you must have, of course; but first you must learn the disciplines of art – for without them, all that you put on paper will be meaningless. Each stroke should contribute to the picture as a whole: better to make one good line than a dozen that are weak and have nothing to say!'

Mr Jameson came to Portland Square each Thursday. Nervousness at first outweighed my pleasure in his visits; for it was clear that what I had already learned was of little worth. Indeed he was, to my surprise, far more interested in the half-finished sketches and random drawings in my notebooks than in other work painstakingly completed, or copied faithfully from some book that I had found. A tall, lean man, with the anxious forehead and constant stoop of one who had studied hard for small reward, he was difficult to please. He would sigh and shake his head when I produced my efforts for the week, saying (in an accent so purely Scottish and musical that his voice, if not his words, delighted me), 'Why now, it is not only what you see, Miss Curwen – it is what you *feel* that gives the work a spirit!'

Observation, he declared, was not enough; and as for copying – that he abhorred as the death of all originality, designed to please only fond mammas who wished to parade the feeble talents of their daughters in society. Instead, he would have me study and learn from the work of other painters; and he would tell me how his own master, Henry Raeburn, had taught himself to capture on his canvases the characters of men – until at length he was, by some, considered better even than Sir Joshua Reynolds, whose portraits he had studied in his youth. Mr Jameson himself was fond of quoting Reynolds to me – though I did not always understand, and even when I came to read his Discourses for myself, was puzzled by the contradictions I discovered there.

With my own work, I persevered – sometimes encouraged, sometimes daunted by the books which almost every week my teacher brought with him: collections of engravings to be examined after he had gone; instructions on line and form, with exercises which, though they wearied me, I always attempted to complete. And then, a treatise on watercolour painting, whose intricacies I must, with Mr Jameson's assistance, try to understand if I was to profit by his lessons and be able, when the better weather came, to paint outdoors again. I almost despaired when from his folder he produced a sketch of the hills at Ambleside – drawn, he said, by Mr Constable more than twenty years before.

It appeared to have been done in haste: a suggestion of wispy summer cloud above the mountains; rocks and a clump of trees standing boldly beside a stream where a mill-wheel turned. Even the colouring was scarcely more than indicated – yet the hues were of a brilliance which startled me; and the whole, though small in size, at once conveyed – as I would have thought impossible – the strength of the Lakeland hills, the brightness of the air, the movement of leaves and water. When at last I turned to Mr Jameson, he was smiling – a rare occurrence with a man so much in earnest.

'I think, Miss Curwen, that there must be rules for painters such as you and I. But for an artist like Mr Constable – there need be none!'

Had it not been for my lessons, I should have found that winter wearisome indeed. The west-coast mists, which in summer always seemed to herald sunlight, in November and December settled close about the town, lying on every surface, silver-black with soot from the Curwen mines. For days the fog would cling to each twig and branch, each fallen leaf upon the stones: then suddenly the rising gale, bearing massive banks of cloud across a sullen ocean, drove the tides inland to meet the already swollen Derwent, filling the marshes where I had searched for Michael Stephens, drowning the ranks of withered iris and the windswept reeds.

Was the fisherman still at Ravenglass? I wondered often; but Jem and his wife had received no further message from him, Peter said. And when at length (as if impelled by some need to confirm what I already knew) I questioned him about the Irish girl, he repeated that she had gone, with her child, to Maryport. Yet he had hesitated, tugging at the sleeves of the jacket I had found him, and fumbling with the harness in his hand. Then I spoke sharply to him, fearing that, as Charles had warned, the boy was not to be believed: later, ashamed of my anger, I tried to dismiss my doubts – but they lingered, pervasive as the mist which hung about the square.

Since that day at Allonby, I had become only too familiar with suspicion and uncertainty. Philip had not seen me, I thought – yet he had not written again, and his note lay unanswered still. His return to England and his meeting with Mary Stephens were only part, perhaps, of that secret life to which my cousin had already, half in jest, referred. Small wonder that Charles had quarrelled with his friend! I too felt betrayed by Philip, who had tried to turn me against my cousin even while guilty, himself, of such deceit. In the shock of recognition I had felt too chilled to entertain such thoughts: but when I reflected on the changed appearance of the girl, once so wild and ragged, now well-clothed and neat, I guessed that only money could have made her so – that Philip, taking her with him back to France perhaps, had (willing or no) become responsible for her, and for her child. For she had looked at me with something almost triumphant in her gaze, as if she knew what I must think of her . . .

But she could not be blamed for turning to him. Why, I myself might one day have sought the help he had offered to me, had I not learned that his kindness at Keswick – everything about him –

had been false. Even his professed regard for Isabella seemed, in this new light, to be part of a gallantry as trivial as that of any Don Juan: perhaps, indeed, I should look for the key to Philip's character in Byron's libertine, rather than in 'The Corsair' – a hero nobly torn between the claims of love and duty!

Had I but paused to think more soberly, I might have asked myself why Philip Earnshaw was of such importance to me. Yet it is so easy, when faced with a certainty which matches all the evidence allowed by circumstance, to overlook a simple truth. I did not know, until too late, how much I cared for him. I did not understand that reason may be led astray by feeling; nor had I learned, as yet, that passion is as quickly turned to anger as to love.

There was little such complexity or scope for self-deception in the nature of my love for Charles. Try as I might, as the winter passed and my aunt's social endeavours grew more tedious to me, I could not accept with any pleasure the approaches other men might make. Even the unhappy Mr Dykes, whose mother proved more determined than himself to make an alliance with the Curwens, at length called off his pursuit and returned (doubtless to his greater satisfaction) to the less frustrating challenge of the hunting season. I could not regret the loss – save perhaps of his rosebeds and pictures: for I had come to anticipate with distaste the touch of his languid fingers, and that speculative stare across the drawing-room. As for the notion of him as a husband, with whom to share my days and nights forever – I recoiled, as I had fled, in dreams, from Horace Chatterton.

Indeed, the very thought of marriage was repugnant to me – save when, in moments of weakening resolve, I allowed myself to imagine Charles at Lorton Grange. For the purchase would be complete by early summer: this much we learned when he came, with his parents, to Portland Square at Christmas-time. The visit had been long expected: my uncle, Richard Curwen, had expressed his wish to see me before retreating to Belle Isle, for like as not bad weather and the dangers of the road across the mountains would prevent his leaving Windermere for several months.

'And Richard was never a one for gallivanting – he'll be content enough with his fishing, and managing the trees, for there's a deal of planting that my brother wishes done, I'm told. Not that Julia will give him any peace, mind; she's friends enough at Kendal and round about to keep her busy – when she isn't fretting to be off to London.'

Aunt Nicolson had made plain her disapproval of my uncle's wife, adding to the unease I felt already at the prospect of our meeting. Despite his kindness in sending me my mother's locket, I could not imagine that his warmth would equal that of Charles or Isabella: after all, I had been at Workington a year and more – surely he might have asked to see me sooner, however strong my grandfather's opposition!

But my Uncle Richard was, I very soon decided, neither so forthright nor so quickly roused to passion as Sir Henry. He lacked, too, his father's impressive bearing: instead, his build was slender, his features those of a scholar – a gentle mouth, and deep-set eyes of the same disconcerting blue as Isabella's. He appeared, as he took my hand and led me to a seat beside him, to be greatly moved, saying (just as my guardian had done on my arrival at Workington), 'How very like you are! I had not thought it possible . . .'

Then for an hour or more we talked together – he with a quiet courtesy and interest, I with a sense of such release that afterwards I wondered how I came to confide so much, quite without my usual fear of self-betrayal. Perhaps, had we known each other sooner (or perhaps, had I remained in Cumberland) his affection might have come to fill the place left empty by my mother's death.

But Julia, his wife, appeared already to suspect me – of what, at first I could not tell. She subjected me, however, to such persistent scrutiny that I blushed with nervous anticipation whenever she addressed me. It was clear that she managed her husband with great competence; so was it she (I could not help but wonder) who had pressed my cousin's marriage to Miss Morgan-Price? From the outset, she appeared a dry, ambitious woman, with a coolly gracious air of patronage – even towards Aunt Nicolson. Whatever he proposed to do, however he might determine to control his own affairs, I was certain that Charles would meet with little understanding from his mother.

Even so, his mood when he arrived that afternoon was exultant. His elation at acquiring Lorton Grange delighted me – yet later I felt uneasy when he seized the chance to say, 'I shall take you to inspect it, one day. But I have said nothing to my parents of my other plans: so you need not fear that my Mamma will pounce on you – she shall know nothing until you have given leave, cousin. But I intend to have my own way – and my father, at least, is just as I predicted, for he sees his sister in you, and must love you for that, whatever Sir Henry may say. Before long, he will want you to go to Belle Isle: *that* will set some feathers flying in the family dovecotes!'

But already, I thought ruefully, your mother quite mistrusts your speaking with me . . . For I could not mistake her hard appraising look, nor the emphasis with which she spoke my name as she leaned forward from her place beside my aunt.

'Miss Georgiana – I understand that you have made a great success across at Ovenby! Mrs Dykes, when I called last month to say goodbye, was most impressed by your knowledge of art, and told me that you spent a considerable time with her son, inspecting the pictures in their gallery. Perhaps there will, before long, be an even greater conquest – for Mr Dykes is often here at Portland Square, I gather . . .'

For an instant, Julia Curwen's gaze rested upon her son, as if she anticipated some reaction from him. And even as I began to answer, 'I cannot think so, ma'am,' my cousin interposed, at once taking up her challenge.

'For heaven's sake, Dykes knows nothing of pictures – he would hang 'em all upside down as soon as look at 'em! Unless, my dear cousin, you were to offer to paint his horse, and himself in the master's scarlet. Now there's a subject for your canvas – but not until you have done a portrait of the Emperor, as you have promised me.'

Charles sounded good-humoured enough; but there was no laughter in the quick glance he gave me, and I knew that if his mother had intended mischief, she must be more than satisfied. But Aunt Nicolson was not to be outdone.

'It is curious,' she remarked, with an innocence of tone which proved her quite as subtle as her adversary, 'that Laetitia Dykes is always so very ready to claim a conquest for her son. It is not so many months ago, if I recall correctly, that she was convinced he would have married Isabella, but for the intervention of Mr Wordsworth. I rather think, indeed, that were we able to produce for him yet another Miss Curwen, Mr Dykes would forget his horses altogether. For he'd not take "no" a third time, I'll be bound – and neither would Laetitia!'

Despite my guardian's timely intervention, I could only interpret Julia Curwen's coldness as a warning. Yet Charles himself remained undeterred: or so I concluded when, on Christmas Eve, a messenger appeared, bearing a large box for myself and hot-house fruit in a basket for Aunt Nicolson. Her surprise and pleasure were evident – though she proclaimed the gift 'a monstrous extravagance' as she examined the label with its inscription of Sutton's Nursery at Carlisle.

'And what have you there, miss?' she demanded. Blushing a little at the sharpness of her glance, I stared first at the ribboned box which bore my name, then in delight at the roses which lay within – their colour (chosen carefully, I guessed) almost the same as that of the summer roses I had gathered in the garden months before. To my relief, my cousin's card carried no greeting, and my aunt could hardly take exception to the gift: yet its meaning was not lost on me. And when at last the flowers faded and their petals fell, I placed them in a little china bowl upon my bookshelf, where their fragrance lingered throughout the empty weeks which followed.

Though I could scarce confess it to myself, my resolve was undermined. Increasingly, as each day passed with no further word from Charles, I longed for him to come again. He loved me, I was certain; my impatience grew; and I had by now transferred to him the trust which once I placed – so foolishly, I thought – in Philip Earnshaw.

For among the packages I had received that Christmas came a letter, in a hand which I recognised at once. I had seen it earlier, upon the note enclosed among the pages of the Byron poems;

yet I opened the letter with reluctance – for whatever Philip
might communicate could only be unwelcome . . .

> I write now from Switzerland, a country more to my taste, with
> its heights and lakes, than Germany or France can ever be –
> and it is peaceful here. I had such hopes of Paris, where I have
> friends whose opinions I knew matched my own. But I was
> detained there long beyond my intention, by events which
> proved more violent and cruel than any I have ever seen – or
> hope to see again. There is much that I could describe, yet will
> not weary you with: sufficient to say I have witnessed the
> capacity of human beings to destroy each other, and their
> failure – as it seems to me – to build new brotherhood upon the
> ruins of the old.
>
> What foolishness: 'A dream of youth, which night and time
> have quenched forever'! Shelley was right – have you read him
> yet?
>
> 'Heartless things are done and said i' the world' – he *was*
> right, and I shall send you his book – if such a thing may be
> found here, my friend . . .

He sounds much distressed, I thought, as I read; and he has been
in some danger too . . . Can I have misjudged him after all? He
makes no reference to having returned to England, cannot then
have seen me that day . . . But no! There was yet a final
paragraph which left me in no doubt. It could only have been as
I had thought at Allonby – and worse, Philip had not the
courage, it appeared, to write of it openly:

> I remain here for several months, owing to a circumstance
> which I cannot remedy. I shall hope that when I return you will
> prove as kind a listener as I remember at Keswick, for there is
> one who, if she recovers health, I wish might meet you. Where
> I would not beg a favour for myself, I must on her behalf, for
> she is that rare creature – one for whom I care sufficiently . . .

Anger at his presumption of my goodwill; shame at my own
foolish longing to find, even yet, the best in such a man; pity for
the Irish girl who now – it was quite clear – depended on him: I
cannot tell which emotion was the strongest as I flung the letter

down. I ignored the address which Philip had enclosed, and endeavoured to forget that I had ever known or sought his friendship.

By now, perhaps, my aunt had become aware of my reluctance to consider marriage; or, wisely, she guessed that only time would lessen my feeling for my cousin. Whatever her reasoning, her taste for society declined almost as rapidly as it had materialised: as soon as the duties of the Christmas season were fulfilled, we retreated – to our mutual relief – behind the heavy curtains and securely bolted doors. A new, more comfortable coexistence was established; and though little enough was said between us, Aunt Nicolson and I, for the present, were content.

Newly resolved, with the turning of the year, to keep at bay the bitter hurt of Philip's evident deceit (unexplained, yet clear enough to me), I determined to put my time to good account. Books which had lain untouched on my guardian's shelves, others borrowed from Mr Jameson or pressed on me by Mrs Sharpe, became scattered about the house, until at last my aunt and Emily rebelled at my untidiness. A small neglected room upstairs was designated mine, cleared of the unused furniture and mice which had accumulated in its corners, and filled again with my painting-things, the newly polished spinning-wheel, and objects which Aunt Nicolson, with alarming zeal, declared superfluous to Humphrey's overcrowded study. Among the curiosities I found (which but for my intervention my aunt would have thrown away) were some splendid shells – great cowries, patterned and glossy; pieces of coral, large as a man's hand; a dull-looking fossil, and another with dark-red bandings of garnet at its centre; more shells, delicately hinged, containing, when I gently prised them open, grains of sand almost silver in the winter light.

A pair of pistols, inlaid with mother-of-pearl, lay in the same drawer; and when I took these to my aunt she laughed, and a gleam of wistful pleasure came into her eyes – reminding me for a moment of that reckless look my cousin often wore . . .

'Why,' my aunt declared, 'Humphrey gave me those as a birthday gift, a year after we were married, on my first voyage with him to Barbados. And I learned to fire them too – but strangely, I never needed them aboard the *Elizabeth*, which was what he always feared.'

Then she told me how she had used them once, at home in Workington, on surprising an intruder in the kitchen.

'Emily was terrified, poor thing,' she concluded with satisfaction, 'but the fellow was merely hungry, as I guessed soon enough. So I packed him off with a warning, and a plate-pie in his pocket; I thought to give him a shot across the bows as he went, but it wasn't necessary, after all!'

Maybe, I thought, as the pistols were duly cleaned and consigned to their drawer again, Aunt Nicolson would have been better born a man of action: for she had told the tale with a satisfaction which betrayed her restless spirit. But her life, like that of many women, ended with her husband's death: small wonder that she sometimes turned her back on Workington, and sought the wider shores of memory and solitude.

Even so, she took an interest in all that Mr Jameson was teaching me, ascertaining from time to time that in this respect, as in others, she was getting good value for her money. From myself, she expected progress, as she made clear.

'Don't thank me, child,' she remonstrated, more than once. 'It's not gratitude I'm after: paint as well as you can, and let Jameson do what he's paid for. If that son of mine had lived, I should have done as much by him; though I doubt that any child of Humphrey's would have been allowed to ruin his eyes as you do, miss. But there it is – you must do the best with whatever gifts the Lord sees fit to give you!'

There was more than a little irony in her remark – since she rarely went to church, defying (and enjoying notoriety, thereby) all the religious prejudices of her friends and relatives. When, if at all, Aunt Nicolson attended any service, she patronised Saint Michael's, the sailors' church, ignoring the impressive, newly-built Saint John's. 'Another of Henry's follies' she sometimes called the latter; but privately I thought it gracious, its proportions quite in keeping with the terraces and neatly laid-out squares of the upper town. More readily, I shared the godless habits of my guardian, impervious to censure – my memories yet fresh of Sabbaths spent in silent misery at

Maidenhead, of pious words which carried no conviction, and a Deity whose vengeance was poised to strike whenever Horace or Matilda Chatterton might call it down upon me.

Now, I spent my Sundays painting, when the light allowed; or I would visit Mrs Sharpe, whose weakness had much increased of late, to my aunt's concern. Hurrying back into the square, I could hear the sea – a distant, uncompromising beat against the harbour wall; the thin cry of a gull on some blackened chimney; the striking of a bell, from the churchyard where I had watched for Peter on a golden summer evening. There were as yet no green shoots in the garden, no signs of hope in the fine sleet which spun in the wind. The chill oppressiveness which precedes spring still hung in the air, making me shiver and seek the fireside, and feel as if that winter had no ending . . .

Imperceptibly, the days had lengthened. Even at four in the afternoon of a Sunday late in February 1831, I was hard at work in my little upstairs room. Fascinated by the complex pattern and the colour – deep, elusive crimson, almost black in certain light – of the garnets at the centre of the fossil lying on my table, I was reluctant to stop, as I must when the lamps were lit. But it was cold, and the fire was low; that morning, when I woke, random snowflakes starred the window, as if an errant schoolboy had flung them against the glass, where they clung like winter's imprint half the day. Uncertain sunlight had erased them at last, but that was fading – soon Emily would bring up tea, which I would take alone.

For more than a week now, Aunt Nicolson had gone daily to Mrs Sharpe. The onset of a fever gave cause for alarm; and my aunt stayed late into the night, unwilling to see a stranger nurse her friend, just as she had cared for me with such devotion almost a year before. Now, she would not let me help her, much as I protested that I could be in no danger; but she spoke ominously of cholera, known to be rife in France in the wake of revolution, and made me promise to remain at home – though I smiled when she reminded me of the pistols in her husband's bureau, bidding me keep the doors and windows barred when evening came. Her instructions were irksome; yet I heeded them, for I had witnessed at Election-time the darker face of Workington, when even sober citizens made wild inflammatory speeches; when tales of violence in other towns rekindled old resentments at neglected promises; and every day the hopeless anger of the poor was fuelled by easy liquor – enough to sink the fleet twice over, so my aunt declared.

It was snowing again, when at last I laid down my brush and went to the window; daylight was almost gone. Below, a heavy door banged shut – the garden door, perhaps, and Peter off to feed the ponies, then away to Jem and Rosa to see his sisters. The sound of another door closing, and the rattle of bolts this time; and at length, footsteps on the wooden staircase from the kitchen. The lamp which I was lighting proved recalcitrant; though I heard a knock at my door I did not answer, absorbed in the task of coaxing a stubborn flame to life.

When, expecting Emily, I turned – it was Charles who stood there. Or rather, he was leaning against the doorway, unsmiling and (as I had never before seen him) quite dishevelled in appearance. Coat and boots were muddied, his face wet with snow; and even as I gathered my wits, he brushed with his hand at his soaking hair, and spoke with some impatience.

'It is all very well, cousin – but I shall catch an ague if I wait here much longer. There was Emily, snoring away, and the kitchen fire gone to ashes: hardly a gracious welcome any day, and less than civil when it's snowing fit to bury a man as he stands on the doorstep! Not a sound, nor a light, and the back-door unlocked . . . And you – hidden away upstairs like a princess in a tower –

'But where,' he asked, as he came into the room, 'is your guardian dragon? Not, I trust, about to drive me off and out again?'

Laughing, I explained Aunt Nicolson's absence, and mended my fire to a more effective blaze – scarcely believing the while that Charles would not vanish as suddenly, and inexplicably, as he had come. Having descended to the kitchen with his coat, I re-lit the stove, despatching Emily (exhausted with her late-night watching for my aunt) to her quarters, and returning upstairs with as hearty a tea as I could muster for my cousin.

He was stretched out on the rug beside the fire, with Minou at his feet; for a moment or two, having closed the heavy door, I watched him, peaceful in the lamplight. After so long a time, so much uncertainty, I could not question his presence – would as soon have sent away the sunshine after winter as have asked him, for convention's sake, to leave me . . .

'Georgiana?'

Had he read my thoughts? Did he know, even as he looked at me then, that I would not make him go?

Whatever his unspoken question, it caused him to frown, and to stir up the fire with a sudden movement which made the sparks and shadows flicker in the dim-lit room. There was a curious constraint between us then; on his part, a cool formality which soon dispelled my joy at seeing Charles again; on my own, a sense that I had angered him, in some way that I did not understand . . .

My aunt did not return that evening. Within the hour, Josh Pratt was stamping and blowing (like one of his carriage horses) on the threshold of the kitchen.

'Waitin' for that Doctor Middleton, were Mistress Nicolson, and like enough he'd tek his time in gettin' there, for all it's no distance – and gettin' paid a fortune for't, that's for certain!'

I cut him short before he could expand still further on the doctor's failings, ascertained that Susan was to bring another message from my aunt next morning, and made fast the door behind him as he departed, whistling, to his night's work at the Green Dragon. Then I took from beside the stove my cousin's heavy coat, welcoming its warmth and the roughness of its texture as I held it in my arms . . . He would need it soon – must soon, I supposed, be gone . . .

But Charles looked grave when I told him that my aunt must remain with Mrs Sharpe.

'It is unwise of her to leave you so: surely there must be someone . . . It's not safe, Georgiana! Why, the door was unlocked when I came.'

'The door is bolted now. And it can be no more unsafe for me, than for you to have come here!'

'But that's just my meaning – which I did not wish to speak of: I did not wish to alarm you. But I must tell you now that I was followed here – why and by whom I can't imagine, but it was so. If I hadn't known of a quicker way to the house – a way I used to take as a child when I wanted to escape my brothers – I might not have come so safely after all!'

He stood up, and crossed to the window; he drew back the velvet curtain, stared out for a moment, then let it fall again. There were streaks of mud on his boots still, I noticed; and now I understood why he had appeared as he had done – by Peter's garden route, perhaps. But if Peter knew that way – then might not others also? . . . And might not my cousin be right – that there was more danger than I realised? The room became, of a sudden, very bleak and cold: and Portland Square, which had seemed to me a haven, was no longer so.

Even Charles, by the window, might have been a stranger standing there, arms folded, his face in shadow. Fleetingly, I remembered Philip's warning – but no, Philip had been wrong, had hurt me by his own evasions more than my cousin ever could . . . Yet why had Charles come here, in weather so cold and wild as this; and who had followed him?

'Will *you* not be careful, as you go back? I have Emily, at least – and Josh is not so far away if we should need him.' I held his coat still, unwilling to lose its safety. He laughed.

'And where is Emily now? Fast asleep again, I'll be bound, in the farthest corner of the house. And nothing will wake a peasant woman once she determines otherwise – however strong her devotion! Why, I could have robbed Aunt Nicolson twice over, and no one the wiser. Maybe, little cousin, I should offer my protection!'

He spoke lightly; but I answered him at once – too quickly, perhaps.

'I cannot think I need it.'

I held out his coat, which he took, shrugging his shoulders. Then he hesitated – as if reluctant to go . . .

'This room is charming, Georgiana. A little on the spartan side, perhaps – but charming, even so.'

Charles had moved to where my easel stood, and was gazing at the painting still upon it.

'A studio is meant for working in,' I reminded him. 'I – I am much indebted to Aunt Nicolson.'

'Then you persist in your ambition – and she supports you in it?' He asked the question quietly, but his eyes were now intent upon me.

'Why yes; she's aware, of course, that I am serious. But I am only just beginning. There's so much I have to learn from Mr Jameson.' I felt uneasy, resentful almost, at his asking. 'I mean to work – to work very hard, cousin.'

'Then you do not mean to marry Thomas Dykes – the *Honourable* Mr Dykes?' His contempt was unmistakable.

I was silent, astounded that he could have thought it. It was several months since I had been at Ovenby. And my refusal of the man had been conclusive – or so I had intended.

'I did not credit it at first,' he went on bitterly. 'How could I do so after – after what had passed between us. Even when Dykes spoke of it himself – a certainty, he called it – still I did not think it. I'd rather have wrung his neck than believe he spoke the truth!'

'He did not do so. I had refused him – more than once.'

'Then why was it all the talk at Christmas, Georgiana? Everywhere I went, I heard it. Even my sister spoke of it, and she was scarcely home with John from Scotland. My mother, too – '

So that was the way of it: Julia Curwen had done her mischief well!

'And is that why you are here – to confirm what you already know?' My voice was hard; I would not let him hear how much his words had grieved me. I shivered, and turned my face to the fireside, away from his accusing gaze.

'I came to speak of business with Aunt Nicolson; to see her, if I could, before Sir Henry comes back from London. It has to do with Mr Wragg – Augustus Wragg, of Lorton. But it must wait – though God knows I wish that I could be at Lorton now, and you there with me – '

I could bear no more, but sprang to my feet, roused by the note of anguish in his voice.

' – and I came because I could not keep away from you! For months I have done so – of necessity at first, and then because it seemed that I was wrong at Keswick, that you did not care for me. Belle Isle has been a prison to me, thinking that I must not come to you . . .

'But now, Georgiana, I must know the truth, you must tell me – Oh, my little love, tell me, for you know I love you! – '

He was not a stranger to me now! Constraint had gone. For I had recognised the passion in his eyes, knew as I looked at him that his longing was a mirror to my own, reflecting all that I had felt for him throughout that dreary winter.

As I crossed the room to Charles, any lingering doubts dissolved, like the morning snowflakes from my window-pane. And I knew that whatever Chance might send me this time, I must welcome – lest it should (by some other chance) just as quickly melt away . . . So at last, compelled by his kisses and warmed by the comfort of his coat, I told him that I loved him; and I did not wish the words unsaid. Nor did I regret the subterfuge which followed – though it changed, irrevocably changed, the pattern of my life thereafter.

How it snowed, that February night, as we lay in the narrow bed within the safety of my room. Firelight, its glow reflected in the smooth brass bedstead-rail; a faint, sweet scent of snowdrops, discovered only yesterday beneath the pear tree; the candle burning low, with sudden gleams, on the table where my mother's letters lay. Perhaps she had known these moments – her lover's breath against her cheek, his arm outstretched, possessing even as he slept, in that half-awakening languor which, towards dawn, is the gentler part of passion.

My painting-smock, stitched with so many hopes, hung on the door, an empty shadow waiting for the morning. Charles would leave me; and I would know, for the first time, that curious sense of drifting unreality which follows such a parting. Sadness, and content; but most of all the sharpening certainty – as one becomes accustomed to the daylight – that so much, in so brief a space, has come and gone again . . .

Chapter 16

And why, reader, did I not reject him? Why did not I, like the youthful heroine of fiction, strive to resist my cousin? Where, indeed, was that sense of virtue which (as the fragile casing of a flower confines its petals till the sun compels them open) should have prevented my ready acquiescence?

'I cannot leave you now, my darling. Or rather – I can, but heaven knows I do not wish it; and it's late now . . .'

I could hear, in the silence of the passageway, the ticking of the moon-faced clock which stood outside my room. How often I had listened to its heavy beat as I lay awake and thought of Charles, so far away each winter night. Now, as he waited there, it seemed – as it always seems to lovers who must part – that there would never be another moment such as this: that he would never come again, unbidden, to my bed; and only marriage might make possible the closeness which – as I now knew – was all I needed from him.

For, when the moment came, it was not love which seemed to threaten me: it was marriage – and possession – which I feared the more. Perhaps, like my mother, I rejoiced too much in love to fear its consequence. Or perhaps I had known too little – far too little – in my childhood, of that warmth of touch and tenderness of glance which others, in their infancy, may take for granted. And so, in casting caution to the winds, I do not think I erred – save in the subsequent deception of my aunt;

and none could have wished me to increase her burden then, at a time when sorrow at her friend's impending death preoccupied each waking minute of her day.

'But Emily?' I asked him, fearful suddenly that she would wonder at his late departure.

'She will think I am gone, since my coat has done so – and if I am seen, returning to the Hall, it would not be the first time that I've left the Dragon in the small hours of the morning. Such, my darling, is my wicked reputation! And can you bear with me, my love? Or must I go, before you tell me that I cannot be reformed as you had hoped – and therefore you cannot let me stay!'

Charles was once again the charming, laughing, reckless cousin who had challenged me, on a summer afternoon, to betray his shirt-sleeves and his lack of courtesy; who had later bidden me decide his future and encourage his defiance of his parents' plans. But this time I did not doubt his feeling – nor could I ignore my own or hope to hide it from him. And when he murmured – gently, yet with such intensity – 'Come, Georgiana', I set aside all hesitation, save for that reserve which only passion's certainty can overcome.

Charles remained at Workington throughout the spring. Frequently, with Susan, I would walk to where the river path wound along the valley to the wooded slopes which lay below the Hall. Here, at a little bridge, I would often find my cousin, sometimes on foot, sometimes astride the Emperor; and always (while Susan gladly took the chance to sit beside the miller's hearth, or play with his children by the tumbling stream) – always Charles prolonged the time we had together, as if he knew that the world, at length, would close about us.

Some love affairs are like that: begun with an intensity of longing, fuelled by absence, or precipitated by the intervention of some unexpected chance. And then, continued in a mood of recklessness which afterwards amazes – as if the very fact of risky subterfuge makes love's commitment stronger even as its time runs out, like a fire which flares too brightly just before it burns itself away.

He did not come to me again at Portland Square. Yet he seemed to be there still, the imprint of his head upon my pillow, the heat of his body close as I lay awake and thought of him, the touch of his hands upon my acquiescent limbs. And I dreamed no longer of those fearful moments of Horatia's suffering: though I never quite forgot them, they tormented me no more, but were replaced by other, gentler memories – of a woman and her lover in the meadow by the Thames.

When, as happened sometimes, we lay together in some hidden woodland glade, or within the shelter of an isolated hut, while the spring rain drifted down on newly opened chestnut leaves, bringing the scent of warmer days to come, it seemed our love was charmed. Yet no promises were made; nor was marriage talked of, save when Charles spoke longingly of Lorton, and how he would take me there. It was as though the burden of the future had been, for the present, briefly set aside by some tacit, subtle understanding; as if each meeting, which confirmed the feelings we acknowledged, yet postponed their consequence; and as if, by telling no one, we could daily recreate the fragile many-coloured bubble which encircled us, enchanted as we were.

'You shall have a summer-house at Lorton, Georgiana. And you can paint there, beside the river – every day if you choose. Or we shall go abroad – to Rome and Paris; and you can improve my taste, fill the drawing-room with pictures to impress our guests . . . if we must have guests, which perhaps, after all, I shall not permit . . .'

Charles laughed, and turned to look where the river, below the hillside, glistened as it flowed toward the sea. He is like a child, I thought – a child who talks of the toys he will buy tomorrow, or of the fortune he will make when he becomes a man . . .

And I said aloud, as if some impulse to destruction prompted me, 'But what of your parents; and Sir Henry, when he discovers everything? Even when the Grange is yours, they will not want me, will prevent your doing as you wish. And there is Aunt Nicolson – she will think, as others may, that I have trapped you and will ruin your life.'

[223]

I believed, indeed, that it would be so; and this time, though he did not say as much, my cousin did not deny it.

'I must speak with Aunt Nicolson – no, not tell her what I plan to do, but with regard to Lorton, and Augustus Wragg.' He hesitated. 'She remembers him, as I told you, from when her husband was alive – and will, perhaps, assist me. There are some difficulties, Georgiana.'

So – however he had meant to purchase Lorton Grange, he needed money: that much was clear. Charles had hoped to see my aunt, I remembered, the night he had remained with me, and even then he had sounded strangely anxious. But the prospect of his speaking to Aunt Nicolson perturbed me, for she had been so much changed of late . . .

The shadow of that winter had not altogether gone from Portland Square. Mrs Sharpe had rallied once, in early March; then she died, without my seeing her again. My aunt had returned withdrawn and silent; and for weeks remained so, as if she did not care how the time was passing. At length, guilty at my preoccupation with my cousin, I begged her to see Doctor Middleton; she refused, as expected, and I could only guess that until the *Elizabeth* returned, and the news was told to Captain Sharpe, Aunt Nicolson would prove immune to all persuasion.

She rarely enquired these days as to the outcome of my lessons with Mr Jameson; and raised no objection when I went with him to purchase more materials at Whitehaven, or to see the studios of painters who he knew were working there. Her generosity, indeed, increased – for she bade me order whatever books I required from Dixon's shop in Workington; then, on my birthday, she gave me a further, larger sum – dismissing my thanks, and remarking wearily, 'I had rather give it to you, child, than have others – who should have more sense of what is right – try to beg or wheedle it from me.'

From this I guessed that my cousin, who at last had called to see her, had been unsuccessful. Her favourite he might have been; but even she, it seemed, was less disposed than ever to support his whims. Yet Charles, when we met again, said nothing of it; and when, a second time, I spoke my doubts aloud, he silenced me.

'Little love,' he said, 'you must trust me, that's all. You shall see – there are ways and means, if one wants a thing enough. As I do – and all will be well!

'There,' he added, taking half a dozen primroses and carefully tucking them into my dress, 'they become you very well . . . And soon there will be primroses in Wastdale, and I mean to take you there!'

What had my mother written? '*Do not marry, save in love & trust.*' The first I was certain of – I loved my cousin still – but the second? I dismissed my doubts; and when the days grew longer, went with him (as I had promised him almost a year before) to Wastdale.

> The road to Wastdale, when I came there with your father, was scarce fit to be call'd a road at all – so narrow, rough & winding that we had to lead our horses half the way; for it pass'd thro' rocky becks and often the bridges or the walls had fallen, leaving boulders strewn across our path. The mountains, rising steep above, at first were green with grass or ferns, but then so precipitous & dark that they seem'd ready to fall about us. Then, to our righthand side, the lake – a black immensity of water, silver-edged, with rising screes reflected, like a mirror full of shadows. And at last, a wide valley, a white farm lying at its head. At our feet, so many flowers – daisies & primroses, & those which they call wind-flowers, that grow in such damp green places; and ev'rywhere, the sound of running water or of singing birds . . .

My mother had described it faithfully. But perhaps she did not see that day, as I did with Charles, the darkness of thunderclouds ahead, above the Scawfell Pikes; or the clear green-golden light of the sky which lay behind as we traversed the valley's length. She may not have felt the same sensation of release on leaving the oppressive height of mountains, the unfathomable lake; nor such a longing to follow the shallow twisting river to the sea.

That river led, I knew, down toward a harbour – Ravenglass. It lay but a few miles along the coast, not far from Calder Bridge, where we were to rejoin my aunt. For all that my cousin was beside me, his hand on mine as the ponies took us slowly home, I wished – for the first time in many months – that I could take the road to Ravenglass, to find what waited for me there.

'Perhaps, Charles, you should see Sir Henry?'

'I should rather wait until I am at Lorton; he is more likely to accept it all once I'm established there. And it won't be long now – Wragg is satisfied, thank God, and soon I shall go to supervise the changes. Then, my little love, you shall come to me at last – to the devil with my parents, so long as Grandfather can be persuaded!'

Somehow – I could not ask him how – my cousin had fulfilled his obligations. But I remained uneasy; and as we walked together through the woodland, I sighed, unable to see how that final obstacle might be surmounted. Already it was May; soon Sir Henry would return from London, where he had been working on the latest plans to implement Reform – for his party had gained control of Parliament at last, and his lifelong dream must soon be realised.

We neared a wicket gate which led into the grounds. But Charles did not, as usual, turn with me to walk as far as time allowed before we parted. Instead, he took my hand, and led me through the gate, saying, 'There's something I wish to show you, Georgiana. Come – I promise no one will notice us – he is away, hardly any servants are about. In any case, the Hall is always quiet; Grandfather lives quite plainly, as you know.'

My aunt had told me long ago of her brother's simple tastes, his preference for shabby clothes, and how he even ate oatmeal porridge (peasant fare, some called it) for his breakfast! And I saw at once, when Charles had persuaded me to enter, that his home reflected not Sir Henry's wealth, but his simplicity. The bleakness of its rough-hewn stone and blackened panelling were softened somewhat by faded dusty tapestries and carpets; rich and glowing once, these were now the relics of a past when Frances, his wife, had entertained the county, or gathered round her the artistic circle of her younger days.

Her portrait hung above the stair. The flowing dress and

graceful pose, set against a background of trees and meadow, richly green – these were the classic attributes of aristocracy, portrayed by Romney with all the mastery for which he had been famous. My grandmother had been among his patrons: yet, as I looked, it seemed that honesty, not flattery, lay in his painting of her direct uncompromising glance; or the mouth, its curve made sweeter by a smile I thought more like my mother's than my own.

'You see?' Charles turned to me. 'That is how Sir Henry will, I am certain, be persuaded. You resemble her so much – the more so lately, I believe, since we have been together . . . He was devoted to her – yet not entirely faithful to her, so they say – '

For an instant I was shocked. Then I remembered.

'But she had a lover, too – a poet who died in France, in the Terror. My mother wrote of it; and afterwards, Grandmother lost her faith in revolution.'

'As so many did. Yes – but there's another tale, that she was loved by Fletcher Christian, who joined the *Bounty* when he was rejected in favour of Sir Henry. Both, of course, were her cousins – and they did not care for one another, not surprisingly. But the mutiny soon severed all connection with the Christian part of the family, excepting for Aunt Nicolson. She dislikes to hear of it – but has managed, at least, to restore her relations with Sir Henry.'

So there was yet another strand in the past disputes among the Curwen family! And I am part of it, I thought – but stand here like a stranger. Charles, if he could, would tie me more closely to them. I might indeed have been a Curwen all my life, belonging here – but for one man, who dominates us, every one of us . . .

My grandfather held the key to happiness with Charles, just as he had had the power to change my mother's life. Yet I had lately believed him to be at heart a man who felt compassion, whom many, including my own mother, had admired and loved: surely he could not repeat his cruelty a second time – no man with any gentleness would do so. When he returned to Workington I would try to see him, to give him the message his

[227]

daughter had charged me with. After so long, he might receive me now – and all might yet be well.

Aunt Nicolson at last, as summer came, appeared improved; yet I had not dared to tell her of Charles' intentions or my own increasing hopes. Something still held me back: a sense, perhaps, that such procrastination might enable our closeness of the winter months to be restored, as I dearly wished. Indeed, I almost welcomed the respite brought by my cousin's leaving Working-ton for Cockermouth, where, from his brother's house, he could set in motion all the alterations planned for Lorton Grange. Then when I paid the visit promised to Isabella in her home at Brigham, I should be able, Charles assured me, to inspect the changes for myself.

Meantime, to my surprise, one morning my aunt declared herself ready for an expedition. We would take the ponies up to Ennerdale, where I might draw the cottages while she visited old Susan – whom she had not seen since our maid had left her grandmother and the hillside home where she was reared.

'You have been looking very pale of late, Georgiana – an excursion will do you good! I feel quite myself again, and I'd rather a pony and the open air than all the calls and drawing-rooms in Cumberland. Folk may think as they please – but if poor Hattie Sharpe had taken exercise, she might be with us still!'

Her enthusiasm, for a time, surpassed my own. And those days were a delight. Long mornings spent in painting, reliving my childhood pleasure in the shapes and colours of grasses, leaves or flowers. The chatter and dazzle of water in the rocky becks; the sound of larks – persistent in their rising song from early hours, when we left the town, until we forsook the moorland for the high-banked tracks which took us home again. Of all the Lakeland places I have known, the rolling hills and hidden waters of that dale are closest to my heart: I remember still the arresting glory of sea and sky, their bands of colour reaching north to south like a gilded cloth – crimson and rose and green – as we rode into the evening light.

Even when, as often happened, a sudden storm of rain pursued us, we would wrap ourselves in heavy waterproofs and press ahead, perhaps to some rough shelter where Josh, who sometimes took us by the wilder paths, would shake his head and mutter unintelligibly. My aunt would counter with, 'There's far worse storms at sea, my man; and many a soul would be glad to be where we are!'; then she would continue, her face into the wind. Emily, on our return, chased her nephew back to the Dragon, telling him my aunt was 'fair worn out'; while I responded, laughing, 'Why, it's the other way about! I tell you, Em, Aunt Nicolson is hardier than southern folk – and she has no mercy on us!'

'I cannat say as to that, miss – but there's something put a bonny spark into you, right enough. Tek a look in the glass, now – and you'll not see a lass that's wastin' away, that's for certain sure!'

She was right: the happiness within me was visible, even to my own reluctant gaze. Surely my aunt must notice such a change – yet Charles had written that I should not speak to her before he came again to Workington himself; then, together, we would go to Isabella, who would surely understand our feeling for each other. His notes came infrequently enough; yet I was satisfied, for he spoke of a future to be shared, in which – so blindly – I believed.

And Sir Henry? It was past midsummer; he was now at home. His carriage had passed me one morning, even as I had approached the gates – but my resolution, when the moment came, had failed me. It was as though that arbitrary fate which sometimes tugged me, almost against my will, in one direction, now withheld its hand, letting me drift unseeing on a different course, towards an unknown shore.

When, as I anticipated, my guardian wearied of riding with me and took up once more the routine of her life in Workington, it was Susan who replaced her. She had kept my secret well throughout the months; and I had learned, moreover, that it was she who drew Josh Pratt so often from the Dragon to frequent our kitchen – much to Emily's voluble annoyance.

Peter, however, had become attached to Josh, learning all he could from him: though he helped me in the garden still, he was determined, he told me, to find himself work with horses when he left us. For I had realised sadly that he would not be needed when next winter came, and I must try to find him something; Charles had said no more to me of his suspicions, but Peter feared him still. And there was now his father to be thought of; for Jem, at last, had brought us news of him.

'He means to take us to Ireland, miss – it cannat be long now, Jem says. He's to go with us to Whitehaven, to meet my father there, for to get a boat he knows of. But I'd rather stay with you – and the little ones will be glad enough to go, I reckon.'

'But he will be grieved to leave you; and you might find the work you want in Ireland.'

'Why no, miss. There's nowt but thieves and beggars in Ireland, Rosa says. And no work neither – he's a fool, she says, to go there. And a fearful long way it is, further than Scotland – and I hates the sea, miss.'

He had said that before, I remembered: perhaps I had been foolish after all to let him come. Michael Stephens might not get away from Ravenglass – but if he did, he would not wish to lose the boy he loved.

I did not try to persuade him further, but waited while he made the ponies ready. Susan was to go with me to fetch a fleece that day from Ennerdale; for I had watched her grandmother spinning the fine grey Herdwick wool, fascinated by the way the old woman's fingers, bent and knotted though they were, had spun so deftly, even in the darkness of her chimney corner. Her husband, long ago, had been one of Sir Henry's shepherds; and she had many tales to tell of how their landlord visited their cottage, eager to learn the skills of rearing upland flocks, and never too proud to sit beside their fire. Sometimes, she said, his little daughter had sat astride his horse in front of him – though often she fell asleep before they left, and he would wrap her in his cloak to keep her warm.

That evening, as we rode down the valley in the dusk, I thought of him – the great Sir Henry and his sleeping child, my mother, who little knew what the future held as they too followed the grassy track to Workington. It was cold now; Susan and I were glad of our heavy cloaks of coarse grey duffle, which warded off the breeze blowing in from the open sea. We had not meant to return so late; but that morning we had waited for the mist to clear. Even so, we had had a chilly ride, though I had, on an impulse before leaving, exchanged my lighter, scarlet cloak for one similar to my companion's – a decision for which, before too long, I was profoundly thankful.

The path was familiar, and there was sufficient early moonlight to take us safely home. Even so, I was relieved when we reached the square, and dismounted to lead the ponies along the narrow passage to the yard. Susan went ahead, lifting the heavy fleece from her mount as she passed into the pool of light shed by the lamp above the wooden door. Her sudden scream, the noise of the startled ponies, brought Josh and Peter from the stable, their shouts increasing the confusion. But I had seen the flash of steel, a knife raised in the lamplight – and heard a voice, which surely I recognised, from the figure running past me down the close.

Pursuit was impossible; bidding Peter catch the ponies, I helped Josh carry Susan to the shelter of the stable. Here, by his lantern, we saw that the fleece – praise God! – had caught the fiercest blow, though it was badly stained already from a shallow wound in Susan's arm. This we bathed with water from the pump, then bound with rags as clean as we could find; and Josh produced from his pocket (I did not ask him how it came to be there!) a brandy flask which quickly proved its value.

'It were better not to tell the mistress – she'll play the very divil if she finds I did not go wi' you. And for the night, the lass would be better at the Dragon wi' Mistress King, I reckon.'

He was right. Susan could walk that little distance, she protested, with his help; and there had been so far no sign that my aunt, from her front parlour, had heard anything amiss. Making them promise to fetch a doctor – 'The young one, mind,' said Josh, 'for t'other's nowt but an owd fool, any road!' – I saw them go; and wearily, with Peter, soon had the ponies safely stabled.

But the boy was weeping when I came to leave him. Gently, my arm about him, I bade him get some rest; but he looked at me despairingly, pointing to the knife which lay, still with the Herdwick fleece, in a corner of the yard. As I retrieved it Peter muttered something which I did not catch. But as I held the knife – of a kind common enough, used by the fishermen for the herring, down on the quay – the boy, still sobbing, showed me a curious mark upon the handle.

''Tis my father's, miss – he marked it, so as he could find it easy in the boat. There! I know for sure it is, for there cannat be another knife the same!'

I could not bear to see the look in Peter's eyes – nor could I reject the fearful certainty which came upon me then. As I took him in my arms and tried to comfort him, I knew that we shared the same conviction – and a grief far worse than on that summer day, a year ago, when he had told me that the fisherman might hang. For then we had believed him innocent; or at worst, his violence had been provoked and was not evil in intent.

But now that violence had come – as Charles had warned – to the heart of Portland Square. Michael Stephens had cause to hate the Curwens, as he himself had told me, in his cottage long ago. That the blow had been intended for myself, I was convinced: only my change of cloak had saved me, for Susan and I were similar in height, hard to distinguish without the conspicuous scarlet which I often wore.

I knew that the fisherman would soon be gone to Ireland. Had he therefore attempted some kind of vengeance upon the Curwens, before escaping there – in spite of the assistance I had given him?

For – though I had not said as much to Peter – I had recognised the voice of the assailant; had glimpsed, in the lamplight, the raven hair of Michael Stephens' sister. Yet one thing puzzled me, as I lay awake that night: why – if she had gone with him from Allonby – had she not remained with Philip Earnshaw? I could find no answer, and the morning brought me none; only Peter, who had known of his father's leaving Ravenglass, might know what had happened to the Irish girl, and where she had fled to now.

But the boy was not in the yard, when I looked for him. Nor did he ever seek me out again. As suddenly and strangely as he came into my life, he vanished. And it was many months before I learned where he had gone.

Chapter 17

It was peaceful at Brigham. Isabella's garden, sheltered by a mellow wall and shaded by the fine old trees so often to be found beside an English rectory, soothed for a time the troubled spirit in which I came from Workington. And it was here I was to learn, at last, of the tricks which love can play with judgement, and how we often most deceive ourselves (and others) when we think we know the truth.

Charles had insisted, on hearing of the danger to which we had been exposed, that Susan and I should go at once to Isabella.

'You will both be safer there. And Aunt Nicolson will not object – indeed, she has mentioned that you planned a visit to my sister.'

He had come in quick response to the letter I had sent, unable any longer to suppress the fear and the uncertainty which darkened every day. Even Mr Jameson had observed my pallor and fatigue, my work unfinished and attention easily distracted from his lesson. And I was afraid that he would soon inform Aunt Nicolson.

'I should have liked to speak to her about you.' I sighed as I spoke, despite my cousin's kiss of reassurance. 'I cannot deceive her any longer, Charles. It is wrong to do so now. And she knows that you have written to me – I have not tried to hide that from her at least.'

Concealment had become a burden, increasingly since I had seen my aunt restored to her usual vigour. And I could not understand why Charles had delayed, yet again, his interview with Sir Henry. He had convinced me, when I confided my purpose to him, that I should not go myself – and now, from Brigham, I should have no chance to do so. Yet still it seemed to me the best, and most honest, hope. As never before, I longed to give my mother's message to her father, to cross the void which must – until one of us should yield that Curwen pride! – remain between us.

Even had Charles not been important to me, I should have wished by now to meet Sir Henry. And though I dreaded the furore which must follow if we told him of our hopes, I could not welcome further secrecy.

'Surely,' I urged, 'he must be still more opposed if we do not tell him soon. He will think me guilty of the same deception as my mother – and will hate me even more because of it. Oh why, when you were so sure he would accept me, love me even – for our grandmother's sake if not my own – must we continue waiting?'

'Because, my darling, there are matters of which you know nothing – which must be dealt with first. If I anger him, he will cut off my means to remain at Lorton, before I am scarcely settled there. I cannot – will not – risk losing the only place I care for. You say you would be happy with me anywhere: but I shall only be content at Lorton – with or without you. I want you there with me, heaven knows I do! But if we are to marry, you cannot ask me to be other than I am!'

'I – would not wish you otherwise,' was my answer – for I loved him still.

Indeed, I could not have wished that he should give up Lorton. Cumberland was his birthplace and his home; and though I had returned, I did not feel the bond so strongly, would never know the power which a place exerts on those whose roots are deeply struck within it. But I was learning now that for men there may be more important things than love – and that sometimes a man would sooner lose his woman than his land.

So I went to Brigham sadly, exhausted by events at

Workington and with no certainty that I might confide in Isabella. And when, as we sat together in her garden, she told me that she expected, in the spring, to have a child, I envied her, and wished that I could bear within myself the assurance of my happiness with Charles.

There are some men, I have observed, who cannot resist a challenge – whether it be a battle, or a gamble, or a woman. For such a man, conquest is all: once gained, the prize may be relinquished, and the pain of loss assuaged by contemplation of another goal, desirable as the first and not as yet reduced to that most irksome state – familiarity. To his friends, he is a charming, reckless fellow; to himself, the epitome of daring, for whom failure is inconceivable, save by some reverse of fortune rather than through any weakness of his own. For a woman caught up by the tide of his determined enthusiasm, there is at first the delightful sensation of inevitability – to which she happily surrenders, knowing nought of consequences, nothing of the empty shore where she is finally cast up, and left alone.

But there are other men to whom such self-betrayal is abhorrent, who prefer to keep their passions to themselves – whose drama, always, is within. The love affairs of such a man seem often casual; yet clearly he has studied their potential and calculated his chances to the nicest degree, so that he may, at their ending, emerge apparently unscathed. Happiness appears not to be relevant to his needs, which may be satisfied as well by one woman as by another; to love him is to court rejection, or at best, uncertainty. For if he cares he will not readily admit it; and there is, with him, no likelihood of self-committal – save in the secrecy of his heart.

More rarely (yet I have known such a one), there is the man who does not seek to conquer or exploit. His love has little guile – and therefore little self-protection in the face of female cruelty, which can destroy as thoroughly as that of any man. But his passion, clear as water from the deepest well, and lacking all the glitter of the shallow stream, will rarely be withheld by mere caprice, or be diverted from its chosen course.

*

'It is Mr Earnshaw, miss. Will I show him to the parlour – or is he to come out to you, miss?'

'Why – is not my cousin down yet? He would rather see her, I am sure.' Whatever Philip might prefer, I did not wish to see him!

'No, miss. Asked particular for Miss Curwen, he did – and says he don't have too much time, neither . . . The mistress will be ready shortly.'

Patiently, the maid was waiting for instructions, while I tried to curb the distress I felt at the thought of meeting Philip. I could not refuse, in another's household. Soon Isabella must appear; John would have left the evening service and be on his way through the churchyard to the garden gate. I need not be long alone with Philip . . .

'Tell him – a moment only. It will soon be dinner-time.'

I had not answered his letter, had heard no word from him since Christmas. Surely, but for the attack at Portland Square, I should by now have forgotten him entirely. Here, I had allowed the quiet garden and my cousin's gentle company to ease the shock of those events; I had even begun, at last, to paint once more. But Philip Earnshaw had come to disturb my peace again . . .

He was, I saw at once, much altered. More grave, older-seeming, careworn almost – less remote, indeed, as he came with outstretched hand toward me, speaking with a warmth to which I could not – must not – respond. As always, when with him, I felt compelled to admit that he exercised such power, that I felt curiously helpless in his presence – and in this respect, at least, he had not changed. But only coldness now, if not open anger, must be my response to such a man as he.

I ignored the proffered handshake, hardened my voice.

'Good evening, Mr Earnshaw.'

He was shocked, even more than I intended. Turning from him, I wished quite desperately that Isabella would come quickly – anything rather than speak to him again.

'Are you well, Miss Curwen? Have I – caused you offence in some way?'

I could almost have laughed at such underestimation of the

truth! As it was, I was trembling – closer to outraged tears than I must let him realise.

'Thank you. I am in perfect health.'

'Then I *have* offended you! Is that why you did not answer my letter?'

I remained silent. A blackbird sang, too close and sweet to be ignored, more ironic than appropriate.

'Can it be that someone – Charles Curwen, perhaps – has influenced you against me? Yet you assured me of your friendship, I remember.'

'Our conversation seems not to have progressed in the year since last we met, Mr Earnshaw. You spoke ill of my cousin then; and now, as then, I prefer to disregard your opinion and maintain my own. If it were not that Isabella might be saddened by it, I should not have spoken with you now. I do not share her illusion as to the goodness of your character.'

The church bells, ringing for the end of evensong, sounded strangely far away. I need wait no longer than a few more moments – surely John would be with us, and I might go . . .

'Then I am sorry that my own illusions were not dispelled the sooner.' It was Philip's turn to be dismissive. 'I believed you would show kindness to – '

Why did his voice, so clear and firm always, falter now, as if some deep emotion troubled him? He looked away, appeared to make an effort to regain composure; then continued: 'I hoped, wrongly it seems, that you and my sister Charlotte might become acquainted. She would have welcomed your friendship had she not – had she returned with me, as I so dearly hoped, and as I wrote – '

Once more he appeared too moved to continue – or to notice the agitation I now felt. Bewilderment, anxiety, a sense that I must have made some grievous error – a tumult of thoughts, discordant as the ringing bells beyond the garden walls. And Philip, staring past me, more distant than if he had been in Paris still, or Switzerland, or anywhere but here beside me.

His sister . . . Charlotte . . . The name, I suddenly recalled, of the girl whose paintings I had seen at Keswick – who had gone, I was told, to Yorkshire with her parents. So it was she of whom

Philip had written in his letter, who had been with him in Switzerland – she, and not the Irish girl! And now there was nothing I could do to repair the breach between us, no way in which I could explain that past confusion, or my present coldness to him.

'Will you – tell me more of your sister?' was all that I could say.

'There is very little.' His finality increased my fear that I had hurt him quite irreparably. Yet he did continue.

'Charlotte is – she was – my youngest sister. More than a year ago she went to Belgium as a governess, against my parents' wishes. While in France I went to see her to persuade her to return – but found her ill, and alone. I took her to Switzerland, to friends, and there I remained – until her death . . . That is all, Miss Curwen . . . I apologise for causing you concern!'

His irony, his scorn, the knowledge that I had added to his grief, were all that I deserved.

I made him the only answer possible.

'No – it is I who must make apology, to you, for my – my deficiency of understanding, for distressing you. I – it is only that I thought – '

How could I go on – how speak of my suspicions? I could not!

'You thought what, Miss Curwen?' He spoke without emotion now.

'It is nothing! Only – only that I thought you were in Cumberland, when I supposed you to be in France. But I was mistaken . . .'

The bells had ceased; the garden lay quite still.

'But I did return to England – from France, before I found my sister. I came to Keswick to consult with Mary and her husband, then went to Carlisle, and south again by the coast – '

'To Allonby?' The question was out before I could prevent it – even as Philip stopped short, and gave me a startled glance.

'It is true! But how can you have learned it? And what more do you know of this – this wretched business of – ' His urgency astonished me.

'Why, I know no more: only that I was with my aunt at Allonby and saw you there with someone who – whom I recognised.' Wearily, for it seemed that my fears were, after all, about to be confirmed, I went on, 'It – it is of no consequence – it matters nothing to me now.'

'But it is of consequence – to both of us, Miss Curwen!'

In the pause which followed I saw that Philip's fingers had tightened upon the whip and gloves he carried; and when he spoke again it was with a quiet fury which he did nothing to conceal.

'It matters because I cannot tell you why I went to Allonby; because my errand there was another's, not my own. And because to tell you more might destroy your happiness – which I have no wish to do. Though God knows I cannot help but wonder if any happiness is worth so much distress!'

His anger, and the cause of it, were beyond my comprehension. At that moment, whatever the truth might be – I did not want to know it! However it had come about, I had only added to the pain he felt already: that was all I knew, and all that mattered to me . . .

'Mr Earnshaw – Philip!' I cried. 'I am only sorry to have grieved you – deeply sorry that any happiness of mine should bring harm to you, or anyone. And I wish with all my heart that I might have known your sister!'

With that I left him. I ran past my cousin as she came down the steps into the garden; and only when I had regained my room did I allow myself, at last, to weep without restraint. But whether they were tears of sorrow or of shame, or even love – I did not know.

Later, in the calmness of reflection, the full significance of Philip's words began to penetrate my mind. He had gone to Allonby, he said, on behalf of another person; and to tell me more could be the ruin of my happiness. I could not disbelieve him this time; and, that being so, could no longer make myself forget his warning – more than a year before – of some kind of danger connected with my cousin Charles.

Yet my cousin too had warned me of danger. He had questioned me closely about the woman who, as I had confessed to him, had struck at Susan with intent to kill me; and when he had learned of Peter's disappearance, Charles had spoken grimly

[239]

(as Aunt Nicolson once had done) of the wicked Irish, making it clear that he believed I had been foolish in my protection of the boy. Though still I had not mentioned Michael Stephens to him, I knew that all the evidence pointed to his complicity in the attack – and I could only wonder now if I should have told my cousin this, and allowed him to bring the fisherman, at last, to the hanging he deserved.

But somehow, I could not forget the sense of total safety I had felt, when I sat with Michael Stephens' arm about me on the windswept shore. Or the look of reluctant affection in his eyes when he spoke of taking me to Ravenglass – 'away from the likes of the Curwens', he had said. Then he had spoken of the injustice of a world where such as he must pay the price of their offences, while other, richer folk went free . . . And he too, as I remembered now, had warned me – of someone who might speak sweetly but would bring me harm, someone whom I should not trust . . .

But whom could I trust now? How could I learn the truth, if none would tell me? Surely, I reasoned, I am not such a child that I must be protected from whatever evil others know; yet men always seem to think a woman must be sheltered from reality, only allowed such knowledge as they judge most fitting for her soft dependent nature, or such as suits their own intentions best. I resolved that when Philip called again, as he had promised Isabella, I would question him. If he refused me, I must ask my cousin Charles why he would not make his peace with Philip. For they had quarrelled, I was certain, over a matter which concerned myself; and I would rather learn the worst, whatever sorrow it might cause me, than remain in ignorance of something which I ought to know.

In the event, however, it was from Isabella that I discovered more of what lay behind that disagreement. And I was glad then that I had told her nothing of my own relationship with Charles, though I had so often longed to do so. She was speaking first of Philip's sister Charlotte, whom she remembered with some sadness from her visits to the Nicolsons at Keswick.

'She looked very like him – tall and dark – and she alarmed me rather, she was so clever and outspoken, and quite determined not to stay at home as her parents wished. My brother, I fear, behaved very foolishly toward her: he has no common sense where young ladies are concerned, and they always let him flatter them. And though he meant no harm by it, Mary and Philip were displeased, as they had every right to be. I even spoke to him myself, but Charles is like any brother – certain always that sisters know nothing at all!'

Isabella sighed, and stitched at the garment she was making for one of John's parishioners: they were always glad, she had averred, of warm things for the children when the winter came.

'And Charles is so impetuous – he was wrong to break with Philip. They were excellent friends at Cambridge; and had it not been for that, my brother would have been in difficulties there. He lost a great deal of money, I think, at Newmarket; I never knew quite what it was all about, but Charles was very much indebted to Philip, and shouldn't forget it so easily.'

So that was why she had sent her brother's friend the Byron poems – in gratitude, as the inscription indicated. And I could see now why Philip Earnshaw had expressed such admiration for her character: for Isabella was, despite her gentleness, firm in her opinions, and clearly not afraid, when needful, to oppose her brother.

But what was I to think of Charles – or of myself? I loved him, yet knew it was beyond my power to understand him. He was elusive, like the sunlight and shadow on an April morning: a man who might persuade any girl, it seemed, to think him perfection – for a time. Perhaps I meant no more to him than any other he had flattered; perhaps there were many he had charmed, convinced – possessed. All that summer, dreaming that he lay beside me or thinking I heard his voice in the song of larks in Ennerdale, I had known – I had surely known – that it might be so.

But he had sought me out, had loved me . . . No, I would not quite believe it yet. He will come again soon, I told myself, from Lorton; he has promised to take me there – and I will not doubt it yet!

*

There is a little school at Brigham. The building which houses it looks severe enough, standing four-square and unadorned upon a rise, halfway between the church and a group of cottages. Beyond these a lane passes through the village, leading toward the hills – which appear, on an early autumn afternoon, sharply defined against the sky, as if a child had drawn them on a card and cut them out, leaving jagged edges where the scissors slipped.

I could see the hills each day, as I walked the parish with Isabella. We visited the sick and aged in their cottages, tried to think of ways and means to help the labourers who had no work – so many facing a cruel northern winter with little hope. Though I disliked to recognise the contrast between their lives and our own, their homes and the comforts of the rectory from which we came, I could only admire the courage with which my cousin set about her tasks. She possessed my uncle Richard's diffidence and kindness rather than her mother's pride – which I had sometimes noticed, as I now admitted to myself, in Charles. But I looked for him still, hoping to see the Emperor tethered at the gate, or Charles riding down the lane, from the hills which lay between us. The distance seemed so short; yet I was daily conscious of my dwindling hopes, of my growing certainty that something grave must be amiss.

Some afternoons, rather than sit in the garden or sew with my cousin, I went instead to the school, where I would help the older children with their reading. The teacher, a man of declining years and uneven temper, was grateful for assistance; and though I had never thought to find teaching any pleasure, it proved, to my surprise, a congenial occupation. Often I would sketch pictures for the children, and ask them to spell the meanings upon their slates or in their copy-books – though I dared not prolong the amusement it afforded, in case of the teacher's disapproval. I little thought that I might one day be glad of even the small experience I gained at Brigham in that mild September: then, I welcomed rather the knowledge that I was of use – reminded often, as I sat among these children, of Peter and his sisters. The boy's disappearance – at a time when his need of me was greatest – grieved me still: I could only hope that when I returned to Workington, before the month was out, I should find him waiting for me.

Late one afternoon, my pupils had been dismissed, and some were lingering at the doorway, when I saw Charles walk quickly past the window of the schoolroom. I had heard a horse go by, only half an hour before – but had repressed the urge to run to the door, had told myself sternly that it was foolish of me to expect my cousin now. Perhaps he spoke to the teacher, or to the children as they scattered down the steps: I remember only that I heard his voice, that he was, within moments, beside me – and that my own eager welcome died on my lips when I saw the look of disapproval in his eyes.

'I am come to escort you home, Georgiana. Though why – ' he glanced about him with distaste – 'you should choose to waste your afternoons in such a fashion I cannot comprehend. You might be riding, or painting out of doors on such a perfect day. Surely Isabella can provide you with better amusement?'

'Isabella would have come herself, I think – but she needs to rest a little now. And besides, the children would be disappointed if neither of us came.'

Hastily I gathered up my pencils, and laid out the copy-books for the teacher to inspect. Hurt and perplexed by Charles' impatience, I tried to conceal my apprehension, recalling that only once before had I seen him so openly ill-tempered. Perhaps, as at Cockermouth, when he met us at the Globe, there was some cause other than my own behaviour: now as then, perhaps, his parents might have urged that he marry a woman of their choice . . .

'I am glad that you came to meet me – though the walk is never a hardship to me. It is less than a mile, and I enjoy it, always.'

No answer. He merely offered me his arm, and accompanied me in silence until we reached the path through the churchyard, the way I usually took. The leaning mossy stones and overhanging elms – their leaves already turning golden, some even fallen among the grass through which we walked – made this a tranquil place, far different from the windswept churchyard of Saint Michael's. Yet today it offered neither peace nor consolation – no shelter from the chill reality within myself.

[243]

For I knew that this time the alchemy of absence had no power to bind me to my cousin. This time he seemed as distant as the hills, though he had come to me; and whatever might have brought about the change in him – that change had only served to harden my resolve. To know the truth could scarcely make me more unhappy; and I could no longer bear to have him walk beside me as a stranger.

'Charles – will you not tell me what is wrong? There is something, some reason why you have not come before.'

At last I had turned to face him. Yet he did not look at me as he answered.

'The reason is simple, Georgiana – and you must, by now, have guessed it. Earnshaw – ' he spoke the name with undisguised resentment – 'Earnshaw has been here: and I do not thank him for it. But it is done; and now – I do not wish you to come to me, to Lorton.'

Indeed I had anticipated it. Yet to be told so plainly, with so little feeling, that he did not want me, was more hurtful almost than to have my fear confirmed. Moreover, his very coolness masked a greater turbulence; his guarded manner, I could sense, hid something of importance – but still I was not allowed to know the cause.

'May I not ask why you do not want me there?' I could scarcely believe my own composure now: perhaps it is always so when such a moment comes at last. And Charles, it was clear, had no wish to answer me.

'Philip has told me nothing, other than the circumstances of his sister's death. He refused, indeed, to tell me more – for my own sake, he said. But why should you – and he – have been so anxious for my safety, yet so determined to keep the reason from me? And now you say I must not come to Lorton – and you will not tell me why!'

Again that silence. The kind of silence which reinforces anger, making one speak openly at last.

'I am weary of deceiving people, Charles. My aunt, your sister, even Sir Henry – we have deceived them all, delayed and evaded because you said it must be so. At first I was willing enough, because I knew you loved me. But now I am weary of

[244]

deception, and of being treated as a child. And if neither you nor Philip will tell me what is wrong, I shall find out by other means.'

Charles had seized my arm, and would have spoken; but I went on, uncaring.

'I shall find out why each of you, at different times, has warned me of danger. It has come close enough to me already; and rather than have Susan hurt again, or Aunt Nicolson alarmed, I shall seek out Mary Stephens and discover why she hates me so. The truth cannot make me more unhappy than I am!'

Almost until the words were said, I had not known what I intended. But even as I spoke, conviction grew; and I knew at once, from the look Charles gave me then, that I had found him out. For there was fear in my cousin's eyes, and his face was pale: my laughing, charming cousin – whom I loved – was, for some reason, quite afraid.

But then he smiled – that easy, ready smile which so often had persuaded me.

'You are an innocent, Georgiana – an innocent, and that is why I love you!' His hand was holding mine, and his eyes were no longer fearful, but warm with the feeling I had longed – until now – to see there.

'That girl would have killed you – would do so now if she knew where to find you. And you think of seeking her out – as if she were a harmless creature, like Emily or Susan. No, my darling, you must be patient: by the time you are in Workington again, Mary Stephens will be gone to Ireland – and then you and I will both be safe enough!'

He tried to kiss me, but I moved away and shook his hand from mine. This time I would not be put off with tender words or gentle condescension.

'And yet I may not come to Lorton – and still you do not tell me why. Nor why she is a danger to you, as well as to myself. How do you know that she will go – and what does Mary Stephens mean to you?'

Charles stared before him, as if making up his mind. Then he looked at me – a hard, quite careless look, from which all persuasiveness was gone.

'Since you insist, little cousin, you shall be told. Mary was – something – to me once: now she is nothing – save a threat to all my hopes. Last year – after Keswick – she was given money; then she demanded more, which Earnshaw gave her. Somehow she came to know of you and of our meetings – though I had thought her still at Allonby, or Maryport. Now she has been paid again, and is quiet enough; and I believe will go to Ireland rather than remain and risk the law. She knows I shall set them after her, as I did her brother – when he threatened me last year, and almost killed a man who came between us; but I will do it only if I must, for then the whole of Workington would hear of it, and at all costs I must keep it from Sir Henry.

'So that, Georgiana, is the woman you would seek – and that boy of yours is another of the clan. I would send the lot of them back to Ireland if I could!'

I had listened to him with a curious detachment, almost as if it were a tale some other man had told – not my cousin who had cared for me. How simply all the pieces of the pattern fitted now, like those of an Eastern puzzle I had found at Portland Square: its secret had eluded me until my aunt had twisted it a certain way – when suddenly, I understood it all.

But Charles was speaking now of Lorton. His voice was low, intense with feeling, his indifference changed to bitterness.

'And so, until Sir Henry makes me otherwise, I am too poor to marry. I dare not let you come to Lorton. I cannot risk the loss of everything. That girl has come between us, just as she meant to do. So Earnshaw, with his philanthropic moralising, claims that I have wronged you both: maybe he is right.' He shrugged his shoulders. 'Yet you at least have loved me in return: but Mary Stephens hates me – and that is also mutual!'

My cousin laughed, stirring at a heap of fallen leaves with the toe of his shiny boot. It was true – I had loved him. But could I love him still?

Suddenly I longed to take him in my arms, to soften that bleak look from his eyes, to bring the warmth back into his laughter, as I had done on that winter evening at Portland Square. I would tell him what he meant to me; there might, even yet, be some hope of happiness with him . . .

But then I remembered the Irish girl as I had seen her first, carefree among the morning fishermen down at the quayside; and later, her curses as she faced me on the cottage step. She had cursed her brother too: no wonder he had hated all the Curwens, and had guessed at once that I was one of them – as now I felt ashamed to be!

And the child? The child I had, so long ago, held in my arms? . . . I was convinced now that it was my cousin's child – but I would never tell him that I knew. Nor should he ever know how I had helped the fisherman: Michael Stephens must go free – that at least the Curwens owed him. For my cousin had betrayed the girl: he had not merely charmed or flattered her, but had discarded her – as a child might throw away a once-loved toy, to replace it with another which has caught his fancy.

'You *have* wronged Mary Stephens, Charles. But as for myself – '

I could not continue, for now I doubted everything: I doubted his love and my own, and wondered whether I had ever known my cousin as he really was.

'And how many other men,' he was saying, 'would have done as much by Mary? She has gained by it, and I have lost. Such women have no feelings!' He folded his arms; and his scorn at once aroused my anger.

'That is untrue,' I cried. 'She feels as much as you, or I, or any other person must. You cannot believe such things: you would not say it if she were your sister – or my own.'

Charles laughed again, this time in disbelief.

'And you, little cousin, know nothing of the world. One does not think of such a creature as one would a sister – as worthy of such respect, or even love. They are different from ourselves!'

'And therefore to be used, and then abandoned?' It was I who was scornful now.

'No, Charles, she is not, of course, my sister – except in my imagination or my dreams, in a way which you will never understand!' I could see his puzzlement begin to turn to anger.

'She is different from myself, or Isabella, only in her circumstance, not in her nature. Had I not been born a Curwen, had not Aunt Nicolson recalled her duty as my guardian, I should have been no better than the like of Mary Stephens. I would have gone from Maidenhead to be a servant – anything to leave the Chattertons; and I would have known the poverty and misery which make such girls as Mary what they are. Unless I had died of cold that winter as so many did, like a wretched woman of the fields . . .'

But there was only incomprehension written on my cousin's face. More than the hills lay between us now – and more, far more, than the threat which a jealous fisher-girl had posed.

'Indeed, I do not understand why you should entertain such notions. I could not tolerate them in a wife of mine – no lady has such thoughts.'

'Then I am not – perhaps will never be – a lady, Charles. I had no thought of marriage when I loved you first; and now – I have no wish to marry you.'

It was the truth, which came upon me without premeditation.

'But perhaps,' I added bitterly, 'a lady would not have cared for you as I have done!'

For an instant only, I could see that I had hurt him; and in that instant, too, I feared that Charles might strike me, as he moved towards me with a sudden violence in his look. But it was, I think, his pride that I had wounded – not his heart. For he restrained himself, and answered with a calculating, mocking tone which he clearly hoped might wound me in return.

'Cousin – you are indeed an innocent. Why, you took me to your bed so willingly – as none of our young ladies with their coquettish airs would do: and yet you seem as careless as any child of how the world would use you if it learnt what you had done. No gentleman would choose to marry such a woman; and I shall consider it my duty as a Curwen to find some other as my wife.'

He walked away from me across the churchyard, to the gate which led to Isabella's garden. I shall not follow him, I thought; and I was, indeed, too exhausted to do more than sink down upon a mossy stone. Resting my head against my arm, heedless of the tranquil dead around me, I did not weep. For I was cold with a sense of loss – of cruel and unremitting loss – which outweighed all other feeling.

'Georgiana.'

For a few moments I did not raise my head to look at Charles. But when at last I did so, and allowed him to take my hand, it was with no hope that all our bitter words might be forgotten. That could never be. Though we returned together to the garden, we were now apart: and this time I had no wish to break the silence which lay between us.

That day I felt despair; then anger – fury of a kind which I had hitherto not known. For it seemed to me that love, which had proved so sweet, had become a tainted thing. Like some tempting, poisoned morsel set before a starving man, it had brought a temporary joy – succeeded by the knowledge that such happiness is bought at the expense of others' pain, and leaves one empty of desire, of all save an instinct to survive.

And Charles was right. I had been an innocent – beguiled not only by the roses and laughter of a summer afternoon, but by a far-off vision of security: a safety which his arms had seemed to offer me, that shared tranquillity I glimpsed beside the Thames at Maidenhead, and which my mother – in her love for Alexander Grieve – had known and lost. So I raged, for a time, against a fate which offers moonbeams to the traveller – illusions of daylight and transient visions of the path which leads him home; I rebelled against the dissolution of my hopes – though I had known they were but winter's random patterns on the glass through which I looked for spring.

But most of all I was angered by my own misjudgement. My blindness, coupled to the whim of circumstance, had caused me to condemn the man I should have trusted. Foolishly, I had ignored that inner prompting which had told me, more than once, that Philip hid his heart, concealed his feelings through necessity: he had known too much of suffering – his own and that of others – to let his inmost thoughts become an entertainment to the world. Whereas Charles had worn his heart so lightly and – I could not doubt it now – would use another's with as little thought or care as he would give, and then withhold, his own. He had wanted love, it seemed, yet had not known its worth: for when at last he spoke of duty – he had meant, I knew, his duty to himself.

As for marriage, he would regard it, clearly, as a means to make himself secure. Society expected him to do so: daily, men and women make transactions of this kind, however often they may speak of love. It is strange, indeed, how so often duty and self-interest coincide! And how a man, renouncing in the name of duty a girl he has seduced, finds that a fortune comes his way – some inheritance, perhaps, of which he might have been deprived had he not recalled his parents or his family name, the opinions of his friends, the expectations of his rank and class. To a gentleman, a girl like Mary Stephens is the diversion of a moment, to be forgotten when the claims of duty call.

And I could not now forgive my cousin for his use of her. Through her child and Peter, through the suffering and pride of Michael Stephens, her life had touched my own; and though, like Charles, I was a Curwen, I had shared with her the same rejection. She might, in her femininity, have been myself – her child, my own.

Though I would, in time, perhaps regain the vision I had lost, for the present I must make a life alone. I had, at least, the challenge of my work: and if to do it well I must lose the right to think myself a lady – why, I did not care to be one, after all!

Chapter 18

Shortly after my return to Workington, Sir Henry Curwen died. The father of the town, its guiding principle for half a century of change, would speak no more in the defence of honest labourers, or challenge Westminster to implement Reform. His death – long wished-for by his enemies, but unexpected when it came – caused the daily work of harbour, mines and mills to cease, as if the spirit of the man who set so much in motion had been a vital spring, which ordered the machine's precision and could never be replaced.

When Josh came running from the Dragon with the news, Emily and Susan wept. My aunt, dry-eyed, at once rebuked them for their weakness, put on her bonnet and went in search of Captain Sharpe, who had become, since the *Elizabeth*'s return, her closest friend. And though I had never spoken to my grandfather, had glimpsed him no more than a dozen times in twice as many months – I mourned him now. In doing so, perhaps I mourned my mother's loss – of the father for whom she had grieved so long before his death; yet I too felt bereft – deeply regretting the opportunity which I had lost. For even had he rejected me again, I should have tried, for my mother's sake, to see him. And now I would come no closer to Sir Henry Curwen than a stranger might, standing in Saint Michael's on the funeral day. With my aunt I watched as he was laid (not far from the tomb of the brave Sir Christopher) in a grave which at his own request remains unmarked by any monument. As I stood there, surrounded for the first and last time by so many Curwens whom I never wished to know, I resolved that I would go from Cumberland.

Contrary to all the rules of fiction, and consistent to himself, Sir Henry left me nothing. Indeed, though his death affected many (including some who knew him only as a name) it brought benefits to few of his relations. He did not die rich; and even my cousin Charles, whose expectations were so great, must have found his grief made the more severe by disappointment. He inherited a farm or two, according to Aunt Nicolson: but, as she remarked with some asperity, my cousin's wants were always greater than his means, and he had never liked to cut his coat according to necessity. So he pursued the course which providence (and prudence) had left open to him: for within three months my cousin Charles was married – to Miss Morgan-Price of Kendal.

My aunt's bereavement, following so soon upon the loss of Mrs Sharpe, went deeper than might have been supposed, for she had loved her brother, however greatly they had been at odds. But in the following spring the Nicolsons removed to Workington from Keswick. Their friendship was a benefit to both of us; and their proximity diverted her from dwelling too much on Sir Henry's death – or upon the former glories of the Hall, now lying empty and neglected. Sometimes, as I passed the gates with little Edith, I remembered how my mother longed to see her childhood home once more: yet had she done so now, she would have grieved to find those silent shuttered rooms, their light and warmth extinguished and her father gone. She had forgiven him, I knew; and as I read her letters once again (more calmly than at any time before) I understood, at last, why she had done so.

My father was proud & hasty, and his feelings were, I think, too strong, too passionate to be easily contain'd. And so he clung the more to principle; but like many men who are quickly mov'd to love or hate, he fear'd to see such passion in a woman. So when he saw his likeness in myself, he condemn'd it all the more, dreading lest I disgrace the family name or add to the rumours us'd against him by men who envied his success. Your Uncle Richard, gentle and upright always, had the virtues which I lack'd – tho even had he lov'd in secret as I did, he would not have paid the price as I have done.

For the world belongs to men, my daughter. They create its laws & order ev'ry instant of our lives, so that we are forc'd to plot & plan in secret when we wish to choose something for ourselves. It will not be so allways; but for us, even the freedoms a woman had when my mother was a girl, are gone. And the right to love is still call'd sin: a child is punish'd for its parents' wrongs. I married so that you might suffer less; yet they took you, to save you from my influence they said, tho I did not trust them & have often fear'd for you. I beleive they lied, & that when my father learns of it he will forgive me – but never those who came between myself and him.

Often we think we know a person whom we love: yet it is not allways so. Sometimes we only know them truly after parting – which is but another kind of death, without its consolation. So with my father – and so also with your own. For I did not see that Alexander was not fitted for the life to which I drew him: tho he cared truly for me, he had not the force which drives a man to fight for what he loves – & yet I should have lov'd him less had he been otherwise. I hope he found the peace he sought, for he suffer'd for my sake. Perhaps we ask too much of men – expect them to be rocks or shields to us, then wonder why their hardness crushes us. And perhaps when women are allow'd to find their freedom for themselves, there will be more gentleness & freindship possible in men. . . .

I could understand my mother now. Her perception and her loving nature, which had led her to unhappiness and loss, had also helped her to forgive the man who wronged her most. I wished, at last, that I had known her all my life; for her letters told me a truth which one learns best in childhood days – that one should love another person for himself, not only for the picture passion paints of him.

*

Several times, in the year which followed Sir Henry's death, Philip Earnshaw came to Portland Square. We did not speak of Brigham or of Charles: all that was past. Although in later years he told me more of how his friendship with my cousin ended, for the present I remained content to hear his news of Isabella and her child, to read the books he brought from London, and – as my plans became more firm – to seek advice about my painting.

For my lessons with Mr Jameson had ceased. He had taught me with care – if not entirely without prejudice; and before returning to his home at Ambleside, had taken two of my paintings to an exhibition at Carlisle. I made him promise to tell no one but myself; for I was at first reluctant, and – once persuaded – certain that he had misjudged their worth. Then there was the question of my name: to sign them as Georgiana Curwen would be to draw attention to myself – 'and you would be well advised,' my teacher told me, 'to take a man's name for the present, if you wish to sell your work.' Though I had no thought of such a thing, I complied, and duly signed my paintings, *G. F. Grieve*; then I wondered whether Mr Jameson might recognise the name, as that of a friend he once had known. But he said nothing to me, and I did not pursue the matter after all: for I had determined that I should not try to find my father now. One day, perhaps, I might attempt to do so; now I would only use the name he never gave to me – for I felt that it was mine.

I told only Philip of my venture; and when to my surprise my work was sold, I shared with him the delight and trepidation which ensued. For I wished to achieve much more; yet when he offered to take some further work to London, I declared it was far too soon to do so. But I began to think that one day I should go there; and though Mr Jameson shook his head at such a notion, I persisted privately in my intention. When the time was right, I would tell Aunt Nicolson of my success – for I owed it to her; but if I told her now I knew that she would say, 'A single swallow doesn't make a summer, child – and don't let it turn your head!'

I worked on steadily and was content – save when my thoughts, despite all resolution, turned to Charles. Almost a year had passed since I had parted from him, and it pained me still. Nothing more had been heard of Mary Stephens; so my cousin was secure, as he had hoped. Yet her brother's children had remained with Jem and Rosa: the fisherman, as far as they could ascertain, had not gone to Ireland after all. And of Peter, there had been no word.

Workington, without its guide and mentor, was, in that year of national agitation, no less restive than any other northern town. There was rumour that the Curwen interests were insecure; the Hall still had no master – for my Uncle Richard had become reclusive at Belle Isle, while Henry, the eldest son and now in Parliament, had made his home at Cockermouth. The farmland and stock were much reduced; and it was clear – with buildings only half completed, ships lying idle in the harbour – that the prosperous times were gone. Those who had relied on Curwen patronage or bounty must look elsewhere for support, and there were some who feared a prospect of ruin for the town.

So when I saw Hugh Nicolson run hatless across the square one morning, and heard men shouting for horses at the corner by the Dragon; when I rushed with Susan to where a group of women, some already weeping, stood in the November chill, their faces white as the mist which crept in from the shore – it was in fear of some confrontation at the mills, or word of a catastrophic loss at sea. But this was disaster of a different kind.

The news had come from Harrington, along the coast, of a pit explosion far below the ground. Great fires, they said, had blazed since dawn, with a fearful brilliance for yards above the shaft – yet the mine was more than ninety fathoms deep. A torrent of water had swept many to their death; others had been blasted – with horses, baskets, and machinery – into a mass of flesh and metal, high into the air or far along the drifts. Of more than a hundred men and boys who worked there, almost half were gone; and with them, the workings of the Curwens' oldest and most valued mine. There was no division now between the lower and the upper towns: genteel and poor alike, there was scarcely a family in Workington which had not suffered loss. My aunt and I grieved with them. For among the names of those who died that day was Peter Stephens – a boy, they said, who had no home, and whose kin could not be found.

[255]

Was it too fanciful to feel that I had caused his death? I was haunted by the thought. Since the morning of my eighteenth birthday, his life had become entangled with my own; and, as with mine, so also with the lives of Mary Stephens and my cousin Charles. And mingled with my sense of guilt was anger – at the wayward fate which wove the strands together: somehow, it seemed, a nameless and uncaring force had made puppets of us all. When I spoke of it to Philip, he was silent for a time; then told me how in Paris he had seen men kill each other in the streets. 'I felt the fault was mine,' he said. 'Yet could it have been so? If you try to right a wrong, and fail – it is more than if you did not care at all.'

There was a postscript to the story. In the spring of 1833, a few months after Peter's death, I returned to Portland Square from a visit to the Nicolsons. Susan met me at the kitchen steps. A man had called, she said, but had refused to give his name. 'Left no message for you, miss – just asked for you. But he left his stick behind.'

It was placed beside the doorway – a heavy staff of ash; and I knew it as the one I had taken to the fisherman. I saw, when I examined it, that Michael Stephens had – while still at Ravenglass, perhaps – made carvings on it with a knife. There were flowers, a ship, a little bird; and at the top, the unicorns and long-haired mermaid of the Curwen crest – like those engraved on the locket which I wore. He must have learned what had happened to the son he loved; I never saw him, and his children were gone from Jem and Rosa's care. But whatever grudge the fisherman had borne against others of my name, I believed from that day on that he harboured none against myself.

The boy is gone; only a white cat plays on the grass beside me . . . I see now, as I write, the girl in the garden – her dark hair tumbled, her feet bare among the rose-petals. How pale she is, how solemn her gaze – and yet she is not unhappy, for there is a lightness in her step, a more challenging set to her shoulders, thin in the blue gown.

I am wearing, at last, my mother's gown, certain that it was hers; I have seen shirts of that same blue, the same coarse weave, on the backs of men in Workington. I know now why she chose to wear it when she left her home – as I shall do. It will remind me of the summer sea, as I saw it from the height beside the church; it is the colour of the harebells which grow among the hills. And I shall remember, when I wear it in the dark street of a far-off city, that we came from Cumberland – I, and my mother, and the blue-dyed gown.

PART II

London, Paris, Ireland

'Hope obeys no man's nor spirit's bidding;
and to resolve is but to fetter flame with
cords of flax.'

Hartley Coleridge

Chapter 19

The city lies beyond the limits of the garden. This garden is leafless, cold; grass browned and rubbed by the boots of many children, the limbs of trees exposed to the northern gale which sweeps across the ridge of hills, down toward London's smoking chimneys. Shining towers and painted steeples, domes white as the breasts of sleeping women, all lie there – like the distant winking promise of an Orient city in its river-watered plain.

From the narrow window of a narrow room – set among the eaves of the tallest house in Highgate – I can see between the moving branches the first of the winter evening lights. I have learned to expect them, have become accustomed to London – or rather to the consciousness of its immensity, a sprawling dormant monster at the forest edge, the ancient forest which extended, centuries ago, from Highgate to the river Thames. Sometimes the monster fascinates, sometimes it repels me: that sense of a massive heaving life beneath the ridged and pitted outer skin of rooftops; the constant exhalation of its drifting breath, chill and dank in winter, steaming and malodorous when summer's heat strikes down from a cloudless sky; those interweaving veins and arteries which both sustain the city and enmesh it with a deadening constriction – endless streets and alleyways so airless, dark and crammed with men and women, children, crying infants, frail as microscopic particles which swirl and sink and vanish as the river bears them to the sea.

Yes, I had grown accustomed to the city – but not yet reconciled. And this evening (dark already though it was but four o'clock), I looked out at it in anger. As the lights became more numerous, and the swaying of the branches ceased with the abatement of the wind, anger was checked by prudence, then turned to determination: I had come to a decision. Without further thought, oblivious now to all save the purpose of my leaving, I put on cloak and bonnet, locked the door, and went out into the darkness of the street.

Halfway down the hill, the outer door of Number 23 was firmly shut. I could not have expected otherwise – today being Sunday and therefore not a day for business: yet I felt a momentary panic as I stood beside the iron railing, and again before pulling at the heavy knob which caused the ringing of a far-off bell. I could hear its notes – a genteel muffled sweetness – which were succeeded by a suitably discreet delay and, at last, by the appearance of a tidy but unsmiling maid. In her wake hovered one Miss Millington – the elder, I believed; behind her I glimpsed the tight grey curls and precisely balanced shawls of the second sister, whom I came to know as Miss Maria. She was small – rounded and lively as the other was languid and slender; but both were dressed with the unassuming care one would have looked for in ladies of their age and occupation. For ladies they undoubtedly were, despite the printed card (so small it escaped the eye of all but the most discerning visitor) pinned to one side of the inner doorway, and announcing their status as high-class milliners and dressmakers to clients of taste and refinement.

I was shown into the front parlour – a room evidently set aside for transactions of a ladylike, yet clearly profitable, nature. (It was to be some months before I was granted the privilege of entrance to the private parlour of the two Miss Millingtons.) My errand, as I knew, needed no explanation; the note I had received the day before had confirmed the sisters' interest in me. They came to the point at once.

'This,' pronounced the elder, 'is what you would be required to do, Miss Curwen. Show her, Maria.'

She subsided, with a slightly weary gesture – as if to indicate distaste – onto a small hard chair of an elegance typical of the establishment, and meant expressly, I concluded later, to discourage clients from too relaxed an attitude toward the serious matter of dress. But Miss Alice Millington herself was perhaps designed more for ornament than usefulness: she continued gracefully silent while the voluble Maria showed me fashion magazines from Paris; patterns of lace, embroidery or beaded decorations; volumes of sketches interleaved with notes of customers' names and requirements. For Miss D— a watered silk with rosebuds and slashed and ribboned sleeves – 'most charming'; the Misses Piercy ('such pretty girls') were to have blue velvet bonnets, each trimmed differently, of course; while the personage of Lady M— appeared to have chosen garments of a singularly *outré* kind – but Miss Maria forbore to criticise this leader of Highgate fashion and arbiter of local taste. And Mrs Perreton – I noticed the name, and remembered it: it seemed unusual. I knew nothing more, as yet, of Mrs Perreton, than her preference in bonnets and the information volunteered by Miss Maria:

'She is married to a Frenchman, and is *very* elegant, my dear!'

During the pause which succeeded this remark, Miss Alice asked with sudden perspicuity:

'But you have, I take it, no experience of this kind of work?'

I admitted that no, I had not.

'You are accustomed to other sorts of copying? And could, when needed, enlarge the details of designs, or even make your own, for the sewing-girls to work from?'

I could do so, I was sure, with sufficient accuracy.

'Good. Then Maria will show you the rooms: one in which you may work, the other for your private use. They have not been let for some time, not since – our circumstances have altered. But we will come to some agreement.' She coughed, with a delicacy which hinted that once, the sisters had known harder times.

The rooms were all that I had hoped. On the second floor, they proved to be large enough, well-lit and neatly furnished, far different from my present shabby quarters. And, though I did

[263]

not know it yet, they overlooked the grounds of Bisham House – home of that same Sophia Perreton whose name (and taste in bonnets) I had so recently observed.

I left well satisfied, indeed elated – as I glanced into the rain-washed windows of the little High Street shops – at the thought of the coming change. The road was steep, the walk eerie and unpleasant by the shadowed hill-top ponds, past the drooping trees and shuttered houses of The Grove: but I did not care. Nor, when I reached the Select Establishment for the Daughters of Gentlemen (*prop. Miss Hannah Brackenbury*) did I feel the least regret to be leaving it again so soon. I ignored the condemnatory looks of the headmistress, my colleagues' enquiring whispers, the quickly stifled laughter of my pupils as I supervised their evening studies. The secret pleasure of my new-found liberty would sustain me through such irritations.

For I expected, in my rooms at Number 23, to be able to paint more freely – even, perhaps, to have sitters if I chose. My duties there would not be negligible, and I must continue to take such private pupils as I might find; but I would labour no more to teach subjects I detested to unwilling girls, or find the demands of my employers so excessive that I could undertake no other work. How gladly now I recalled my chance encounter with Miss Maria Millington, as I waited one morning to purchase pens and water-colours at the Highgate stationers! I could be thankful, even, for the scathing criticism levelled at me by Miss Brackenbury, and the silent fury with which I had left our interview only this afternoon: for that had spurred me to action, after months of unexpressed rebellion on my part. And at last, perhaps, I might dare to hope for some reward for the three long years of disappointment which had passed since I left Cumberland.

'The world does not care for independent women, Georgiana.'

Aunt Nicolson had warned me – and events had proved her right. I had come to London with such eager expectations, built, it is true, upon the frail foundation of a small success. But I had sold no further work, and had begun of late to fear I might never do so: it would, indeed, be many years before I should

[264]

understand the true importance of those early paintings, executed with such youthful hope. Their purchaser (a Carlisle mill-owner, so I had been told, who yearned to spend his hard-won profits as a patron of the local arts) would have smiled to see the effects of his encouragement: to what heights my optimism had aspired – only to be crushed by the indifference of the London dealers to whom I showed my work.

I had been to several during those early months, and though more than one had praised the execution, all had condemned my choice of subject. A young lad seated on the harbour steps; a fisher-girl with her laden baskets; pit-men returning, grimed and weary, to their tumbled cottages: such themes were thought too 'low' – too lacking in noble inspiration for the refined taste of the metropolis. Even the scarlet-flowered geranium, which had flourished in the old man's sunlit porch at Portland Square, was considered a trifle vulgar; but some drawings of wild and garden plants met with a better response: 'Yes, now those might sell – flowers are the very thing, of course, for a young *lady* artist such as yourself.' Roses, or exotic blooms from the conservatory, would prove the most desirable; and portraits – those would 'do very well', provided the sitter were sufficiently attractive or important. But nothing humble – whether human or horticultural – would suit the present market: that much was made quite clear.

And clearer still (from the embarrassment with which I was received, the visible relief with which the dealers saw me from their premises) was the truth which Mr Jameson had from the first attempted to impress upon me. A woman was allowed to paint, if her subject were acceptable; she might even show her work at exhibitions – to do so could not offend against propriety, though the selection of pictures was of necessity made by men. But a female artist ought to remain an amateur, with independent means: she should not try to make a living from her paintings – she was bound to fail. A man might survive the deprivations and the struggle to succeed, but even the best required some patronage or private wealth to support his talent. And just as he – by making art his profession rather than his pastime – could no longer be considered quite a gentleman, so a woman must relinquish any claim to be a lady.

I had ceased long since to care about respectability – yet knew that without it I would never gain commissions or any kind of recognition for my work. Marriage (by which most girls seek their freedom) was out of the question: for husbands wish for virtue in exchange for the security they give – damaged goods are unacceptable, unless glossed over by the glitter of a fortune. And I had neither innocence nor money; nor could I even (as I thought then) offer love: that I had left in Cumberland with Charles.

So when, within six months of leaving Workington, I found myself faced with the prospect of returning, all my hopes abandoned – I took the only other course then open to a single woman. Teaching, it seemed, would enable me to stay in London. With the small allowance which my aunt had insisted I retain, I might earn enough to pay for lessons in the studio of some established artist – if I could find one willing to take me, with or without a chaperone. For a girl could not even copy pictures in a gallery without the presence of an older, married woman; and I obtained the necessary student's ticket only by using, once again, my father's name. Soon after my arrival, I had sent drawings in my own name to the Royal Academy, hoping to gain admission to the famous Schools: 'regretfully,' came prompt reply, 'its courses were not available to female artists'. My request for advice went unheeded, further letters were ignored; and bitterly I vowed that if I ever found success I should not set foot within that sacred institution. Had I but known how many painters – including Constable himself – had suffered like rejection, I should perhaps have been encouraged at being included in their number! As it was, I felt beset by obstacles at every turn: only persistence, or perhaps deception, would help me overcome them.

I will not dwell upon my experience at Miss Brackenbury's school. Others have described the tribulations of a teacher's life, its petty and exhausting trials which make one hate the very word of education. I can, however, verify the tales which others tell as fiction: for I went there with independence as my goal, only to become the slave of a worthless system. It was only one of several schools in Highgate at the time; yet I cannot think I should have done better had I chosen any other.

As a man, indeed, I might have fared far worse. At the least, I had food and shelter – though they cost me dear enough. But I pitied from the bottom of my heart the handsome, hungry-looking drawing master who went from place to place in search of pupils – only to be turned away because the parents disapproved of the temptation to their daughters, whilst the teachers quarrelled as to which of them might catch him in the end. He came throughout one spring; then suddenly he ceased to visit our establishment. His pupils were assigned to me; and it was some little time before I learned that he had thrown himself, in desperation, from the bridge above the Archway Road.

Then, I had almost left my post, longing to go back home to the security of Portland Square. Shocked by the waste of a fellow-artist's life, and by the indifference of those with whom I worked, I was prepared to pack my few belongings and return to quiet spinsterhood at Workington. But something – a residue of Curwen pride, perhaps, or a sense that to do so would be but another kind of death – something had prevented me. So I remained, painting as best I could by the fitful candle in my narrow room, and supported by those dreams which alone make daily disappointment less difficult to bear.

Aunt Nicolson had written to me several times, with more affection flowing from her pen than ever she had shown me whilst I stayed with her. Yet she had, indirectly, been the cause of my coming here to Highgate. Immune at first to all my arguments that I must go to London, she had (with her usual sudden change of tack) given in when Chance intervened on my behalf. A letter from Mrs Heywood, widow of Humphrey Nicolson's old friend, had repeated earlier invitations – which my aunt had consistently refused. This time, she determined that I should go instead of her: within weeks, and efficient as any quartermaster, she had organised my clothes and my finances, my tickets and the necessary escort southward. She supplied me, too, with the address of Nicolson & Curwen's London premises: 'It may be useful: Mr Backhouse is the agent there – and you may trust him with anything, that's for sure!' (Could she have foreseen, I wonder, that the day would come

[267]

when I should be more than glad of the good offices of Mr Backhouse?)

Several months in Mrs Heywood's home at Regent's Park proved quite sufficient for us both. She was all effusiveness at first; but though we went to galleries and exhibitions, and I became acquainted with her more artistic friends, I could not readily confide my hopes. Indeed, she had a patronising manner and an acid tongue, which at length became too much to tolerate. Her accounts of Captain Heywood's life as a young midshipman on the *Bounty*, and his part in the famous mutiny, were interesting enough – the more so because my aunt had told me so little. But before long Mrs Heywood bored me with her constant reminiscence; and when one day she spoke slightingly of Henry Curwen, I felt bound to come to my grandfather's defence. Whereupon she eyed me shrewdly and remarked: 'Well, miss – it's easy to tell that *his* blood is in your veins, at any rate!'

Her insinuation – for such it seemed to me – was not to be ignored, though till then I had been sure that she could know little of my story. From that time I wished to go elsewhere; and when (with the same notion in mind, perhaps) Mrs Heywood spoke of the schools she had known at Highgate, her former home, I resolved to seek a post in one of them. Her words had only made me the more determined to remain in London, rather than go back to be a poor relation of the Curwens: for nothing could be worse, I thought, than to return a failure to my aunt in Workington.

Only Philip knew the truth of my first unhappy years at Highgate. And his visits had been the cause of that final quarrel with Miss Brackenbury. My immorality was proven, the headmistress claimed, by my having been observed with him (and on a Sunday morning, which made the matter worse), walking in the direction of Hampstead. She had only allowed his visits as a favour, so she said, because of his acquaintance with Dr Gillman of The Grove; and because he professed to have known the poet, Mr Coleridge. But the latter was, in any case, deceased, and could not therefore provide a reference for Mr Earnshaw. Triumphantly, she concluded with an ultimatum:

either the gentleman must come no more, or I must leave her house – for the sake of her pupils, and the reputation of her school.

'And what have you to say, Miss Curwen?' she had, with a shake of her well-ringed finger, then demanded of me.

After a silent moment – during which I hated all the more her little slaty eyes, the row of pious books so carefully displayed beneath the badly varnished portrait of her clerical papa, and every moment I had wasted in that over-principled establishment – I answered:

'Nothing, ma'am – save that your accusation, as to my immorality, is not the truth. And that even if it were, I should not care!'

With that I left her, glad of the look of shock upon her face, and wishing only that I had spoken all the bitterness which I had harboured for so long. Later, as I came back from my visit to the two Miss Millingtons, I felt that I had reached a turning-point: one of those moments which – if only we could prise it open, like a shell containing hidden grains of sand, or a bud which keeps the secret of a future flower – must hold within it all the strange complexities that lie ahead.

That winter – the first of the young queen's reign – caps and bonnets *à la reine Victoria* were all the rage. Sophia Perreton wore hers precisely as recommended in *La Belle Assemblée*: red velvet, with a little veil, for her festive New Year calls; black, with a matching muff, upon more sober occasions – though these were less numerous in her social calendar, to judge by the frequency with which the lady ordered her evening gowns and mantles from my new employers. Even before we met, I had formed my judgement by her choice of clothes: pleasure-loving, yet not ostentatious – her taste was rarely to be faulted; young, of course – or at least, little older than myself, for I might have chosen styles the same, though her height was less than mine. She must be rather capricious, altering her mind as to this or the other detail with 'isconcerting speed; yet she could not be ill-natured, since when some error had occurred, she spoke of it most charmingly, so Miss Maria said.

I too was disarmed to receive one morning a little delicately scented note, expressing Mrs Perreton's delight at the new designs embroidered on her muslin dresses: she would consult me, when she called again, as to the decoration for a summer cloak she had in mind. Her praise, and the thought of meeting her, could only give me pleasure. For I had long ago rejected the notion that such work might be too trivial: an artist, I had learned, must welcome anything that gives his hand more practice or helps him exercise his judgement. Nothing, it seemed, could be so degrading as those hours passed with my reluctant pupils, tracing dull, ill-chosen pictures or compelled to finish off their drawings to impress their parents or the school inspectors. No wonder I had welcomed (until Miss Brackenbury made her disapproval plain) the times when Philip came with architectural plans for me to copy or to tint with water-colour. Though often I had worked into the night to get them done, they had meant some small addition to my savings – destined for the studies which I might, one day, be able to pursue.

Now, it was enough that even Miss Alice Millington was pleased with me. She, unlike her sister, had little patience with those in her employ: the sewing-girls who came each morning to collect the day's assignment often went home in tears or – which was worse – unpaid, if their efforts failed to satisfy; whilst those who worked in the cramped and stuffy room beyond the private parlour might chatter to each other under Miss Maria's supervision, but never when Miss Millington was present. Good workmanship, however, she respected – as a fitting complement for the expensive fabrics which (as I had soon discovered) were her passion. She alone was allowed to choose them, or to show them to her clients, who rarely seemed to question her opinion. But Mrs Perreton was clearly a woman of independent taste; and though Miss Alice was far too refined to say so openly, she could not afford to offend so influential a customer.

'Mrs Perreton comes of one of Highgate's oldest families. I knew her mother as a girl; and her father is a publisher in the city – but very well connected, all the same – ' Miss Alice paused, as if to emphasise the fact. 'She is his only child. Her mother died when she was very young, so Mrs Perreton has spent a good deal of time with him. He has built a splendid house, of course, on the Southwood hill, where the air is excellent.'

'But Bisham House is very pretty.'

I could see it from the window of my upstairs room; and I thought Sophia Perreton could not want a more delightful home. True, it was not particularly large, and had an old-fashioned air with its red-tiled roof and high chimneys – but there was a garden, sloping down toward a lichened wall, and its trees, even in winter, were gracious. I should prefer it, I was sure, to the newer, fashionable villas which the prosperous families of Highgate occupied, up on the healthy heights looking toward the city.

'And this part of the village is more interesting,' I added, though I guessed that Miss Millington would not agree.

Already, I had come to like the High Street with all its busy comings and goings; tradesmen passing, children on their way to school, or sometimes drovers taking the ancient way to the London markets. And though Number 23 stood on the border, as it were, between gentility and commerce – with houses of like respectability below and opposite, but shops, taverns and little dirty courtyards on each side of the cobbled street above – it seemed to me a perfect situation. But then, I had no wish to find a place among the gentlefolk of Highgate – not if it meant a return to Miss Brackenbury's school!

'Then you are happy here, Miss Curwen?'

The question took me quite by surprise. So far removed were my present circumstances from the unrewarding toil and isolation I had known before, that I had not realised the sisters might be anxious as to whether I would wish to stay with them. Rather, I had been daily apprehensive that my work might not meet with Miss Millington's exacting standard; and the past three months had been, I was all too conscious, a period of probation. Only today, having been summoned to the private parlour and handed the note from Mrs Perreton, had I felt certain that I was giving satisfaction.

'Your copying is excellent. And these new designs are good – unusual perhaps, but good: my sister and I are agreed as to that. So, now that you are becoming used to our requirements, you must feel free to pursue your own interests as well – just as we arranged. But if you can do this kind of thing' – Miss Alice indicated the drawings on the table beside her – 'for our special clients, we shall be more than glad to have you remain with us.'

For Miss Alice Millington to show enthusiasm was a rare event. Even as I smiled and murmured my agreement, she resumed her usual cool demeanour, handed the drawings to me, and returned to her close inspection of a parcel of fine lace, newly arrived from Brussels. But she had made her point: at last I was free to paint, just as I had hoped – but it was important that Sophia Perreton should continue to approve my work.

There were children at Bisham House. Their laughter rang among the frosty trees – for even in the coldest weather two small figures, muffled in hoods and mittens, took their exercise beyond the wall which bounded the garden. Later, on better days, there would be a groom leading a sleepy-looking pony; but in the winter season the children ran with their hoops along the sloping path, or chased each other, careless of the remonstrations of the nursery-maid who guarded them. As I worked at my easel near the window, I found myself wondering sometimes (remembering Mary Nicolson playing with her children in the Keswick garden) whether Mrs Perreton were as devoted to her little daughters as to the details of her dress. For I saw – but only once or twice – a woman watching from the terrace beside the house. Tall and elegant, she corresponded to my image of her; but she did not linger – and she had, so far, paid no further visit to the Misses Millington, though half a dozen finished garments had been carefully packed and sent round to Bisham House.

My curiosity remained unsatisfied. And in the meantime, as the grass grew brighter with the green of spring, and the leaves began to open, I observed another figure in the garden: a gentleman, to whom the children ran, to be swung by the hand or lifted in his arms. He must be the Frenchman, the children's father, I supposed.

A footpath – treacherous, at first, with mud or frozen ruts – led from the High Street toward the open fields and woods which stretched along the hillside, above the mists and shadows of the London plain. Often, as I followed the path beside the curving garden wall, I would hear the children calling; or I would see them, as the days lengthened, walking with the maid, and gathering the flowers which – almost magically, so sudden was the transformation – now appeared on the grassy banks and verges. The little girls, seated together on a fallen tree to make their daisy-chains, or reaching to shake the pollen from the lowest catkins in the hazel hedge, looked happy enough. Yet their father, on the few occasions when I saw him with them, was preoccupied and grave. Perhaps, indeed, I should not otherwise have noticed him: for his silence seemed to isolate him from the world about him, from the movement and laughter of his children, from the leaves and sunlight, even the song of birds. I did not think, as he passed, that I should ever know the cause.

Chapter 20

'Miss Curwen – you are to go to Bisham House!'

Maria Millington, her cap askew with haste and excitement, stood in the doorway of my room.

'That is,' she modified, 'my sister says she wishes you to go with her as soon as you are able. But she would prefer it to be at once, this afternoon.'

In spite of all my interest in Mrs Perreton, I was annoyed at this unexpected summons. With Miss Alice, such a request was not to be ignored; yet there was other work to be considered, not least the portrait on which I was engaged. It was of Mrs Heywood, with whom I had made my peace some weeks before, when she descended without warning on her old acquaintances, the Misses Millington. Delighted at my change of occupation (of which I had felt bound to write and tell her), she had ordered her summer bonnets and requested a pastel drawing of herself. I had pocketed my pride and made some sketches there and then; now there was further preparation to be done – for tomorrow Mrs Heywood was to come again, to take me back with her to Regent's Park. Miss Alice had agreed to spare me for a day or two, so I dared not risk displeasing her. But I did not conceal my reluctance from Maria.

'I should rather go next week, after I have been to town. But I suppose that Mrs Perreton has asked to see some more designs – and of course, she will not want to wait for them. It is strange,' I added, as unwillingly I gathered up my things, 'that she has not wished to see them sooner.'

The family had gone to Bath for Easter, so Maria (always eager to impart such information) had told me some time ago. But now it was almost May; the sisters were fully occupied, and would not welcome a request for another set of summer gowns – even for a special client – when already the sewing-girls were working late into the night to get the orders done. I had even begun to wonder if Mrs Perreton had changed her mind, and no longer liked the patterns she had praised before: but that, it seemed, was not the case.

'You are to take as many drawings as you can – the new ones, in particular, so Alice said. They will be needed for some special dresses – bonnets, too – but Mrs Perreton is too unwell to come herself, so Annie told me when she brought the message round. And, my dear,' – Maria's voice dropped to a discreet whisper, 'you ought to know, I think – she was very ill at Bath, with another – '

The appearance of her sister, impeccably attired for walking (even for the little distance we would go), effectively ended Maria's breathless speech. But, had Mrs Perreton been Queen Victoria herself, the news of her illness could scarcely have been invested with more significance: and I guessed at once – from the pinkness of Maria's cheeks and the embarrassed glance she gave Miss Millington, that their client had suffered the misfortune of another stillborn child. No wonder, I reflected, that she sought distraction in expensive clothes: my annoyance was forgotten as I hurried with Miss Alice down the stair and in, by the iron gate, to the grounds of Bisham House.

We passed through a kitchen garden, neatly ranged below the mossy wall, against which clouds of pear and cherry blossom rose, perfuming the air and reaching up to the slanting gables of the High Street houses. Then a second, lower wall, and another gate, overhung with trails of clematis, its buds already touched with pink and almost open to the noisy searching bees; and beyond, an expanse of green, rising up to a curving bank and the terrace steps. There were flowers everywhere: celandines, and paler primroses, among the uncut grass; a mass of daffodils around the ancient mulberry tree, whose newly opened leaves cast a golden, moving pattern of light and shade upon the brighter gold beneath.

Flowers, too, in the garden room beyond the terrace, high above the sloping lawn, the shimmer of Highgate woods in springtime, the distant, whitening blur of London. A heavy scent of hyacinth; sunlight, diffused by muslin curtains; an enclosing wall of glass. And Sophia Perreton – white-gowned among the shining leaves, the coloured waxen petals and the delicate, attenuated fronds of fern.

Sophia Perreton was bored. Or so I thought, observing the listless inclination of her head: her hair, red-gold against the pallor of her hand, appeared to curl in defiance of the fashionable bands which held it in its place; her mouth, almost childlike in the fullness of its curves, hinted at sadness, or caprice, or even petulance. I should have liked to paint her – in the instant before she turned, smiling, to greet Miss Millington. For she seemed – in that restless and yet curiously passive pose – to represent the yearnings of so many women, tied too early in their lives to home and hearth.

Yet only one or two, of the many drawings which I later made of her, show Sophia as I saw her then. For she always rejected such interpretations as too melancholy; and always, if any thing distressed her by its ugliness or imperfection, she would remove, or at the very least ignore it. Error, even carelessness, in others, she allowed – for her instinct was affectionate; but she was harder with herself. She could bear no defect in her features or her dress, no lapse of conduct or of taste, no fault even among the flowers which – next to her children and her clothes – were her chief delight. Once I saw her throw away a hot-house plant whose shape displeased her when it failed to match the perfect picture in her book; and so it was with the sketches for the portrait which (though I had despaired) I at last completed to her satisfaction, if not to my own. She preferred to see herself as beautiful – a static image in a gilded frame upon the wall. I tried to draw Sophia as she was: imperious and often wilful, quickly moved to anger or delight, and – like the flowers by which she was surrounded – possessed of a transient perfection, easily destroyed.

That afternoon, I was astonished by the eagerness with which she welcomed us.

'You are very kind to come, Miss Millington.' She held out both her hands to my companion. 'And Miss Curwen – I had hoped to meet you sooner, but – no, I am not ill at all, it is only that tiresome doctor who insists that I must rest a little longer.'

Laughing and perfectly at ease, she shook her head at Miss Alice's concern and, leaning back against her cushions, gazed at me.

'Forgive me – but you are so much younger than I had expected! Miss Millington will not mind my saying so – she has known me for so long and understands me thoroughly – but I am so glad that you have come to her. It is strange – our taste seems to coincide exactly in the matter of designs; and you draw so beautifully, I can tell at once how they will look when they are done. Since I was a child, I have wished that I could draw, and paint my flowers in particular – but I must have been the despair of half the masters in London, for I failed most dreadfully!'

I could not believe her insincere – but I was quite unused to so much praise, and at a loss to find an answer. I was conscious, as I had not been since leaving Cumberland, of a sudden wish that such grace of manner, and such confidence, were mine; that I did not wear a dark, uninteresting gown beside so bright a creature; and that I had not chosen so hard a way to live my life. Yet I could not quite forget that first brief glimpse of another, far less happy woman – gazing from her cushioned couch toward the world beyond her garden room.

'But you have other gifts, and a home to care for,' I began, 'whilst I – I have one talent, and one occupation only. Fortunately – and thanks chiefly to Miss Millington, of course – the two now coincide. Yet I should like, all the same, to have time or opportunity for other interests.'

'But you might find them less rewarding – or might care about them less. You see – ' Sophia Perreton looked ruefully toward a pile of books which lay unopened on the table at her side ' – I say I don't have time to read them, yet I should, if I truly cared to. They are in French – and therefore I am idle about them. My husband insists that the children speak French a good deal of the time that he is with them; but though I learned at school, I speak it far less well than he does English – and so I do not try as I ought – '

She sighed, then added, with more animation, 'But Louis has promised that we shall go to Paris when I am quite recovered, and that is why I must have some new clothes made. I long to see more of your designs . . .'

I glanced nervously at Miss Millington, fearing that she might have become impatient; but she remained absorbed in setting out the patterns she had brought.

'I hope you will like them, for I draw chiefly the things which give me pleasure. And some of them are very simple – leaves or grasses, sometimes flowers; and shells, or feathers perhaps – '

Sophia listened carefully while I described how I tried to find shapes and colours which would harmonize with the fabrics that she chose, or might best suit the different kinds of ornamental thread in which the decoration would be worked. But I told her nothing of my paintings: after all, I was there as an employee of the Misses Millington – and though they rarely treated me as such, I must always be conscious of the fact. It was no wonder that I seemed to her (as Sophia later told me) so reserved and cold: I had no thought of friendship with her then, could not have imagined the affection that would spring between us – or the grief which would bring it to an end.

Yet I was, that afternoon, already fascinated by Sophia: by the expressive intonation of her voice, the quickly changing moods reflected in her unambiguous gaze, the swift but always graceful movement of her hands. Spoiled and frivolous, perhaps – yet she made her decisions with intelligence and care. And when, with a reverence worthy of some ancient ritual, my employer spread upon the table several lengths of silk, Sophia's eyes – large, and a curious golden-brown in colour – glowed with delight. She was, I realized, not merely a devotee of fashion but (more, even, than Miss Millington) a woman with a sense of beauty, which found its chief fulfilment in her clothes.

Was it that deeper quality, or her elegance alone, which had drawn to her a man like Louis Perreton? I was to ask myself the question many times during the months which followed: but now – save for the first strange moment of unease when I saw Sophia waiting in her garden room – my mind was innocent of thoughts so dangerous.

I scarcely remember how Louis looked that day. He must have been, as usual, hatless, with his hair unruly and his manner quite abstracted, as he entered from the terrace, followed by the little girls. One of them was, like himself, dark-haired and neatly made; the other fair and taller, with her mother's curls and golden-coloured eyes. They came in together from their walk, laughing and bringing the fragrance of the garden to the over-heated brightness of the glass-walled room. The father bowed and spoke with courtesy to my companion; to me, he said nothing, and his glance – elusive yet intent – told me nothing more about himself.

But I recollect how then he crossed the room, so swiftly, to Sophia's couch. And the children stood beside him as he bent toward their mother with a gesture of concern. They were, as we left them there, a perfect group: a picture which – like a brown, forgotten photograph – I find again, long after its reality has faded.

Miss Millington, on our returning home, informed Maria that she must engage another sewing-girl at once. Soon the summer Season would be at its height: there would be further unexpected orders, or alterations to be made to favourite gowns, for customers impatient to secure – at a minute's notice – something special for tomorrow's garden-party or excursion. There would, indeed, be work for two more girls in the coming months: but two, said Miss Alice, would be an extravagance – the others must work longer hours, as was expected of them at such a busy time of year.

However, she refused my offer to postpone my visit to Mrs Heywood, declaring herself well satisfied with our success at Bisham House. For had not Mrs Perreton ordered several dresses, to be made at once, in consequence of being 'quite in love' with my designs? And had not she requested to keep a number of the drawings, to consider at her leisure before making up her mind?

'Maria must go up to Southcott House tomorrow, first thing in the morning. They have a girl there, Mrs Southcott says, whose needlework is quite exceptional. You can bring some samples back with you, Maria – plain sewing and embroidery as well: unless she is able to do both, there's no point in our considering her. And of course, the sooner she can start the better.'

For once, it was Maria who was silent. She seemed, for a moment, about to protest; then evidently thought better of it, and only murmured faintly: 'I am sure that you know best, sister . . . But did you not once say that you had rather not employ such girls as – as those . . .'

'Needs must when the devil drives, Maria! And besides, if what I hear from Mrs Southcott is the truth – and I have no reason to doubt it -- the women there are quite reformed. I would expect, of course, to give a lower wage to such a girl – but as to her morals, she may be a savage or a Hottentot for all I care, so long as her work is good enough. You may go and see about it in the morning.'

Rarely had I heard her speak so forcibly. Yet more than once I had suspected that beneath the studied, genteel femininity there lurked an interesting mind. Maria, outwardly more cheerful and resilient, always yielded to her sister, knowing that her fragile air concealed a steely resolution – especially in business matters. The sisters could afford no disregard of rank or riches: yet Miss Alice seemed inclined to despise the fads and foibles of their more pretentious clients, preferring those like Sophia Perreton who showed discrimination in their taste. I knew (for Maria had confided in me readily) that their father had been a self-made man, supplying silks and other fabrics to the city trades. Until the ruin of his enterprise, he had been respected as a wealthy citizen of liberal principles – outspokenly expressed before Reform became a general cause: so I wondered sometimes whether – even though she paid lip-service to convention – Alice Millington retained her father's more progressive views.

When, on my coming first to Number 23, I had felt bound to tell her why I wished to leave my former post, she had altogether lost her languid manner, with a sharp response.

'I think, Miss Curwen, that Hannah Brackenbury's notions are not mine. An artist – whether man or woman – cannot work well if so rigidly confined. You will be free to come and go in my establishment; and I should prefer to make my judgement of you after three months' trial, if you please!'

She had surprised me then; and now, in this matter of her choice of another seamstress, did so again. For Jeremiah Southcott and his wife, of Southcott House, were proprietors of an institution of a most unusual kind, which had been the cause of rumour and controversy for several years. A Home for Penitents they called it: but it was, as everyone in Highgate knew, a refuge for some of London's fallen women – outcasts from respectable society. Abandoning his trade as brewer (and supplier of the liquor that so many sought as the only solace in their prostitution) Mr Southcott had turned his wealth to a philanthropic cause – only to discover that he was, for a time, himself an outcast among his friends and neighbours. Some became reconciled, believing that in Highgate's cultivated atmosphere even such degraded creatures (few cared to speak of them as harlots, save in sermons from the pulpits on a Sunday) could not help but be reformed. Others took to walking by a different route, or made their protest with self-consciously averted eyes – lest they be contaminated by the sight of a sinner at a window, or in the garden behind the ugly laurel hedge.

The inmates of Southcott House, meantime, were set to useful work. Only one, I heard, had been sent back to the streets from which she came – she had been found in the courtyard of the Angel Inn, trying (and not without success) to ply her former trade among the customers. Another – whose fate Miss Brackenbury had described with satisfaction as 'only what the girl deserved' – had run away last winter, and was thought to have drowned in one of Highgate's several ponds, though her body was not found.

As for the girl Maria Millington engaged – I saw her on the morning after my return from town. She was sullen, silent, pale.

Yet she worked hard, Maria soon reported, and some of her sewing was quite exquisite. Her hands, I noticed, were not coarse but finely shaped; her figure, far too thin. Although her gown was old, it had been patched with care, and had once been of good quality, I thought – while the spotless, well-starched pinafore above it must have been supplied from Southcott House. The other seamstresses ignored her, and she worked apart, in a quiet corner of the room: she had been the first to come that morning, I was told – and at ten o'clock that night, she was the last to leave.

The sittings with Mrs Heywood had gone well. And when she spoke of recommending me among her friends, I felt it would be foolish to refuse. After all, I was treading in the well-worn path which even the greatest painters had to follow: though I should not wish to toil at portraits all my life, they might enable me, one day, to venture something more ambitious. I would want, I knew, to show the world how working people lived – in the fields or in the city streets; to choose subjects which – though they might never hang in drawing-rooms – would speak the truth, and move the watcher to feel something more than envy or complacency.

When – in those moments of despair which every artist knows and learns to dread – self-doubt and disillusion overcame me, the words of Mr Constable would sometimes come to mind: 'You must listen to your own voice first, and paint the vision you alone can see. Study the great, Miss Curwen – but ignore the rest, and paint as you believe: it is the only way.' He paused, and for an instant I thought I saw a younger and less weary man – as he had been before the lines of grief and illness marked his face. Then he had said, more bitterly, 'As for the Academy – they have no soul, and you may do without them.'

I had visited him only once, when, after several months in London, I had found the courage to use the letter of introduction Mr Jameson had given me. Certain that their early friendship would not have been forgotten, my teacher had warned me, even so, that Constable could be unkind, and had no time for flatterers or fools. Yet my fears and hesitation had proved groundless. He spoke with fondness of his visit to the Lakes, and with respect of Robert Jameson; then he looked keenly at the watercolour sketches I had taken with me, noting here and there – in a curious slanting hand – how I might make some improvement in their light and shade. 'Man,' he declared, 'is a creature of the landscape in which he moves; and it is light which makes that landscape come alive.' But he did not care for mountain scenery – its loneliness and grandeur were oppressive; rather, he preferred the sheltered vales, the sunlit, tranquil meadows, and the quiet corners of domestic countryside.

He was working on such a scene that afternoon at Charlotte Street: a large canvas, with a distant house, a river, and a boat beneath the trees. A painting of calm simplicity: and yet the whole of its complex surface seemed to move – from each separate, minute point of light upon the water to the restless, shifting strokes of leaves, the curves and trailing vapour of the clouds. The figures in the boat were young; but there was a hint of sadness in the overshadowed landing-place, a note of melancholy in the picture's mood, which made me wonder if it was, perhaps, the ageing artist's image of his youth. And I could not but recall the brightness of a day on Derwentwater, with two lovers in a white-sailed boat; the moment of their coming to that hidden shore – the uncertain light and darkness of my love for Charles.

That was my own, as yet uncharted, past. But this of Constable's – the distillation of so much that he had known and loved – would surely live long after he himself had gone. It was intended, so he said, for that summer's exhibition at the Royal Academy. And when I went to find it there, among a thousand other pictures, I was glad that I had seen it as he painted it – in daylight and away from all the false pretension of the fashionable world.

I resolved that I would ask no favours: he had inspired me, and that would be enough. His notes I kept and studied carefully, intending that one day, should I visit him again, I would prove that I had learned from his advice. But Constable, within two years, was dead; and I, meantime, had gone to Highgate, where I found myself embarked upon an unknown course – a journey which, in times of desperation, seemed as if it had no purpose, and would never end.

Philip Earnshaw was in town. He called at Mrs Heywood's during our sitting on my second day at Regent's Park – when my subject's mood was more amenable, and I had persuaded her that the portrait would not be improved by another change of dress, or the adoption of an altogether different pose from that with which we had commenced.

I had not seen Philip since I came to the Miss Millingtons. Work (and pleasure also, I supposed, though he did not say as much) had taken him abroad that spring; and I was in any case reluctant to do anything which might incur my employers' disapproval. Now he had plans commissioned for some cottages at Twickenham, and for a city banker's house at Hampstead: he would be in London for some time, and would be free to come to Highgate when I wished. We might, if I could make arrangements, go to some galleries together, and to the Summer Exhibition.

It was three years since that last, decisive, visit to the Royal Academy. I had been cut off from the artistic world, as completely as if I had remained in Workington. Now, with my confidence renewed, I was eager to visit exhibitions, to see the work of other painters – even to try my fortunes with the dealers once again. Miss Millington, moreover, went each week to town: for some of her city clients patronised a small (but most expensive) Bond Street shop in which she was a partner – to the exclusion, so it seemed, of the less talented Maria. She had suggested that when my work allowed I might like to go with her, and I wondered if she hoped to employ my talents in this other enterprise.

If so, she did not choose to speak of it that morning in mid-May, when we drove together out of Highgate and along the London road. My companion was composed and silent, unobtrusively attired in gray – though the cut and fabric of her clothes, as always, were quite faultless. Today I did not envy her. I felt in a joyous, early-summer mood, wearing (like the countryside through which we passed) a fresh green gown, embroidered to my own design; on the carriage seat beside me lay my first commissioned portrait, now completed; and I had, in a gesture of defiant vanity, put on my Curwen locket once again – as if challenging the shadows of the past to darken such a day.

Even the brash new villas – white scars along the leafy lanes by which we came to Regent's Park – displeased me less than usual; and Mrs Heywood, with whom I waited while my employer continued into town, was in the best of humours, flourishing her latest bonnet and eager to show me a recent letter from my aunt.

'She is lonely without you, my dear: I can tell it, though the last thing Lizzie Nicolson would do is to complain of it. But she hopes you will agree to go there with me at the end of June. I shall be in Workington a week at least, and you could stay there while I tour the Lakes, then travel south with me again. It is a perfect plan: I am sure Miss Millington will spare you – in fact, I intend to ask her myself when we meet her at Bond Street this afternoon.'

At once I became alarmed. Miss Alice would dislike it, I was certain; and I had, besides, my own reasons for preferring not to go. I was determined not to let myself be overruled – not knowing that a time would come when I should wish with all my heart I had decided otherwise.

'You are very kind: but I cannot think of leaving Highgate for some time. Miss Millington is very busy; and there will be some more commissions of my own, I hope – I should need to stay for those. But I will write and explain to Aunt Nicolson, of course.'

'Very well.' Mrs Heywood was offended: I could tell it by the vigour with which she re-tied her bonnet, gathered up her reticule and gloves and crossed the morning-room – precisely at the moment when the doorbell rang.

'I hope you won't regret it, Georgiana: it would be a pity if your aunt were to think you ungrateful after all that she has done. But there, young women will never listen to advice.'

I might have answered that my aunt, at least, respected my desire for independence, and that I was, at twenty-six, scarcely so very young! Yet my conscience was uneasy on the subject of

Aunt Nicolson: her letters had, of late, seemed somewhat strained – almost as if she had been reluctant to undertake the writing of them. And I had missed her more than I could readily admit: had it not been for the prospect of an empty life, too close to Lorton and my cousin Charles, I should have long ago abandoned my ambitions and returned to Workington. Now, I had put such lingering regrets behind me: my aunt would surely understand that I must seize new opportunities – and that I would return when I no longer needed to depend on her . . .

Mrs Heywood was waiting for me in the hall. Philip glanced quickly at me, guessing perhaps that something had been amiss. Then we were seated in the carriage, where Mrs Heywood's temper was restored as she speculated who, of all her wide acquaintance, might or might not be present at the Summer Exhibition. She did not mention Cumberland again; Philip, to my relief, appeared more tolerant than usual of her persistent monologue; and my spirits lifted as each moment brought us further into town.

Even before we reached St Martin's Lane, it seemed as if the freshness of the air, the morning's clarity, the blue and white and green to which we were accustomed on the northern heights, had swept before us with the summer breeze – into the very heart of London. London itself was poised expectantly, filled with unusual optimism – almost as if the city itself had undergone some change of heart. The new white buildings near Trafalgar Square shone with a brightness rivalled by the dazzle of many-coloured parasols and gowns, the flash of livery and harness, the gleams of golden light which burnished weathercocks and spires. Carriage-boys and flower-sellers shouted cheerfully, their urgency or rancour dissipated with the winter's chilly fogs and fumes; even the ragged children on the steps beside the church looked warmer in the sunlight – like the eager sparrows fluttering among the remnants of last autumn's leaves.

It was, I knew, only the thinly varnished surface of the day that hid the poverty and desperation of those fragile lives. There was filth on the cobbles and the pavements; every stone beneath our well-shod feet was treacherous with city grime; there was no scent of leaves or summer flowers – only the pervasive odour of the streets. Patriotic ribbons, pictures of Victoria, were everywhere: the young queen's coronation, scarcely a month away, had brought a temporary brightness into town. A new prosperity, a hopeful spirit (so the comfortable doctrine went) would soon transform the nation: London, at the heart of England's greatness, would be recognised for what she was – the centre of the world. Yet, it would make little difference to the poor: they were like the particles of dust in London's streets – so many, and so insignificant, that they must be trodden underfoot, or brushed aside to fester in the sun.

The galleries were crowded. Half of London's well-informed society, it would appear, was gathered in the foyer, waving catalogues and nodding greetings, gracefully determined to display artistic taste. We had scarcely reached the pictures before Mrs Heywood had discovered some acquaintance, in whose company (and at a speed which I felt disinclined to share) she circumnavigated the exhibits in the first saloon. Loudly, she declared approval of the lofty well-lit rooms: 'The Academy were always *very* cramped, of course, at Somerset House'; then, clearly quite impatient with her role as chaperone, she engaged to meet us in the foyer after half an hour.

Philip was, as always, reticent, ironic, kind. He humoured my desire to linger here and there; shared my distaste for Wilkie's massive canvas of Victoria (so young, yet so imperious already) with the members of her Council; and smiled when I expressed despair at my inability to paint, as Mr Etty could, the symmetry of human form, the nuances of flesh.

'I cannot think you ought to wish to do so – or that Mrs Heywood thinks his work so admirable. In fact – ' he looked extremely grave ' – I am certain I have heard her say it is immoral – decadent, indeed!'

I laughed. I knew Philip well enough to recognise his earnestness as feigned, and prompted chiefly by his wish to rouse me to a passionate defence of my artistic freedom. He enjoyed provoking argument; while I had learned to tell his mood, and whether I might risk the sudden and destructive scorn with which he sometimes answered me, a scorn against which (even after years of friendship) I could not protect myself.

'But of course Mr Etty's paintings are not moral – they are not truly meant to be so! He may call his people nymphs and shepherds, goddesses or gods, and say they are from fables or from fairy-tales – but they are living, breathing men and women: that is why the moralists dislike them, for they come too near to life. And that – as I believe you know already – is the reason why they move me; and if to paint as well as Mr Etty makes me decadent – I would not wish it otherwise!'

This time, however, Philip did not smile.

'You should be careful, Georgiana. If you cross the moralists, your work will not survive. Even Etty had to fight for his success, till he was over forty – and now, the world is grown more prudish even than it was. Besides, since he is so successful, Etty may fall in love with the women whom he paints, and no one will object – or not enough to damage him. And a man is allowed to paint from life, as you, I am afraid, are not!'

I was silent, knowing (only too well) that he was right. And his scorn this time was reserved for others, not directed at myself. He had told me once that William Etty was a humble baker's son from Yorkshire, that he had struggled for many years without the benefit of patrons or commissions, until his *Cleopatra* made him famous overnight. Since then his paintings of the nude, though controversial, had become accepted; and he was, so Philip often said, the only painter, save for Turner, whom he could admire.

Sometimes, I thought the key to Philip's character lay in his taste: though outwardly so cool, he was not the puritan he seemed, but a man of feeling – which he chose not to express. He rarely spoke of love, save with contempt; yet he had grieved for his sister Charlotte, whom he said that I resembled – and for her sake (rather than my own, I was convinced) had helped me with my work. His deeper passions lay concealed, like the unseen waters of the frozen river where we met. Always, still, there was a sense of something unfulfilled – as if the thread which circumstance had spun about us from the first had never quite been broken, yet had never been complete. Once, I believed he might have cared for me; but always now the shadow of my cousin Charles would lie between us . . .

Together, we moved away from Etty's sleeping nymphs, towards the second picture-room. There were fewer people here; and most were grouped before a pair of canvases whose style and colouring – flamboyant, elemental and disturbing – were unique. I had experienced Turner's paintings once before: and then, as now, had seen upon the faces of the crowd expressions of bewilderment, of outrage or contempt. His *Burning of the House of Lords and Commons* had departed from their expectations: careful observation and the faithful rendering of fact were what they looked for in the record of so recent an event. Instead they were shown his vision of a panic-stricken city, and the power of fire. And I, in that first London winter, had been ill-equipped to comprehend the revolutionary force of Turner's work; in spite of Philip's protestations, I had been inspired by Constable: his mood had fitted mine, and his world was one which I could share and understand.

This time, I stood and marvelled. Turner's colour seemed to be applied at random and in haste – and yet the canvas glowed with an iridescent light, as if the crimson, azure, ochre, white had been fragmented, forced apart, and fused together by the painter's hand. His theme was ancient Italy; and he had drawn the ruined temples, towers and walls with lines so delicate that all their substance was dissolved in heat, their transient splendour merging with the southern sky. Turner had created, from the distant past, a visionary world; and as I gazed at it, I saw once more (as from a high imagined vantage-point) the sunlit mountain pinnacles beyond the golden mist of Keswick Vale.

The group of people had dispersed. Only a dark-haired gentleman remained, apparently absorbed in close perusal of the second painting of the pair. I remembered Mrs Heywood waiting for us, and I moved away.

But Philip murmured, 'Tell me, Georgiana, who is that man? He seems to know you . . .'

Surprised, I looked again – but Louis Perreton had gone.

Chapter 21

'He seems to know you, Georgiana.' There was no reason why those words should mean anything to me – and yet, throughout that summer when I came to know Sophia well, they lingered in my mind, like the faint but lasting imprint of a stranger's footstep on the fallow land. I had no premonition of a love which took possession quietly; there was no sudden revelation, no clarity of vision to illumine such an empty road as mine. I had forgotten love: or rather, I had driven it beyond the bounds of conscious thought, believing it could not return.

'But it was Earnshaw whom I noticed first. He is so very arrogant and tall. A tall proud Englishman, I thought – a type one recognised. And you – '

Louis pauses, gives me that quick, dark, solemn glance which is familiar to me now; then, smiling a little, spreads his fingers (neat and practical, yet thin, and always expressive of his feeling) in a gesture of uncertainty.

'You – I am not very sure – perhaps I did not see you after all! You went so quickly away – ' He laughs, enjoying my puzzlement.

' – But no, I did see you; and I thought it very strange that you should be alone with such a man, and yet you could not be his wife. First, you stood so long with him at Etty's painting, which is so immodest – *that* I considered curious for an English lady; and then you were looking at the Turners for so long . . .

But at first I had not recognised you – for with Miss Millington you were so silent, so reserved; and in the gallery I saw a different woman – someone who had come to life . . .'

His voice becomes more foreign-sounding as he searches for the words, tries to describe his feeling to me. Sometimes, I wonder if there are such barriers between us that we cannot ever know each other well: yet there are other moments when one does not need to seek for words, as if our meeting and communication have (without our aid) been fashioned long ago.

'And that is why I stared at you so much – and your friend Philip Earnshaw was, I think, not pleased.'

So, he had seen me. But he did not speak of it for many months – those months when I came to feel affection for his wife and children; months when, all unwittingly, I must have listened for the sound of Louis' voice, or welcomed the knowledge of his presence in the house – as we become accustomed to the light to which we waken, or the pleasure of the objects in a place we know and love.

When I went a second time to Bisham House, he came into the morning-room, where I was waiting for Sophia.

'You have come to see my wife, Miss Curwen? And to collect your drawings, so I believe. But may I speak to you about them first, if you please?'

I murmured an answer, surprised at his eager manner, which belied the formal words and the studied care with which he placed my drawings on the table.

'Sophia has been called to the nursery – she will be a moment only, but I cannot wait, since I have an appointment in town. And this – this I must explain to you, if you will be so kind . . .'

With even greater care he laid upon the table a large book, leather-bound and with slips of paper placed between the leaves. Rubbed and timeworn as the covers were, within, the pages of the book were crisp and clean; and though I could not understand the language, I exclaimed with pleasure at the finely printed foliage and flowers, small animals and birds, all delicately drawn to form a decorative border to the text.

Louis Perreton was watching me, as, with a sigh, I closed the book.

'You think that you could do so well, Miss Curwen?'

'I?' Alerted by the suddenness with which he put the question, I looked at him: but no, he did not seem to be mocking me – though there was surely a hint of humour in the gravity with which he returned my glance.

'Indeed, no – I could not!' It was the truth: however hard I tried, I would never achieve such splendour, such simplicity.

'You are right to say it.' This time he smiled, quite frankly. 'It is the work of France's greatest printer – that is why! But that is the standard I must set myself, though I know that I shall never print so well. This is a book for the church – a Book of Hours you call it here, I think – and therefore, it must be perfect. It has lasted for three hundred years – nothing that I can do will last as long, or look as beautiful. But, I intend to try.

'So, what I require are drawings for my books. I design them for Sophia's father – he is the publisher, not I myself. Already I have two engravers working for me; one of them – a woman – she is very good. She can cut the wood so finely that you might, if you wish, do some very delicate designs. I look at the drawings you have done here – and at once I think that they are exactly what I want – '

Louis stopped abruptly, aware perhaps of the extent of my astonishment and doubt. Then he shrugged his shoulders, turned away from me – but not before I had noticed the look of disappointment, almost sadness, which tightened the lines about his eyes and mouth. I had rarely seen, I thought, so sensitive a face, or one which would be so difficult to paint.

'But I was wrong, maybe . . . It does not interest you . . .'

Already, the book was in his hand; he was about to go. I could not let him misunderstand my hesitation.

'No – it is not that. It is only that I cannot tell if I can do anything as intricate, as detailed. I should like to try – but first I must consult Miss Millington, of course. She has said that I am free to take whatever work I wish, but even so . . . and then, I should need to know exactly what you want, to see some books, perhaps – '

I had remembered, from long ago, the carvings in Saint Michael's church at Workington: those age-old patterns cut in wood and stone. And the flowers or ferns I used to find among the rocks of Ennerdale; the little moorland birds which often I had tried to draw ... Somewhere, I knew, I had those early sketchbooks still ...

'Then you will consider it? We will talk about it when you come again. And my wife will tell you more about my work – '

Sophia was standing in the doorway. I heard the rustle of her gown, and felt, rather than observed, the conscious grace with which she moved – or glided almost – across the room. She looked less frail than when I saw her first; yet even now the whiteness of her skin, the slender contours of her shoulders and her neck (too fragile, surely, to support the mass of burnished hair so carefully arranged) had all the vulnerable beauty of a hot-house flower – too tender and exotic for the ordinary world.

'Miss Curwen, I am glad that you are here: there is so much to discuss. Louis has spoken to you, then, about his books?' And, turning quickly to him, 'But Louis, you must go. My father will be here at any moment – and he hates to be kept waiting.'

With a hasty, awkward nod in my direction, and a murmur of apology, he was gone; while Sophia sank into a chair, laughing a little and exclaiming, 'Louis is always so *distrait* – so vague! And when he is talking about his work he has little sense of time, and Papa is always *very* punctual indeed. So you must forgive me if I seem discourteous – but you will become used to us, I hope, and will be here often if you are to help my husband with his books. He is quite perfectionist about them – but when I showed him your designs he said they reminded him of some rare French bindings that he has, and that you are too good an artist for Miss Millington. He meant no disrespect to her, of course: indeed, I think he believes, as I do, that even clothes should be as beautiful and well designed as possible.

'But then – ' she sighed – 'I have so little else to interest me! I hate domestic things, and lately everything has been extremely dull. I need to see new people and new places – and I am determined that soon I shall be well enough to go to Paris. I have lived all my life in Highgate, and now I find it too respectable and earnest: though I have everything I need – it seems, somehow, that I do not have enough!'

Sophia paused, and gazed around her at the pretty, tasteful room, with its polished furniture; at the gilt-framed pictures on the walls, the flowers in their crystal vases, and the ticking, painted clock upon the blue-veined marble of the chimney-piece. Above it hung a heavy, ornate mirror; and as she rose from her chair, I saw her glance, with some distaste, at the image of herself reflected in the glass. She crossed to the window and looked out into the garden.

'But there,' she said, 'you will think me foolish and ungrateful: if I go out into the air, I shall feel quite differently. Will you go with me, and we will meet the children from their walk? I should like them to know you . . .'

'I should like it very much,' I answered.

Then, impulsively, I added (for I could not bear to see her look so sad, and so angry with herself), 'You *will* feel better, out of doors – it is the best of things when one has been unwell and out of spirits. Once, at home in Cumberland where I was very ill, it was the garden, I believe, that cured me. And I shall be glad to come again – as often as my work allows me to!'

Afterwards, returning to the quiet gentility of Number 23, I wondered if I had imagined it: that almost instantaneous friendship with Sophia, that sense of empathy with a woman whose life had been so very different from my own. Yet in one respect, I was to learn, we were alike: for she had never known a mother's or a sister's love, while her father was a formal, distant-seeming man, an autocrat of whom Sophia (and the three unmarried aunts who brought her up) had been afraid. So there grew between the two of us the kind of bond that one imagines sisters share – yet without the rivalry or rancour which exists so often where two girls are close in age. Sometimes, when Sophia's little daughters quarrelled, I would marvel at the ease with which their childish joy could turn to anger or to tears. But then, I did not know that from my feeling for their mother there would one day spring a sorrow that would overshadow all our lives.

'My wife has been too much alone, Miss Curwen.'

It is the height of summer now. July – and although the garden is in full bloom, the air refreshed by the gentle breeze which hovers about the Highgate hillside, Sophia still prefers to rest indoors. The heat of her glass-walled room, the scent of its many-coloured flowers, oppress me; and I welcome an escape to the cooler panelled study where her husband works. Several times a week, I come to Bisham House; the little girls are to have their portraits painted soon, before departing, with their mother and the nurse, for a holiday beside the sea. They will go to Ramsgate, or some other quiet resort; Brighton is Sophia's favourite, of course – but she will forgo its fatiguing social pleasures for her Paris visit, promised for September.

'My wife – ' Louis hesitates, almost as if his thoughts are far off, and he can only speak them by some concentrated effort of his will. He has more work for me, to be undertaken while Sophia is away; yet it is not this, to my surprise, which he wishes to discuss with me.

'She was too much alone after we returned from Bath. I cannot tell you how much changed she is since you have come. She was so sad before you came – unwilling to enjoy her life as always she used to do. Now I think she has become herself again – '

'But you must not thank me for it! Her friendship is the greatest pleasure to me. And – and I hope it will continue, even when she is restored to health.'

'That is as I wish it, too, Miss Curwen. I have been anxious for Sophia for many months; now, I am able to work again, to think of other things. And maybe, when I am in Paris, I can be of some service to you – if, that is, you will permit me.'

As soon as he looks directly at me, rather than before him at the plans and drawings on his desk, I can see that the hesitation and the diffidence are only in his voice. His glance is full of feeling – a warmth which must surely come from his affection for Sophia, and his relief that she is almost well again. For Louis loves his wife. His daily care for her, his evident distress at her continued weakness, have already shown me that. I know now why he was so grave, preoccupied, when I saw him with his children in the garden, or walking with them in the early days of spring.

Yet I am glad – surprised and glad – that he should think well of me. I do not know what use he can be on my behalf in Paris; but he does not listen to my protestations.

'There is someone to whom I should like to show your work. He is an artist, like yourself; he has some influence – but his work is very different from yours. No – ' Louis smiles at my unspoken question – 'you will not have heard of him, though one day I am sure he will be known in England, too. Gavarni, they call him now – when we were young and together in Paris, I knew him by another name. You see, some of us changed our names after the Revolution; and some, like myself, left Paris altogether.

'It was a strange time – before I met Sophia's father, and before I came to England. One day, perhaps I will tell you more about it all . . .'

I think how curious it is, that this man has had another country and another life – even, perhaps, a different name. Almost like myself, he has a past of which others know so little. And how changed he seems when speaking of it: how much less distant and abstracted he becomes . . .

'But in France, we are kinder to our artists. Here, they are respected less, and have to fight for everything. Blake – how the English persecuted him! And Constable – he was ignored, and so was Bonington; and yet, in France they were recognised as great . . . But then, we French do other, more barbaric things to one another – things which here you do not tolerate.'

Louis' voice has lost its usual gentle hesitance. And there is surely bitterness, as if he has suffered in some way, in the curve of his mouth, the sudden hardening of his gaze as he stares before him once again . . . What was it Philip said to me, so long ago? How in France he saw men dying in the streets, and somehow felt to blame for standing by at such a time . . . And Louis Perreton: was he, perhaps, in Paris then?

'Those things, Miss Curwen, and those times, are best forgotten now.'

He was right; and so we did not speak of them again that day. But if there was a moment at which I ceased to see him only as Sophia's husband, I must suppose that it was then.

Chapter 22

Philip disliked my friendship with Sophia. He often came to Highgate now, and sometimes I would return from Bisham House to find him taking tea with the two Miss Millingtons. Miss Alice had approved him from the first; she found his gravity, perhaps, congenial to her own; while Maria was flattered by his courtesy – after all, such masculine attention rarely came her way. There had been a brother in the family once. His portrait occupied a proud position in the ladies' private parlour, hanging above the decorative plaster fruit and flowers which framed the fireplace: and whenever Philip came, I noticed that Maria glanced more often at the picture – with the kind of tearful reverence one sometimes sees in women's faces when they pause before the altar of a church.

Increasingly, I felt the weight of Philip's disapproval. I knew him well enough to sense it in the studied air with which he asked about the progress of my work, in the silence with which he listened as I told him of the drawings I would do for Louis Perreton.

'So that is why you go so frequently to Bisham House.'

The words, when at last they came, were spoken lightly. Yet there was sufficient censure in Philip's tone to anger me. He had been waiting while I dried and put away my brushes; we were to walk as far as Kenwood House that afternoon with Miss Maria. But suddenly, I did not wish to go.

'Yes – it is for that, in part. And also, the children are sitting for their portraits, and I want to do as much as possible before they go away.' He had no right, I felt, to make me justify myself; yet I must not let him see that I resented it.

'When they are gone,' I added, 'I shall have more time – '

'More time for what – for yet more work? To shut yourself away each afternoon, when you might, at the very least, be painting in the open air, as you used to do in Cumberland?'

His manner was abrupt, peremptory, like that of a father with a wilful child. And it puzzled me, for I could not think I was at fault.

'But I am happy here, and I am often in the garden with the little girls. Besides, you understand – surely – the reason why I choose to work . . .'

'I do not understand why you should let your work destroy you, Georgiana! Why, when there are others who would help you, must you be so proud? I thought, when you left Miss Brackenbury, that you would try to find some easier way – and yet you take on pupils still, and every time I come you tell me of some new commission. You do not seem to care that such constant application may affect your health – as well as making you forget your friends. And this, for Perreton – ' He glanced with contempt at the drawings on the table. 'He thinks that you will work more cheaply than another artist would: he wishes to exploit you, that is all!'

The accusation shocked me, as he must have known it would. As so often in the face of Philip's scorn, I could not find the words of self-defence; nor, in the ensuing silence, did I think of any argument that might explain my trust of Louis Perreton. Perhaps, instinctively, I knew that nothing will out-weigh convictions based (as Philip's must have been) on one man's jealous apprehension of another.

Silence, indeed, proved the more effective answer. For Philip, after several minutes, picked up his gloves, examined them with care, and turning to me, said, 'If you are ready, let us go and find Miss Maria. It's a pity to waste the afternoon – and it must almost be a year since you and I have walked to Hampstead.'

This last rebuke, implicit though it was, distressed me most of all. For I had never told him of the reason why I quarrelled with Miss Brackenbury, nor of her description of our meetings as immoral. He had known I was unhappy at her school; but he had always, until now, encouraged me to persevere with my ambition. Yet I supposed that he must remember Charlotte still, and how her bid for independence led to loneliness, to fever, and to death. Perhaps I had neglected to consult him as I should: the Perretons were strangers to him, after all – and perhaps I had indeed been tempted to forget that Philip was my closest friend . . .

I resolved to be more prudent, and said nothing of Louis' wish to take my work with him to Paris. In August and September, while Sophia and her family were away, I resumed my walks with Philip. When Miss Alice felt she could be spared, Maria Millington went too; and sometimes Philip's nephew, George (now working in the city offices of Nicolson & Curwen), came to Highgate on a Sunday afternoon. George had not lost the open, easy manner which I used to like so much – and though something of a dandy in his dress, he had retained the Cumbrian intonation in his voice.

Hearing the familiar cadence once again, I felt as if the past had entered with him through the door of Number 23. As Maria bobbed in and out with tea-things, in a voluble frenzy of attention to the gentlemen's requirements, I would listen with a strange detachment to the latest news of Workington, or to George's reminiscences of Keswick days. And when, in the evening quietness of my room, I thought of Charles – of those moments I had tried to bury in the dark recesses of my mind – it pained me less. I was not ready to go back to Cumberland: yet now, with George's coming, I did not fear the prospect as I had. Something had changed me – but what it was, I could not tell.

Mindful of Philip's admonition, I painted out of doors as often as I could. My employers were less busy, since many of their customers were out of town; so I was often free to find some sheltered place to draw. My subjects were the kind beloved of Constable: a drover with his herd, some gypsies on the common land, the water-carrier with his ancient battered cart which laboured in the dusty heat up Highgate Hill. I sketched the shops and cottages, the toll-house and the ponds – hopeful that I would sell the finished work when winter came. My savings had increased, my skill improved, yet still there was so much to learn. For I was conscious now of something lacking in my work, some vital element which might one day transform it to that higher level which I sought: only constant practice and experiment would show me what it was. I knew that competence alone was not enough – there had to be, there *must* be something more. 'An artist should accept his limitations, Georgiana': Philip had said it to me more than once. And yet, unless I tried – however frequently I failed – I should never know the limit of my powers.

Sometimes I walked along the leafy hill-top lane past Southwood, where Sophia's aunts, the three Miss Longmans, lived; and beyond, past her father's house – the newly-built reward of his prosperity, a square white monument to enterprise and thrift. Through the surrounding trees I glimpsed the wide expanse of fields and wooded groves, the slender spires of churches gleaming in the sun. A landscape which had a dreamy quality, an air of timelessness – as if the encroaching city, its inexorable northward march, held no reality for those who lived above it in their tranquil fortresses, among their sheltered garden walks and croquet-lawns, the summer-houses set between the scented limes.

But if I took a different path, the open road beyond the gate-house and the castle-yard, I came to Southcott House. From its pillared entrance I could see the grey-clad inmates spreading linen on the grassy banks to bleach. The women took in laundry work as well as sewing, so Maria said; and I wondered how they bore the dull monotony of ceaseless toil, so far removed from any friends or family they might have known. What circumstance had made them what they were, what chance had brought them here, from among the thousands haunting London's streets, its fashionable parks and thoroughfares, its filthy alleys or disreputable courts?

The young girl whom Miss Millington engaged remained a mystery. Even Miss Maria (her curiosity outweighing moral scruple) had confessed defeat: we knew her name, Grace Evans –

nothing more. When I passed her, trudging with her heavy basket up the hill, she recognised me, sometimes nodded to me; but she did not smile. She might have been any stranger walking by – save that her glance, I noticed, rested longer than a stranger's might upon the painting-things I carried with me.

She had continued to work the longest hours of all the sewing-girls. They had ceased to mock her quiet demeanour, and the scandal of her having come from Southcott House had long since passed. There had been some talk of her dismissal, when the summer orders lessened; but Miss Alice was reluctant to dispense with someone whose sewing was so fine. Yet I observed, when I went into the workroom one September day, that she had not taken up her needle; a garment lay in front of her, but she only sat and stared at it – until she saw me watching her, and then, with a sigh, she picked it up again.

Later, I overtook her on the road, halfway between the Angel and the turn which led into The Grove. I said 'Good morning' as I passed, but she made no answer; then I happened to look back, and saw the girl still standing there, gazing at her basket on the ground. I waited; but she did not move, and on an impulse I returned to where she stood.

'Is something wrong?' I asked. 'Why are you not at work?'

It was not midday; and I knew that only some pressing reason could have made her leave so long before the usual time. But she looked so startled when I spoke that I wondered if she thought I had been told to take her back; so I tried to reassure her.

'I am sorry – you are unwell, perhaps. Has Miss Maria sent you home?'

'Home?'

It was I who was startled now – by the blankness of her look, by her uncomprehending echo of the word, the sudden flash of anger which succeeded it.

'Home? Why, yes – I suppose that Southcott House must be my home!'

Before I could say more she turned away, and took her basket, and was gone beyond the hilltop, out of sight.

Grace Evans' work was faulty, so Maria said. Yes – it was unusual; that morning she had complained of seeing badly and had been allowed to go. She ought to be dismissed, of course – she was nothing but a trouble to the other sewing-girls! Miss Millington had disagreed, and her sister had no choice but to comply. It was clear to me that Miss Maria disliked the girl, but privately I thought Miss Alice was the better judge. Within a day or two, Grace Evans had returned; and though convinced she was not idle or deceitful as Maria claimed, I could tell that there was something strange about her. Perhaps it was the hesitancy in the way she moved, the air of apprehension as she looked about her when she took her usual place.

Then, to my surprise, she sought me out. I had returned from walking late one afternoon, and found her waiting by the door, at the foot of the narrow stair which led up to my rooms. The other seamstresses had gone; and she held her bonnet in her hand – so that I noticed yet again how delicate her features were, how dark the shadows of fatigue upon the pallor of her skin, how marked the lines about her eyes and mouth. She was no more than seventeen, I guessed: yet her face already bore the signs of weariness and toil one might have seen in a woman twice as old. And I thought, as she followed me upstairs, of a girl whom I had seen from a carriage window long ago – another whom capricious Chance had cast aside.

Was that why I could not disbelieve the tale she told? Why, after she had gone, I did not heed the doubts which cautioned me that she had been (despite her youth) a whore, whose character was lost beyond recall? Or was it, perhaps, some premonition of a time to come – when I should feel myself rejected by society, an object of the moralists' reproach? . . . Whatever prompted me to listen, it was clear that only a desperate kind of resolution led her to confess her secret to me; and I wondered later that she had succeeded in concealing it so long.

Grace had been apprenticed to a milliner at thirteen years of age. Her mother had been a needlewoman, too: daily, from dawn till after midnight, she had stitched her life away as an 'improver' in the sewing-trade – supplying finery to ladies who (with careless irony) might call themselves the slaves of fashion! Having nursed her mother, having seen her die from lack of warmth and food, Grace had returned to find another girl employed. And so, like many others, she had sold herself on London's streets – for virtue matters little to a hungry child, or to a father desperate for work. But she was luckier than most, she said: for a year or more, she had been the mistress of a painter, who had used the money which she earned from other men to buy materials, until one day he vanished, leaving her alone.

'He was good to me – and he was Irish, so sometimes I could not understand the way he spoke. But he laughed a lot, and I was sorry that he went away. That was when Mr Southcott found me. And when he knew I had a trade, he said that he could find me work – only I didn't know he would take the money for himself . . .'

The girl had hesitated then, and looked at me as if afraid.

'So every week I kept a little, so that I could take it to my father. And on Sundays, when we are supposed to go to church, I sometimes walk to Islington to take the money there; but lately I haven't earned enough, and Mr Southcott was angry when they sent me back, that day you spoke to me . . .'

Her voice was low; and I could see her fingers shaking as she twisted the ribbon of her bonnet and gazed beyond me to the window, to where my easel stood, an unfinished painting still upon it.

'That is why I came to you – to ask if you might know of any other work. I am afraid that I will lose my place, that Miss Millington will make me go.'

'But Miss Millington is pleased with you,' I said at once. 'Whatever Mr Southcott says, she will want to keep you.'

I was convinced of it. And surely, if she knew, she would be as angry as myself that Mr Southcott's charity did not extend to those who were too ill to work: for only industrious sinners, so it seemed, could with profit be reformed!

'Come,' I added gently, ' – you need not be afraid to tell her. She is very fair, and perhaps will let you rest more until the winter orders must be done. As for the money – '

[303]

'No!' she cried. 'I did not come to beg from you. But I could earn it – if you would let me sit for you; I have done it before – for the Irish painter, very often. And I must go on sewing, if I can: but I – I may be ill again; and Miss Millington won't want me if she knows . . .'

Suddenly, I realised that she had not told me all. And, what was it that had puzzled me of late? . . . Something about the way she moved her head, and looked uncertain – just as she did now, searching for the basket she had placed beside her on the floor . . .

Even as she turned to me again, and put her hand up to her eyes in a gesture of despair, I understood.

'I cannot tell her,' she was saying quietly. 'I have to work. But, soon, I am afraid I shall be blind.'

Her likeness grows beneath my hand. Beside me, a heap of sketches; palette, pencils; brushes with tips like little sable eyebrows, finely drawn. A disarray of colours out of which an image, by degrees, is formed, fleshed in and made substantial – every feature new, and yet, by now, well known.

Philip comes; and yet again, he finds Grace Evans sitting for me. I cannot walk with him: as soon as I began this work, I knew it would absorb my whole attention. There is an urgency, such as I have never felt before. He is a distraction, an intruder from that other place – of drawing-rooms and hot-house flowers, and voices which will tempt me to abandon what I wish to do. I will try to show the life that Grace has lived, discarded like an outworn garment faded long before its time: a world of hunger, cold, and dirt, of youth long past and darkness still to come. And something elusive, which the autumn light illumines as she sits before me with her basket at her side: the innocence retained, and yet the virtue gone; a child, who wears a woman's clothes.

The Perretons, said Mrs Heywood, were a charming pair. *She*, of course, had been the belle of Highgate: it was a wonder that her father had allowed the match, and the three Miss Longmans were against it from the start. But then, Sophia had always been a headstrong girl, and he was glad enough to have her settled near to him. Only it was a pity (here Mrs Heywood paused, giving her words the weight of all her national prejudice), such a pity that the husband was so very *French*!

Laughing, I answered that I thought perhaps it was the reason that Sophia married him. But Mrs Heywood did not seem amused: the Captain, as she pointed out, had often in the Indies fought against the French.

'And do you know, when Captain Heywood sold him Bisham House, he said that he wished to leave it as it was, and to make no changes – *I* always found it very old and inconvenient. It was Sophia, I believe, who had the terrace made; and the conservatory cost a deal of money – all that glass is so expensive, and most of her plants, they say, have come from Kenwood. I suppose that Lady Mansfield must have felt obliged . . . but there, Mr Longman has such influence in Highgate, and Sophia is still his daughter, after all.'

'I think that she prefers to go to Mr Cutbush. His nursery is very good – and I am sure she likes to patronise him if she can.'

I did not care for Mrs Heywood's gossip, and felt bound to defend Sophia. Since her return from Paris, she had taken up her social life once more, and I had become absorbed in work; we had, in consequence, been together less. But our friendship had, if anything, increased: she embraced me warmly when we met, and soon I would begin her portrait – a present for her father, and therefore a secret from Mrs Heywood, who could rarely keep her counsel, as I knew.

'She would rather be closer to her father's house, I hear; and the air is better there, of course. I was asking Sara Coleridge the other day, but she hadn't heard if Perreton would move . . .' She looked expectantly at me.

But I would not let myself be drawn, and answered cautiously, 'I did not realise they were acquainted.'

When I came to London first, Sara Coleridge had lived at Hampstead – at the address which her brother Mr Hartley had written in my book, five years before. With Philip, I had visited her cottage several times; and we had spent some pleasant hours, talking of her brother and our Keswick friends. It was only lately that we had met again, for now she was a neighbour of Mrs Heywood, at Regent's Park.

'Well, I would not say that Sophia knows her *intimately*, dear. But Mr Longman is a publisher, with intellectual friends; and Sara's father was a literary man, of course, and as a poet, so well known – they were bound to meet at Doctor Gillman's, in The Grove, while Coleridge was still alive. Now she does not often go to Highgate; even so, at Regent's Park, you know, we hear of everything that's going on!'

Yes, I thought – and now I am accepted by the Perretons, you are glad enough to take me up again, to introduce me as an artist to your friends. How I wished that I had no need of fashionable patronage; and how annoyed I was by the look of triumph in her eyes, the note of malice in her voice. It was no wonder that Sophia sometimes seemed to hate the place which she had always called her home, or that Alice Millington disliked her more pretentious customers. There could be no escape from idle curiosity; from the more persistent scrutiny of moralists like Hannah Brackenbury; or the scandal whispered over teacups in the afternoons.

Just then, Maria Millington came in, to summon Mrs Heywood for the fitting of a gown. I was relieved to see them go; Grace Evans had been waiting patiently for over half an hour. Since the girl had come to sit for me, I was out of favour with Maria: she had not said so openly, but I knew it all the same. At first she had tried to dissuade her sister; then, having failed, had simply murmured 'shocking' or 'ridiculous' whenever I encountered her, until one day Miss Alice overheard and bade her hold her tongue. For Miss Millington had gone to Mr Southcott on the girl's behalf, and persuaded him to give her laundry work, in hope that a change of occupation might delay her loss of sight; and in place of sewing, she could help deliver orders to the customers – however much Maria might complain.

I wondered what Mrs Heywood might have thought if I had told her who my sitter was, or what her former life had been. And perhaps I painted into Grace's picture some part of my anger at her helplessness, my sense of guilt that there was so little else that I could do. I spoke of it to no one; this time, not even Philip shared my thoughts, or understood the meaning of my work.

For though I did not know it fully at the time, those months of labour brought about a change. What was it Constable had said? 'You must paint the vision you alone can see...' Something had been restored, which had been lacking in my life since I left Cumberland. It could not be my love for Charles — the innocence which vanished like the snow in spring, the trust which withered when the autumn came. Not my aunt's embrace, nor the sense of safety I had known at Portland Square; not even the sound of singing larks in Ennerdale, nor anything that I had yearned for when I sat alone and watched the city lights.

It was Peter whom Grace Evans had brought back to me. A ragged boy; a white cat playing on the grass; an ugly, senseless death. The father who had loved and lost his son; the fisherman, with whom I might have gone to Ravenglass...

Chapter 23

More than a year has passed since first I came to Bisham House. It is a calm mid-summer afternoon. Tea is to be brought into the garden, where we sit in a shadowed circle: Louis and Sophia; myself and the little girls, one on either side. The older child, Virginia, holds in the hollow of her hand a thrush's egg, which she found beside the path while walking with me earlier in the day. She is looking at it now – a perfect blue, a perfect shape. Helen, small and dark, intense at times just as her father is, bends closer to her sister, tries to see more easily – and suddenly, the egg is crushed. There is momentary anger; tears; Sophia beckoning the maid to take the little girls inside: they will take tea in the nursery, after all . . .

Even by dusk, the heat remains. The windows, and the glass doors of the garden room, are open wide; moths drift in among Sophia's flowers, brushing at the petals with intrusive wings, then moving on toward the lamplight in the hall. Soon the dinner-table candles will be lit, the curtains drawn; Louis will come in, carrying a book or papers – proofs, perhaps – which he wishes me to see before I go. And when he glances at me, I will guess his thought; even before the words are said, he asks the question – and, as always now, I shall refuse.

'No, I mustn't stay; Miss Millington expects me soon.'

*

Sophia has been ill again. The atmosphere is strained. It is impossible to know, from day to day, how I shall find her: lying on her couch, as if she has no strength to rouse herself from inward thoughts; or wandering from room to room, looking for some trifle she has lost – maybe a handkerchief, a button from her gown. Her conscience, her anxieties, are focused on such odd or unexpected things: the colour of her stockings or the whiteness of her gloves obsess her mind for hours; even the falling of the petals from a blossom causes her distress.

Louis, I can tell, is becoming weary. Sometimes, when we work together, he will sit at his desk across the room, eyes closed, head leaning forward on his hand. Often now, he seems much older than his forty years – save when his features are illumined by a smile in which I see him as a boy, eager and without reserve. I have thought, of late, that he is more a father than a husband to Sophia; he cannot always hide the anger that he feels when she is wilful and demands his whole attention – only to reject him with her sudden tears, or with a laugh which once was sweet, but has become discordant, meaningless.

At such moments she will often turn to me, hold out her hands, and say, 'You are not angry, Georgiana? You will help me to be happy, will you not? . . . And I will try – '

And then we go together to her glass-walled room, the place where she is most at peace; and to please her I will draw the flowers that she loves. Or, until she tires and sleeps at last, I read to her, as if she were a child. Perhaps tomorrow, when I come again, I shall find her as I knew her first . . . Yet even then, her happiness had been a transitory, brittle thing which, like the ice upon the surface of a winter pool, might break beneath the burden of her thoughts.

Highgate at Christmas-time. Coloured cakes and candles in the windows of the village shops; a sound of bells, which echo out across the London plain. A wagon-load of holly pulling up the hill to Southwood, where the lighted lamps make little misty suns above each gate; the cottage children running to pick up a fallen, berried branch, or standing on the step of Number 23, hopeful that Miss Maria will give a penny for a seasonable song.

Soon there will be skating on the ponds; the trees, their twigs encased in ice, will shake and tinkle in the bitter wind, which penetrates the shutters and, at length, bears snow upon its breath.

It was at this time, when Sophia held her New Year party, that I saw it first: the frailty of her hold upon the world, her fear of anything that marred her own perfection, threatening her image of herself.

She had come down to greet her guests. Most of them were Highgate people – family and friends, with whom I found myself surprisingly at ease. I had not wished to go, had pleaded headaches, or the risk of further snow. But Sophia had insisted that she could not do without me: her father wished to know me, so she said – he was delighted with the portrait I had done. The Miss Millingtons would be there; and Miss Gillies, with her sister Margaret, who painted miniatures and was a friend of Sara Coleridge. And I would meet – at last – Gavarni, who had come back with the Perretons from France. Louis had told me that his friend was sketching scenes of London life for the Paris magazines, and for a week or two would stay at Bisham House: he would like to take the opportunity to talk to me about my work.

The conservatory looked charming, everyone declared. Lamps, and a little fountain, had been set among the plants, which seemed to glow with heat and light – a coloured, artificial world, enclosed above the winter garden and the snow. Sophia had spent hours, with Mr Cutbush and his boy, preparing it: and the effect was perfect, as she wished.

When Louis came to find me I was looking at the flowers with Miss Maria.

'I can remember,' she was saying, 'when I was a girl – before my father was *unfortunate*, that is – Mamma would always send to Mr Cutbush for her flowers. But I do not recollect that there was ever anything particular about them – nothing as unusual, I should say, as these of Mrs Perreton's! I wonder if – '

'Miss Curwen.' Louis spoke with urgency, and glanced at my companion, as she turned away to watch the fountain for a moment.

'Georgiana!' Now he took me by the arm, and led me to the doorway of the garden room.

'I am anxious for Sophia. She was with me for a time, when everyone arrived. Then I saw her with her father, and he tells me that she felt unwell, and went upstairs. I cannot go to her — there are too many here, you understand. But you could go to her, perhaps, and come to tell me what is wrong . . . It would be very kind —'

I found Sophia in her room. She did not answer to my knock at first; but after I had waited for a moment, tapped a second time, she came — and I could see at once that she had been in tears. As soon as I had closed the door behind me, she began to weep again — quite heedless of the blood which, as she held her hands up to her face, was flowing from her fingers, falling on the whiteness of her gown. And behind her, in the pretty, ordered room, her gloves lay on the bed: a pair of empty twisted things upon the coverlet of rose.

For an instant, in my shock, I could not speak or move to go to her. But then I led her to a chair and seized her gloves, with which I tried to stem the bleeding from the cuts — irregular and deep — across the palm and fingers of one hand. Sophia scarcely seemed to hear me as I rang for water and some linen; but, at length, I made her take a little wine, and she appeared to be herself again. I spoke of fetching Louis — but, to my surprise, she would not let me go.

'You must not — he will only be alarmed. I — I will change my dress, and then — perhaps I can come down again.' She hesitated, glancing with aversion at her hand.

'It was foolish of me to be terrified, of such a little thing. But there was so much blood — I couldn't bear it, Georgiana — and I thought that I should die, just as I believed I should at Bath when I was ill . . .'

She shivered suddenly, despite the shawl I placed about her shoulders, and the glowing fire which she kept burning in her room. Her fears were real enough. For I remembered how she avoided going to the nursery when the little girls were sick; and how she told me once that she would sooner die than bear another child. Sophia hated pregnancy, I knew: to see her

[311]

perfect figure swollen, and to feel her strength diminished, grieved and frightened her. Yet later, when I saw her carrying her last, and fatal, child, I thought how beautiful she looked – as if the burden of a second life had given her unconscious dignity and grace.

Now, as she trembled, pulled the shawl more tightly round herself and stared into the fire, I loved and pitied her. Perhaps, if I had known that I would one day injure her, I would have gone from Highgate then . . .

'Will you tell me how it came about?' I asked. 'It isn't foolish to be frightened – and to speak of it may help you – '

Sophia looked uncertainly at me, and sighed.

'It is foolishness to do as I have done – I should have been content to leave it as it was . . . It was that little orange-tree, which stands next to the window in the garden room. When Mr Cutbush came this afternoon, he moved it for me, so that it would be beside the fountain. But after he had gone, I didn't like it – but I left it, all the same. Then I went to see if all the lamps were lit, before the guests arrived; and the orange-tree looked wrong. I thought that I could trim a branch away – '

Although Sophia's voice was steadier, I noticed that her amber-coloured eyes were very large and, like the firelight, flickered with a curious, unsteady brightness: and it was as if, though seeing me, she had forgotten I was there.

'And so I took the pruning-knife, the one I often use outside – it tells you how in Mr Loudon's book. I – think it slipped somehow, or I held it wrongly – I don't know what happened quite. But there was blood upon the floor, and on the tree, and in the little pool . . . I thought that Louis would be very angry if he knew – he often says that I should take more care. I would not let the servant fetch him; and then the bleeding stopped. I put a handkerchief beneath my glove – I hadn't time to come upstairs again . . . But as I waited in the hall, when everybody came, I knew that there was something wrong. My hand was wet. And then I saw that blood was coming through my glove . . .'

Later, I stood beside my window and looked out across the grounds of Bisham House. I saw the terrace lamps, their pattern like the threads of shining beads that decorate a garment's hem.

Sophia would be sleeping now, her garden room deserted and her guests gone home. And Louis? Seated in his study, with an open book, unread, upon his desk: his thoughts, his heart, and his uncertainties still centred on his wife.

That night I had begun to understand his fear for her. The cuts upon Sophia's hand would heal: but there was something more, a deeper wound within herself, which no one – save herself – could hope to mend.

The bitter cold continued until Candlemas. The seamstresses could scarcely work, Maria said, their fingers were so numb; and yet they must, for there were ball-gowns to repair, an opera-cloak or fancy-dress to be completed, or another batch of bonnets to be trimmed. My pupils had a holiday; and during the dark midwinter weeks Grace Evans was confined to Southcott House: I would begin another painting of her in the spring.

What would become of her, I wondered, when next winter came? Her family would not be able to support her, it was clear; Mr Southcott would not keep her if she was incapable of work; and though I did not say as much to Grace, I doubted if Miss Millington, though kind enough at present, could continue to employ the girl so long. To think of her alone and blind, a prey to all the dangers of the city streets, appalled me. She would have been far better off without the intervention of the Southcotts' charity: they, perhaps, had eased their prosperous consciences and saved her fallen soul from further sin – but Grace had lost her sight.

Yet while she was sitting for me, she often seemed more cheerful. As we became accustomed to each other, she would tell me of her early childhood on the Kentish coast, from where her parents, like so many village people, had been drawn to London by the hope of work; their few possessions dwindled until none was left, and only the mother's skill at needlework had kept the family from destitution, till her death. And one day, smiling a little, Grace told me of a time when the Irish painter came to her with country flowers, and put them in her hair and at her feet, and wondered why she wept. Her story moved me: for I could imagine how another artist – young and penniless, perhaps – must have wished to paint her as she looked to him, before the lines of weariness had marred her face. I should like to draw her in the countryside, I thought, for that is where she comes from, where she rightfully belongs. The city, with its degradation and its artifice, destroys her kind.

I took my studies of her to Gavarni, when he came. I had not meant to do so – for they had been shown to no one else. At the New Year party, when we met, he had alarmed me; and my own preoccupation with Sophia, when at last she joined her guests again, had made me even more reserved. He was not a handsome man, despite his elegance and wit; and Louis seemed the younger of the two. Gavarni's face was narrow, neatly bearded, and his forehead high, with a mass of curly greying hair; his eyes were very bright: they noticed everything, and penetrated (as I was to find his drawings did) the truth beneath the fashions of society, the beggar's rags, the poet's melancholy air. But here in Highgate – as he bowed and smiled with calculated courtesy, and studied every woman in the room – he looked eccentric, out of place.

He approached me as I was about to leave. Miss Millington was tired; but Maria, I suspected, would have liked to stay beyond the time convention (and her sister) had decreed. As it was, she seemed quite dazzled by Gavarni's air, his purple velvet jacket and his lilac-coloured gloves. In Paris I would discover that, with him, appearances deceived: he could be what he wished – immaculate, bizarre, even dishevelled if he chose. And when he spoke (with a voice more heavily accented than his friend's) he sounded charming and persuasive, yet amused.

'Ladies, you will forgive – may I speak a moment with Miss Curwen? You do not go already? It is early yet; we have to talk, I think?'

'I am sorry – yes, we are just going home.' I was wary; yet I wondered what he might have said of me to Louis . . . 'I shall come to see Sophia, perhaps, before you leave. You will return to Paris soon, I understand.'

'Yes; I shall not be in London very long. But it need not prevent – you see, Louis has already shown to me your work. It did not please me: I have to say it to you.' He shrugged his shoulders, shook his head.

[314]

'I am sorry; it was the best that I could do.' I tried not to let him see my disappointment. But then to my surprise he laughed.

'No, no, Miss Curwen, that is not my meaning. Your drawing, it is good – but you will not make a fashion artist. That is what I am myself, you understand. Some of my work, it is for magazines – *La Mode*, especially; you could not do that, I think.

'The designs you do for Louis, and your designs for the clothes – I like them, yes. But they are for earning money; and for your bread, they are as good as anything. But for an artist, they are not enough. It is your other work – whatever you have done; that I must see, if you please.'

'There is my portrait of Sophia,' I answered hesitantly.

'That I see at Mr Longman's house. But she is difficult, *la belle Sophie*. Not only beautiful – ' his tone became thoughtful – 'but, to try to paint her . . . it is hard, to paint a woman who always hides herself from you. But no, you did not fail; only you will do better, possibly . . .'

'I – have done other things. In the summer, drawings of Highgate and . . .' I could not have explained my reluctance to discuss my work; somehow, in the face of his persistence, and his charm, I felt uncertain.

'No, Miss Curwen! I do not want the views – they are for the public. Louis, he tells me that you are – *mystérieuse* – you do not speak to him about your paintings. But to me – you will do so!'

I acquiesced – yet not without misgiving. Paul Gavarni would not hesitate to crush the few illusions left to me; and this time it was not (as when I went to Constable) approval of my talent that I sought. Rather, I feared he might destroy my certainty that suffering and toil were subjects which a woman – like a man – must be allowed to see, to understand, to paint. And Gavarni was undoubtedly a worldly man; more of a cynic, I supposed, than even Philip Earnshaw was: I resolved to tell him nothing more of Grace than that she was a seamstress, whom (through my work for Alice Millington) I chanced to know.

But even so, he guessed. He examined all the drawings carefully, having laid them out upon the table in Sophia's morning-room: and then, he picked up one, to look at it again. He held it out to me.

[315]

'Is it possible, in Highgate? That you see a girl like this? The lady, the Miss Millington — she cannot know of it, of course! But I think that you must know it, surely . . . And myself, I see such women in the streets in town — there are so many more in London than in Paris. But I do not understand how you could find her — you will tell me, if you please.'

The drawing had been made one afternoon when Grace had told me of the Irish painter. She had taken off the apron that she usually wore, and had unpinned her hair, which fell about her shoulders, reaching almost to her waist. I sketched her as she talked, half smiling at her thoughts, and with an arm upraised to hold her hair: an attitude in which (as Gavarni recognised) seductiveness and innocence were curiously combined.

'So, Miss Curwen, you are serious, I think. You will continue with this kind of work — I am correct?'

I assured him that was so. For in spite of my resolve, I had described to him not only Grace's circumstances, but my own.

'But here in England, it is difficult. To be an artist, to have freedom, for a woman — is impossible almost; in France also, it is hard. But there, you may paint as you like; though to study — that is a different affair. But in Paris, you would be with artists, learn from them; and I think you must go there. You must work here first, so that you earn money to come to France. And when you come, I shall take you to the *ateliers* — the studios — and perhaps one accepts you; if not — you work more, and others will help you.'

Gavarni gathered up my sketches, gave them to me with a flourish of his hand. Yet he had not mocked me as I feared; and I was grateful to him, as I said at once.

'As for Paris, I will think of it, and try to do as you suggest. But it will take some time before — '

'That I understand. But Louis, he will talk to you — if you permit, I tell him what you do; you learn some French with him, perhaps. He is interested in you, that is evident. And we have been friends, many many years — '

He paused, and looked at me, almost as if he were about to tell me something more; but then, he smiled, and shrugged, and added, 'Louis, if he had remained with us, he would not be so —

so changed. Like you, he always must be respectable – he is in a trap, in England. Always, before, he was happy – full of ideas; now he is the businessman, he cannot go back to what he was.

'In Paris, maybe, he would live *la vie de Bohème* – the artist's life. But France – it is no more his home; he has become an Englishman!'

The force with which he spoke the final words amused me; and, at the time, I did not think Gavarni right. In Paris, when I met his friends – men who had been close to Louis in his youth – I changed my mind.

Before I left him, he fetched from another room some drawings of his own. Most of these were for the public eye: studies of the fashionable crowd; theatrical designs; or comic sketches for the magazines. But some, he said, were for himself; and it was these which finally dispelled my doubts. He was sophisticated and urbane, a libertine, perhaps – I did not know. Whatever Paul Gavarni proved to be, one thing was clear: he was an artist of extraordinary skill, whose sympathies I understood. For the people he had sketched in London's streets were those whom Grace had spoken of: drunkards, women with naked children in their arms; thieves with furtive eyes and greedy hands; beggars, huddled on the churchyard steps; and whores in feathered hats and furs, waiting on the benches in the public parks. They were drawn with feeling; yet there was no sentimental gloss: the lines were bold, the observation true; and the message (though he might have said that there was none) as clear as light.

'I am a connoisseur – of women, clothes, and poverty,' he said – and I believed it to be true.

Gavarni's sketches haunted me. The look of anguish in the women's eyes, the hopelessness which I had sometimes seen in Workington, and never dared record: a world I entered only when I followed Peter, in my thoughts, into the filthy tenements that scarred the hillside, far below the Curwen park, my mother's childhood home. I had walked through the lower town; but I had lived within the sunlight of a sheltered square. Often I had wondered what became of Mary, of the child my cousin Charles (with such unconcern) had fathered, and I held beside the transitory warmth of Michael Stephens' hearth. But I had done nothing for such people – nothing more than stand upon the threshold of the places where they lived and died. And in London, I had done nothing with my life except indulge ambition's fancy, stubbornly pursuing dreams which held no hope for others, and little profit for myself.

Yet if I were, in future, to do no more than paint the portraits, landscapes, flowers, that society expected of me, then I might as well return to Cumberland, to be a comfort to my aunt, to lead the life of a useful spinster, taking charitable gifts into the homes of those in need. I did not despise such women: I had seen my cousin Isabella welcomed into cottages, bringing the only comfort that the sick or workless might expect. Then, I knew that Henry Curwen's vision of Reform was good; yet neither he nor those who followed him had guessed how slowly and how painfully reforms would come. All I could do (as my grandfather had done) was follow in my chosen path; to use the only talent I possessed, seeking the freedom that my mother was denied.

Gavarni had both daunted and encouraged me: but while I worked to go to Paris – it would take a year, perhaps, to save enough – I would not be content to paint the Highgate scene. Now, I wished to go where he had gone; to find the truth he had portrayed, and had not tried (as so many other artists did) to make less shocking, by the use of gentle shading, softer colours, sentimental light. There was poverty and dirt among the green of Highgate; even tragedy, as I would come to know, within the walls of elegant and tasteful homes. But I would see Grace Evans' world, the city's darker face – which I had glimpsed only from the windows of a carriage, from the white steps of the exhibition rooms, from the narrow sheltered enclave of the class where I belonged.

The sky was the blue of thrushes' eggs, a colour pure and clear, before we left. But here, beside the Thames, there seems to be no sky – only a veil of smoke and dust, and the damp which rises round us as we walk. Somewhere perhaps, there has been morning light; midday; and afternoon: yet here it must be evening – uniform, monotonous and grey – from dawn until the weight of darkness presses out what little light there is upon the water, on the angles of the leaning rails, the worn-down edges of the steps.

My two companions are silent, watchful as we cross the bridge, toward the moorings and the rotting wooden stairs along the farther bank. Already we have found it difficult to move among the crowd; like the sullen, pallid river, far below the curving span, the press of people ebbs and flows, and bears us on the surface of its tide. Yet no one troubles us. For this is not the noisy, ribald throng that jeered us as we passed through Covent Garden or Saint Giles – where even children, drunk with gin, linked arms with laughing women at the corners of the streets. Nor are we followed now by those furtive ragged boys who lingered by Saint Dunstan's church, where the chiming clock, the twisted gothick towers, shone bright and new above the Fleet Street dirt. I saw the looks of menace in the faces there, and I was more than glad of Louis' arm, thankful that I had not been so foolish as to try to come alone.

Here on London Bridge we are among the very poorest of the city's poor. Old men, cripples, girls with babies at their breast, all drifting (like the city's putrid refuse on the tide below) in one direction, seeking shelter from the coming darkness and the bitter wind. They are too cold and hopeless to do more than stare at us, to turn away and stumble on towards the shadow of the steps, the iron pillars or the benches made of stone, even the railings at the water's edge – to any corner where they might find refuge for the night.

Behind, a driver cursing at the children in his path; the wail of infants, women chiding; and, beside the sloping parapet, a weeping, half-clad creature – blind or crazed perhaps – is reaching out to touch us as we pass.

Gavarni glances at her, looks at me, his eyes expressionless; and murmurs, 'So, Miss Curwen – you have seen enough? . . .'

I cannot answer him. I know that there is more, far more than this. Yet in that woman's face I recognise not one, but all the girls and women I have ever known: the sum of all that I have seen, or wish to see.

Chapter 24

That spring, Sophia's children learned to ride their pony, took their customary walks, and had new dresses made. Sometimes, when they came to find me, I would see them running down the path, across the grass, and through the iron gate; I heard their laughter as they clattered up the stairs; a sudden silence till they tapped the door, their faces eager as they watched me put away my work and find my outdoor things.

They were too young, perhaps, to notice how their mother changed. Sophia loved them, yet her affection seemed more childlike than their own – as if she were too self-absorbed to offer them the love that she, in childhood, was denied. She rarely laughed or sang with them; and while they played she often sat alone, withdrawn as any spell-bound princess in her shining tower, staring out across the newly budding trees toward the city and the smoke. One day she might intend to visit friends – but I would find her standing in her room among discarded clothes, her puzzled maid dismissed; she would delay, protest with furrowed brow and brimming eyes, declare she could not go. And tomorrow she might suddenly be driven by the restless spirit that I noticed when I knew her first: then for a time she would scarcely be at home, would walk or ride or dance with a compulsion that alarmed me even more. For I knew she must return at last, exhausted and afraid, to weep in Louis' arms or lie upon the couch among her flowers.

Since Sophia's party, I had come to realise that the woman who had captivated me a year ago – the wife whom Louis Perreton had loved – was gone. She could be delightful still; her beauty was no less: yet somehow her love of beauty, her distress at imperfection, had become a threat. Wilfully, and yet against her will, she was enclosed within a world from which we were locked out, from which at times she longed to be released. For neither I nor Louis could dispel the fear that filled Sophia's mind, or ease the hurt from which she fled.

When, at last, I spoke of it to him, Louis gazed to where his daughters ran ahead of us along the sunlit path.

'Sometimes,' he said, 'I think that Sophia wants still to be a child, and not a woman – to be always in the nursery, where it is so safe. But then she has bad dreams and wakens – it is dark, she is alone, afraid . . . But no – '

He smiled, watching the little girls; yet it was a bitter smile, that I could hardly bear to see.

'A child, if a father tells her "No", then she accepts; if you give her what she wants, she is content. But Sophia – never!'

She had told me so herself, I suddenly remembered: *'I have so much, and yet I do not have enough . . .'*

What was it that she sought? 'I should have died, I think, had he not married me. It meant so much – it would be an escape, I thought, to leave my father's home. How could I know that Louis would make me stay in Highgate? When I met him first he meant to live in France again one day – and Paris would have been our home. But then my father found that he could use him here; and he told me that Paris would be too unsafe . . .'

What had made Louis change his mind, I wondered? Would his children, and his wife, have led so different a life if they had gone to France? Whatever she was looking for, I knew Sophia hated Highgate; and, as I recalled her words, I thought of how my mother wanted to escape, to leave the home she loved, in search of something that she never found . . .

And yet Sophia was afraid of life, of its imperfection, and its disappointments; she could not bear the thought of pain, the sight of blood. No wonder Louis wished to spare her from reality, from whatever cruelties he had known and left behind.

[321]

Here, she could live protected, far from the sights that I had seen on London Bridge: high above them, in the safety of her glass-walled room.

'Maybe,' Louis was saying as we walked beneath the trees, 'maybe it is I who am at fault – I do not know ... Or perhaps she is like the girl you tell me of, the girl you paint – '

We came to a turning in the path, and saw that Helen, coming back to us, had fallen, lost her hat; her sister was picking up the scattered flowers. And as we went to them, I understood what Louis meant. Their mother, now, had gone alone into a darker world: Grace Evans was imprisoned by her blindness – and Sophia, by her self.

Philip Earnshaw was to marry, so they said. I heard it first – of course – from Mrs Heywood. *She* had heard it, she asserted, from her daughter, Lady Belcher, who had learned of it in Hampstead, where it seemed the happy pair had met. And Captain Belcher knew the lady's father well: he was an architect – Sir Robert Pennethorne; Mrs Heywood could not recollect the daughter's name. But she was certain of the rest: 'and what a pity' she concluded (with such conscious emphasis) 'that *you*, my dear, are not as fortunate!'

I had been aware for quite some time that she considered I had been remiss. After all, as she reminded me, Mr Earnshaw was more eligible now, for since his father's death he had inherited a quite substantial sum. How she had acquired this latter information I was at a loss to know, for Philip rarely spoke of his affairs; and as for marriage, he had told me once that he considered it a kind of death – and that he had no wish to waste his life in mourning for himself! He had laughed; but I was certain that he meant it all the same.

Now I was determined to ignore the rumours, and to believe in Philip's marriage only when he spoke of it himself. Yet I was apprehensive: for so long, his friendship had been all-important to me – and the loss of it was terrible to contemplate. Only when faced with such an unexpected possibility could I admit how much of my affection he had claimed ...

Within a week of hearing it from her, I began to think that Mrs Heywood's gossip must be true. For Maria Millington came, her eyes and cheeks aglow with ill-suppressed excitement, into the little parlour at Number 23, where her sister was in consultation with me as to silk for Lady Mansfield's new spring gown.

'I believe this is exactly what she has in view. And it would match exactly with the velvet mantle; and perhaps the feathered trim – the one with the little pearls, that you designed. What do you think, Miss Curwen?'

I agreed with her, though my mind was not upon my work. That afternoon, Grace Evans had not come: whether she was detained at Southcott House by unexpected tasks, or for some other, more alarming reason, I could only guess.

It was clear that Maria had something special to impart. She was visibly put out when Miss Alice bade her wait until she had measured out the silk. At length, she was allowed to speak.

'It is Mr Earnshaw!' she announced, unable to resist a sidelong glance at me. 'No wonder that he has not been to see us for so long!'

I had told her, when she mentioned it before, that I believed that Philip had been kept in Yorkshire in the weeks that followed on his father's death. And he had been to Cumberland, of course, to Mary Nicolson – though I had not said as much to Miss Maria. Evidently she thought she had far better information than my own . . .

'But we shall see much more of him in future, I should think. He is to marry a Miss Pennethorne, you know. I heard it from Sir Robert's sister, just this morning, when she came to change that bonnet – the one she took last week and did not care for when she got it home. It was her brother, so she says, who built her house at Hampstead, and Mr Earnshaw helped him there – '

'I think you mean Sir Robert *planned* the house, Maria!'

'Well, yes – it is the same of course – but it was there they met, you see. And – ' she paused dramatically – 'this is the most important part: Sir Robert is to buy Elm Court. He will be a neighbour, almost; and his daughter will be bound to come to us for all her wedding-things.

'Yet it is a pity – ' Unknowingly, she echoed Mrs Heywood's words; and her small, quick eyes were fixed, with open curiosity, on me. 'For we hoped, when Mr Earnshaw came so frequently . . . We wondered, sister, did we not – ?'

But Maria Millington had gone too far.

'Whatever *you* had hoped,' Miss Alice stated, calmly but with unmistakable distaste, 'Mr Earnshaw's personal affairs are of concern to no one save himself. It does not do, as I have often said, to mention confidences made to us by clients: you will, in future, not forget!'

Poor Maria – she had not meant me any ill; she had so little of excitement to enjoy. Yet I was thankful that Miss Alice intervened, for by now the subject (and the speculation) had become a painful matter to me.

It was in April that I learned the truth. Philip had returned; and he called – at last – one Sunday afternoon. He was good-humoured, looking fit and brown, as if he had been walking in the sun. Yes, he admitted, he had spent a month in Italy; he had disliked the thought of London, after so much travel – in the summer, he might go abroad again. Maria, I could tell, was mystified; but she found out nothing else. And she would have been more puzzled still had she known that I would go, quite soon, to Twickenham, to see the cottages that Philip had designed. I should be glad, I thought, to spend the day away from Highgate. I should enjoy the company of Sara Coleridge and George – for Mrs Heywood, to my great relief, had said she would not go.

The day proved fine and warm. There were daffodils beneath the trees at Hampton Court, and sailing-boats at Richmond, on the Thames. We walked beside the river; laughed at the antics of the ducks; and watched the swooping gulls above the graceful bridge. The cottages were duly seen, and I thought them pretty, set on rising ground, with their gardens along the river banks. Philip planned to build another for himself, so we were told: surprised, I reminded him that he had always hated London – whereupon he smiled, and said that he had changed his mind.

We took our luncheon on the grass, beneath the chestnut trees. And it was afterwards, when Sara Coleridge and George set off to look at Turner's house, that Philip leaned across to me and said: 'There is something I must tell you, Georgiana.'

I had expected it. Yet when the moment came, it was as if the river, flowing smoothly past us, ceased to move; as if the trees, their branches idly swaying in the April air, had closed about us and shut out the light.

Philip knew what he had done. He did not look at me, but stared before him at the daisies in the grass – almost as if he did not wish to know.

'I may marry, very soon.'

And then he looked at me, with sudden laughter in his eyes.

'You say nothing – you are not surprised?'

'I – congratulate you . . .'

'You are premature. I have not asked the lady yet – but when I do, she will accept.' He paused. 'Her name is Laura Pennethorne.'

'It is a charming name.'

'She is a charming girl. I have known her almost since she was a child. Her father is the architect – you must have heard me mention him. We have worked together in the past, and now he wishes it to be a partnership. Also, he requires a son-in-law: I seem to suit on both accounts.'

His voice was light; his manner arrogant; his eyes, amused. I found it shocking that he could speak so, of her, and of himself.

'You are quite sure that it is what you want?' I could not keep back the question, though I had determined not to ask.

'No. But I may do it all the same. I am thirty-five, the age at which – as Mrs Heywood never tires of telling me – society expects a man to settle down. I shall become, I must suppose, domestic, very tame – and very bored. But as an architect, I shall be certain of success.'

I almost laughed; and yet, I was so close to tears. Why, Philip Earnshaw was no different from any other man! He was like Charles – his marriage a transaction, made to suit a parent's whim, or to ensure a safe career. Or like Louis' marriage to Sophia: the daughter young and longing to escape, the father glad to see her off his hands, the husband trapped into respectability. Yet Louis, surely, cared about his wife; while Philip, though he talked of marriage, did not speak of love. And I would rather he had told me that he loved Miss Laura Pennethorne, than speak with so little feeling: I had known him far too well, still cared for him too much, to wish him such unhappiness . . .

'And does she care for you?' I asked him this – for I could not ask him what I truly wished to know.

'I am certain that she does. And so?'

'Then, I suppose that she is very suitable . . .'

'I see. You are like all the rest, like Mrs Heywood: you will be glad to know I have been caught at last!'

Philip stood there, gazing down at me. And I had not time to answer, or do more than comprehend the fleeting look of pain, the force of anger in his words: he seized me by the arm, and pulled me up to face him as he spoke.

'You are heartless, Georgiana. I have thought it for some time. You care for nothing but your work – it seems to blind you to all else. And it has made you hard: you have no understanding of me, even after you have known me for so long. Until lately, I have always wished to help you: now, I would sooner that a woman had no work, than that – like you – she had no heart!

'As for my marrying – I thought that it might matter to you, but I see that I was wrong.'

It was true that I did not comprehend him then: his inconsistency seemed strange to me, his scorn, unjustified. It grieved me that he did not know how much I feared the loss – to him and to myself – that a marriage such as this might bring. And why, I asked (though I could not say the words aloud), must Philip always try to hide his feeling from me – when he knew as well as I that it had lain so long beneath the surface of our friendship; that it might, but for my cousin Charles, have turned to love?

Yet now, it was as if he read my thoughts.

'I used to think you cared for Curwen still. But I believed you would forget – perhaps you have . . . But you have forgotten everything: your aunt, and Cumberland, myself – and all you live for is your painting, and your Highgate friends!'

His accusation hurt me, as it had when he had made it months before. But this time I remembered Louis' need, Sophia's distress; and my hopes to go to Paris, my concern for Grace – all that

Philip had not shared of late, and that I feared he might not understand . . .

'I have the right,' I answered, shaking off his arm, 'to do my work, to choose my friends – as you, or any man, may do. And I will not give it up. I have forgotten Charles. No, not forgotten; only – he does not matter to me now . . .'

I had not thought that I could ever say such things. And yet I did, while Philip listened silently, his mouth compressed: his anger, I believed, was gone, but I had caused him pain – and that I could not bear.

'You matter more to me than Charles. Your marriage – that will matter to me; and your happiness – much more than you can ever know!'

For the first time, almost, I was not afraid of him. Perhaps he realised: for he smiled a little wrily, and replied, 'In that case, whether I marry Laura Pennethorne or no, we shall continue friends . . .'

At last, that look of Philip's I remembered from so many years before. His eyes expressive, dark, and yet their meaning still concealed: all that I had longed to know of him, and now, perhaps, could never hope to know.

'But I wish,' he murmured, as he turned away, his voice so low that I could scarcely hear, ' – I wish to God that you had said it long ago!'

Before the month was out we met again, at Regent's Park. Mary Nicolson was there with Edith for a week or two, before going on to Bath. Philip's niece had been a schoolgirl when I saw her last: she was a self-possessed young lady now – yet she had not forgotten how we used to go for walks together, and how she taught me to use her mother's spinning-wheel. But Mary, in the forthright way that I remembered well, declared I must be a thorough Londoner by this time; and I did not mistake the note of disapproval in her voice. For when I told her I should not wish to stay in Highgate above another year, she asked at once:

'And shall you come to Cumberland at last? Aunt Nicolson has missed you greatly.'

I assured her that I planned to be in Workington for several months; I did not speak of Paris – I would prefer to tell my aunt of that myself. To my relief, Mary did not press the point. But she proved more than equal to Mrs Heywood when the conversation turned (as I guessed it would) to Philip's marriage.

'It is far from settled, Mrs Heywood,' Mary stated with considerable force. 'My brother does not seem inclined to hurry into matrimony – so I should not count my chickens there, if I were you!'

How blunt and honest northerners could be! I had forgotten – and Mary had sounded almost like Aunt Nicolson herself, her manner alarmingly straightforward when compared with Maria's cunning hints, or Mrs Heywood's cultivated interest. And after luncheon, when we went upstairs, she left me in no doubt as to her view of Laura Pennethorne.

'She is a pretty little thing, of course, but Philip would be bored within a month – and I pity any woman living with my brother when he's bored! I cannot think what he's about. He's a wanderer by nature, I believe; but if he ever settles down he should marry someone like yourself – though I doubt if he would have the common sense!'

Would she have spoken so, I wondered sadly, if she had heard what Philip, only days before, had thought of me? I did not think so. But in later years, when she showed me greater kindness than ever I deserved, I knew that she saw me not merely as a woman whom her brother might have married, but as myself, and as a friend.

Mary had brought from Workington a parcel and a letter from my aunt:

> You will be sad to hear that Captain Sharpe has died. They brought him back on the *Elizabeth*, when she came home from Barbados, just a month ago. I shall miss him greatly, but it is as well that Harriet, poor thing, was taken first – she would not have lasted long without him.

I could not help but smile a little, to remember how often, and how vigorously, she had criticised the frailty of her friend: my aunt had altered very little, so it seemed. Yet she would miss the captain, with his eccentricities, though she would not admit to such a weakness in herself! . . .

> I am sending you this box, which will be of use to you, I hope. It came from the *Elizabeth* – my husband always kept it in his cabin, for he liked to paint a little when he was away. But it has a history, which Mrs Heywood knows.
> It was given to Humphrey with some pictures by Captain Heywood, when he retired and gave up his command. He had had it for many years – since he was on the *Bounty* with my cousin, Fletcher Christian. But it belonged to Fletcher first. He had it made before he went to sea; he taught Peter how to paint, and gave the box to him, not long before the mutiny.
> So if you will use it, it will stay within the family. I have written to Mrs Heywood, and I do not think she will object . . .

It was a rosewood box. The corners and the lock were silver, smooth and bright; inside, the brushes and the palette were a little worn, but the colours must have been renewed. I was touched, both by my aunt's consideration, and by Mrs Heywood's generosity. For when I went downstairs, she insisted that she did not wish to keep it for herself.

'I remember that Peter always said he did not care to use it after Fletcher went; and he would not speak of anything to do with that terrible affair. He was so very young, of course – but fourteen years of age when he went on board the *Bounty*! Fletcher was very kind to him, and whatever they may say, he was a good and honest man – a splendid officer, so Peter thought . . . But you must read all about it in my daughter's book.'

I promised I would do so, and that I would show the box to Lady Belcher when she came. Mrs Heywood had told me several times that her daughter's story of the mutiny was written with a view to clearing Fletcher Christian's name; but I had paid her less attention than I ought: I had no notion, at the time, that it might prove of any interest to me . . .

Philip came back with me as far as Highgate. He laughed when I said I should, in future, think less ill of Mrs Heywood.

'Wait,' he said, 'until you plan to marry, or do something of which the gossips disapprove: you will find you have been very rash in saying such a thing.'

It was planned that he should call for me again next morning, if Miss Alice did not object. We were to go with Mrs Heywood and the Nicolsons out into the country, to the home of Mr Windus at Tottenham Green. He collected paintings, and had in particular an interest in Turner's work: there was a room devoted wholly to his watercolours, which he was sure would please me, Philip said.

He was in good spirits, and we did not speak of what had passed at Twickenham. I had always known that Philip could be kind: yet now it was as if he had not ever uttered words that caused me grave distress; as if I had never hurt him by my wish for independence, by my inability to understand his need. For that little space of time, as the carriage moved between the meadows to the northern hills, we were at peace.

Perhaps we knew such true communication comes but rarely in our lives; perhaps we knew it could not be prolonged. For sometimes there are moments when, within our hearts, we know that soon a storm will break – and afterwards, when we look back, we see that momentary calm, the gentle waters of the haven we have left behind.

Another afternoon. Light rain is drifting onto summer leaves and upturned flowers, onto the window-panes of Louis' workroom, and the fine suspended threads that spiders weave against the corners of the glass.

It is here that Louis likes to make his proofs, amid the papers, neatly stacked; the wooden blocks, engraving tools; the smell of ink and turpentine – the comforting familiarity of things a craftsman uses, knows and loves. Beside the window is a little iron press, its shape the same as larger ones which I have seen at Mr Longman's premises at Saint John's Road: I have watched the printers working there, have marvelled at the speed with which they can produce – from the magical conjunction of the massive presses' weight and the precision of each separate piece of type – a perfect page.

Louis is happy in this little room. He can lose all sense of time as he prepares and inks the blocks, appraises each impression, works to a rhythm that can ease the harsher certainties to which he must return each day. Sometimes the children come to find him; and he smiles as they search among the types for the letters of their names, then place them carefully upon the press for him to print. It grieves him, I can tell (though he does not speak of it), to think that his daughters are cut off, increasingly, from the affection that they need.

This afternoon, we are alone. I notice the deftness of his fingers, stained with ink; he has taken off his jacket and pushed back his sleeves and, with his hair awry, is careless of propriety. The sound of rain is more persistent now, enclosing us within the room: and Louis seems to me, at last, a man in harmony with what he does, and with himself.

Chapter 25

'It is impossible, Miss Millington. I cannot take responsibility for her: Grace Evans cannot stay at Southcott House!'

The speaker, a loud-voiced man of large proportions, appeared discomfited – both by the hardness of the small gilt chair on which he sat, and the cool but nonetheless contemptuous look Miss Alice gave him as reply. His folded hands began to fidget nervously upon the shiny fabric of his suit (ill-cut, and distinctly second-rate), where it attempted to restrain his ample stomach – the size of which suggested that he had not altogether given up the self-indulgence of a lifetime, whatever the privations he imposed upon the sinners in his charge.

There had been complaints, Mr Southcott had informed us, from the other inmates at the Home. Grace worked much less, so the women there had said, yet she received the same as they; and as her benefactor pointed out, there were many other needy persons who would be glad enough to take her place. (He avoided mention of their calling, since he was with ladies; but we knew his meaning, just the same.) No, he did not know of any institution that might take the girl: her family must support her, he supposed.

I could see that Miss Alice, like myself, was angry and perplexed. There was not room to spare at Number 23, and Grace had now too little sight to do her former work of taking orders to the Highgate customers; besides, the sewing-girls and Miss Maria would make her life unpleasant – that I could not doubt. Already Grace had found it difficult to cross the busy London road; sometimes she was afraid to come at all, and I could not imagine how she would survive alone. He would keep her for a fortnight more, Mr Southcott stated as he took his leave; then, she must find some other place to go.

It was Louis who suggested Bisham House. I had told him of Grace when Paul Gavarni came; he had seen my drawings of her, and her story had distressed him even then – more than it had his friend, who was (as I later found in Paris) a much harder man, where women were concerned.

'Perhaps the housekeeper could use her – for the laundry, or some other work? If Miss Millington would speak for her, I do not think Sophia would object.'

I disagreed: Louis did not understand, I thought, how women viewed such girls as Grace – surely Sophia would not wish to have her in the house.

'But she is little older than a child – and she is very quiet, a gentle girl like that can do no harm. She is honest, I am sure.'

Louis had seen her several times with me when we were walking in the lane that spring; he had been struck, he told me, by her delicate appearance and her patient air. He persuaded me at length to ask Miss Alice's advice – and she, to my amazement, was in favour of the plan. Whether she acted out of liberal conviction, from dislike of Mr Southcott, or simply in a spirit of perverse defiance of Maria's prejudice, I did not know. Within a day she had consulted with the housekeeper; had pointed out the saving to be gained by the use of Grace as laundry-maid, instead of sending half the washing up to Southcott House; and had taken it upon herself to guarantee her character if she were to be employed.

As for Sophia, I realised that she was becoming quite indifferent to such things. When, with some misgiving, I spoke to her of Grace, she merely looked surprised, and said that Mrs Harris mentioned something of the sort.

Then she smiled, and kissed my cheek in her impulsive way, saying that I had not been to see her quite so much of late.

'And when you come, you are so very solemn, Georgiana! Is there something wrong? You are not angry with me? Oh, I do not know why I am so dreadfully unkind: sometimes, I cannot bear to think how much I hurt you – yet I do, and I cannot help myself, somehow!'

I tried to reassure her. For I knew that now her eyes would fill with tears. She would torment herself with such reproach that she would be incapable of any other thought; and would lie upon her couch in silent misery, or would destroy a favourite flower in the garden room – as punishment for her imagined wickedness.

Such times were dreadful to me. Sophia had, one afternoon, been angered by some sketches I had made, when she was sitting on the terrace with the little girls. Suddenly she took a drawing from my hand and tore it up, throwing the pieces to the ground. I had been hurt and horrified; but it was Sophia's remorse that made it harder – not the deed itself. She remembered it for many weeks, in spite of all my protestations that our friendship was the same.

Now, as always, I was apprehensive that her mood would alter and that, yet again, I had unwittingly destroyed her fragile peace.

'You have not changed your mind?' she pressed. 'You are to come with us, you know. The children would be very sad if you did not after all – and I have promised them . . .'

'Of course I want to come! Miss Millington has said I need a holiday: the summer is a quieter time for her, and in any case, I can take some work with me if necessary. It is all arranged.'

To my relief, Sophia laughed. How strange it is, I thought, that when she is so anxious, she looks almost ugly, with her features sharpened by the tautness of her skin; her eyes too large, their colour clouded and their animation gone. Now they glowed with pleasure, with an amber brightness and a warmth which told me that, in spite of everything, her affection for me would remain.

'I am glad!' she cried. 'We should be so dull without you. The coast can be very boring if one does not have the company one likes. And you must help me to decide what clothes to take.'

[334]

She seemed to be herself again. And I should be so happy to be gone from Highgate for a time. A month, in which to walk beside the sea, to breathe the sharpness of the air and hear at last the sound of waves upon a pebbled shore: so much that I had left behind, had remembered with such longing and so little hope . . .

But I was fortunate. And Sophia, perhaps, would be improved in spirits by a change from Highgate; even the thought of leaving had restored a little of the happiness that she had lost. By August, I reflected, Grace would be quite settled here for, unless some chance should intervene, she would be safe at Bisham House . . . It seemed, that afternoon, as if the blue midsummer sky might be untouched by cloud; the warmth that rose from leaves and flowers and new-cut hay could never turn to autumn mist; and winter, with its end to all illusion, would not come.

I never met Miss Laura Pennethorne. By the time she came to Highgate with her father, to Elm Court, in the spring of 1840, I was gone. As to the young lady's rumoured marriage, Miss Maria (no doubt to her chagrin) was wrong: the speculated wedding-dress and trousseau were not needed after all – indeed, the last I heard of Laura Pennethorne was that she kept her father's house, a spinster still. But whether she was jilted cruelly (as of course the gossip later went) I do not know, for Philip never spoke to me of her again.

He had not visited me since the Nicolsons left town: he had gone with them to Bath, so Mrs Heywood said. But by the end of June, when I had heard no further news of him, I began to fear that Philip had been hurt that day at Twickenham – much more, even, that I had supposed. Yet at Mr Windus's he had been his usual self: composed and enigmatic in his sister's company; provocative, or absorbed in thoughtful inspection of the paintings, when with me.

There, I had been once more astonished by the power of Turner's work, and fascinated by the colours he employed: the room, with pictures crowded on the walls, propped up against the chairs and tables, had seemed alive with light. I was determined, after I returned, to begin another painting, more ambitious that anything I had achieved so far.

By the summer, the preliminary drawings had been made. I used my notes and sketches of the Thames, of those who lived – existed rather – on its banks, beneath the bridges, or among the courts and alleys not far from the water's edge. The day that Louis and Gavarni took me to the city, I had not wished to make a record of the sights we saw: it seemed to me as if too much indignity and suffering existed there – that I could not let such things become a spectacle, to be callously observed. Yet I was drawn by them and went, in the succeeding months, perhaps a dozen times.

When Miss Alice made her customary journeys into town, I would go as far as Bond Street, to her little shop. Last autumn, I had become acquainted with a dealer whom she knew; he had bought some paintings, and I had since made several visits to him with my work. But now, each time I went, the driver took me further on – at first, with some reluctance, past Saint Paul's and down to London Bridge; and later, since he had discovered that I paid him well, to safer places where he stopped to let me make the sketches I required. I told Miss Millington that I had been to exhibitions, which on one or two occasions was the truth; for by now, I knew I had to do such things alone – after all, if I went to Paris, I would not wish to take a chaperone!

My drawings and my notes were scattered round the room, the evening Philip came. He had called earlier, Maria said, and left a message that he would return at six; I was surprised, for as a rule he waited and had tea. But it was evident, when he arrived, that he had something on his mind: he had been walking all the afternoon. Placing his hat and gloves upon the table, he did not even wait until I had sat down; instead, he walked to where my easel stood.

'How came you to do such work as this?'

At once I was defensive, all my resolution gone.

'Must you always censure what I do?'

'I did not come for that. But I was waiting for you earlier – Miss Maria said you might not be too long. I came up here, of course. And I wish to know how you have been to places such as this: it is Perreton again, I must suppose!'

'You are unjust. He does not know that I have been.' It was true that I had not told him of my further visits: even Louis would have been alarmed to know that I had gone alone.

'In any case' – I was angered now by his presumption – 'I shall go where I choose, if it concerns my work. You have said already that you do not care for what I do – how can it matter to you where I go?'

Philip was incensed: his tone grew more deliberate, his glance was hard.

'I am amazed that you can ask me that. You told me that you cared about me – even more than Charles!' He gestured with contempt at the drawing at his side. 'Yet you do not care what risks you take – with yourself, or with your reputation. You are seen with men like Perreton; you go alone – you say – to places where a woman should not go.

'You say you care. Yet you go against advice – exactly as you did in Cumberland. I warned you then: and you ignored me, just as now. Even Mrs Heywood says you choose your friends unwisely: Louis Perreton, a foreigner; his wife, who they say is going mad. And that girl – whom you have never told me of: she sits for you – but they found her on the streets, she was a whore – '

Perhaps it was my look that silenced him. Perhaps it was the way in which I handed him his hat and gloves.

'You warned me of the gossips, too – and yet you listen to them, evidently. You know nothing of my friends; when you were asked to Bisham House, you would not go. I am not a child – but you are just the same as any other *gentleman*: it suits you to believe a woman is a child, and knows only things that little children are allowed to know. I cared, because once you did not treat me so. But now – I do not care for you at all . . .'

I turned my back on Philip, hoping he had not noticed the sudden faltering of my words, that he would not guess how close I was to tears. I waited for the door to close behind him . . . But instead, I felt his hand upon my shoulder, heard his voice, speaking with a note of gentleness that I had never known him use before.

'Come, we are not children – you are right, we should not quarrel so. I did not come for that. And I don't wish to listen to Mrs Heywood or Maria Millington – it makes me angry when they pry, or tell me things I hate to hear.

'But when I think you have behaved unwisely, it distresses me. As for Louis Perreton, I cannot judge him: but I believe you have a right to know the things I learned of him in France – not rumour, but the truth!'

He led me to a chair, and I listened silently while Philip told me that he had, in Paris recently, made some enquiries as to Louis and his friends. At first I was resentful that he should have thought of doing so; yet I was too weary and unhappy now to argue further with him. In spite of my defiance, he had filled me with self-doubt: any further anger on his part, and I knew I should despair.

'I recognised the name,' he said, 'from years ago. When I was in Paris – you remember – I wrote to you from there. The fighting had just stopped, and people whom I knew were killed. They were liberals, of course; I had believed in them – most of us at Cambridge felt that they were right. They wanted freedom for the people – yet it was the people who betrayed them in the end.

'Perreton was at the barricades, of course. There were students, writers, printers, men who wanted the régime to end, some who wanted any kind of change . . . But it ended nothing! It was a waste of all those lives, and those of us who went there afterwards could see it had been useless after all.'

Even now, I saw it moved him just to think of what had happened then. Our quarrel was forgotten as I listened, and remembered how (ten years ago, almost) his letter showed me that he was a man who cared about such things. Since then, Philip had not spoken often of his principles; his cynicism was too strong, it seemed, for him to wish for change, as he had done when first we met . . .

And Louis – what had been his part in all that happened? Was it this that made him stay in England – to become, as Paul Gavarni said, respectable, 'an Englishman'. . . ?

'You said you recognised the name . . .'

Philip's look was sharp, and when he spoke again his voice had something of an edge to it – but I did not choose to wonder why.

'Yes. And at first I thought no more of it. But then, when I enquired, I learned that he was indeed the same. Louis Perreton was something of a leader at the time: he was a journalist, and wrote against the government, of course. Then when everything went wrong, there was a plot and some of the new establishment were killed. I could not learn much more than that – but he was certainly a violent man, and they do not want him there. They don't easily forget the past in places such as France – and there will be other revolutions, I don't doubt.'

He moved to the window, and looked out – as I had done so many times – across the little lane, the curving wall, the garden where so often Louis walked, and where his children played.

'But why,' I asked, 'should you suspect him now? You used to sympathise with men like that, yet you seem to think he should not be – a friend . . .'

I tried to speak of him as coolly as I could: it mattered to me, but I did not want to anger Philip even more. Yet his glance was keen, and this time his hostility was plain to see.

'He is unsuitable to be a friend. The men he knew in Paris, painters, intellectuals, are leading lives that here, in England, we would not tolerate. They call themselves Romantics, or Bohemians: but they are all the same, and his morals, possibly, are not any different from theirs. That artist – Paul Gavarni as he calls himself – who was over here some time ago, no doubt you met: he is another of them. He is notorious in Paris as a womaniser, as a rake. Society there does not object, perhaps; but here it cannot be the same – even to be seen with men like that is quite enough to make them dangerous to know.'

What would he have said, I wondered instantly, if he had known where I had been with them? Yet they had cared – far more than Philip seemed to care – about the lives of others, in that world which I was not allowed to enter, either with them or alone.

'I do not want to hurt you, or to seem ungrateful that you are

[339]

concerned for me,' I answered slowly, 'yet I – I am not certain that you can be right. Whatever Louis did – '

'Forget him, Georgiana!'

Philip was gazing at me now, with an expression that I could not understand.

'You must forget them all. You seem to think they are artistic, fascinating in some way. But you are wrong: they are dangerous, corrupt. If you married me you would not need to think of them; you could be a painter, anything you wish – but you would have no need to work with people of that kind. Why should you choose to be with them, when you might be with me?'

I was astonished by his words, and almost frightened by the way in which he spoke – with feeling, yet with a detachment too dispassionate to make it credible to me. Was it truly marriage that he meant – or did he simply seek to overrule me? For, just as with Laura Pennethorne, he did not speak of love: and though I knew I cared for him, as I had always done, I could not wish to marry Philip, if he meant to form my judgement, have possession of me – rather than remain my closest, and my dearest, friend.

He took my silence, I suppose, as a refusal; and, as in so many things, he could not bear my opposition, would not have his will denied.

'How can you want more? Or is it that I am not, as I have believed, acceptable to you? I suppose I am not what you hoped, not good enough for you – as Curwen was, as Perreton will be!'

At the time, I wondered why he mentioned Louis in that way, with a contempt as great as that with which he spoke of Charles. Later, I was to wonder how he guessed at what my life would be . . .

'It is not that.'

I was distressed that he should think it. Even had he not alarmed me so, I knew that any marriage would affect my work, and restrict the freedom that I had (and at such cost) already won. But there was another reason why I could not marry – something of which I could not speak to Philip, or to any man . . .

[340]

'I do not see how I could be a wife that you – would want. I would wish to make you happy, and I do not know if that is possible . . .'

He did not listen to me. He was already by the door, and would not wait to hear what I might have to say. Philip was proud: once he had made up his mind, he would never be persuaded that he might be wrong.

'There is no point in saying any more. I thought it might be otherwise; I see it is not so.'

His calm, his apparent lack of all emotion terrified me. His air of resolution might mean anything.

'What shall you do?' I scarcely dared to ask.

'I shall do as I have always done when you – or any woman – has rejected me.'

He laughed, in a way that was quite terrible to me.

'I shall find some other woman: willing, young and less difficult to please. And I shall use her – as all women, I believe, deserve! . . . What else, Miss Curwen, is there left to do?'

After he had gone – to where, and for how long a time, I could not guess – I sat unmoving at the table where I often worked. And at length, on impulse, I took some paper and a pen. It was Philip's face I drew – long known, and yet remote; far off, yet so clearly visible within my mind. A smoothly curving lock of hair, still dark as when I knew him first, almost as black as stone or the rainwashed slate of Cumberland. The eyes deep-set, the brows above more finely marked than is usual in a man, and slightly raised in mockery or disbelief; and the eyes' expression – impossible to draw, just as it was impossible for me, for anyone perhaps, to understand. There were the forehead lines, the high-boned cheeks, the angles of the jaw; and the mouth, a touch of fullness in the lower lip the only sign of feeling in that face . . .

I could do no more. Philip had never sat for me, would never do so now. Whether he had truly wanted me, or had spoken so from pride or out of pique, I would not know: but whatever he had felt, I could not have married him.

For there was that other reason, which – like the presence of my cousin Charles – had always overshadowed us. Philip had not been in Cumberland throughout that time: that winter when the snow had drifted on the step at Portland Square, that spring when I had lain among the fallen leaves, in love with an elusive dream – of roses, laughter, and the sound of singing on a darkened lake. A dream for which I gladly gave the purity men prize in women whom they wish to make their wives: a virtue which, it seems, means more to men than women's power to love – for it gives to men possession, just as if it were a kind of talisman they wear, to give them pride and proof that manhood conquers all.

It was that untouched self that Philip, just like any other man, required of me. Or so I must believe, since he had taken such a moral stance, and since he did not speak a single word of love – which was all that I had left to give. Like my mother – who had told me in her letters of a marriage empty of all passion; of the grief of bearing children to a man who gave her nothing but a name she would not use – I feared to face a loveless wedded life. And if Philip wanted something that I could not give, I would not now be blinded by regret – unless I lost his friendship, which meant more to me than marriage, even more than love.

How had Philip guessed? How had he foreseen a feeling that I had not yet acknowledged to myself – the love which would, before the summer's end, become a threat to friendship and to all I had achieved? Perhaps it was the way I spoke of Louis; maybe it was that hostility which Philip could not hide, and had already felt. Or perhaps his insight had begun that day at the Academy, when he had noticed Louis' look, detecting in it, by some premonition, what the future held . . .

Louis has no doubt.

'For me it did begin that day – I am quite sure of it. But you see, I did not think of it again for many weeks. I did not know you would be often in the house, that she would come to care for you so much. Then, I was glad that Sophia had a friend – she needed you: it made her happy, to be young and talk so much with you. So I did not let myself be anxious; but I liked to see you with the children, hear you laugh with them – my mother, she was dark, I can remember, just as you are, and Hélène . . .'

Today he seems to wish to stay much longer than his custom is. There are times when I almost dread his coming here, for I know that an hour, or two, or half a day, slips past so quickly and is gone – leaving to their slow progression all the minutes, hours, and days that pass until he comes to me again. Often, the sense of loss oppresses me; and then I work much harder, walk across the heath in wind and rain, anything rather than sit and stare into the fire, as I used to do at first. For now I know that Louis will not suddenly abandon me: that fear, which made me feel bereft beyond all reason, which at times deprived me of all peace, no longer haunts me as it did.

'My mother – she was a peasant, and my father found her in the fields, near the village where she came from in the north of France. He was an *aristo*, of course, and took her back with him to Paris; there were other mistresses, but she – he married her. It was after I was born; he did not own me as his child at first, but then he changed his mind. You see – ' Louis smiles, and takes my hand in his – 'it is a romantic story, is it not?'

'But why did he choose to marry her, and not another?'

'She was intelligent, and loyal – and he wished to have a son, as I should like . . .' He shrugs his shoulders, looks a little sad. 'It is from pride – one should not care about such things as names, and yet one does. In Paris, there are others like my mother – singers, actresses, perhaps, who have been beautiful and poor, and marry men above them, or become their mistresses . . .'

Already I have seen that Louis, though a revolutionary once, is fiercely proud of his aristocratic name – all that can remain, I must suppose, of his Gallic heritage. And perhaps, within, he feels a sense of disappointment in Sophia, who does not wish to bear another child, and has not given him the son he needs.

'So now, my love – you see I am two men. I am a peasant sometimes, maybe that is why I like to work, to use my hands; and the other – he is what the English people much prefer – a patrician, I suppose. You may have whichever one you choose!' There is that fleeting brightness in his eyes, the little smile that makes him younger suddenly.

'I love two men!' I answer, delighting in his laughter – heard so rarely in the months, the many months, when being close to him in Highgate was a torment to me, when I wanted both to go, and to remain . . .

'But Gavarni says you are an Englishman – I am not sure that that is what I want . . .'

'Paul knows I don't forget. He speaks of outside things: I wear the clothes or speak the words perhaps, but no, I am not changed. He is afraid I shall become a *bourgeois*: he is wrong – that I cannot be!'

Louis is emphatic now, and I can tell how much it means to him: he has forgotten me – he is the foreigner, the stranger whom I used to see across the garden, whom I never thought to understand.

'It is true that I am tired of bloodshed, that I do not wish to fight, but I care about my country still. Paul wants me to go back, to live as he does. But it is too late. It is unsafe, for a wife and family: I have my work, which here I need not use for politics but in the way I wish. Besides – there is Sophia: she needs the doctors here, she needs her father, too: it is impossible for me to go to France . . .'

I know he will never leave Sophia. I could not wish it otherwise, for still I grieve for the affection that she felt for me. And though Louis comes to me, I am sure that he will not neglect his wife; her nurse is conscientious, and the housekeeper was always, I remember, competent to manage everything. Even before I went from Highgate, it was clear to me that Sophia had become too inward-looking for our friendship to survive; yet I miss the light that seemed to move with her, when she came into a room; the gladness of her welcome when I went to her; the grace and gentleness she lost.

Yet sometimes, even then, I felt she was destroying Louis. It seems she cannot live without him; for she clings to him, like an ivy that will slowly drain the life from the branch that is its main support. And he – he had despaired. For when he sought me, on that summer's day beside the sea, he said he would have killed himself, had he not found me there . . .

*

Sophia had agreed to go to Broadstairs for her holiday. Brighton, it was clear, would not be possible: she needed somewhere quieter, the doctor said. I was relieved; there would be noise and crowds and too much that was new to me at Brighton. We would have instead some quiet comfortable rooms in Nelson Place, which had been recommended by a friend of Sara Coleridge: it was close to the shore, and perfect for the little girls.

I had been glad to go at last. For after Philip left me I was tempted (as I always was at times of grief or strain) to go at once to Workington to see my aunt. She would have asked no questions, would not have upbraided me: she would have looked me up and down, in that unambiguous way she had, and bade me take some exercise or find a useful task to do. Yet had I gone, how different the future might have been: Sophia might have stayed at home; and Louis – but I could not tell what Louis might have done if I had been so far away.

For several weeks he had been silent and morose. Often before, he was abstracted, troubled – not, as now, beyond my reach. Since Philip's warning, I had been more wary of him: it was as if, by those few words, an innocence was lost, as if some subtle poison had been scattered in the summer air and had destroyed a mutual trust. I did not work alone with Louis now; and did not stay beyond the lighting of the lamps, for sometimes we had walked together through the garden to the iron gate.

Those July days were long and very hot. Dust rose from every footstep's touch, and at Number 23 the workroom windows had been opened wide. As a rule Miss Alice kept them tightly shut; but this year she relented when the sewing-girls complained of faintness or fatigue: I was glad that Grace was not among them. By August, I found the glaring heat and light impossible to bear.

It was hot beside the sea. Yet here there was a breeze, which cooled the surface of the stones, and stirred the grasses, coarse along the margin of the beach. Between our lodging and the sea lay corn, a lesser ocean with its golden surface undulating in the motion of the wind. Along its edges, flowers: the red of poppies, fallen petals scattered, drops of blood upon the chalky roughness of the path; chickory, and harebells, blue and delicate; convolvulus among the bramble clumps, or staring white among the dark of nettles, with a waxen whiteness like lilies that Sophia grew at home. In evening, there was a touch of autumn chill; we would often walk along the cliff, above a shore from which the colour faded, and beneath a sky where narrow bands of cloud were made translucent by the brightness of a rising moon. And sometimes when we went so far as Dampton Stairs, we watched the sudden shining of the man-made stars ahead of us – the warning lights upon the Goodwin Sands.

Sophia and the children rested in the afternoon. But I disliked to be indoors, and took my painting-things to a patch of shade beneath the cliff. It was a respite – from the ever-present consciousness of treading carefully, and from Sophia's frailty, which made each day uncertain, almost any word a danger to us all. Beside the shore, I found release: it was all that I had hoped.

I saw him walking there that afternoon. A figure in the distance, pausing to watch the waves, and once he bent to take a pebble which he threw far out into the sea. There was no mistaking him – slight of build, dark-haired, no hat, his jacket swinging from his hand.

For a moment as he stood beside me, his shadow still upon the stones, I felt as if he had been always there. But Louis had remained in Highgate; and now I saw that he had changed, within the space of days. He looked as if he had not slept – and yet his eyes were more intent, with a brightness partly fevered, partly purposeful, a look which told me all.

'I thought that I would find you here.'

'How did you know?'

'You like to be outside. I knew it would be so.'

'But Sophia – and the children; they are not with me. They always take a rest, it is so hot . . .'

'I did not come for them. I came for you.'

No smile, just words; and Louis' hand on mine, his fingers hard and brown, and cool against my skin.

'I could not stay at home. The house is empty, terrible to me. I cannot be alone there any more: there are shadows everywhere . . . No, no' – and now he smiles a little – 'you are thinking, "he is ill perhaps". But no, it is not that. It is – I have to come to find you, tell you that I need you to be there.'

'You cannot say these things.'

'I must. I cannot only think them any more. It is no good: Sophia – she is gone from me, I cannot know her any more. But – you I must not lose. I came to say it. And if you had not been here, I think – '

His eyes are very dark, and I see in them a certainty, a purpose which I do not wish to understand. Yet I have seen the way his life has lost its meaning. I have known Sophia, have watched the way she changed: I cannot wonder, now, that Louis too is changed . . .

'I know – ' he says, 'I know that if I had not found you, I could not want to go back home. I would not want to live.'

Chapter 26

It is not true, the myth they put about, that women have no feelings in these things. We feel as much as men, our needs & our desires are just as great: it is only that we dare not speak of them, cannot acknowledge to the world that we are not as pure or modest as we seem. For men, my daughter, wish us to be subject to their will; but if we have the need & passion which they think are only masculine, they risk the loss of their domain – they are made less than us because we question ev'rything.

Yet sometimes it is women who are wrong and hard. They seem to promise what they will not give, or let their beauty be a lure to men, who love them & then find that they are cold. It is no wonder that they go to whores, or lose their faith in women's gentleness, & take revenge upon us all: for when a woman acts in such a way, she uses men and makes a mockery of love . . .

I would not say these things to anyone save you; for they are truths which often people cannot bear to hear. I write them down, in the beleif that one day you will read & understand . . .

My mother, long ago, had written as she might have spoken to me had she lived. I thought my own capacity for love was gone, that I had left behind such youthful hopes, that need and passion – all such things – were past. Now, I found it was not so.

I went from Highgate in the spring. There was no other choice, for once the silence had been broken it was clear that Louis, like myself, found subterfuge impossible to bear. Without intention, I believe, we had become too close for further self-deceit: if, for so long, we had not recognised, could not acknowledge it, it was perhaps because we had an inward fear of doing so – a certainty that once the words were spoken all the pain of loving must begin.

We had no hope that such a feeling might one day bring joy: what little comfort we might give each other always must be modified by guilt. It seemed, as each day passed, that we were locked together by Sophia's need. She wanted both of us – and yet she had no consciousness that we, together or alone, had fears of which she was the cause. Increasingly I feared that Louis' care for her might turn to hatred or despair; while he, I knew, was anxious lest she turn against me suddenly, and cause me more distress.

Perhaps I should have gone to Workington; or to Paris, as I had hoped. Yet the decision proved too hard: I could not go so far away. There were commissions to fulfil; my painting of the Thames to be prepared, for exhibition possibly; and my obligations to my pupils and Miss Millington – so many reasons why I must remain in London . . . All of this was true; but more compelling was the thought that maybe things would change, that the love which had come unbidden might prove less difficult to bear; that even my return to Highgate might be possible one day. Unknowingly, the roots of those affections I had come to need had struck too deep: not only Louis but his children and Sophia, had grown essential to my life.

There was a cottage, at the far side of the heath, in Hampstead. It had been let, some years ago, to Sara Coleridge, and would be the very thing if I wished to be more independent; she believed it had been empty for some months. I remembered it as small, but with a pretty view between the trees; but I could not live alone entirely, if I wished to keep my reputation . . . I thought of Grace: she was not strong, and had begun to find the laundry work too much; yet she was happier at Bisham House than ever in her life before, so she had told me once. There was some hope, too, that her sight could possibly be saved. Sophia's doctor had seen many cases at the Moorfields Hospital, of milliners' apprentices or seamstresses like Grace: if they continued working, often as much as eighteen hours a day, their blindness was a certainty, he said. If she had rest and care, she might recover yet. It was this that finally persuaded her to come with me; at first she had, from pride, refused to give up work, but when I pointed out that I should find her useful, worth her keep, she was won over, and agreed to go.

The Miss Millingtons were sad to lose me, they declared. Privately, Miss Alice made me promise to return if I had need; she would continue to require designs from time to time. But I knew I would be glad to be away from the attention of Maria's eyes, her constant flow of information as to the habits of the neighbourhood; already I suspected that she had been gossiping too much of Grace – and I dreaded lest her speculation should extend to Louis, and myself.

For Louis was (exactly as Gavarni once had said) unable to escape the Highgate trap: it was his chosen home, and with Sophia's need of a physician's care becoming more acute, he had to stay. I went as little as I could to Bisham House, towards the winter's end, telling myself that my decision must be strong. Yet inwardly I wept to think of him. And one day when, at Sophia's persuasion, I remained a little longer than I meant, he came to find us in the garden room. He was beside Sophia's couch, and looked across to where I sat. There was no passion in that gaze, nor even longing, but a steady certainty of need so powerful that it made my resolution fail.

Before I reached the garden gate he was beside me. There was frost already forming on the grass, ice among the pebbles at our feet.

'You will not go?'

He knew the answer.

'Yes,' I said.

It was months before Louis came to me at Hampstead. A summer empty of all warmth and meaning, such as I had never known. I painted, and walked among the trees, sat in the little garden, talked with Grace: yet none of it engaged me – almost as if I were a creature made of brittle glass, through which I saw the outer world as from a distance, from the hollow, barren centre of my self. There were days when I could not work, nights when I knew no rest; times when in imagination I would cross the dusty heath, to Highgate and to Bisham House.

I did not believe that he would seek me out. Yet when he came at last, there was no choice – I would not make him go away. Each time, it was the same: the pain of loss, the guilt, and the necessity of his return.

Even so, throughout, I missed Sophia. She had occupied the place my mother might have filled, had I felt the love whose voice I heard across the vacancy of years. Sophia's need for sisterhood had been as great as mine: had we met long before, she might have suffered less from those destructive fears that so obsessed her mind.

'Sophia does not care,' said Louis once – the only time we quarrelled bitterly. 'She thinks of no one but herself.'

I knew that he was right – and yet it was a partial truth. For her selfishness was born of inner pain, an inability to turn the cruelty of life to a more bearable reality. Where others proved resilient or patient, she could not: even my mother, lonely and tormented as her letters showed, had put her suffering to some account – had given me, her child, the insight she had gained. But Sophia had offered me affection when I needed it the most; and even Louis' love, which now sustained me so, had grown from all that she had given to me first.

'You cannot understand,' I said to Louis then. 'She needs you more than I. She has more right to you than I can ever have.'

He went from me, with words which afterward I used against myself – as if driven by a sense of guilt that I had made him go. There was a time of emptiness again, as deep as the January snow which lay across the heath in folds, as if it meant to shut him out forever from the peace he sought with me. When he returned at last, we lay together in the little upstairs room, beneath the shadows of the angled roof; we heard the steady falling of the April rain, and found once more that harmony which seemed – by some strange interchange of time – to have existed long before that night.

With Charles I had known passion, but little peace. For Louis I felt passion tempered by a calm that must, it seemed to me, derive from him not from myself. For I knew my outward composure to be but a frail shell, painfully constructed and presented to a world I was determined should not witness my turmoil, nor overhear my inner dialogues.

These latter were frequent, and for the most part unresolved. How could I wish to harm Sophia, whose friendship had come to mean more to me than that of any human creature I had encountered before coming to London? How hurt her children – Louis' children – in whose company I found such delight, whose eyes I had opened to the shine of starlings' wings on the window-sill, the delicate hardness of shells brought back from our seaside excursions? And yet – how much of my own pleasure in these things, and in the sharing of them with his daughters, had derived from Louis himself? I had known with Charles that heightened awareness which accompanies love; that sensitivity to sound and colour and form which can sharpen, almost unbearably, the ticking of a clock in the still bedroom; or brighten the leaves and darken the shadows between them, hardening to a dazzle the sunlight burning through willow branches beyond the window.

So now, with Louis. And yet more so: I knew the need to capture such moments, to translate them through pen and brush into something more than the faithful drawings of hill and lake, rock and tree, in which I had distilled my love for Charles and my sense of homecoming in the early days in Cumberland. Here in London, I not only knew desire and rejoiced in its fulfilment – I also recognised within myself the power to create. What I did not understand, as I filled page upon page of my sketchbook with strange forms and fantasies, was that deeper frailty which is born of great feeling. My outer defences were indeed secure against the murmurings of the world: the strength of my inward peace had yet to be tried and tested.

*

There was a sudden knocking at the cottage door, one fine September afternoon. It could not be Louis: he had gone to Broadstairs with his daughters; they would remain there with their governess when he returned to Highgate in a day or two. Callers were rare enough; I painted sitters or visited my pupils in their homes, and for the past few months, since Louis came to me again, I had discontinued working for Miss Millington, for I feared Maria's curiosity might be an even greater danger now. Grace had proved a loyal friend; we lived quite frugally, yet were content. I knew I must leave Hampstead soon. All summer I had tried to make decisions, only to postpone, delay – as if some instinct warned me that, before too long, I should be forced by circumstance to follow paths I had not wished to choose.

'Mr Backhouse, miss. Miss Curwen, I believe?'

He was a little, wizened, nut-brown man, with bright blue eyes: a Cumbrian, I knew at once.

In the dusty parlour, which we seldom used, he told me he had come from Mr George – George Nicolson, of course. I was to be with him by six o'clock, to go to Workington.

'Yes, miss. It's urgent, so he says. You may get there in time, but you'll need to get the Mail tonight; I am to wait, while you get ready, if you please – my man will take us down to Mr George.'

Why had I not gone sooner? Yet how could I have known? My aunt had written to me only a month before, when all was well.

'It happened very sudden, miss. But she's a strong one, Mistress Nicolson, she'll weather it, you may be sure.'

But Mr Backhouse knew, as well as I, that she would only send to me in an extremity: my aunt would not give in, but even she – in spite of a hardy constitution and unyielding will – was not immune from danger such as this.

Within an hour I was prepared. Grace would remain, with a girl from the nearest cottage as companion until she heard from me again. A note for Louis – he would come to find me when he came back from the coast. There was some uncompleted work but that would wait – how long, I could not tell. Yet perhaps I sensed already that my time in Hampstead must, within the next few weeks, be at an end.

For as, with Mr Backhouse facing me, I started on that journey home at last, I thought of one thing more that I must do.

'Is there time?' I asked him, as we came to Highgate, to take the London Road.

'Ten minutes, miss,' he answered, looking at his watch. 'We've another hour till six.'

At Bisham House the curtains of the downstairs rooms were drawn across; but everything was just as I remembered . . . I followed Annie through the hall. The nurse was in the morning-room, alone.

'You may go through, Miss Curwen – Mrs Perreton is very quiet today. But it's best you shouldn't stay with her too long.'

Sophia was there, among her flowers. A glance of recognition and her hands outstretched; no smile, just a look of mild reproach.

'Why, Georgiana, I have missed you! You did not come here yesterday – I wondered why.'

She stooped to cut a blossom from a little bush. I thought how delicately beautiful she was: her hair an unchanged reddish-gold, and her complexion with a touch of colour. I had known that she was carrying another child, for Louis had, some months ago, admitted it; I had been alarmed for her – and yet she had an air of strange serenity, such as I had never known in her before.

Her task resumed, I was forgotten so I thought, and turned to go. But then she looked up suddenly and said:

'You see – I have another orange-tree: the old one died. I pruned it wrongly, Louis said. It bled to death, poor thing: they sometimes do, you know. But this one is much stronger – I am sure – yes, sure, that it will live . . .'

The scars were on her hand, quite plain to see; but they were now as nothing to those deeper scars, which from this time, it was too clear to me, would never fade.

Chapter 27

In death, Aunt Nicolson looked scarcely less uncompromising than she had when first we met. And now, as then, I felt afraid and insignificant when I beheld the sternness of those deep long lines across the brow; the lips so tightly closed, as if she had just uttered some rebuke (no doubt deserved); the folded hands, their fingers long and unadorned, save for the solitary prominence of Humphrey's wedding-band. 'It is what he would have wished,' she said so often, when she chose to justify some whim, or a decision she had made: yet he would have grieved to see her as she was that autumn day – the clear blue eyes concealed beneath their heavy lids, her restless spirit still.

It was my aunt – of all the people in my life – who had been most instrumental in the changes I had known. And I had not regretted that she brought me to her, though she had sometimes spoken of her own regret that I came to Cumberland so late. She had tried to make amends, not only for her own but for my grandfather's neglect: yet it was I who felt a shame far deeper now – for a neglect which seemed, as I stood beside her bed, to have far less excuse than hers. 'What's done is done – it's no use fretting, child!': she would have scorned to weep, would have said my tears were useless – as indeed they were.

She had died, so Susan told us, only hours before we came to Workington. It was dark; yet every detail of the square was clear as daylight in my mind. There would be a narrow passage by the high stone wall, in which the garden door was set; a patch of lamplight on the cobbles and the fallen chestnut leaves, already brown; the white-scrubbed step, of which Emily was rightly proud. And, as we hesitated by the shuttered house, a smell of soot and salt, so curiously mingled in the misty air. We had driven fast along the lakeside road: Kendal, Windermere and Keswick; Cockermouth – and home. But when we paused to give the horses rest, beneath the shoulder of a barren fell, I knew already that we were too late, that I should not see my aunt alive again.

Mary Nicolson was there when we arrived; and Hugh, with Doctor Richards, who remembered me, and was, of course, no longer inexperienced and young. Susan and Josh were married: they had been living in as cook and gardener to my aunt, for Emily had grown too old and frail to be of use; mostly she dozed, with Minou on her lap, in the chimney corner by the kitchen stove. No one, save Emily, upbraided me: 'You should've come before,' she said – and nodded off to sleep.

At Portland Square, in January, my son was born. A New Year's gift, so Susan called him, for she was childless still, and loved him from the start. I had meant to stay no more than a month or two in Workington; I would find a lodging somewhere, so I thought. But Mary had already guessed, and to my amazement, would not hear of it.

'If you go, I shall go with you,' she asserted. 'You cannot be alone at such a time. Aunt Nicolson would not have wanted it. The house is yours, and you have a right to stay.'

She was quite adamant – yet I maintained I could not continue there: few would have been so charitable in their views as Mary seemed.

'Aunt Nicolson would have disowned me,' I replied. 'I cannot let her home be mine, and – and bring disgrace to all of you.'

My decision had been made already; yet I was exhausted now, and knew that I dreaded being somewhere strange. I should have left Hampstead long before this time: I had not told Louis so, but I had planned to find somewhere far from Highgate, knowing that he already had too much to bear.

Mary was more clear-sighted than myself.

'This *is* your home – at the very least until you are strong and can choose another where you wish. You will have sufficient means: it is very foolish to consider doing otherwise. No one here knows anything as yet, except myself; and if we are very careful, no one needs to know – in winter, we all keep to our homes so much.

'And remember,' she added, with a steadiness that gave me courage – more than I could have imagined possible, 'Aunt Nicolson had lost a child – and I know what that can mean. Lately, she used to talk of how he would have looked, or what he might have been one day: she was much gentler in the time before she died. Susan was six months gone when she and Josh were married – it happens often to the country girls. I thought Aunt Nicolson would turn her out, but she didn't after all; and when the baby died, she was very good to Susan – as she would have been to you.'

At length I had told Mary everything. She had listened patiently: perhaps she saw how great was my relief, or perhaps there was another reason, which she did not express to me. For she asked, when I had done, 'Does Philip know of this?'

And when I answered 'No', she said at first, 'Thank God'; but then she looked at me, with her direct Yorkshire gaze, and added, 'But I wish he had not been so blind; he has left everything too late.'

She would never speak of it to him, I knew; like my aunt, she could keep her counsel if she chose.

For Aunt Nicolson (I now discovered) – my upright and plain-speaking aunt – had concealed the truth from me. To my shame at first, she had bequeathed me all her property: her house and Humphrey's boats, investments and some cottages – as if I had, indeed, been the child for whom she grieved. I was bewildered by it, for I believed that I had forfeited what little right I had to anything, by leaving Cumberland. Yet this was the lesser shock: for Hugh and Mary Nicolson assured me that my aunt had told them her intentions, and had made it plain that she had cared for me, and considered me her heir.

But she had not told me everything about myself. Her honesty (which I had never doubted) had not been at fault; she had not lied – yet there were omissions in those explanations she had given me so long ago. And in a letter which she wrote to me some little time before her death, she set them out – knowing, I suppose, that she might never speak of them, that I might not return.

> I write to you, dear Georgiana, because there are things that you should know. I have been remiss; yet until my brother Henry died I hoped he would accept you – as I believe he would have done had he seen you for himself. For he had doubted, always, that your mother was his child, though Frances maintained that he was wrong, & since her death he must have regretted his mistake. Yet he was always proud, & would not listen when I told him that he had been misled: to me, your likeness both to him & Frances proved that there could be no other, foreign blood in you. I thought to write much sooner of it all, when I sent you my cousin Fletcher's box – for in a way, it all began with him.
>
> He enlisted on the *Bounty* when Frances would not marry him, when she came from Ireland first. It was no secret, & made Henry jealous, first of Fletcher, & later of other men whom Frances knew. In particular there was a Frenchman, who stayed with them some months, an exile from the Revolution, I believe; later he went back, but Henry thought your mother might have been his child.

'*A poet whom she lov'd was kill'd in Paris*': so had my mother written to me, when she told me of her childhood here in Workington. And Charles, I remembered, had spoken of Frances Curwen's lovers when we saw her portrait, hanging by the stair, so long ago . . .

> Henry might, perhaps, have forgiven & forgotten everything; but later – almost twenty years, it must have been – there were rumours that Fletcher Christian had come back to Cumberland from Pitcairn. He was said to be hiding on Belle Isle, where your grandmother was staying at the time; it must have been untrue – yet Henry was incensed, of course. There was an Election imminent, & the Lowthers were always glad to seize on rumours of any kind to use against my brother if they could.

[358]

Then, when your mother ran away from home, he feared a scandal even worse might break, & ruin all his chances – all his hopes to bring about Reform. I knew of it, of course, for your mother came to me in great distress before she left the Hall; I was always fond of her, for Frances seemed to me to be too careless with her children. Your mother had tried to run away from school, & then had met your father secretly whilst she was with Frances on Belle Isle – Henry knew nothing of it, & was rightly angry when he knew how careless Frances must have been. He refused to take your mother back; yet he loved her dearly, & would have been less harsh to her, I do believe, had she written to him, or shown him that she cared about him, in spite of being such a willful girl.

Later, I realised that something, somehow, must have gone amiss. For my mother had written to Sir Henry, so her letters told me; she was sure he had forgiven her – and she had longed to see her home and parents once again. Now, I could only feel distress: for my mother chiefly, for she had brought upon herself (through loving one man, with too little prudence) not only Henry Curwen's wrath but retribution for another's wrong. I felt grief for Frances, too. Whether Sir Henry's jealousy was justified or not, she had lost her daughter, and her husband's trust. Yet Sir Henry Curwen, like my cousin Charles, had not lived a blameless life: it was not for nothing that he had been called 'the father of the town' – but such things are allowable in men, and not in women, it would seem. Men may breed children with impunity, may still pursue their calling or career: but a woman's life is ruined if she leaves the narrow path of virtue, and is seen to go astray.

More than anything, perhaps, I regretted that my aunt (understandably enough) had kept the truth from me until it was too late. I had been as proud and unforgiving as any other Curwen until just before Sir Henry's death: then, I had longed to go to him, to tell him of my mother's love, as she had wished me to. Whatever else had come between the two of them in later years, had not been of their doing, I was sure: and had I gone to find my grandfather, he might not only have accepted me – that other deeper breach, which had lasted from my birth until my mother's death, might have been explained at last.

As for the rest, I realised somewhat ruefully that even Mrs Heywood had known more than I. Her dislike of Henry Curwen, which had angered me, had had some reason in it after all. For Fletcher Christian had been her husband's friend; and she had told me several times of Captain Heywood's certainty that Fletcher had secretly returned to England, long after the scandal of the mutiny was past. Twenty years had gone she said, when Peter saw his friend in Plymouth, near the quayside where the Captain's ship was moored. If so, I mused, then it was possible that Henry Curwen had been right to be alarmed – that Fletcher might have gone to Belle Isle after all . . . But that was something neither I myself, nor anyone, would ever know.

There had been no word from Louis since I came to Workington – none, save for one short note which I received a few days after I arrived. He had been to Hampstead, had seen Grace; I must tell him of my plans – he would want to be with me, and with our child, for a little time at least. 'Please, you are not to go too far from me . . .'

So he had guessed that I would not return to Hampstead. Later I wrote to tell him that I should remain in Cumberland until the early spring: he need not be afraid that I should want for anything, I was fortunate to be with friends . . .

And so I was. I had come to see that Mary had been right. There were my aunt's possessions to be dealt with, all the legal matters for which I needed Hugh Nicolson's advice; at their suggestion, I wrote to Mr Backhouse, requesting that he should try to find some relative – her father or her sister, possibly –who would go to live with Grace. For I had decided that the cottage should be rented for her use: I could afford it easily – it was the least that I could do. And one day, maybe, I might return to London . . . But as yet, I had no further plans: I would wait until my child was born.

I was more than glad of Mary then, and of Doctor Richards' care. For the birth proved long and difficult, and left me very weak: I could share so easily Sophia's dread, the anguish and resentment that she felt at the thought of future suffering. And now I understood my mother's grief at bearing children to a man she did not choose.

For in spite of Louis' absence, our son was a delight. Whatever fears or doubts I entertained, whatever difficulties lay ahead, I knew that I was luckier than many others were: thanks to Aunt Nicolson, we both would be secure. During those early days, before I realised that the child I nursed might never know the man who fathered him, I did not feel despair, but joy – that in my son I saw the features of the man I loved.

And it was my child, perhaps, who helped me most of all to bear the hardest of the truths Aunt Nicolson communicated to me. For there was a final revelation in the letter that she left – and having read it once, I knew that I should never wish to look at it again. And even at this time, as I set it down myself, I find what it contained unbearable to contemplate.

There is one more thing, dear child, which I can only tell you now: and if I could have kept it from you longer, I should have chosen so to do, for it will cause you sorrow, as it has myself.

Your mother's death was not, as you supposed, an accident. Her husband, Mr Pirrip, sent to me from Rochester not only the package, with her letters, which I gave to you, but a note which she had left for him. In this she made it plain that, by the time he should return that day, she would have put an end to her own unhappy life. She asked him to communicate to me her final wish, that I should become your guardian and give a home to you, for she never trusted those with whom you had, since infancy, been placed.

The note I have destroyed, of course; for it was given out that she had fallen from the window of her room by accident – so she rests, her husband told me, in consecrated ground, which otherwise had not been possible.

I can only ask you to forgive the long delay which, as you know, elapsed before I implemented the request your mother made. I have done all that lay within my power to make amends.

Your loving guardian and aunt
E. Nicolson.

*

[361]

My room at Portland Square, the room my aunt prepared so carefully when she received me first, had not been changed. There was the table, with a pewter candlestick, beside my bed; my mother's letters lying, as I left them, locked within the drawer. The harbour lights, the distant masts and sails, were as I had remembered; and when I lay in bed, a baby in my arms, I watched the firelight flicker on the walls, casting its moving shadows as it had when I had lain and watched it long ago, with Charles.

Along the passage, in my painting-room, my smock hung on the door, and my easel waited for me – though for several months I could not even think of using them. But at last, in February, when the early snowdrops had appeared, and Mary had declared my confinement at an end, I made the first of many sketches of my son. I would send them, so I thought, to Louis, when I wrote to him again. I never did so; before the month was out, I heard from him at last.

He had received my note, which told him that his son was safe, and I recovering my health. He longed to see us both.

'I love you, need' you, but I cannot come to you – I don't know when it will be possible to come . . . Sophia . . .'

Sophia had died at Christmas-time. Her child, another girl, had lived.

> I cannot find it in my heart to care about the Spring: a winter darkness seems to cling about me, to penetrate my being, chill my limbs . . . as though my strength will never be renew'd. Even my baby (Pip they call him) has no claim to make me long for life . . .

Now I shared my mother's wish to end it all. There was no hope in me, that spring in Cumberland; even my son brought no delight. If ever I had thought there was a God, I should have cried against Him at that time. There seemed no justice, only retribution undeserved, for those who suffered in the darkness of this world: for Peter, a fisher-boy who met a fearful end; for those whom I had seen, in a life far worse than death, on London Bridge; for Sophia, who died in childbirth, which she dreaded so ... And for my mother, another Georgiana, choosing, in her final desperation, to leave sorrow far behind at last.

Why must they, and all the other innocents whom fate had so uncaringly destroyed, be given little, whilst others had so much? And why should I be spared? How could I, having seen all this, prefer to live?

There were no answers, only the unceasing turmoil of my troubled mind. And yet at length there came a day, toward the end of March, when I went down to the kitchen and took the ashen stick which had been left, since Michael Stephens brought it, in a corner by the door. I put on the heavy woollen cloak, which once Aunt Nicolson had worn, and set out across the square.

I did not take the harbour path; nor the wider road which led beyond the trees, past the gateway of the empty Hall, where my family had lived. I went by the narrow track between stone walls, inland toward the hills of Ennerdale. And for an hour or so, through the clarity of morning air, I walked.

From the hillside, when at last I stopped, I looked down upon the shining roofs of Workington – the upper and the lower towns, the harbour and the sea. Below me, on a little rise, Saint Michael's church, its square tower bleak and grey; across the Solway, the Scottish hills; and far ahead, their tops in mist, the mountains of the Isle of Man, where Fletcher Christian had been born. Northward, along the mainland coast, I would come to Allonby and Maryport . . . and to the south, a sheltered harbour – Ravenglass, where I had never been.

This was my mother's country, and my own. Now that I knew her story, I understood more fully why she longed, at times of pain or sorrow, to come home.

Most of all, I recognised her thoughts of death as mine. I shared at last her longing to escape from what she had created – a world within herself, to keep the truth at bay. '*My dreams keep me alive . . .*': those dreams, more real to her than any other part of her sad life, the dreams which in the end she lost. I too had found a world, now gone: so should I now compound that loss by self-destruction? A simple remedy, for so common a complaint – the cure for love unrequited, lost or unfulfilled; the snuffing of a faint flame burning to no purpose, like the candle-ends of childhood, little comfort in the darkened room. Yet was not such self-pity fruitless – now, just as it had been then?

At last I recognised it as self-pity, as perhaps my mother, too, had recognised her own. Did she know that she would live through me, that her personality would overshadow mine even as I shared her name? Should my own child know no more of me than a shared name, a bare shred of my self with which to comfort his wakefulness?

As I turned and looked out across the valley I saw a thread of smoke rise from old Susan's cottage chimney; I knew exactly where she would be sitting, huddled in her blanket beside the ashes, her brown face wrinkled against the smoky heat of the chimney corner, a hen at her feet, a snuffing pig at her door. Susan, who remembered my mother as a girl . . . Somewhere in my long-forgotten sketchbook were drawings of the cottage, and one of Susan, too: when I left for Paris, I would remember to take them with me.

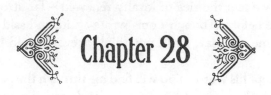

Chapter 28

In France I lived as Georgiana Grieve. And there I knew, for the first time in my life, the sense of independence that sufficient means – and perhaps a change of name – can give. Upon my marriage finger, it was true, I wore a ring: it was a compromise, but a necessary one. Nothing, I determined, should be allowed to jeopardise the safety of my future with my child: he might not ever know a father's care, or the protection of another's name, but he would have as good a start, as much security, as I was able to provide. And more than anything, I wished my son to have the love which I, throughout the days of childhood, never knew.

Once more I was glad of Mary Nicolson's advice. She was practical about the hazards for a woman travelling alone; and it was at her persuasion that, at length, I asked Josh and Susan if they wished to go with me. The house in Portland Square was to be let, not sold – in case I should return; yet I was sure, increasingly, that I should never make my home in Cumberland.

And by the time we left, in May, I knew that I should not be part of Louis' life. He would remain in London, for his work and for his children's sake; I could not ever go to him, unless I wished to cause him more unhappiness. For even had I done so, there would always be, at Bisham House, the shadow of Sophia. Now, when I thought about her death, it did not only cause me pain: there was – perhaps would always be – a deeper sense of guilt, which I guessed that Louis shared. Had he not gone from me in anger, intending never to return, Sophia's child might not have been conceived: she would not have suffered so, and Louis' children would have had their mother still. So often, after some betrayal, we feel the ties of loyalty renewed – far stronger than they were before. Though Louis wrote again, and said he would come to me one day, I did not think it ever would be so.

Gavarni kept his word. 'You will find me through the papers – the journals,' he had said; '*La Presse*, or *La Mode* perhaps, anyone who writes for them will know where I am to be found.' Within three days of my arrival at the small hotel in Saint Germain, he came to see me there. As before, he was amused and charming, yet direct.

'Louis?' he queried, looking at the infant in my arms. And when I murmured yes, he shrugged, and said, 'It happens always.'

Then, with a smile which I thought curiously sad, he went on, 'But I think my friend was fortunate – more fortunate than I, or you yourself, madame . . .'

Later, when I learned much more of him, I found that Paul had not experienced a deep relationship: he had known many women in his life, yet never one whom he had loved. The girls he drew – the dainty *lorettes*, with their laughing eyes and pretty clothes – were a diversion from the other face of Paris, which Gavarni knew so well and, like Daumier, felt a compulsion to record. With myself he was gallant yet detached: I was a fellow artist first, and secondly, the lover of his friend.

When I told him of Sophia's death, he was thoughtful for a moment, then he said, 'You know, she only cared about his name, his history, I think. She wanted him to rescue her, as if he were a knight – *chevalier* – in an old story, a romance. But he is made of flesh, like any man. It is no good to marry women who are beautiful, they are so often cold . . .

'But no, I will not say more; now, he will be faithful to her memory – a man devoted to his family, of course . . . And you, madame?'

Had I come to work, to learn, he asked. If so, he would advise, but it would perhaps be difficult, as he had warned. First, I would need apartments – somewhere quiet but not far from the Louvre, so that I could study there, until a studio might take me, possibly . . .

'But do not hope too much: the *ateliers*, the establishments of art, are meant for men, as anywhere. And if a well-known painter takes a pupil, gifted like yourself, I tell you what will happen to her: she will study for a time, she falls in love with him – her *maître* – then she either dies of love, or marries him perhaps. Or she becomes his mistress: either way, she helps him with his work, forgets her own – and so, the end of all her hopes, of everything!'

Gavarni laughed out loud. Yet he could see that I was troubled, apprehensive. Supposing I had come so far, for nothing, after all? And yet where else would I have gone? But as he left he touched my arm in sympathy.

'You were quite right to leave. In England you would both be persecuted. Here, you will not be accepted by the *bourgeoisie*, but it need not trouble you. There are alternatives, in France. And there are women here who do things more outrageous than you think of, or will ever do, my friend.'

He was right. For when Paul took me with him to meet some of them, I saw what he had meant. There was Madame Sand, with her masculine attire and air of carelessness: not beautiful, but striking certainly – more truly independent than I should ever be. Or Madame Sabatier, younger and more elegant, with hair the colour of Sophia's and a smile which I thought enchanting: Apollonie, Paul called her when we visited her *salon* in the rue Frochot, on the Butte Montmartre where he also had his home. These were women of intelligence and wit – of an order worlds removed from the stolid down-to-earth Parisian wives with their market-baskets on their arms, their servants hovering behind the massive, formidable skirts.

For it was to this Bohemia that Gavarni introduced me, rather than to that other and more suspect satellite society, which had already grown corrupt and decadent. I did not wonder that Philip had been alarmed. For in Paris, I saw so many men who called themselves Romantics yet were merely mirrors of an intellectual world which they could only imitate and not attain; they were pitiable, often mad or living in a dream of absinthe and Byronic aspiration, a delusion which often ended in despair and fashionable suicide. Gavarni seemed to know them all. But the artists and writers whom I met through him were greater men than these; and I realised, before too long, that I should never reach the heights to which, as a painter, I aspired.

Even before I left for France, I had begun to suspect that my ambition had outreached ability. For though I had completed my painting of the Thames, I knew it failed to show my meaning, that it brought together elements too disparate to be completely reconciled. I had wanted to portray the splendour of the city landscape Turner saw – the colours and the light – beside the wretchedness of lives within the London streets: a vision of unearthly beauty; a reality of chaos that so many people knew. It took two years or more to paint, at a time of inner questioning and much distress. Some smaller paintings – portraits – had been accepted for an exhibition at the British Institute; encouraged, I meant to try again, with a work which brought together all that I had cared for, everything I wished to do. And even when this was rejected, I believed it was worthwhile and had been misunderstood.

Now I was not so sure. For here in Paris I saw that I lacked judgement; here there were painters such as Delacroix, whose work had such terrifying power that my efforts seemed as trivial as when, so many years ago, Mr Jameson had shown to me that sketch of Constable's – so small and yet so meaningful. I would not give up the search. I would study, hope to learn – yet perhaps what I would find would be those limitations which I knew existed, which must now dictate my course.

There is a cobbled square behind the church of Saint Germain des Près: sometimes its warmth and intimacy make me think of home. Here is that certainty one finds in ancient gentle-coloured stone, a peace which the massive walls of churches, or their misty spires, so often give.

It is impossible to live in Paris and to be without emotion. In Highgate, or in London's vastness, I succeeded in forgetting Charles: so constant was my purpose there that he receded from my consciousness – as Louis never will. I hear the intonation of his voice each day; and when I see his son in Josh's arms, coming to meet me at the Louvre steps or walking just ahead of me along the *quai*, across the bridge, I wonder how it would have been with Louis here, in the city which he knew and loved.

There are chestnut flowers beside the river. The fine brown dust they cast is quickly ground into the dirt beneath the tread of many feet; their scent is in the air, and the brightness of their leaves reflected in the water of the Seine, among the coloured boats, the drifting refuse, and the gleams of light. It is two years since we were in Hampstead, in another, transient summer land . . .

Paul says that Louis wished to see me when he came to Paris a few weeks ago. I would not let him do so: it would have been impossible to be with him again, and then to part, not knowing for how long. Yet now I have the knowledge that I caused him pain; and I have learned anew a feeling which I thought had gone.

It was in this second summer that I was at last accepted by a studio. The *atelier* of the painter Delaroche, it was well known as a place of study for aspiring artists; that year, its acknowledged leader was Charles Gleyre, whose latest canvas caused a stir at the Paris *Salon* where I saw it first. But this, which he had called *Le Soir*, was an enigmatic and disturbing picture, redolent with symbolism which I did not understand: and at first I found the man himself aloof and cold. Later I discovered that his sight had been impaired whilst he was travelling in the East: I marvelled at how much he had achieved in spite of such a disability.

With several other students I was set to work to copy drawings Gleyre had made in Greece and Turkey, and along the Nile; there were many of them – landscapes, portraits, studies of interiors, meant to document as faithfully as possible his journeys to those far-off places, and another, more exotic way of life. The brilliance of his watercolours; the detail of the people's clothes; the features of men and women from a distant alien world – I was fascinated by them all. Unknowingly I had been well prepared in Highgate: faithful reproduction, subtle tinting, these were necessary now. I did not lament the fact that as a woman I was barred from formal classes: there was discipline and training to be gained from careful study of the work which Gleyre, himself a classicist and once a student of the English painter Bonington, had so painstakingly achieved. My imagination, too, was fired by the scenes he had depicted: one day, when my son had far less need of me, I would try to travel to the East, to places of which Philip wrote to me, or where Humphrey Nicolson had sailed so many years before . . .

There were other English students whom I met at Gleyre's; but they seemed reluctant to acknowledge me – their prejudice was clearly carried beyond their native shore. But I had no need of them: there were others, chiefly French or Swiss (like Gleyre himself) who readily advised me, talked about their work, as Paul Gavarni led me to expect. With some, at least, there was an easy comradeship, which I knew would have been lacking had I been a younger woman or less serious about my work. In particular there was an Irishman, whose talents far outweighed the rest: his clothes were worn, his health precarious, yet his wit and ready laughter rarely failed. Arthur O'Conor he was called; and he became, apart from Paul, my closest friend while I remained in France.

We were returning together from the studio one afternoon, when I saw my cousin Charles. Instead of turning right toward the rue Jacob, the way to my apartment, we had gone ahead and come to Nôtre Dame; and there, among a little group of people, stood my cousin, with a woman leaning on his arm. He recognised me, I was sure, for we had to pass close by; but it was clear at once that neither of us meant to speak. I thought him remarkably unchanged – and yet the power he once exerted was entirely gone. Afterwards, I could not understand how I had felt so little, save for a momentary shock: it was, I must suppose, that even someone whom we once have loved becomes, at last, a mortal like the rest.

Arthur came with us when, in the spring of 1845, we moved into the countryside. Already he had found our peaceful square congenial, for he had wearied of the noise and squalor of the lodging where he lived with other painters: it was becoming impossible to work, he said. For a time, he shared the room I had set aside to be a studio; even then he must have had some premonition of his early death, for he painted with a fevered energy, as if there were too little time in which to utilise his gifts.

I too had begun to find the city irksome. It seemed, as I came to know it, a dangerous place in which to rear a quick and lively boy, as William promised to become. I had given him his father's second name, and liked to think I saw in him already Louis' gentleness and unpredictable intensity. He was a little spoiled by Susan, but soon her own child would be born, and she would be much preoccupied. In the country, I would be able to give my son much more of my attention; he had become attached to Arthur, whose companionship, for another year, was to prove invaluable to us. He was much younger than myself, and spoke with bitterness of how he failed, in London, to gain any patronage or recognition for his work. I did not wish to become his lover; but I gladly gave him help when it was needed – for his painting, it was clear, was of more significance than mine would ever be.

It was he who told me first of Barbizon. A village south of Paris, in the Forest of Fontainebleau, for some painters whom we knew it was an escape from the rivalries of the artistic world – a place where truth was to be found. For O'Conor it became at once an inspiration – like the Irish countryside for which he longed; for myself it was a journey back to childhood, to the woods of Berkshire and the water meadows by the Thames. Where we settled, it was river country, rich with trees and flowers. Yet for the peasants, existence was primitive and hard; I was drawn by their simplicity, and by the unchanging rhythm of their days. Once there, I knew I should not yearn for city life; and when at length I went from France, it would be a green and gentle landscape that I sought.

'Mamma – there is a gentleman . . .'

It had been a long quiet summer. Often I walked with William to the shady margins of a little pool, where moorhens swam among the reeds. Above the stream there was a wooden bridge, from which we saw the lazy cattle drinking at the ford, where stones made the water foam and bubble down to the smoothness of a wider reach. Sometimes I would paint, while William played or looked in the shallows for the darting fish; perhaps I would sketch him where he lay outstretched among the grasses, and when he fell asleep, I watched him, wondering how long our peace would last.

Arthur had gone to Ireland; he was unlikely to return. From Paris came rumours of disturbances, precursors of that greater storm which would, within a year or so, be set to break. Already Josh and Susan talked of going back to England; I dreaded it, yet it was likely that there might be no alternative.

'Mamma – '

There was indeed a gentleman, standing beside the narrow path which led toward the house. Strangers seldom came, and so far no one had disturbed us in our sheltered place beside the stream. This man was tall and slightly stooping, his hair worn long and almost white; his face was pale, fatigued and lined. He was not anyone I knew.

William ran to him, ahead of me. I called him back. But as the stranger, still unsmiling, held his arms out to my child, there was something about his gesture that I recognised . . .

'You are Georgiana Curwen . . .'

His voice was deep; yet it was not this that now arrested me – but his use of my other name, which I had not heard since leaving Cumberland.

I could not answer him; I stared, uncomprehending still.

He smiled; and this time when he spoke, there was such feeling in his voice, and in his eyes –

'I am Alexander Grieve.'

My father – for at last I could believe that it was he – had been searching for me almost since the time I left for France. I marvelled that it could have taken him so long, until he told me that at first he had not known the object of his search – had been ignorant, indeed, that my mother, when he parted from her, was already carrying their child. After she had gone from Cumberland, he had learned that she was married; then he had despaired. He had become the curate of the living that was offered to him by the Lowthers, and had lived alone in a little house beside the church on their estate – at Ravenglass.

As he spoke of this, I could see why my mother cared for him so much. His gentleness was of a kind that often men despise: yet it was not weakness that had made him so. He had an air of sensitivity which, even as I watched him hold my son, made me see that he would have been too proud to follow where my mother went, if he believed it was against her wish.

'She sent no word to me,' he said. 'I was told that Sir Henry had forbidden her to write, that she was ill – and then I heard that she had gone. Perhaps, if I had been less poor, I should have thought she loved me still – '

'Indeed she did!' I cried – for his look of sorrow was too much to bear. 'She left me letters when she died; and I believe she cared for you, and for myself, for all of us – until she – '

Did my father know that she had killed herself, in such distress? Already he had borne much loneliness and grief: I could not add to it by telling him of such a thing. Already any anger I had felt toward him was quite gone. Later, we would discover how greatly both of them had been deceived; for the present, it was a wonder to me that he bore no grudge, but felt himself at fault in bringing sorrow to my mother and, unwittingly, to me. But how had he discovered my existence? Why had he searched so long?

'Four years ago,' he said, 'I was paid a visit by a friend whom I had not seen for a decade – more perhaps; he owns a mill outside Carlisle, and as a self-made man, he is interested in the arts – for he had little education in his youth. He had collected paintings, so he told me – including some which he had bought at an exhibition, by an artist who he thought might be a relation of my own. For Grieve is not a common name in Cumberland: the pictures were of Workington, and the signature upon them, G. F. Grieve. The painter, so my friend believed, was a woman – but that was all he knew . . .'

Here my father paused and sighed. Then he took my hand, which he held so tightly in his own that I understood, for the first time since he came to me, how much he needed my affection, after so many years alone.

'At first I thought little of it. But it seemed too strange, for I had never had connections with that place, save through your mother and her family . . . When I went, on impulse, I found the Hall was shut; there were no Curwens left in Workington, and, though I made enquiry, no one by the name of Grieve. So I went back to Ravenglass, to my studies and my empty house, my empty life – for so it always seemed, though I had thought myself, till then, content. The past was gone, forgotten, I believed . . . But then – '

Then he had written to his friend. He had learned of Mr Jameson, my teacher, who had arranged for my pictures to be shown and knew, of course, that I had used my father's name . . .

Highgate, Hampstead, Workington and France . . . At every place where Alexander Grieve had sought his child, he had arrived too late. Until, at last, he came to me at Barbizon. My father's faith, his persistence after so many years of loneliness and loss, convinced me that there are some moments in our lives when fate or circumstance (whatever we may call it) makes some reparation, after all.

Together, in the early spring, we went from France. Paris was by then unsafe, and we did not linger there. But I saw Gavarni, who confirmed that we were wise to leave.

'Soon, I and others – we shall need to go to England, too. Perhaps we will be there for years, who knows. For me – it is not so bad, I have my work; but for most, it will be difficult, and sad. When a country tears itself apart, as France will do – and other places, Italy and Germany perhaps . . . But you, you will go to Louis now?'

I told him I should not. He sighed and murmured that it had been long – but maybe it was wiser, who could know. But we would meet again in London, very possibly?

Again, I told him no.

For we had made our plans. We were to go to Cumberland, where we should need to spend some time, to deal with property and other practical affairs, my father's and my own. When all was finished we should sail, within a year we hoped, to

Ireland, where my father had always wished to go: and it was here, we had agreed, that we should make our home.

But first of all, as soon as we reached England, there was another matter to be settled: only then, when that was done, could we look forward to the future, and shake off the shadow of the past.

Chapter 29

In the windswept marshland, not far from the sea, there is a churchyard, where we found my mother's grave. Like others in that dreary place it was untended, overgrown with nettles, which obscured the small smooth stones of several lesser mounds, close by. Those were for her children, of whom she had written to me long ago, from her home in the village which we saw between the distant trees – a grey low-lying group of houses, insignificant beneath the deeper greyness of the banks of cloud, the emptiness of sky.

From the window of her room, my mother had gazed out across the marsh, had thought with longing of the man who stood beside me now. How thin and frail he looked to me, and careworn as he stared in silence at her resting-place, beside the husband whom she never loved. Of him we knew so little, nothing of the children she had mourned; but I noticed, as I read their names, that one which I had thought to see was, after all, not there. '*Pip they call him*,' so my mother wrote – and as she nursed him she had hoped that, though the last and weakest of the infants she had borne, he might survive. I wondered what could have happened to him, where he might be now: had his childhood hopes and expectations, like my own, been few, and founded on his untold, inward dreams? Perhaps he too knew something of the cruelties and inconsistencies of fate, or the illusions of that happiness we seek in love . . . There was no way of knowing; but I wished him well.

We had come that day from Rochester. While there, my father had enquired at an address not far from the cathedral yard. It was the same as that upon the package which contained the letters that my mother wrote; for it was her husband who had sent it to my aunt. '*Chatterton & Pirrip, Co.*': I had not forgotten it – and there it was, on a plate upon the door. The brass was dusty, the engraving worn; the door was locked. Mr Pirrip had died long since, we learned; but our informant had never known a Mr Chatterton. Mr Pirrip's father had the business long ago, he thought; but now the place was sold – to whom he could not tell.

'*Never put your trust in lawyers, Georgiana – for they lie.*' I had told my father of my certainty that somehow he, my mother and Sir Henry Curwen must have been deceived: how else could so long a silence be explained, when each had written several times, receiving no reply? I had not forgotten Horace Chatterton, and the fear that he inspired not only in myself, but in his servants, in his children and his wife. He had had charge of me – though why, I never knew; and he had left it to my aunt to tell me of my mother's death, though surely he must have known of it before I left his home. There was some mystery, still unexplained. And if the answer did not lie in those empty premises at Rochester, nor at the house (now occupied by strangers) where my mother lived – then we must go to Maidenhead, where Horace Chatterton had taken me, so many years ago . . .

My father went alone. I was glad – I had no wish to see that place again. I waited for him, with my son, at a little inn at Slough, where the road to London crossed the river Thames. Josh and Susan had already gone ahead to Cumberland; and now I longed to see the hills and lakes again. If I let myself remember that we were so close to London, I should think of Highgate too; of Sophia, within the glass walls of her garden room, as I so often saw her when I walked across the grass to Bisham House; of Hampstead, where a blind girl sat beside the fire; of Louis' voice as he murmured to me in the darkness of an attic room – where he had spoken of his feeling for a child whom he would never see . . . Soon I should leave it all behind: I should be gone to Ireland, to another far-off place.

*

Horace Chatterton had died, only a year before. So my father told me as we travelled north.

'But I saw his daughter – she has lived there since his death. She did not wish to speak to me at first, disclaimed all knowledge of you – and I guessed at once that there was something that she wished to hide.'

Horatia had, of course, remembered me. But though my father was persistent, she refused to let him in; he had told her his relationship to me, and she had disbelieved him, so it seemed. He went away discouraged, puzzled, angry when he realised that she was withholding information of importance to us both. He had returned within the hour. And this time she had taken him across the hall into the study where (as I had not forgotten) Horace Chatterton had worked.

'She said that you had done a kindness to her once. What it was she did not say, but it was clearly troubling her conscience. This time, I was allowed to look among the papers, where she told me she had seen the name of Curwen mentioned several times. I looked for an hour or more, and found the proof we need: letters from Sir Henry, in which he spoke of the allowances he made your mother whilst she was alive. And another, final one, written in October 1827 – '

That was the date, as I already knew, of my mother's death. I was right. Horace Chatterton had known of it: for there was a note which stated that Sir Henry's money, meant for her, would cease; and since I would from that time have another guardian – my aunt – there was no need for his support. Yet nothing, all the time that I had been with him, had come to me; and my mother also must have been cheated of her due. No wonder Horace Chatterton had been alarmed, when I, unwittingly, had questioned his authority; and now I knew at last why he had kept me ignorant of everything connected with the Curwens and myself.

My father's letters, and my mother's – all had been withheld, as far as we could guess. The consequences we already knew too well, but we could only surmise why my grandfather had trusted such a man. It had to do, perhaps, with Curwen pride – which had prevented him from seeking out his child, had caused him to mistrust his wife, and to reject me – certain that he must be right. He would have wanted to ensure that his enemies would not discover secrets they could use against him: such is the need of politicians to protect the virtue of their name!

There was nothing more that either I or Alexander Grieve could wish to know. But as we neared our journey's end, my father turned to me.

'I have a gift for you. At first I thought I would keep it – and give it to you for your birthday. After all,' he smiled, with the affection which had lain untouched for many years, 'I have never had the chance before. But I think I should let you have it now; Miss Chatterton was wearing it, and gave it to me when I left.'

It was a ring, with little pearls set round a centre-piece in which lay strands of hair, their colour almost black beneath the glass – hair which was the colour of my own . . .

'She said she found it in her father's desk, among the papers there. And I believe I recognise it as the same I saw upon your mother's finger once – '

It must have been the same: the ring which she had sent to me (though my father did not know it yet) in a letter long ago, a letter I had not received. She too had meant it as a birthday gift.

We took the west-coast route to Cumberland. Across the smooth expanse of Morecambe Bay – so flat that we could scarcely see the ocean far beyond the ripples of the shore: a place so treacherous in winter that a coach could vanish, so they said, in the waiting quicksands or the fast approaching tide. Then Ulverston, with reeds and bright green turf beside the water's edge; where sheets of silver lay upon the dark-brown sand, sea-birds drowsing in the early-morning sun. Hawthorn bushes, blossom white along the margins of a winding road; a line of hillside pale beneath the clouds, becoming clearer as we came inland: turrets and gables set among the trees, with cattle grazing in the park – the ancient priory of Conishead, aloof and undisturbed.

At last, the shoulder of a mountain which my father called Black Combe. A wooded valley, curving out ahead of us toward the sea, where a sandbank stretched like an enclosing wall, as if to hold the ocean back from the narrow sheltered harbour – Ravenglass.

So often I had been there in my mind. With Michael Stephens, when he left me on the lonely shore, where ragged tinkers scanned the refuse scattered by the tide. And later, in those moments when I wished that I had never known the name of Curwen, when I longed to seek some haven from the troubles and the passions of the world.

But when I stood beside the row of cottages, whose staring windows face the water where the sea-birds cry and wheel incessantly, I knew that once I had a dream of Ravenglass, of coming in a boat which landed at the pebbled beach. And the stranger whom I looked for at the cottages was no one I had seen before. He was – he must have been – my father: who had come to France, and now had brought me to the harbour, which throughout my time in Cumberland had been his home.

The house my father found for us near Dublin was neglected, quiet and old. Around it bramble thickets grew, and swaying elms; from the upper windows there were glimpses of the sea. Grass, which in summer would be turned to hay, had long since covered flowerbeds and garden paths; but we liked it so, and left it, fragrant with its intermingled clover, buttercups and meadow-sweet.

Here in my little island of security, I learned of famine, revolution, death. In Paris there was civil war; in London cholera was rife; and in Ireland's capital, so near at hand, there was starvation, on a greater scale than ever had been known before. There was little, to our shame, that we could do. We had been warned; but nothing had prepared us for the sights we saw along the quays, or in the spacious squares, among the city's many noble buildings, even in the quieter tree-lined streets. Yet in this country where, in those grim years, there seemed so little hope, we found the people gentle, courteous, good-humoured even in their poverty. And to our amazement, when the English queen, Victoria, arrived in state, the city welcomed her ungrudgingly – more so perhaps than we ourselves, who had by then so few political illusions left.

No one troubled us. But sometimes, when I talked with people at their cottage doors, or when they came to beg for food or clothes, I discovered that there were among the oldest of them several who had known my grandmother in the years before she left and went to Workington. She was remembered with affection – genuine enough. It pleased me, for I had thought of her as proud, perhaps capricious – yet it appeared she was not so. Later, in Dublin, when I came to know the artists and the writers of that city where there was more freedom than I had expected, I found that Frances Curwen's independent spirit long ago had left its mark. For though young she had learned to care for painting, poetry and music; and, in an age more liberal in some ways than our own, had been respected for her gifts, and for her intellect. I had come to Ireland as a stranger; yet I was to find that there were deeper roots, to which I had returned.

England began to seem remote, unreal. But even so, the letters came.

Mary Nicolson was well; her daughter Edith had a son; George was to be married very soon – he would like to buy the house at Portland Square . . . Philip was travelling in Africa; Morocco, Mary thought, was dangerous and hot – she wished he would return.

To my surprise, Mrs Heywood sent me news from Highgate. Miss Millington, I would be sad to know, had died quite suddenly, while walking to a client in The Grove. And her sister, Miss Maria, had married (quite beneath her, Mrs Heywood thought); her husband was Allinson the grocer, who had had a little High Street shop – yet Maria was quite content, to everyone's surprise . . . It seemed that Bisham House was to be sold; the Frenchman, Perreton (I must remember him) had gone – to where, and for what reason, no one knew.

A communication came from Mr Backhouse, of Nicolson & Curwen. Miss Evans and her father would give up the tenancy in three months' time; if I wished, the lease could be renewed, if not,

[381]

arrangements could be made. Miss Evans sent her grateful thanks – she and Mr Evans would return to Kent.

My father was contented. He had proved, as well as a devoted guardian of my son, a very able tutor. So William had not gone away to school; I should have him at home a little longer yet. Occasionally, artists whom I knew from Paris came to visit us. At first there was O'Conor; but his health, which while we were at Barbizon had been precarious, had failed. He had died, a victim of the fever which had spread through Dublin, shortly after we arrived.

Sometimes my father went to London, taking with him paintings that I wished to sell. They were chiefly landscapes now, or studies of the people whom I met in the villages and lanes; I had relinquished all ambition, yet my work of late was much improved. I should never give it up . . .

Or so I thought, until a letter came from Mary, bringing word to me of Philip's death. He had been travelling alone, she wrote, in country where he had not been before. There had evidently been a guide, who had returned without him, having warned him of the dangers that he faced. But Philip had ignored advice and gone ahead into a desert area, where other travellers were known to have succumbed. He was not found for several weeks . . . Yet he was usually so prudent; it was very strange.

For months I could not paint, and scarcely slept. Until a year before, he had written to me; then there was a silence, which I did not understand. And now his death.

At length I would see more clearly why I grieved for him; first, there was no feeling, only coldness – quite unlike the anger of my sorrow for Sophia. I had loved him, I suppose, without the certainty of touch, or the comfort that such closeness brings. And yet he had possessed me in a deeper way, which even though he went so far from me continued, long after he had gone.

I have received a letter from Louis. He will visit Dublin in the spring and wishes to see his son. He tells me that his daughters are becoming quite grown-up; Virginia, especially, was like her mother, I remember . . .

As I write at my table beside the window I see that William has fallen asleep, with his schoolbook beside him – at times he looks so like Louis, at other times he puts me in mind of Charles. I have written to Louis telling him that he may come. After so long a silence, I know that now I cannot wish to keep him from his child. I cannot forget how my mother lost her father; and how I, at last, have found my own.

This morning the sun's rays seem to reach a little further beyond the elm tree. The days are beginning to lengthen; soon it will be spring. Around me, as I sit writing in the stillness, I seem to hear an echo of my mother's words: '*There must be – there must be more to my existence than waiting, forever, beside an open window . . .*'